CLOUDS OF WITNESS

and

THE UNPLEASANTNESS
AT THE BELLONA CLUB

WIMSEY, Peter Death Bredon, D.S.O.; *born* 1890, *2nd son of* Mortimer Gerald Bredon Wimsey, 15th Duke of Denver, and of Honoria Lucasta, *daughter of* Francis Delagardie of Bellingham Manor, Hants.

Educated: Eton College and Balliol College, Oxford (1st class honours, Sch. of Mod. Hist. 1912); served with H. M. Forces 1914/18 (Major, Rifle Brigade). *Author of:* "Notes on the Collecting of Incunabula," "The Murderer's Vade-Mecum," etc. *Recreations:* Criminology; bibliophily; music; cricket.

Clubs: Marlborough; Egotists'. *Residences:* 110A Piccadilly, W.; Bredon Hall, Duke's Denver, Norfolk.

Arms: Sable, 3 mice courant, argent; crest, a domestic cat crouched as to spring, proper; motto: As my Whimsy takes me.

Clouds of Witness

AND

The Unpleasantness
at the
Bellona Club

BY

DOROTHY L. SAYERS

HARPER & ROW, PUBLISHERS
NEW YORK, EVANSTON, AND LONDON

CLOUDS OF WITNESS
All rights reserved

THE UNPLEASANTNESS AT THE BELLONA CLUB

Copyright 1928, 1956 by Dorothy Leigh Sayers Fleming

Printed in the United States of America

THE SOLUTION OF
THE RIDDLESDALE MYSTERY

WITH

A REPORT

OF THE TRIAL OF

THE DUKE OF DENVER

BEFORE THE HOUSE OF LORDS

FOR

MURDER

———

The inimitable stories of Tong-king never have any real ending, and this one, being in his most elevated style, has even less end than most of them. But the whole narrative is permeated with the odour of joss-sticks and honourable high-mindedness, and the two characters are both of noble birth.

—*The Wallet of Kai-Lung.*

Clouds of Witness

CONTENTS

CHAPTER I

"OF HIS MALICE AFORETHOUGHT"

O, who hath done this deed?

—Othello.

LORD PETER WIMSEY STRETCHED HIMSELF luxuriously between the sheets provided by the Hôtel Meurice. After his exertions in the unravelling of the Battersea Mystery, he had followed Sir Julian Freke's advice and taken a holiday. He had felt suddenly weary of breakfasting every morning before his view over the Green Park; he had realised that the picking up of first editions at sales afforded insufficient exercise for a man of thirty-three; the very crimes of London were over-sophisticated. He had abandoned his flat and his friends and fled to the wilds of Corsica. For the last three months he had forsworn letters, newspapers, and telegrams. He had tramped about the mountains, admiring from a cautious distance the wild beauty of Corsican peasant-women, and studying the vendetta in its natural haunt. In such conditions murder seemed not only reasonable, but lovable. Bunter, his confidential man and assistant sleuth, had nobly sacrificed his civilised habits, had let his master go dirty and even unshaven, and had turned his faithful camera from the recording of finger-prints to that of craggy scenery. It had been very refreshing.

Now, however, the call of the blood was upon Lord Peter. They had returned late last night in a vile train to Paris, and had picked up their luggage. The autumn light, filtering through the curtains, touched caressingly the silver-topped bottles on the dressing-table, outlined an electric lamp-shade and the shape of the telephone. A noise of running water near by proclaimed that Bunter had turned on the bath (h. & c.) and was laying out scented soap, bath-salts, the huge bath-sponge, for which there had been no scope in Corsica, and the delightful flesh-brush with the long handle, which rasped you so agreeably all down the spine. "Contrast," philosophised Lord Peter

3

sleepily, "is life. Corsica—Paris—then London. . . . Good morning, Bunter."

"Good morning, my lord. Fine morning, my lord. Your lordship's bath-water is ready."

"Thanks," said Lord Peter. He blinked at the sunlight.

It was a glorious bath. He wondered, as he soaked in it, how he could have existed in Corsica. He wallowed happily and sang a few bars of a song. In a soporific interval he heard the valet de chambre bringing in coffee and rolls. Coffee and rolls! He heaved himself out with a splash, towelled himself luxuriously, enveloped his long-mortified body in a silken bath-robe, and wandered back.

To his immense surprise he perceived Mr. Bunter calmly replacing all the fittings in his dressing-case. Another astonished glance showed him the bags—scarcely opened the previous night—repacked, re-labelled, and standing ready for a journey.

"I say, Bunter, what's up?" said his lordship. "We're stayin' here a fortnight y'know."

"Excuse me, my lord," said Mr. Bunter, deferentially, "but, having seen *The Times* (delivered here every morning by air, my lord; and very expeditious I'm sure, all things considered), I made no doubt your lordship would be wishing to go to Riddlesdale at once."

"Riddlesdale!" exclaimed Peter. "What's the matter? Anything wrong with my brother?"

For answer Mr. Bunter handed him the paper, folded open at the heading:

RIDDLESDALE INQUEST.
DUKE OF DENVER ARRESTED
ON MURDER CHARGE.

Lord Peter stared as if hypnotised.

"I thought your lordship wouldn't wish to miss anything," said Mr. Bunter, "so I took the liberty——"

Lord Peter pulled himself together.

"When's the next train?" he asked.

"I beg your lordship's pardon—I thought your lordship would wish to take the quickest route. I took it on myself to book two seats in the aeroplane *Victoria*. She starts at 11.30."

Lord Peter looked at his watch.

"Ten o'clock," he said. "Very well. You did quite right. Dear me!

Poor old Gerald arrested for murder. Uncommonly worryin' for him, poor chap. Always hated my bein' mixed up with police-courts. Now he's there himself. Lord Peter Wimsey in the witness-box—very distressin' to feelin's of a brother. Duke of Denver in the dock—worse still. Dear me! Well, I suppose one must have breakfast."

"Yes, my lord. Full account of the inquest in the paper, my lord."

"Yes. Who's on the case, by the way?"

"Mr. Parker, my lord."

"Parker? That's good. Splendid old Parker! Wonder how he managed to get put on to it. How do things look, Bunter?"

"If I may say so, my lord, I fancy the investigations will prove very interesting. There are several extremely suggestive points in the evidence, my lord."

"From a criminological point of view I daresay it is interesting," replied his lordship, sitting down cheerfully to his *café au lait,* "but it's deuced awkward for my brother, all the same, havin' no turn for criminology, what?"

"Ah, well!" said Mr. Bunter, "they say, my lord, there's nothing like having a personal interest."

.   .   .   .   .

"The inquest was held to-day at Riddlesdale, in the North Riding of Yorkshire, on the body of Captain Denis Cathcart, which was found at three o'clock on Thursday morning lying just outside the conservatory door of the Duke of Denver's shooting-box, Riddlesdale Lodge. Evidence was given to show that deceased had quarrelled with the Duke of Denver on the preceding evening, and was subsequently shot in a small thicket adjoining the house. A pistol belonging to the Duke was found near the scene of the crime. A verdict of murder was returned against the Duke of Denver. Lady Mary Wimsey, sister of the Duke, who was engaged to be married to the deceased, collapsed after giving evidence, and is now lying seriously ill at the Lodge. The Duchess of Denver hastened from town yesterday and was present at the inquest. Full report on p. 12."

"Poor old Gerald!" thought Lord Peter, as he turned to page 12; "and poor old Mary! I wonder if she really was fond of the fellow. Mother always said not, but Mary never would let on about herself."

5

The full report began by describing the little village of Riddlesdale, where the Duke of Denver had recently taken a small shooting-box for the season. When the tragedy occurred the Duke had been staying there with a party of guests. In the Duchess's absence Lady Mary Wimsey had acted as hostess. The other guests were Colonel and Mrs. Marchbanks, the Hon. Frederick Arbuthnot, Mr. and Mrs. Pettigrew-Robinson, and the dead man, Denis Cathcart.

The first witness was the Duke of Denver, who claimed to have discovered the body. He gave evidence that he was coming into the house by the conservatory door at three o'clock in the morning of Thursday, October 14th, when his foot struck against something. He had switched on his electric torch and seen the body of Denis Cathcart at his feet. He had at once turned it over, and seen that Cathcart had been shot in the chest. He was quite dead. As Denver was bending over the body, he heard a cry in the conservatory, and, looking up, saw Lady Mary Wimsey gazing out horror-struck. She came out by the conservatory door, and exclaimed at once, "O God, Gerald, you've killed him!" (Sensation.)*

The Coroner: "Were you surprised by that remark?"

Duke of D.: "Well, I was so shocked and surprised at the whole thing. I think I said to her, 'Don't look,' and she said, 'Oh, it's Denis! Whatever can have happened? Has there been an accident?' I stayed with the body, and sent her up to rouse the house."

The Coroner: "Did you expect to see Lady Mary Wimsey in the conservatory?"

Duke of D.: "Really, as I say, I was so astonished all round, don't you know, I didn't think about it."

The Coroner: "Do you remember how she was dressed?"

Duke of D.: "I don't think she was in her pyjamas." (Laughter.) "I think she had a coat on."

The Coroner: "I understand that Lady Mary Wimsey was engaged to be married to the deceased?"

Duke of D.: "Yes."

The Coroner: "He was well known to you?"

Duke of D.: "He was the son of an old friend of my father's; his parents are dead. I believe he lived chiefly abroad. I ran across him

* This report, though substantially the same as that read by Lord Peter in *The Times,* has been corrected, amplified and annotated from the shorthand report made at the time by Mr. Parker.

6

during the war, and in 1919 he came to stay at Denver. He became engaged to my sister at the beginning of this year."

The Coroner: "With your consent, and with that of the family?"

Duke of D.: "Oh, yes, certainly."

The Coroner: "What kind of man was Captain Cathcart?"

Duke of D.: "Well—he was a Sahib and all that. I don't know what he did before he joined in 1914. I think he lived on his income; his father was well off. Crack shot, good at games, and so on. I never heard anything against him—till that evening."

The Coroner: "What was that?"

Duke of D.: "Well—the fact is—it was deuced queer. He—— If anybody but Tommy Freeborn had said it I should never have believed it." (Sensation.)

The Coroner: "I'm afraid I must ask your grace of what exactly you had to accuse the deceased."

Duke of D.: "Well, I didn't—I don't—exactly accuse him. An old friend of mine made a suggestion. Of course I thought it must be all a mistake, so I went to Cathcart, and, to my amazement, he practically admitted it! Then we both got angry, and he told me to go to the devil, and rushed out of the house." (Renewed sensation.)

The Coroner: "When did this quarrel occur?"

Duke of D.: "On Wednesday night. That was the last I saw of him." (Unparalleled sensation.)

The Coroner: "Please, please, we cannot have this disturbance. Now, will your grace kindly give me, as far as you can remember it, the exact history of this quarrel?"

Duke of D.: "Well, it was like this. We'd had a long day on the moors and had dinner early, and about half-past nine we began to feel like turning in. My sister and Mrs. Pettigrew-Robinson toddled on up, and we were havin' a last peg in the billiard-room when Fleming—that's my man—came in with the letters. They come rather any old time in the evening, you know, we being two and a half miles from the village. No—I wasn't in the billiard-room at the time—I was lockin' up the gun-room. The letter was from an old friend of mine I hadn't seen for years— Tom Freeborn—used to know him at the House——"

The Coroner: "Whose house?"

Duke of D.: "Oh, Christ Church, Oxford. He wrote to say he'd seen the announcement of my sister's engagement in Egypt."

The Coroner: "In Egypt?"

7

Duke of D.: "I mean, *he* was in Egypt—Tom Freeborn, you see—that's why he hadn't written before. He engineers. He went out there after the war was over, you see, and, bein' somewhere up near the sources of the Nile, he doesn't get the papers regularly. He said, would I 'scuse him for interferin' in a very delicate matter, and all that, but did I know who Cathcart was? Said he'd met him in Paris during the war, and he lived by cheatin' at cards—said he could swear to it, with details of a row there'd been in some French place or other. Said he knew I'd want to chaw his head off—Freeborn's, I mean—for buttin' in, but he'd seen the man's photo in the paper, an' he thought I ought to know."

The Coroner: "Did this letter surprise you?"

Duke of D.: "Couldn't believe it at first. If it hadn't been old Tom Freeborn I'd have put the thing in the fire straight off, and, even as it was, I didn't quite know what to think. I mean, it wasn't as if it had happened in England, you know. I mean to say, Frenchmen get so excited about nothing. Only there was Freeborn, and he isn't the kind of man that makes mistakes."

The Coroner: "What did you do?"

Duke of D.: "Well, the more I looked at it the less I liked it, you know. Still, I couldn't quite leave it like that, so I thought the best way was to go straight to Cathcart. They'd all gone up while I was sittin' thinkin' about it, so I went up and knocked at Cathcart's door. He said, 'What's that?' or 'Who the devil's that?' or somethin' of the sort, and I went in. 'Look here,' I said, 'can I just have a word with you?' 'Well, cut it short, then,' he said. I was surprised—he wasn't usually rude. 'Well,' I said, 'fact is, I've had a letter I don't much like the look of, and I thought the best thing to do was to bring it straight away to you an' have the whole thing cleared up. It's from a man—a very decent sort—old college friend, who says he's met you in Paris.' 'Paris!' he said, in a most uncommonly unpleasant way. 'Paris! What the hell do you want to come talkin' to me about Paris for?' 'Well,' I said, 'don't talk like that, because it's misleadin' under the circumstances.' 'What are you drivin' at?' says Cathcart. 'Spit it out and go to bed, for God's sake.' I said, 'Right oh! I will. It's a man called Freeborn, who says he knew you in Paris and that you made money cheatin' at cards.' I thought he'd break out at that, but all he said was, 'What about it?' 'What about it?' I said. 'Well, of course, it's not the sort of thing I'm goin' to believe like that, right bang-slap off, without any proofs.' Then he said a funny thing. He said, 'Beliefs don't matter

8

—it's what one *knows* about people.' 'Do you mean to say you don't deny it?' I said. 'It's no good my denying it,' he said; 'you must make up your own mind. Nobody could *dis*prove it.' And then he suddenly jumped up, nearly knocking the table over, and said, 'I don't care what you think or what you do, if you'll only get out. For God's sake leave me alone!' 'Look here,' I said, 'you needn't take it that way. I don't say I do believe it—in fact,' I said, 'I'm sure there must be some mistake; only, you bein' engaged to Mary,' I said, 'I couldn't just let it go at that without looking into it, could I?' 'Oh!' says Cathcart, 'if that's what's worrying you, it needn't. That's off.' I said, 'What?' He said, 'Our engagement.' 'Off?' I said. 'But I was talking to Mary about it only yesterday.' 'I haven't told her yet,' he said. 'Well,' I said, 'I think that's damned cool. Who the hell do you think you are, to come here and jilt my sister?' Well, I said quite a lot, first and last. 'You can get out,' I said; 'I've no use for swine like you.' 'I will,' he said, and he pushed past me an' slammed downstairs and out of the front door, an' banged it after him."

The Coroner: "What did you do?"

Duke of D.: "I ran into my bedroom, which has a window over the conservatory, and shouted out to him not to be a silly fool. It was pourin' with rain and beastly cold. He didn't come back, so I told Fleming to leave the conservatory door open—in case he thought better of it—and went to bed."

The Coroner: "What explanation can you suggest for Cathcart's behaviour?"

Duke of D.: "None. I was simply staggered. But I think he must somehow have got wind of the letter, and knew the game was up."

The Coroner: "Did you mention the matter to anybody else?"

Duke of D.: "No. It wasn't pleasant, and I thought I'd better leave it till the morning."

The Coroner: "So you did nothing further in the matter?"

Duke of D.: "No. I didn't want to go out huntin' for the fellow. I was too angry. Besides, I thought he'd change his mind before long—it was a brute of a night and he'd only a dinner-jacket."

The Coroner: "Then you just went quietly to bed and never saw the deceased again?"

Duke of D.: "Not till I fell over him outside the conservatory at three in the morning."

The Coroner: "Ah yes. Now can you tell us how you came to be out of doors at that time?"

9

Duke of D. (hesitating): "I didn't sleep well. I went out for a stroll."

The Coroner: "At three o'clock in the morning?"

Duke of D.: "Yes." With sudden inspiration: "You see, my wife's away." (Laughter and some remarks from the back of the room.)

The Coroner: "Silence, please. . . . You mean to say that you got up at that hour of an October night to take a walk in the garden in the pouring rain?"

Duke of D.: "Yes, just a stroll." (Laughter.)

The Coroner: "At what time did you leave your bedroom?"

Duke of D.: "Oh—oh, about half-past two, I should think."

The Coroner: "Which way did you go out?"

Duke of D.: "By the conservatory door."

The Coroner: "The body was not there when you went out?"

Duke of D.: "Oh, no!"

The Coroner: "Or you would have seen it?"

Duke of D.: "Lord, yes! I'd have had to walk over it."

The Coroner: "Exactly where did you go?"

Duke of D. (vaguely): "Oh, just round about."

The Coroner: "You heard no shot?"

Duke of D.: "No."

The Coroner: "Did you go far away from the conservatory door and the shrubbery?"

Duke of D.: "Well—I was some way away. Perhaps that's why I didn't hear anything. It must have been."

The Coroner: "Were you as much as a quarter of a mile away?"

Duke of D.: "I should think I was—oh, yes, quite!"

The Coroner: "More than a quarter of a mile away?"

Duke of D.: "Possibly. I walked about briskly because it was cold."

The Coroner: "In which direction?"

Duke of D. (with visible hesitation): "Round at the back of the house. Towards the bowling-green."

The Coroner: "The bowling-green?"

Duke of D. (more confidently): "Yes."

The Coroner: "But if you were more than a quarter of a mile away, you must have left the grounds?"

Duke of D.: "I—oh, yes—I think I did. Yes, I walked about on the moor a bit, you know."

The Coroner: "Can you show us the letter you had from Mr. Freeborn?"

Duke of D.: "Oh, certainly—if I can find it. I thought I put it in my pocket, but I couldn't find it for that Scotland Yard fellow."

The Coroner: "Can you have accidentally destroyed it?"

Duke of D.: "No—I'm sure I remember putting it—— Oh"—here the witness paused in very patent confusion, and grew red—"I remember now. I destroyed it."

The Coroner: "That is unfortunate. How was that?"

Duke of D.: "I had forgotten; it has come back to me now. I'm afraid it has gone for good."

The Coroner: "Perhaps you kept the envelope?"

Witness shook his head.

The Coroner: "Then you can show the jury no proof of having received it?"

Duke of D.: "Not unless Fleming remembers it."

The Coroner: "Ah, yes! No doubt we can check it that way. Thank you, your grace. Call Lady Mary Wimsey."

The noble lady, who was, until the tragic morning of October 14th, the fiancée of the deceased, aroused a murmur of sympathy on her appearance. Fair and slender, her naturally rose-pink cheeks ashy pale, she seemed overwhelmed with grief. She was dressed entirely in black, and gave her evidence in a very low tone which was at times almost inaudible.*

After expressing his sympathy, the coroner asked, "How long had you been engaged to the deceased?"

Witness: "About eight months."

The Coroner: "Where did you first meet him?"

Witness: "At my sister-in-law's house in London."

The Coroner: "When was that?"

Witness: "I think it was June last year."

The Coroner: "You were quite happy in your engagement?"

Witness: "Quite."

The Coroner: "You naturally saw a good deal of Captain Cathcart. Did he tell you much about his previous life?"

Witness: "Not very much. We were not given to mutual confidences. We usually discussed subjects of common interest."

The Coroner: "You had many such subjects?"

Witness: "Oh, yes."

* From the newspaper report—*not* Mr. Parker.

The Coroner: "You never gathered at any time that Captain Cathcart had anything on his mind?"

Witness: "Not particularly. He had seemed a little anxious the last few days."

The Coroner: "Did he speak of his life in Paris?"

Witness: "He spoke of theatres and amusements there. He knew Paris very well. I was staying in Paris with some friends last February, when he was there, and he took us about. That was shortly after our engagement."

The Coroner: "Did he ever speak of playing cards in Paris?"

Witness: "I don't remember."

The Coroner: "With regard to your marriage—had any money settlements been gone into?"

Witness: "I don't think so. The date of the marriage was not in any way fixed."

The Coroner: "He always appeared to have plenty of money?"

Witness: "I suppose so; I didn't think about it."

The Coroner: "You never heard him complain of being hard up?"

Witness: "Everybody complains of that, don't they?"

The Coroner: "Was he a man of cheerful disposition?"

Witness: "He was very moody, never the same two days together."

The Coroner: "You have heard what your brother says about the deceased wishing to break off the engagement. Had you any idea of this?"

Witness: "Not the slightest."

The Coroner: "Can you think of any explanation now?"

Witness: "Absolutely none."

The Coroner: "There had been no quarrel?"

Witness: "No."

The Coroner: "So far as you knew, on the Wednesday evening, you were still engaged to deceased with every prospect of being married to him shortly?"

Witness: "Ye-es. Yes, certainly, of course."

The Coroner: "He was not—forgive me this very painful question —the sort of man who would have been likely to lay violent hands on himself?"

Witness: "Oh, I never thought—well, I don't know—I suppose he might have done. That would explain it, wouldn't it?"

The Coroner: "Now, Lady Mary—please don't distress yourself,

12

take your own time—will you tell us exactly what you heard and saw on Wednesday night and Thursday morning."

Witness: "I went up to bed with Mrs. Marchbanks and Mrs. Pettigrew-Robinson at about half-past nine, leaving all the men downstairs. I said good night to Denis, who seemed quite as usual. I was not downstairs when the post came. I went to my room at once. My room is at the back of the house. I heard Mr. Pettigrew-Robinson come up at about ten. The Pettigrew-Robinsons sleep next door to me. Some of the other men came up with him. I did not hear my brother come upstairs. At about a quarter past ten I heard two men talking loudly in the passage, and then I heard someone run downstairs and bang the front door. Afterwards I heard rapid steps in the passage, and finally I heard my brother shut his door. Then I went to bed."

The Coroner: "You did not inquire the cause of the disturbance?"

Witness (indifferently): "I thought it was probably something about the dogs."

The Coroner: "What happened next?"

Witness: "I woke up at three o'clock."

The Coroner: "What wakened you?"

Witness: "I heard a shot."

The Coroner: "You were not awake before you heard it?"

Witness: "I may have been partly awake. I heard it very distinctly. I was sure it was a shot. I listened for a few minutes, and then went down to see if anything was wrong."

The Coroner: "Why did you not call your brother or some other gentleman?"

Witness (scornfully): "Why should I? I thought it was probably only poachers, and I didn't want to make an unnecessary fuss at that unearthly hour."

The Coroner: "Did the shot sound close to the house?"

Witness: "Fairly, I think—it is hard to tell when one is wakened by a noise—it always sounds so extra loud."

The Coroner: "It did not seem to be in the house or in the conservatory?"

Witness: "No it was outside."

The Coroner: "So you went downstairs by yourself. That was very plucky of you, Lady Mary. Did you go immediately?"

Witness: "Not quite immediately. I thought it over for a few minutes; then I put on walking-shoes over bare feet, a heavy covert-coat,

13

and a woolly cap. It may have been five minutes after hearing the shot that I left my bedroom. I went downstairs and through the billiard-room to the conservatory."

The Coroner: "Why did you go out that way?"

Witness: "Because it was quicker than unbolting either the front door or the back door."

GROUND PLAN

x:- Old Oak Chest.

At this point a plan of Riddlesdale Lodge was handed to the jury. It is a roomy, two-storied house, built in a plain style, and leased by the present owner, Mr. Walter Montague, to Lord Denver for the season, Mr. Montague being in the States.

14

Witness (resuming): "When I got to the conservatory door I saw a man outside, bending over something on the ground. When he looked up I was astonished to see my brother."

The Coroner: "Before you saw who it was, what did you expect?"

Witness: "I hardly know—it all happened so quickly. I thought it was burglars, I think."

The Coroner: "His grace has told us that when you saw him you cried out, 'O God! you've killed him!' Can you tell us why you did that?"

Witness (very pale): "I thought my brother must have come upon the burglar and fired at him in self-defence—that is, if I thought at all."

The Coroner: "Quite so. You knew that the Duke possessed a revolver?"

Witness: "Oh, yes—I think so."

The Coroner: "What did you do next?"

Witness: "My brother sent me up to get help. I knocked up Mr. Arbuthnot and Mr. and Mrs. Pettigrew-Robinson. Then I suddenly felt very faint, and went back to my bedroom and took some sal volatile."

The Coroner: "Alone?"

Witness: "Yes, everybody was running about and calling out. I couldn't bear it—I——"

Here the witness, who up till this moment had given her evidence very collectedly, though in a low voice, collapsed suddenly, and had to be assisted from the room.

The next witness called was James Fleming, the manservant. He remembered having brought the letters from Riddlesdale at 9.45 on Wednesday evening. He had taken three or four letters to the Duke in the gun-room. He could not remember at all whether one of them had had an Egyptian stamp. He did not collect stamps; his hobby was autographs.

The Hon. Frederick Arbuthnot then gave evidence. He had gone up to bed with the rest at a little before ten. He had heard Denver come up by himself some time later—couldn't say how much later— he was brushing his teeth at the time. (Laughter.) Had certainly heard loud voices and a row going on next door and in the passage. Had heard somebody go for the stairs hell-for-leather. Had stuck his head out and seen Denver in the passage. Had said, "Hello, Denver, what's the row?" The Duke's reply had been inaudible. Denver had bolted into his bedroom and shouted out of the window, "Don't be

15

an ass, man!" He had seemed very angry indeed, but the Hon. Freddy attached no importance to that. One was always getting across Denver, but it never came to anything. More dust than kick in his opinion. Hadn't known Cathcart long—always found him all right—no, he didn't *like* Cathcart, but he was all right, you know, nothing wrong about him that he knew of. Good lord, no, he'd never heard it suggested he cheated at cards! Well, no, of course, he didn't go about looking out for people cheating at cards—it wasn't a thing one expected. He'd been had that way in a club at Monte once—he'd had no hand in bringing it to light—hadn't noticed anything till the fun began. Had not noticed anything particular in Cathcart's manner to Lady Mary, or hers to him. Didn't suppose he ever would notice anything; did not consider himself an observing sort of man. Was not interfering by nature; had thought Wednesday evening's dust-up none of his business. Had gone to bed and to sleep.

The Coroner: "Did you hear anything further that night?"

Hon. Frederick: "Not till poor little Mary knocked me up. Then I toddled down and found Denver in the conservatory, bathing Cathcart's head. We thought we ought to clean the gravel and mud off his face, you know."

The Coroner: "You heard no shot?"

Hon. Frederick: "Not a sound. But I sleep pretty heavily."

Colonel and Mrs. Marchbanks slept in the room over what was called the study—more a sort of smoking-room really. They both gave the same account of a conversation which they had had at 11.30. Mrs. Marchbanks had sat up to write some letters after the Colonel was in bed. They had heard voices and someone running about, but had paid no attention. It was not unusual for members of the party to shout and run about. At last the Colonel had said, "Come to bed, my dear, it's half-past eleven, and we're making an early start tomorrow. You won't be fit for anything." He said this because Mrs. Marchbanks was a keen sportswoman and always carried her gun with the rest. She replied, "I'm just coming." The Colonel said, "You're the only sinner burning the midnight oil—everybody's turned in." Mrs. Marchbanks replied, "No, the Duke's still up; I can hear him moving about in the study." Colonel Marchbanks listened and heard it too. Neither of them heard the Duke come up again. They had heard no noise of any kind in the night.

Mr. Pettigrew-Robinson appeared to give evidence with extreme reluctance. He and his wife had gone to bed at ten. They had heard the quarrel with Cathcart. Mr. Pettigrew-Robinson, fearing that something might be going to happen, opened his door in time to hear the Duke say, "If you dare to speak to my sister again I'll break every bone in your body," or words to that effect. Cathcart had rushed downstairs. The Duke was scarlet in the face. He had not seen Mr. Pettigrew-Robinson, but had spoken a few words to Mr. Arbuthnot, and rushed into his own bedroom. Mr. Pettigrew-Robinson had run out, and said to Mr. Arbuthnot, "I say, Arbuthnot," and Mr. Arbuthnot had very rudely slammed the door in his face. He had then gone to the Duke's door and said, "I say, Denver." The Duke had come out, pushing past him, without even noticing him, and gone to the head of the stairs. He had heard him tell Fleming to leave the conservatory door open, as Mr. Cathcart had gone out. The Duke had then returned. Mr. Pettigrew-Robinson had tried to catch him as he passed, and had said again, "I say, Denver, what's up?" The Duke had said nothing, and had shut his bedroom door with great decision. Later on, however, at 11.30 to be precise, Mr. Pettigrew-Robinson had heard the Duke's door open, and stealthy feet moving about the passage. He could not hear whether they had gone downstairs. The bathroom and lavatory were at his end of the passage, and, if anybody had entered either of them, he thought he should have heard. He had not heard the footsteps return. He had heard his travelling clock strike twelve before falling asleep. There was no mistaking the Duke's bedroom door, as the hinge creaked in a peculiar manner.

Mrs. Pettigrew-Robinson confirmed her husband's evidence. She had fallen asleep before midnight, and had slept heavily. She was a heavy sleeper at the beginning of the night, but slept lightly in the early morning. She had been annoyed by all the disturbance in the house that evening, as it had prevented her from getting off. In fact, she had dropped off about 10.30, and Mr. Pettigrew-Robinson had had to wake her an hour after to tell her about the footsteps. What with one thing and another she only got a couple of hours' good sleep. She woke up again at two, and remained broad awake till the alarm was given by Lady Mary. She could swear positively that she heard no shot in the night. Her window was next to Lady Mary's, on the opposite side from the conservatory. She had always been accustomed from a child to sleep with her window open. In reply to a question from the Coroner, Mrs. Pettigrew-Robinson said she had never felt there was a real, true affection between Lady Mary Wimsey and deceased. They seemed very off-hand, but that sort of thing was the fashion nowadays. She had never heard of any disagreement.

Miss Lydia Cathcart, who had been hurriedly summoned from town, then gave evidence about the deceased man. She told the Coroner that she was the Captain's aunt and his only surviving relative. She had seen very little of him since he came into possession of his father's money. He had always lived with his own friends in Paris, and they were such as she could not approve of.

"My brother and I never got on very well," said Miss Cathcart, "and he had my nephew educated abroad till he was eighteen. I fear Denis's notions were always quite French. After my brother's death Denis went to Cambridge, by his father's desire. I was left executrix of the will, and guardian till Denis came of age. I do not know why, after neglecting me all his life, my brother should have chosen to put such a responsibility upon me at his death, but I did not care to refuse. My house was open to Denis during his holidays from college, but he preferred, as a rule, to go and stay with his rich friends. I cannot now recall any of their names. When Denis was twenty-one he came into £10,000 a year. I believe it was in some kind of foreign property. I inherited a certain amount under the will as executrix, but I converted it all, at once, into good, sound, British securities. I cannot say what Denis did with his. It would not surprise me at all to hear that he had been cheating at cards. I have heard that the persons he consorted with in Paris were most undesirable. I never met any of them. I have never been in France."

John Hardraw, the gamekeeper, was next called. He and his wife inhabit a small cottage just inside the gate of Riddlesdale Lodge. The grounds, which measure twenty acres or so, are surrounded at this point by a strong paling; the gate is locked at night. Hardraw stated that he had heard a shot fired at about ten minutes to twelve on Wednesday night, close to the cottage, as it seemed to him. Behind the cottage are ten acres of preserved plantation. He supposed that there were poachers about; they occasionally came in after hares. He went out with his gun in that direction, but saw nobody. He returned home at one o'clock by his watch.

The Coroner: "Did you fire your gun at any time?"

Witness: "No."

The Coroner: "You did not go out again?"

Witness: "I did not."

The Coroner: "Nor hear any other shots?"

Witness: "Only that one; but I fell asleep after I got back, and was wakened up by the chauffeur going out for the doctor. That would be at about a quarter past three."

The Coroner: "Is it not unusual for poachers to shoot so very near the cottage?"

Witness: "Yes, rather. If poachers do come, it is usually on the other side of the preserve, towards the moor."

Dr. Thorpe gave evidence of having been called to see deceased. He lived in Stapley, nearly fourteen miles from Riddlesdale. There was no medical man in Riddlesdale. The chauffeur had knocked him up at 3.45 a.m., and he had dressed quickly and come with him at once. They were at Riddlesdale Lodge at half-past four. Deceased, when he saw him, he judged to have been dead three or four hours. The lungs had been pierced by a bullet, and death had resulted from loss of blood, and suffocation. Death would not have resulted immediately—deceased might have lingered some time. He had made a post-mortem investigation, and found that the bullet had been deflected from a rib. There was nothing to show whether the wound had been self-inflicted or fired from another hand, at close quarters. There were no other marks of violence.

Inspector Craikes from Stapley had been brought back in the car with Dr. Thorpe. He had seen the body. It was then lying on its back, between the door of the conservatory and the covered well just outside. As soon as it became light, Inspector Craikes had examined the house and grounds. He had found bloody marks all along the path leading to the conservatory, and signs as though a body had been dragged along. This path ran into the main path leading from the gate to the front door. (Plan produced.) Where the two paths joined, a shrubbery began, and ran down on both sides of the path to the gate and the gamekeeper's cottage. The blood-tracks had led to a little clearing in the middle of the shrubbery, about half-way between the house and the gate. Here the Inspector found a great pool of blood, a handkerchief soaked in blood, and a revolver. The handkerchief bore the initials D. C., and the revolver was a small weapon of American pattern, and bore no mark. The conservatory door was open when the Inspector arrived, and the key was inside.

Deceased, when he saw him, was in dinner-jacket and pumps, without hat or overcoat. He was wet through, and his clothes, besides being much blood-stained, were very muddy and greatly disordered through the dragging of the body. The pocket contained a cigar-case and a small, flat pocket-knife. Deceased's bedroom had been searched for papers, etc., but so far nothing had been found to shed very much light on his circumstances.

The Duke of Denver was then recalled.

The Coroner: "I should like to ask your grace whether you ever saw deceased in possession of a revolver?"

Duke of D.: "Not since the war."

The Coroner: "You do not know if he carried one about with him?"

Duke of D.: "I have no idea."

The Coroner: "You can make no guess, I suppose, to whom this revolver belongs?"

Duke of D. (in great surprise): "That's my revolver—out of the study table drawer. How did you get hold of that?"—(Sensation.)

The Coroner: "You are certain?"

Duke of D.: "Positive. I saw it there only the other day, when I was hunting out some photos of Mary for Cathcart, and I remember saying then that it was getting rusty lying about. There's the speck of rust."

The Coroner: "Did you keep it loaded?"

Duke of D.: "Lord, no! I really don't know why it was there. I fancy I turned it out one day with some old Army stuff, and found it among my shooting things when I was up at Riddlesdale in August. I think the cartridges were with it."

The Coroner: "Was the drawer locked?"

Duke of D.: "Yes; but the key was in the lock. My wife tells me I'm careless."

The Coroner: "Did anybody else know the revolver was there?"

Duke of D.: "Fleming did, I think. I don't know of anybody else."

Detective-Inspector Parker of Scotland Yard, having only arrived on Friday, had been unable as yet to make any very close investigation. Certain indications led him to think that some person or persons had been on the scene of the tragedy in addition to those who had taken part in the discovery. He preferred to say nothing more at present.

The Coroner then reconstructed the evidence in chronological order. At, or a little after, ten o'clock there had been a quarrel between deceased and the Duke of Denver, after which deceased had left the house never to be seen alive again. They had the evidence of Mr. Pettigrew-Robinson that the Duke had gone downstairs at 11.30, and

that of Colonel Marchbanks that he had been heard immediately afterwards moving about in the study, the room in which the revolver
produced in evidence was usually kept. Against this they had the
Duke's own sworn statement that he had not left his bedroom till
half-past two in the morning. The jury would have to consider what
weight was to be attached to those conflicting statements. Then, as
to the shots heard in the night; the gamekeeper had said he heard
a shot at ten minutes to twelve, but he had supposed it to be fired
by poachers. It was, in fact, quite possible that there had been poachers about. On the other hand, Lady Mary's statement that she had
heard the shot at about three a.m. did not fit in very well with the
doctor's evidence that when he arrived at Riddlesdale at 4.30 deceased had been already three or four hours dead. They would remember also that, in Dr. Thorpe's opinion, death had not immediately
followed the wound. If they believed this evidence, therefore, they
would have to put back the moment of death to between eleven p.m.
and midnight, and this might very well have been the shot which the
gamekeeper heard. In that case they had still to ask themselves about
the shot which had awakened Lady Mary Wimsey. Of course, if they
liked to put that down to poachers, there was no inherent im-
possibility.

They next came to the body of deceased, which had been discovered by the Duke of Denver at three a.m. lying outside the door of
the small conservatory, near the covered well. There seemed little
doubt, from the medical evidence, that the shot which killed deceased
had been fired in the shrubbery, about seven minutes' distance from
the house, and that the body of deceased had been dragged from that
place to the house. Deceased had undoubtedly died as the result of
being shot in the lungs. The jury would have to decide whether that
shot was fired by his own hand or by the hand of another; and, if the
latter, whether by accident, in self-defence, or by malice aforethought
with intent to murder. As regards suicide, they must consider what
they knew of deceased's character and circumstances. Deceased was
a young man in the prime of his strength, and apparently of considerable fortune. He had had a meritorious military career, and was liked
by his friends. The Duke of Denver had thought sufficiently well of
him to consent to his own sister's engagement to deceased. There was
evidence to show that the fiancés, though perhaps not demonstrative,
were on excellent terms. The Duke affirmed that on the Wednesday
night deceased had announced his intention of breaking off the en-

gagement. Did they believe that deceased, without even communicating with the lady, or writing a word of explanation or farewell, would thereupon rush out and shoot himself? Again, the jury must consider the accusation which the Duke of Denver said he had brought against deceased. He had accused him of cheating at cards. In the kind of society to which the persons involved in this inquiry belonged, such a misdemeanour as cheating at cards was regarded as far more shameful than such sins as murder and adultery. Possibly the mere suggestion of such a thing, whether well-founded or not, might well cause a gentleman of sensitive honour to make away with himself. But was deceased honourable? Deceased had been educated in France, and French notions of the honest thing were very different from British ones. The Coroner himself had had business relations with French persons in his capacity as a solicitor, and could assure such of the jury as had never been in France that they ought to allow for these different standards. Unhappily, the alleged letter giving details of the accusation had not been produced to them. Next, they might ask themselves whether it was not more usual for a suicide to shoot himself in the head. They should ask themselves how deceased came by the revolver. And, finally, they must consider, in that case, who had dragged the body towards the house, and why the person had chosen to do so, with great labour to himself and at the risk of extinguishing any lingering remnant of the vital spark,* instead of arousing the household and fetching help.

If they excluded suicide, there remained accident, manslaughter, or murder. As to the first, if they thought it likely that deceased or any other person had taken out the Duke of Denver's revolver that night for any purpose, and that, in looking at, cleaning, shooting with, or otherwise handling the weapon, it had gone off and killed deceased accidentally, then they would return a verdict of death by misadventure accordingly. In that case, how did they explain the conduct of the person, whoever it was, who had dragged the body to the door?

The Coroner then passed on to speak of the law concerning manslaughter. He reminded them that no mere words, however insulting or threatening, can be an efficient excuse for killing anybody, and that the conflict must be sudden and unpremeditated. Did they think, for example, that the Duke had gone out, wishing to induce his guest to return and sleep in the house, and that deceased had retorted upon

---

* Verbatim.

him with blows or menaces of assault? If so, and the Duke, having a weapon in his hand, had shot deceased in self-defence, that was only manslaughter. But, in that case, they must ask themselves how the Duke came to go out to deceased with a lethal weapon in his hand? And this suggestion was in direct conflict with the Duke's own evidence.

Lastly, they must consider whether there was sufficient evidence of malice to justify a verdict of murder. They must consider whether any person had a motive, means, and opportunity for killing deceased; and whether they could reasonably account for that person's conduct on any other hypothesis. And, if they thought there *was* such a person, and that his conduct was in any way suspicious or secretive, or that he had wilfully suppressed evidence which might have had a bearing on the case, or (here the Coroner spoke with great emphasis, staring over the Duke's head) fabricated other evidence with intent to mislead—then all these circumstances might be sufficient to amount to a violent presumption of guilt against some party, in which case they were in duty bound to bring in a verdict of wilful murder against that party. And, in considering this aspect of the question, the Coroner added, they would have to decide in their own minds whether the person who had dragged deceased towards the conservatory door had done so with the object of obtaining assistance or of thrusting the body down the garden well, which, as they had heard from Inspector Craikes, was situated close by the spot where the body had been found. If the jury were satisfied that deceased had been murdered, but were not prepared to accuse any particular person on the evidence, they might bring in a verdict of murder against an unknown person, or persons; but, if they felt justified in laying the killing at any person's door, then they must allow no respect of persons to prevent them from doing their duty.

Guided by these extremely plain hints, the jury, without very long consultation, returned a verdict of wilful murder against Gerald, Duke of Denver.

CHAPTER II

THE GREEN-EYED CAT

And here's to the hound
With his nose unto the ground——
—Drink, Puppy, Drink.

SOME PEOPLE HOLD that breakfast is the best meal of the day. Others, less robust, hold that it is the worst, and that, of all breakfasts in the week, Sunday morning breakfast is incomparably the worst.

The party gathered about the breakfast-table at Riddlesdale Lodge held, if one might judge from their faces, no brief for that day miscalled of sweet refection and holy love. The only member of it who seemed neither angry nor embarrassed was the Hon. Freddy Arbuthnot, and he was silent, engaged in trying to take the whole skeleton out of a bloater at once. The very presence of that undistinguished fish upon the Duchess's breakfast-table indicated a disorganised household.

The Duchess of Denver was pouring out coffee. This was one of her uncomfortable habits. Persons arriving late for breakfast were thereby made painfully aware of their sloth. She was a long-necked, long-backed woman, who disciplined her hair and her children. She was never embarrassed, and her anger, though never permitted to be visible, made itself felt the more.

Colonel and Mrs. Marchbanks sat side by side. They had nothing beautiful about them but a stolid mutual affection. Mrs. Marchbanks was not angry, but she was embarrassed in the presence of the Duchess, because she could not feel sorry for her. When you felt sorry for people you called them "poor old dear" or "poor dear old man." Since, obviously, you could not call the Duchess poor old dear, you were not being properly sorry for her. This distressed Mrs. Marchbanks. The Colonel was both embarrassed and angry—embarrassed because, 'pon my soul, it was very difficult to know what to talk about in a house where your host had been arrested for murder; angry in a dim way, like an injured animal, because unpleasant things like this had no business to break in on the shooting-season.

24

Mrs. Pettigrew-Robinson was not only angry, she was outraged. As a girl she had adopted the motto stamped upon the school note-paper: *Quæcunque honesta*. She had always thought it *wrong* to let your mind *dwell* on anything that was not really nice. In middle life she still made a point of ignoring those newspaper paragraphs which bore such headlines as: "ASSAULT UPON A SCHOOLTEACHER AT CRICKLEWOOD"; "DEATH IN A PINT OF STOUT"; "£75 FOR A KISS"; or "SHE CALLED HIM HUBBYKINS." She said she could not see what *good* it did you to know about such things. She regretted having consented to visit Riddlesdale Lodge in the absence of the Duchess. She had never liked Lady Mary; she considered her a very objectionable specimen of the modern independent young woman; besides, there had been that very undignified incident connected with a Bolshevist while Lady Mary was nursing in London during the war. Nor had Mrs. Pettigrew-Robinson at all cared for Captain Denis Cathcart. She did not like a young man to be handsome in that obvious kind of way. But, of course, since Mr. Pettigrew-Robinson had wanted to come to Riddlesdale, it was her place to be with him. She was not to blame for the unfortunate result.

Mr. Pettigrew-Robinson was angry, quite simply, because the detective from Scotland Yard had not accepted his help in searching the house and grounds for footprints. As an older man of some experience in these matters (Mr. Pettigrew-Robinson was a county magistrate) he had gone out of his way to place himself at the man's disposal. Not only had the man been short with him, but he had rudely ordered him out of the conservatory, where he (Mr. Pettigrew-Robinson) had been reconstructing the affair from the point of view of Lady Mary.

All these angers and embarrassments might have caused less pain to the company had they not been aggravated by the presence of the detective himself, a quiet young man in a tweed suit, eating curry at one end of the table next to Mr. Murbles, the solicitor. This person had arrived from London on Friday, had corrected the local police, and strongly dissented from the opinion of Inspector Craikes. He had suppressed at the inquest information which, if openly given, might have precluded the arrest of the Duke. He had officiously detained the whole unhappy party, on the grounds that he wanted to re-examine everybody, and was thus keeping them miserably cooped up together over a horrible Sunday; and he had put the coping-stone on his offences by turning out to be an intimate friend of Lord Peter

25

Wimsey's, and having, in consequence, to be accommodated with a bed in the gamekeeper's cottage and breakfast at the Lodge.

Mr. Murbles, who was elderly and had a delicate digestion, had travelled up in a hurry on Thursday night. He had found the inquest very improperly conducted and his client altogether impracticable. He had spent all his time trying to get hold of Sir Impey Biggs, K.C., who had vanished for the week-end, leaving no address. He was eating a little dry toast, and was inclined to like the detective, who called him "Sir," and passed him the butter.

"Is anybody thinking of going to church?" asked the Duchess.

"Theodore and I should like to go," said Mrs. Pettigrew-Robinson, "if it is not too much trouble; or we could walk. It is not so *very* far."

"It's two and a half miles, good," said Colonel Marchbanks.

Mr. Pettigrew-Robinson looked at him gratefully.

"Of course you will come in the car," said the Duchess. "I am going myself."

"Are you, though?" said the Hon. Freddy. "I say, won't you get a bit stared at, what?"

"Really, Freddy," said the Duchess, "does that matter?"

"Well," said the Hon. Freddy, "I mean to say, these bounders about here are all Socialists and Methodists. . . ."

"If they are Methodists," said Mrs. Pettigrew-Robinson, "they will not be at church."

"Won't they?" retorted the Hon. Freddy. "You bet they will if there's anything to see. Why, it'll be better'n a funeral to 'em."

"Surely," said Mrs. Pettigrew-Robinson, "one has a *duty* in the matter, whatever our private feelings may be—especially at the present day, when people are so terribly *slack*."

She glanced at the Hon. Freddy.

"Oh, don't you mind me, Mrs. P.," said that youth amiably. "All *I* say is, if these blighters make things unpleasant, don't blame me."

"Whoever thought of blaming you, Freddy?" said the Duchess.

"Manner of speaking," said the Hon. Freddy.

"What do you think, Mr. Murbles?" inquired her ladyship.

"I feel," said the lawyer, carefully stirring his coffee, "that, while your intention is a very admirable one, and does you very great credit, my dear lady, yet Mr. Arbuthnot is right in saying it may involve you in some—er—unpleasant publicity. Er—I have always been a sincere Christian myself, but I cannot feel that our religion demands that we should make ourselves conspicuous—er—in such very painful circumstances."

Mr. Parker reminded himself of a dictum of Lord Melbourne.

"Well, after all," said Mrs. Marchbanks, "as Helen so rightly says, does it matter? Nobody's really got anything to be ashamed of. There has been a stupid mistake, of course, but I don't see why anybody who wants to shouldn't go to church."

"Certainly not, certainly not, my dear," said the Colonel heartily. "We might look in ourselves, eh, dear? Take a walk that way I mean, and come out before the sermon. I think it's a good thing. Shows *we* don't believe old Denver's done anything wrong, anyhow."

"You forget, dear," said his wife, "I've promised to stay at home with Mary, poor girl."

"Of course, of course—stupid of me," said the Colonel. "How is she?"

"She was very restless last night, poor child," said the Duchess. "Perhaps she will get a little sleep this morning. It has been a shock to her."

"One which may prove a blessing in disguise," said Mrs. Pettigrew-Robinson.

"My dear!" said her husband.

"Wonder when we shall hear from Sir Impey," said Colonel Marchbanks hurriedly.

"Yes, indeed," moaned Mr. Murbles. "I am counting on his influence with the Duke."

"Of course," said Mrs. Pettigrew-Robinson, "he must speak out—for everybody's sake. He must say what he was doing out of doors at that time. Or, if he does not, it must be discovered. Dear me! That's what these detectives are for, aren't they?"

"That is their ungrateful task," said Mr. Parker suddenly. He had said nothing for a long time, and everybody jumped.

"There," said Mrs. Marchbanks, "I expect you'll clear it all up in no time, Mr. Parker. Perhaps you've got the real mur—the culprit up your sleeve all the time."

"Not quite," said Mr. Parker, "but I'll do my best to get him. Besides," he added, with a grin, "I'll probably have some help on the job."

"From whom?" inquired Mr. Pettigrew-Robinson.

"Her grace's brother-in-law."

27

"Peter?" said the Duchess. "Mr. Parker must be amused at the family amateur," she added.

"Not at all," said Parker. "Wimsey would be one of the finest detectives in England if he wasn't lazy. Only we can't get hold of him."

"I've wired to Ajaccio—poste restante," said Mr. Murbles, "but I don't know when he's likely to call there. He said nothing about when he was coming back to England."

"He's a rummy old bird," said the Hon. Freddy tactlessly, "but he oughter be here, what? What I mean to say is, if anything happens to old Denver, don't you see, he's the head of the family, ain't he—till little Pickled Gherkins comes of age."

In the frightful silence which followed this remark, the sound of a walking-stick being clattered into an umbrella-stand was distinctly audible.

"Who's that, I wonder," said the Duchess.

The door waltzed open.

"Mornin', dear old things," said the newcomer cheerfully. "How are you all? Hullo, Helen! Colonel, you owe me half a crown since last September year. Mornin', Mrs. Marchbanks, Mornin', Mrs. P. Well, Mr. Murbles, how d'you like this bili-beastly weather? Don't trouble to get up, Freddy; I'd simply hate to inconvenience you. Parker, old man, what a damned reliable old bird you are! Always on the spot, like that patent ointment thing. I say, have you all finished? I meant to get up earlier, but I was snorin' so Bunter hadn't the heart to wake me. I nearly blew in last night, only we didn't arrive till 2 a.m. and I thought you wouldn't half bless me if I did. Eh, what, Colonel? Aeroplane *Victoria* from Paris to London—North-Eastern to North-allerton—damn bad roads the rest of the way, and a puncture just below Riddlesdale. Damn bad bed at the 'Lord in Glory'; thought I'd blow in for the last sausage here, if I was lucky. What? Sunday morning in an English family and no sausages? God bless my soul, what's the world coming to, eh, Colonel? I say, Helen, old Gerald's been an' gone an' done it this time, what? You've no business to leave him on his own, you know; he always gets into mischief. What's that? Curry? Thanks, old man. Here, I say, you needn't be so stingy about it; I've been travelling for three days on end. Freddy, pass the toast. Beg pardon, Mrs. Marchbanks? Oh, rather, yes; Corsica was perfectly amazin'—all black-eyed fellows with knives in their belts and jolly fine-looking girls. Old Bunter had a regular affair with the inn-keeper's daughter in one place. D'you know, he's an awfully suscepti-

ble old beggar. You'd never think it, would you? Jove! I am hungry.
I say, Helen, I meant to get you some fetchin' crêpe-de-Chine undies
from Paris, but I saw that old Parker was gettin' ahead of me over the
bloodstains, so we packed up our things and buzzed off."

Mrs. Pettigrew-Robinson rose.

"Theodore," she said, "I think we ought to be getting ready for
church."

"I will order the car," said the Duchess. "Peter, of course I'm exceedingly glad to see you. Your leaving no address was most inconvenient. Ring for anything you want. It is a pity you didn't arrive in
time to see Gerald."

"Oh, that's all right," said Lord Peter cheerfully; "I'll look him up
in quod. Y'know, it's rather a good idea to keep one's crimes in the
family; one has so many more facilities. I'm sorry for poor old Polly,
though. How is she?"

"She must not be disturbed to-day," said the Duchess with decision.

"Not a bit of it," said Lord Peter; "she'll keep. To-day Parker and
I hold high revel. To-day he shows me all the bloody footprints—it's
all right, Helen, that's not swearin', that's an adjective of quality. I
hope they aren't all washed away, are they, old thing?"

"No," said Parker, "I've got most of them under flower-pots."

"Then pass the bread and squish," said Lord Peter, "and tell me
all about it."

The departure of the church-going element had induced a more
humanitarian atmosphere. Mrs. Marchbanks stumped off upstairs to
tell Mary that Peter had come, and the Colonel lit a large cigar. The
Hon. Freddy rose, stretched himself, pulled a leather armchair to
the fireside, and sat down with his feet on the brass fender, while
Parker marched round and poured himself out another cup of coffee.

"I suppose you've seen the papers," he said.

"Oh, yes, I read up the inquest," said Lord Peter. "Y'know, if
you'll excuse my saying so, I think you rather mucked it between
you."

"It was disgraceful," said Mr. Murbles, "disgraceful. The Coroner
behaved most improperly. He had no business to give such a
summing-up. With a jury of ignorant country fellows, what could
one expect? And the details that were allowed to come out! If I could
have got here earlier——"

"I'm afraid that was partly my fault, Wimsey," said Parker penitently. "Craikes rather resents me. The Superintendent at Stapley sent to us over his head, and when the message came through I ran along to the Chief and asked for the job, because I thought if there should be any misconception or difficulty, you see, you'd just as soon I tackled it as anybody else. I had a few little arrangements to make about a forgery I've been looking into, and, what with one thing and another, I didn't get off till the night express. By the time I turned up on Friday, Craikes and the Coroner were already as thick as thieves, had fixed the inquest for that morning—which was ridiculous—and arranged to produce their blessed evidence as dramatically as possible. I only had time to skim over the ground (disfigured, I'm sorry to say, by the prints of Craikes and his local ruffians), and really had nothing for the jury."

"Cheer up," said Wimsey. "I'm not blaming you. Besides, it all lends excitement to the chase."

"Fact is," said the Hon. Freddy, "that we ain't popular with respectable Coroners. Giddy aristocrats and immoral Frenchmen. I say, Peter, sorry you've missed Miss Lydia Cathcart. You'd have loved her. She's gone back to Golders Green and taken the body with her."

"Oh, well," said Wimsey. "I don't suppose there was anything abstruse about the body."

"No," said Parker, "the medical evidence was all right as far as it went. He was shot through the lungs, and that's all."

"Though, mind you," said the Hon. Freddy, "he didn't shoot himself. I didn't say anything, not wishin' to upset old Denver's story, but, you know, all that stuff about his bein' so upset and go-to-blazes in his manner was all my whiskers."

"How do you know?" said Peter.

"Why, my dear man, Cathcart'n I toddled up to bed together. I was rather fed up, havin' dropped a lot on some shares, besides missin' everything I shot at in the mornin', an' lost a bet I made with the Colonel about the number of toes on the kitchen cat, an' I said to Cathcart it was a hell of a damn-fool world, or words to that effect. 'Not a bit of it,' he said; 'it's a damn good world. I'm goin' to ask Mary for a date to-morrow, an' then we'll go and live in Paris, where they understand sex.' I said somethin' or other vague, and he went off whistlin'."

Parker looked grave. Colonel Marchbanks cleared his throat.

"Well, well," he said, "there's no accounting for a man like Cathcart, no accounting at all. Brought up in France, you know. Not at all like a straightforward Englishman. Always up and down, up and down! Very sad, poor fellow. Well, well, Peter, hope you and Mr. Parker will find out something about it. We mustn't have poor old Denver cooped up in gaol like this, you know. Awfully unpleasant for him, poor chap, and with the birds so good this year. Well, I expect you'll be making a tour of inspection, eh, Mr. Parker? What do you say to shoving the balls about a bit, Freddy?"

"Right you are," said the Hon. Freddy; "you'll have to give me a hundred, though, Colonel."

"Nonsense, nonsense," said that veteran, in high good humour; "you play an excellent game."

Mr. Murbles having withdrawn, Wimsey and Parker faced each other over the remains of the breakfast.

"Peter," said the detective, "I don't know if I've done the right thing by coming. If you feel——"

"Look here, old man," said his friend earnestly, "let's cut out the considerations of delicacy. We're goin' to work this case like any other. If anything unpleasant turns up, I'd rather you saw it than anybody else. It's an uncommonly pretty little case, on its merits, and I'm goin' to put some damn good work into it."

"If you're sure it's all right——"

"My dear man, if you hadn't been here I'd have sent for you. Now let's get to business. Of course, *I'm* settin' off with the assumption that old Gerald didn't do it."

"I'm sure he didn't," agreed Parker.

"No, no," said Wimsey, "that isn't your line. Nothing rash about you—nothing trustful. You are expected to throw cold water on my hopes and doubt all my conclusions."

"Right ho!" said Parker. "Where would you like to begin?"

Peter considered. "I think we'll start from Cathcart's bedroom," he said.

. . . . .

The bedroom was of moderate size, with a single window over-looking the front door. The bed was on the right-hand side, the dressing-table before the window. On the left was the fireplace, with an arm-chair before it, and a small writing-table.

"Everything's as it was," said Parker. "Craikes had that much sense."

"Yes," said Lord Peter. "Very well. Gerald says that when he charged Cathcart with bein' a scamp, Cathcart jumped up, nearly knockin' the table over. That's the writin'-table, then, so Cathcart was sittin' in the armchair. Yes, he was—and he pushed it back violently and rumpled up the carpet. See! So far, so good. Now what was he doin' there? He wasn't readin', because there's no book about, and we know that he rushed straight out of the room and never came back. Very good. Was he writin'? No; virgin sheet of blottin'-paper——"

"He might have been writing in pencil," suggested Parker.

"That's true, old Kill-Joy, so he might. Well, if he was he shoved the paper into his pocket when Gerald came in, because it isn't here; but he didn't, because it wasn't found on his body; so he wasn't writing."

"Unless he threw the paper away somewhere else," said Parker. "I haven't been all over the grounds, you know, and at the smallest computation—if we accept the shot heard by Hardraw at 11.50 as *the* shot—there's an hour and a half unaccounted for."

"Very well. Let's say there is nothing to show he was writing. Will that do? Well, then——"

Lord Peter drew out a lens and scrutinised the surface of the armchair carefully before sitting down in it.

"Nothing helpful there," he said. "To proceed, Cathcart sat where I am sitting. He wasn't writing; he—you're sure this room hasn't been touched?"

"Certain."

"Then he wasn't smoking."

"Why not? He might have chucked the stub of a cigar or cigarette into the fire when Denver came in."

"Not a cigarette," said Peter, "or we should find traces somewhere —on the floor or in the grate. That light ash blows about so. But a cigar—well, he might have smoked a cigar without leaving a sign, I suppose. But I hope he didn't."

"Why?"

"Because, old son, I'd rather Gerald's account had some element of truth in it. A nervy man doesn't sit down to the delicate enjoyment of a cigar before bed, and cherish the ash with such scrupulous care. On the other hand, if Freddy's right, and Cathcart was feelin' unusually sleek and pleased with life, that's just the sort of thing he would do."

"Do you think Mr. Arbuthnot would have invented all that, as a matter of fact?" said Parker thoughtfully. "He doesn't strike me that way. He'd have to be imaginative and spiteful to make it up, and I really don't think he's either."

"I know," said Lord Peter. "I've known old Freddy all my life, and he wouldn't hurt a fly. Besides, he simply hasn't the wits to make up any sort of a story. But what bothers me is that Gerald most certainly hasn't the wits either to invent that Adelphi drama between him and Cathcart."

"On the other hand," said Parker, "if we allow for a moment that he shot Cathcart, he had an incentive to invent it. He would be trying to get his head out of the—I mean, when anything important is at stake it's wonderful how it sharpens one's wits. And the story being so far-fetched does rather suggest an unpractised story-teller."

"True, O King. Well, you've sat on all my discoveries so far. Never mind. My head is bloody but unbowed. Cathcart was sitting here——"

"So your brother said."

"Curse you, *I* say he was; at least, somebody was; he's left the impression of his sit-me-down-upon on the cushion."

"That might have been earlier in the day."

"Rot. They were out all day. You needn't overdo this Sadducee attitude, Charles. I say Cathcart was sitting here, and—hullo! hullo!"

He leaned forward and stared into the grate.

"There's some burnt paper here, Charles."

"I know. I was frightfully excited about that yesterday, but I found it was just the same in several of the rooms. They often let the bedroom fires go out when everybody's out during the day, and relight them about an hour before dinner. There's only the cook, housemaid, and Fleming here, you see, and they've got a lot to do with such a large party."

Lord Peter was picking the charred fragments over.

"I can find nothing to contradict your suggestion," he sadly said, "and this fragment of the *Morning Post* rather confirms it. Then we can only suppose that Cathcart sat here in a brown study, doing nothing at all. That doesn't get us much further, I'm afraid." He got up and went to the dressing-table.

"I like these tortoiseshell sets," he said, "and the perfume is *'Baiser du Soir'*—very nice too. New to me. I must draw Bunter's attention to it. A charming manicure set, isn't it? You know, I like being clean and neat and all that, but Cathcart was the kind of man who always impressed you as bein' just a little *too* well turned out. Poor devil! And he'll be buried at Golders Green after all. I only saw him once or twice, you know. He impressed me as knowin' about everything there was to know. I was rather surprised at Mary takin' to him, but, then, I know really awfully little about Mary. You see, she's five years younger than me. When the war broke out she'd just left school and gone to a place in Paris, and I joined up, and she came back and did nursing and social work, so I only saw her occasionally. At that time she was rather taken up with new schemes for puttin' the world to rights and hadn't a lot to say to me. And she got hold of some pacifist fellow who was a bit of a stumer, I fancy. Then I was ill, you know, and then I got the chuck from Barbara and didn't feel much like botherin' about other people's heart-to-hearts, and then I got mixed up in the Attenbury diamond case—and the result is I know uncommonly little about my own sister. But it looks as though her taste in men had altered. I know my mother said Cathcart had charm; that means he was attractive to women, I suppose. No man can see what makes that in another man, but mother is usually right. What's become of this fellow's papers?"

"He left very little here," replied Parker. "There's a cheque-book on Cox's Charing Cross branch, but it's a new one and not very helpful. Apparently he only kept a small current account with them for convenience when he was in England. The cheques are mostly to self, with an occasional hotel or tailor."

"Any pass-book?"

"I think all his important papers are in Paris. He has a flat there, near the river somewhere. We're in communication with the Paris police. He had a room at the Albany. I've told them to lock it up till I get there. I thought of running up to town to-morrow."

"Yes, you'd better. Any pocket-book?"

"Yes; here you are. About £30 in various notes, a wine-merchant's card, and a bill for a pair of riding-breeches."

"No correspondence?"

"Not a line."

"No," said Wimsey, "he was the kind, I imagine, that didn't keep letters. Much too good an instinct of self-preservation."

"Yes. I asked the servants about his letters, as a matter of fact. They said he got a good number, but never left them about. They couldn't tell me much about the ones he wrote, because all the out-going letters are dropped into the post-bag, which is carried down to

the post-office as it is and opened there, or handed over to the post-
man when—or if—he calls. The general impression was that he didn't
write much. The housemaid said she never found anything to speak
of in the waste-paper basket."

"Well, that's uncommonly helpful. Wait a moment. Here's his
fountain-pen. Very handsome—Onoto with complete gold casing.
Dear me! entirely empty. Well, I don't know that one can deduce anything from that, exactly. I don't see any pencil about, by the way. I'm
inclined to think you're wrong in supposing that he was writing letters."

"I didn't suppose anything," said Parker mildly. "I daresay you're
right."

Lord Peter left the dressing-table, looked through the contents of
the wardrobe, and turned over the two or three books on the pedestal
beside the bed.

"*La Rôtisserie de la Reine Pédauque, L'Anneau d'Améthyste,
South Wind* (our young friend works out very true to type), *Chro-
nique d'un Cadet de Coutras* (tut-tut, Charles!), *Manon Lescaut.*
H'm! Is there anything else in this room I ought to look at?"

"I don't think so. Where'd you like to go now?"

"We'll follow 'em down. Wait a jiff. Who are in the other rooms?
Oh, yes. Here's Gerald's room. Helen's at church. In we go. Of course,
this has been dusted and cleaned up, and generally ruined for purposes of observation?"

"I'm afraid so. I could hardly keep the Duchess out of her bedroom."

"No. Here's the window Gerald shouted out of. H'm! Nothing
in the grate here, naturally—the fire's been lit since. I say, I wonder
where Gerald did put that letter to—Freeborn's, I mean."

"Nobody's been able to get a word out of him about it," said
Parker. "Old Mr. Murbles had a fearful time with him. The Duke
insists simply that he destroyed it. Mr. Murbles says that's absurd.
So it is. If he was going to bring that sort of accusation against his
sister's fiancé he'd want *some* evidence of a method in his madness,
wouldn't he? Or was he one of those Roman brothers who say simply: 'As the head of the family I forbid the banns and that's
enough'?"

"Gerald," said Wimsey, "is a good, clean, decent, thoroughbred
public schoolboy, and a shocking ass. But I don't think he's so
mediaeval as that."

"But if he has the letter, why not produce it?"

"Why, indeed? Letters from old college friends in Egypt aren't, as a rule, compromising."

"You don't suppose," suggested Parker tentatively, "that this Mr. Freeborn referred in his letter to any old—er—entanglement which your brother wouldn't wish the Duchess to know about?"

Lord Peter paused, while absently examining a row of boots.

"That's an idea," he said. "There were occasions—mild ones, but Helen would make the most of them." He whistled thoughtfully. "Still, when it comes to the gallows——"

"Do you suppose, Wimsey, that your brother really contemplates the gallows?" asked Parker.

"I think Murbles put it to him pretty straight," said Lord Peter.

"Quite so. But does he actually realise—imaginatively—that it is possible to hang an English peer for murder on circumstantial evidence?"

Lord Peter considered this.

"Imagination isn't Gerald's strong point," he admitted. "I suppose they *do* hang peers? They can't be beheaded on Tower Hill or anything?"

"I'll look it up," said Parker; "but they certainly hanged Earl Ferrers in 1760."

"Did they, though?" said Lord Peter. "Ah, well, as the old pagan said of the Gospels, after all, it was a long time ago, and we'll hope it wasn't true."

"It's true enough," said Parker; "and he was dissected and anatomised afterwards. But that part of the treatment is obsolete."

"We'll tell Gerald about it," said Lord Peter, "and persuade him to take the matter seriously. Which are the boots he wore Wednesday night?"

"These," said Parker, "but the fool's cleaned them."

"Yes," said Lord Peter bitterly. "M'm! a good heavy lace-up boot —the sort that sends the blood to the head."

"He wore leggings, too," said Parker; "these."

"Rather elaborate preparations for a stroll in the garden. But, as you were just going to say, the night was wet. I must ask Helen if Gerald ever suffered from insomnia."

"I did. She said she thought not as a rule, but that he occasionally had toothache, which made him restless."

"It wouldn't send one out of doors on a cold night, though. Well, let's get downstairs."

They passed through the billiard-room, where the Colonel was making a sensational break, and into the small conservatory which led from it.

Lord Peter looked gloomily round at the chrysanthemums and boxes of bulbs.

"These damned flowers look jolly healthy," he said. "Do you mean you've been letting the gardener swarm in here every day to water 'em?"

"Yes," said Parker apologetically, "I did. But he's had strict orders only to walk on these mats."

"Good," said Lord Peter. "Take 'em up, then, and let's get to work."

With his lens to his eye he crawled cautiously over the floor.

"They all came through this way, I suppose," he said.

"Yes," said Parker. "I've identified most of the marks. People went in and out. Here's the Duke. He comes in from outside. He trips over the body." (Parker had opened the outer door and lifted some matting, to show a trampled patch of gravel, discoloured with blood.) "He kneels by the body. Here are his knees and toes. Afterwards he goes into the house, through the conservatory, leaving a good impression in black mud and gravel just inside the door."

Lord Peter squatted carefully over the marks.

"It's lucky the gravel's so soft here," he said.

"Yes. It's just a patch. The gardener tells me it gets very trampled and messy just here owing to his coming to fill cans from the water-trough. They fill the trough up from the well every so often, and then carry the water away in cans. It got extra bad this year, and they put down fresh gravel a few weeks ago."

"Pity they didn't extend their labours all down the path while they were about it," grunted Lord Peter, who was balancing himself precariously on a small piece of sacking. "Well, that bears out old Gerald so far. Here's an elephant been over this bit of box border. Who's that?"

"Oh, that's a constable. I put him at eighteen stone. He's nothing. And this rubber sole with a patch on it is Craikes. He's all over the place. This squelchy-looking thing is Mr. Arbuthnot in bedroom slippers, and the goloshes are Mr. Pettigrew-Robinson. We can dismiss all those. But now here, just coming over the threshold, is a

37

woman's foot in a strong shoe. I make that out to be Lady Mary's.
Here it is again, just at the edge of the well. She came out to examine
the body."

"Quite so," said Peter; "and then she came in again, with a few
grains of red gravel on her shoes. Well, that's all right. Hullo!"

On the outer side of the conservatory were some shelves for small
plants, and, beneath these, a damp and dismal bed of earth, occupied,
in a sprawling and lackadaisical fashion, by stringy cactus plants and
a sporadic growth of maidenhair fern, and masked by a row of large
chrysanthemums in pots.

"What've you got?" inquired Parker, seeing his friend peering into
this green retreat.

Lord Peter withdrew his long nose from between two pots and
said: "Who put what down here?"

Parker hastened to the place. There, among the cacti, was certainly the clear mark of some oblong object, with corners, that had
been stood out of sight on the earth behind the pots.

"It's a good thing Gerald's gardener ain't one of those conscientious
blighters that can't even let a cactus alone for the winter," said Lord
Peter, "or he'd've tenderly lifted these little drooping heads—oh!
damn and blast the beastly plant for a crimson porcupine! *You* measure it."

Parker measured it.

"Two and a half feet by six inches," he said. "And fairly heavy, for
it's sunk in and broken the plants about. Was it a bar of anything?"

"I fancy not," said Lord Peter. "The impression is deeper on the
farther side. I think it was something bulky set up on edge, and
leaned against the glass. If you asked for my private opinion I should
guess that it was a suit-case."

"A suit-case!" exclaimed Parker. "Why a suit-case?"

"Why indeed? I think we may assume that it didn't stay here very
long. It would have been exceedingly visible in the daytime. But
somebody might very well have shoved it in here if they were caught
with it—say at three o'clock in the morning—and didn't want it to be
seen."

"Then when did they take it away?"

"Almost immediately, I should say. Before daylight, anyhow, or
even Inspector Craikes could hardly have failed to see it."

"It's not the doctor's bag, I suppose?"

"No—unless the doctor's a fool. Why put a bag inconveniently in a damp and dirty place out of the way when every law of sense and convenience would urge him to pop it down handy by the body? No. Unless Craikes or the gardener has been leaving things about, it was thrust away there on Wednesday night by Gerald, by Cathcart—or, I suppose, by Mary. Nobody else could be supposed to have anything to hide."

"Yes," said Parker, "one person."

"Who's that?"

"The Person Unknown."

"Who's he?"

For answer Mr. Parker proudly stepped to a row of wooden frames, carefully covered with matting. Stripping this away, with the air of a bishop unveiling a memorial, he disclosed a V-shaped line of footprints.

"These," said Parker, "belong to nobody—to nobody I've ever seen or heard of, I mean."

"Hurray!" said Peter.

> "Then downwards from the steep hill's edge
> They tracked the footmarks small

(only they're largish)."

"No such luck," said Parker. "It's more a case of:

> They followed from the earthy bank
> Those footsteps one by one,
> Into the middle of the plank;
> And farther there were none!"

"Great poet, Wordsworth," said Lord Peter; "how often I've had that feeling. Now let's see. These footmarks—a man's No. 10 with worn-down heels and a patch on the left inner side—advance from the hard bit of the path which shows no footmarks; they come to the body—here, where that pool of blood is. I say, that's rather odd, don't you think? No? Perhaps not. There are no footmarks under the body? Can't say, it's such a mess. Well, the Unknown gets so far—here's a footmark deeply pressed in. Was he just going to throw Cathcart into the well? He hears a sound; he starts; he turns; he runs on tiptoe —into the shrubbery, by Jove!"

"Yes," said Parker, "and the tracks come out on one of the grass paths in the wood, and there's an end of them."

"H'm! Well, we'll follow them later. Now where did they come from?"

Together the two friends followed the path away from the house. The gravel, except for the little patch before the conservatory, was old and hard, and afforded but little trace, particularly as the last few days had been rainy. Parker, however, was able to assure Wimsey that there had been definite traces of dragging and bloodstains.

"What sort of bloodstains? Smears?"

"Yes, smears mostly. There were pebbles displaced, too, all the way—and now here is something odd."

It was the clear impression of the palm of a man's hand heavily pressed into the earth of a herbaceous border, the fingers pointing towards the house. On the path the gravel had been scraped up in two long furrows. There was blood on the grass border between the path and the bed, and the edge of the grass was broken and trampled.

"I don't like that," said Lord Peter.

"Ugly, isn't it?" agreed Parker.

"Poor devil!" said Peter. "He made a determined effort to hang on here. That explains the blood by the conservatory door. But what kind of a devil drags a corpse that isn't quite dead?"

A few yards farther the path ran into the main drive. This was bordered with trees, widening into a thicket. At the point of intersection of the two paths were some further indistinct marks, and in another twenty yards or so they turned aside into the thicket. A large tree had fallen at some time and made a little clearing, in the midst of which a tarpaulin had been carefully spread out and pegged down. The air was heavy with the smell of fungus and fallen leaves.

"Scene of the tragedy," said Parker briefly, rolling back the tarpaulin.

Lord Peter gazed down sadly. Muffled in an overcoat and a thick grey scarf, he looked, with his long, narrow face, like a melancholy adjutant stork. The writhing body of the fallen man had scraped up the dead leaves and left a depression in the sodden ground. At one place the darker earth showed where a great pool of blood had soaked into it, and the yellow leaves of a Spanish poplar were rusted with no autumnal stain.

"That's where they found the handkerchief and revolver," said Parker. "I looked for finger-marks, but the rain and mud had messed everything up."

Wimsey took out his lens, lay down, and conducted a personal tour of the whole space slowly on his stomach, Parker moving mutely after him.

"He paced up and down for some time," said Lord Peter. "He wasn't smoking. He was turning something over in his mind, or waiting for somebody. What's this? Aha! Here's our No. 10 foot again, coming in through the trees on the farther side. No signs of a struggle. That's odd! Cathcart was shot close up, wasn't he?"

"Yes; it singed his shirt-front."

"Quite so. Why did he stand still to be shot at?"

"I imagine," said Parker, "that if he had an appointment with No. 10 Boots it was somebody he knew, who could get close to him without arousing suspicion."

"Then the interview was a friendly one—on Cathcart's side, anyhow. But the revolver's a difficulty. How did No. 10 get hold of Gerald's revolver?"

"The conservatory door was open," said Parker dubiously.

"Nobody knew about that except Gerald and Fleming," retorted Lord Peter. "Besides, do you mean to tell me that No. 10 walked in here, went to the study, fetched the revolver, walked back here, and shot Cathcart? It seems a clumsy method. If he wanted to do any shooting, why didn't he come armed in the first place?"

"It seems more probable that Cathcart brought the revolver," said Parker.

"Then why no signs of a struggle?"

"Perhaps Cathcart shot himself," said Parker.

"Then why should No. 10 drag him into a conspicuous position and then run away?"

"Wait a minute," said Parker. "How's this? No. 10 has an appointment with Cathcart—to blackmail him, let's say. He somehow gets word of his intention to him between 9.45 and 10.15. That would account for the alteration in Cathcart's manner, and allow both Mr. Arbuthnot and the Duke to be telling the truth. Cathcart rushes violently out after his row with your brother. He comes down here to keep his appointment. He paces up and down waiting for No. 10. No. 10 arrives and parleys with Cathcart. Cathcart offers him money. No. 10 stands out for more. Cathcart says he really hasn't got it. No. 10 says in that case he blows the gaff. Cathcart retorts, 'In that case you can go to the devil. I'm going there myself.' Cathcart, who has previously got hold of the revolver, shoots himself. No. 10 is seized with remorse. He sees that Cathcart isn't quite dead. He picks him

41

up and part drags, part carries him to the house. He is smaller than Cathcart and not very strong, and finds it a hard job. They have just got to the conservatory door when Cathcart has a final hœmorrhage and gives up the ghost. No. 10 suddenly becomes aware that his position in somebody else's grounds, alone with a corpse at 3 a.m., wants some explaining. He drops Cathcart—and bolts. Enter the Duke of Denver and falls over the body. Tableau."

"That's good," said Lord Peter; "that's very good. But when do you suppose it happened? Gerald found the body at 3 a.m.; the doctor was here at 4.30, and said Cathcart had been dead several hours. Very well. Now, how about that shot my sister heard at three o'clock?"

"Look here, old man," said Parker, "I don't want to appear rude to your sister. May I put it like this? I suggest that that shot at 3 a.m. was poachers."

"Poachers by all means," said Lord Peter. "Well, really, Parker, I think that hangs together. Let's adopt that explanation provisionally. The first thing to do is now to find No. 10, since he can bear witness that Cathcart committed suicide; and that, as far as my brother is concerned, is the only thing that matters a rap. But for the satisfaction of my own curiosity I'd like to know: What was No. 10 blackmailing Cathcart about? Who hid a suit-case in the conservatory? And what was Gerald doing in the garden at 3 a.m.?"

"Well," said Parker, "suppose we begin by tracing where No. 10 came from."

"Hi, hi!" cried Wimsey, as they returned to the trail. "Here's something—here's real treasure-trove, Parker!"

From amid the mud and the fallen leaves he retrieved a tiny, glittering object—a flash of white and green between his finger-tips.

It was a little charm such as women hang upon a bracelet—a diminutive diamond cat with eyes of bright emerald.

MUDSTAINS AND BLOODSTAINS

*Other things are all very well in their way, but give me Blood
. . . We say, "There it is! that's Blood!" It is an actual matter
of fact. We point it out. It admits of no doubt. . . . We must
have Blood, you know.*—David Copperfield.

"HITHERTO," SAID LORD PETER, as they picked their painful way
through the little wood on the trail of Gent's No. 10's, "I have always
maintained that those obliging criminals who strew their tracks with
little articles of personal adornment—here he is, on a squashed fungus
—were an invention of detective fiction for the benefit of the author.
I see that I have still something to learn about my job."

"Well, you haven't been at it very long, have you?" said Parker.
"Besides, we don't know that the diamond cat is the criminal's. It
may belong to a member of your own family, and have been lying
here for days. It may belong to Mr. What's-his-name in the States, or
to the last tenant but one, and have been lying here for years. This
broken branch may be our friend—I think it is."

"I'll ask the family," said Lord Peter, "and we could find out in
the village if anyone's ever inquired for a lost cat. They're pukka
stones. It ain't the sort of thing one would drop without making a fuss
about—I've lost him altogether."

"It's all right—I've got him. He's tripped over a root."

"Serve him glad," said Lord Peter viciously, straightening his back.
"I say, I don't think the human frame is very thoughtfully constructed
for this sleuth-hound business. If one could go on all-fours, or had
eyes in one's knees, it would be a lot more practical."

"There are many difficulties inherent in a teleological view of crea-
tion," said Parker placidly. "Ah! here we are at the park palings."

"And here's where he got over," said Lord Peter, pointing to a
place where the *chevaux de frise* on the top was broken away. "Here's
the dent where his heels came down, and here's where he fell forward
on hands and knees. Hum! Give us a back, old man, would you?
Thanks. An old break, I see. Mr. Montague-now-in-the-States should

43

keep his palings in better order. No. 10 tore his coat on the spikes all the same; he left a fragment of Burberry behind him. What luck! Here's a deep, damp ditch on the other side, which I shall now proceed to fall into."

A slithering crash proclaimed that he had carried out his intention. Parker, thus callously abandoned, looked round, and, seeing that they were only a hundred yards or so from the gate, ran along and was let out, decorously, by Hardraw, the gamekeeper, who happened to be coming out of the lodge.

"By the way," said Parker to him, "did you ever find any signs of any poachers on Wednesday night after all?"

"Nay," said the man, "not so much as a dead rabbit. I reckon t'lady wor mistaken, an 'twore the shot I heard as killed t'Captain."

"Possibly," said Parker. "Do you know how long the spikes have been broken off the palings over there?"

"A moonth or two, happen. They should 'a' bin put right, but the man's sick."

"The gate's locked at night, I suppose?"

"Aye."

"Anybody wishing to get in would have to waken you?"

"Aye, that he would."

"You didn't see any suspicious character loitering about outside these palings last Wednesday, I suppose?"

"Nay, sir, but my wife may ha' done. Hey, lass!"

Mrs. Hardraw, thus summoned, appeared at the door with a small boy clinging to her skirts.

"Wednesday?" said she. "Nay, I saw no loiterin' folks. I keep a look-out for tramps and such, as it be such a lonely place. Wednesday. Eh, now, John, that wad be t'day t'young mon called wi' t'motor-bike."

"Young man with a motor-bike?"

"I reckon 'twas. He said he'd had a puncture and asked for a bucket o' watter."

"Was that all the asking he did?"

"He asked what were t'name o' t'place and whose house it were."

"Did you tell him the Duke of Denver was living here?"

"Aye, sir, and he said he supposed a many gentlemen came up for t'shooting."

"Did he say where he was going?"

"He said he'd coom oop fra' Weirdale an' were makin' a trip into Coomberland."

"How long was he here?"

"Happen half an hour. An' then he tried to get his machine started, an' I see him hop-hoppitin' away towards King's Fenton."

She pointed away to the right, where Lord Peter might be seen gesticulating in the middle of the road.

"What sort of a man was he?"

Like most people, Mrs. Hardraw was poor at definition. She thought he was youngish and tallish, neither dark nor fair, in such a long coat as motor-bicyclists use, with a belt round it.

"Was he a gentleman?"

Mrs. Hardraw hesitated, and Mr. Parker mentally classed the stranger as "Not quite quite."

"You didn't happen to notice the number of the bicycle?"

Mrs. Hardraw had not. "But it had a side-car," she added.

Lord Peter's gesticulations were becoming quite violent, and Mr. Parker hastened to rejoin him.

"Come on, gossiping old thing," said Lord Peter unreasonably. "This is a beautiful ditch.

> From such a ditch as this,
> When the soft wind did gently kiss the trees
> And they did make no noise, from such a ditch
> Our friend, methinks, mounted the Troyan walls,
> And wiped his soles upon the greasy mud.

Look at my trousers!"

"It's a bit of a climb from this side," said Parker.

"It is. He stood here in the ditch, and put one foot into this place where the paling's broken away and one hand on the top, and hauled himself up. No. 10 must have been a man of exceptional height, strength, and agility. I couldn't get my foot up, let alone reaching the top with my hand. I'm five foot nine. Could you?"

Parker was six foot, and could just touch the top of the wall with his hand.

"I *might* do it—on one of my best days," he said, "for an adequate object, or after adequate stimulant."

"Just so," said Lord Peter. "Hence we deduce No. 10's exceptional height and strength."

"Yes," said Parker. "It's a bit unfortunate that we had to deduce his exceptional shortness and weakness just now, isn't it?"

"Oh!" said Peter. "Well—well, as you so rightly say, that *is* a bit unfortunate."

"Well, it may clear up presently. He didn't have a confederate to give him a back or a leg, I suppose?"

"Not unless the confederate was a being without feet or any visible means of support," said Lord Peter, indicating the solitary print of a pair of patched 10's. "By the way, how did he make straight in the dark for the place where the spikes were missing? Looks as though he belonged to the neighbourhood, or had reconnoitred previously."

"Arising out of that reply," said Parker, "I will now relate to you the entertaining 'gossip' I have had with Mrs. Hardraw."

"Humph!" said Wimsey at the end of it. "That's interesting. We'd better make inquiries at Riddlesdale and King's Fenton. Meanwhile we know where No. 10 came from; now where did he go after leaving Cathcart's body by the well?"

"The footsteps went into the preserve," said Parker. "I lost them there. There is a regular carpet of dead leaves and bracken."

"Well, but we needn't go through all that sleuth grind again," objected his friend. "The fellow went in, and, as he presumably is not there still, he came out again. He didn't come out through the gate or Hardraw would have seen him; he didn't come out the same way he went in or he would have left some traces. Therefore he came out elsewhere. Let's walk round the wall."

"Then we'll turn to the left," said Parker, "since that's the side of the preserve, and he apparently went through there."

"True, O King; and as this isn't a church, there's no harm in going round it widdershins. Talking of church, there's Helen coming back. Get a move on, old thing."

They crossed the drive, passed the cottage, and then, leaving the road, followed the paling across some open grass fields. It was not long before they found what they sought. From one of the iron spikes above them dangled forlornly a strip of material. With Parker's assistance Wimsey scrambled up in a state of almost lyric excitement.

"Here we are," he cried. "The belt of a Burberry! No sort of precaution here. Here are the toe-prints of a fellow sprinting for his life. He tore off his Burberry; he made desperate leaps—one, two, three—at the palings. At the third leap he hooked it on to the spikes.

46

He scrambled up, scoring long, scrabbling marks on the paling. He reached the top. Oh, here's a bloodstain run into this crack. He tore his hands. He dropped off. He wrenched the coat away, leaving the belt dangling——"

"I wish you'd drop off," grumbled Parker. "You're breaking my collar-bone."

Lord Peter dropped off obediently, and stood there holding the belt between his fingers. His narrow grey eyes wandered restlessly over the field. Suddenly he seized Parker's arm and marched briskly in the direction of the wall on the farther side—a low erection of un-mortared stone in the fashion of the country. Here he hunted along like a terrier, nose foremost, the tip of his tongue caught absurdly between his teeth, then jumped over, and, turning to Parker, said:

"Did you ever read *The Lay of the Last Minstrel?*"

"I learnt a good deal of it at school," said Parker. "Why?"

"Because there was a goblin page-boy in it," said Lord Peter, "who was always yelling 'Found! Found! Found!' at the most unnecessary moments. I always thought him a terrible nuisance, but now I know how he felt. See here."

Close under the wall, and sunk heavily into the narrow and muddy lane which ran up here at right angles to the main road, was the track of a side-car combination.

"Very nice too," said Mr. Parker approvingly. "New Dunlop tyre on the front wheel. Old tyre on the back. Gaiter on the side-car tyre. Nothing could be better. Tracks come in from the road and go back to the road. Fellow shoved the machine in here in case anybody of an inquisitive turn of mind should pass on the road and make off with it, or take its number. Then he went round on shank's mare to the gap he'd spotted in the daytime and got over. After the Cathcart affair he took fright, bolted into the preserve, and took the shortest way to his bus, regardless. Well, now."

He sat down on the wall, and, drawing out his note-book, began to jot down a description of the man from the data already known.

"Things begin to look a bit more comfortable for old Jerry," said Lord Peter. He leaned on the wall and began whistling softly, but with great accuracy, that elaborate passage of Bach which begins "Let Zion's children."

.   .   .   .   .

"I wonder," said the Hon. Freddy Arbuthnot, "what damn silly fool invented Sunday afternoon."

He shovelled coals on to the library fire with a vicious clatter, waking Colonel Marchbanks, who said, "Eh? Yes, quite right," and fell asleep again instantly.

"Don't *you* grumble, Freddy," said Lord Peter, who had been occupied for some time in opening and shutting all the drawers of the writing-table in a thoroughly irritating manner, and idly snapping to and fro the catch of the French window. "Think how dull old Jerry must feel. 'Spose I'd better write him a line."

He returned to the table and took a sheet of paper. "Do people use this room much to write letters in, do you know?"

"No idea," said the Hon. Freddy. "Never write 'em myself. Where's the point of writin' when you can wire? Encourages people to write back, that's all. I think Denver writes here when he writes anywhere, and I saw the Colonel wrestlin' with pen and ink a day or two ago, didn't you, Colonel?" (The Colonel grunted, answering to his name like a dog that wags its tail in its sleep.) "What's the matter? Ain't there any ink?"

"I only wondered," replied Peter placidly. He slipped a paper-knife under the top sheet of the blotting-pad and held it up to the light. "Quite right, old man. Give you full marks for observation. Here's Jerry's signature, and the Colonel's, and a big, sprawly hand, which I should judge to be feminine." He looked at the sheet again, shook his head, folded it up, and placed it in his pocket-book. "Doesn't seem to be anything there," he commented, "but you never know. 'Five something of fine something'—grouse, probably; 'oe—is fou'—is found, I suppose. Well, it can't do any harm to keep it." He spread out his paper and began:

"Dear Jerry,—Here I am, the family sleuth on the trail, and it's damned exciting——"

The Colonel snored.

Sunday afternoon. Parker had gone with the car to King's Fenton, with orders to look in at Riddlesdale on the way and inquire for a green-eyed cat, also for a young man with a side-car. The Duchess was lying down. Mrs. Pettigrew-Robinson had taken her husband for a brisk walk. Upstairs, somewhere, Mrs. Marchbanks enjoyed a perfect communion of thought with her husband.

Lord Peter's pen gritted gently over the paper, stopped, moved on again, stopped altogether. He leaned his long chin on his hands and stared out of the window, against which there came sudden little swishes of rain, and from time to time a soft, dead leaf. The Colonel snored; the fire tinkled; the Hon. Freddy began to hum and tap his fingers on the arms of his chair. The clock moved slothfully on to five o'clock, which brought teatime and the Duchess.

"How's Mary?" asked Lord Peter, coming suddenly into the firelight.

"I'm really worried about her," said the Duchess. "She is giving way to her nerves in the strangest manner. It is so unlike her. She will hardly let anybody come near her. I have sent for Dr. Thorpe again."

"Don't you think she'd be better if she got up an' came downstairs a bit?" suggested Wimsey. "Gets broodin' about things all by herself, I shouldn't wonder. Wants a bit of Freddy's intellectual conversation to cheer her up."

"You forget; poor girl," said the Duchess, "she was engaged to Captain Cathcart. Everybody isn't as callous as you are."

"Any more letters, your grace?" asked the footman, appearing with the post-bag.

"Oh, are you going down now?" said Wimsey. "Yes, here you are —and there's one other, if you don't mind waitin' a minute while I write it. Wish I could write at the rate people do on the cinema," he added, scribbling rapidly as he spoke. "'DEAR LILIAN,—Your father has killed Mr. William Snooks, and unless you send me £1,000 by bearer, I shall disclose all to your husband.—Sincerely, EARL OF DIGGLESBRAKE.' That's the style; and all done in one scrape of the pen. Here you are, Fleming."

The letter was addressed to her grace the Dowager Duchess of Denver.

. . . . .

From the *Morning Post* of Monday, November—, 19—:

"ABANDONED MOTOR-CYCLE

"A singular discovery was made yesterday by a cattle-drover. He is accustomed to water his animals in a certain pond lying a little off the road about twelve miles south of Ripley. On this occasion he saw that one of them appeared to be in difficulties. On going to the rescue, he found the animal entangled in a motor-cycle, which had been driven into the pond and abandoned. With the assistance of a couple of workmen he extricated the machine. It is a Douglas, with dark-grey side-car. The number-plates and licence-holder have been carefully removed. The pond is a deep one, and the outfit was entirely submerged. It seems probable, however, that it could not have been there for more than a week, since the pond is much used on Sundays and Mondays for the watering of cattle. The police are making search for the owner. The front tyre of the bicycle is a new Dunlop, and the side-car tyre has been repaired with a gaiter. The machine is a 1914 model, much worn."

"That seems to strike a chord," said Lord Peter musingly. He consulted a time-table for the time of the next train to Ripley, and ordered the car.

"And send Bunter to me," he added.

That gentleman arrived just as his master was struggling into an overcoat.

"What was that thing in last Thursday's paper about a number-plate, Bunter?" inquired his lordship.

Mr. Bunter produced, apparently by legerdemain, a cutting from an evening paper:

"NUMBER-PLATE MYSTERY

"The Rev. Nathaniel Foulis, of St. Simon's, North Fellcote, was stopped at six o'clock this morning for riding a motor-cycle without number-plates. The reverend gentleman seemed thunderstruck when his attention was called to the matter. He explained that he had been sent for in great haste at 4 a.m. to administer the Sacrament to a dying parishioner six miles away. He hastened out on his motor-cycle, which he confidingly left by the roadside while executing his sacred duties. Mr. Foulis left the house at 5.30 without noticing that anything was wrong. Mr. Foulis is well known in North Fellcote and the surrounding country, and there seems little doubt that he has been the victim of a senseless practical joke. North Fellcote is a small village a couple of miles north of Ripley."

"I'm going to Ripley, Bunter," said Lord Peter.

"Yes, my lord. Does your lordship require me?"

"No," said Lord Peter, "but—who has been lady's maiding my sister, Bunter?"

"Ellen, my lord—the housemaid."

"Then I wish you'd exercise your powers of conversation on Ellen."

"Very good, my lord."

"Does she mend my sister's clothes, and brush her skirts, and all that?"

"I believe so, my lord."

"Nothing she may think is of any importance, you know, Bunter."

"I wouldn't suggest such a thing to a woman, my lord. It goes to their heads, if I may say so."

"When did Mr. Parker leave for town?"

"At six o'clock this morning, my lord."

. . . . .

Circumstances favoured Mr. Bunter's inquiries. He bumped into Ellen as she was descending the back stairs with an armful of clothing. A pair of leather gauntlets was jerked from the top of the pile, and, picking them up, he apologetically followed the young woman into the servants' hall.

"There," said Ellen, flinging her burden on the table, "and the work I've had to get them, I'm sure. Tantrums, that's what I call it, pretending you've got such a headache you can't let a person into the room to take your things down to brush, and, as soon as they're out of the way, 'opping out of bed and trapesing all over the place. 'Tisn't what I call a headache, would you, now? But there! I daresay you don't get them like I do. Regular fit to split, my head is sometimes—couldn't keep on my feet, not if the house was burning down. I just have to lay down and keep laying—something cruel it is. And gives a person such wrinkles in one's forehead."

"I'm sure I don't see any wrinkles," said Mr. Bunter, "but perhaps I haven't looked hard enough." An interlude followed, during which Mr. Bunter looked hard enough and close enough to distinguish wrinkles. "No," said he, "wrinkles? I don't believe I'd see any if I was to take his lordship's big microscope he keeps up in town."

"Lor' now, Mr. Bunter," said Ellen, fetching a sponge and a bottle of benzene from the cupboard, "what would his lordship be using a thing like that for, now?"

"Why, in our hobby, you see, Miss Ellen, which is criminal investigation, we might want to see something magnified extra big—as it might be handwriting in a forgery case, to see if anything's been altered or rubbed out, or if different kinds of ink have been used. Or we might want to look at the roots of a lock of hair, to see if it's been torn out or fallen out. Or take bloodstains, now; we'd want to know if it was animals' blood or human blood, or maybe only a glass of port."

"Now is it really true, Mr. Bunter," said Ellen, laying a tweed skirt out upon the table and unstoppering the benzene, "that you and Lord Peter can find out all that?"

"Of course, we aren't analytical chemists," Mr. Bunter replied, "but his lordship's dabbled in a lot of things—enough to know when anything looks suspicious, and if we've any doubts we send to a very famous scientific gentleman." (He gallantly intercepted Ellen's hand as it approached the skirt with a benzene-soaked sponge.) "For instance, now, here's a stain on the hem of this skirt, just at the bottom of the side-seam. Now, supposing it was a case of murder, we'll say, and the person that had worn this skirt was suspected, I should examine that stain." (Here Mr. Bunter whipped a lens out of his pocket.) "Then I might try it at one edge with a wet handkerchief." (He suited the action to the word.) "And I should find, you see, that it came off red. Then I should turn the skirt inside-out, I should see that the stain went right through, and I should take my scissors" (Mr. Bunter produced a small, sharp pair) "and snip off a tiny bit of the inside edge of the seam, like this" (he did so) "and pop it into a little pill-box, so" (the pill-box appeared magically from an inner pocket), "and seal it up both sides with a wafer, and write on the top 'Lady Mary Wimsey's skirt,' and the date. Then I should send it straight off to the analytical gentleman in London, and he'd look through his microscope, and tell me right off that it was rabbit's blood, maybe, and how many days it had been there, and that would be the end of that," finished Mr. Bunter triumphantly, replacing his nail-scissors and thoughtlessly pocketing the pill-box with its contents.

"Well, he'd be wrong, then," said Ellen, with an engaging toss of the head, "because it's bird's blood, and not rabbit's at all, because her ladyship told me so; and wouldn't it be quicker just to go and ask the person than get fiddling round with your silly old microscope and things?"

"Well, I only mentioned rabbits for an example," said Mr. Bunter. "Funny she should have got a stain down there. Must have regularly knelt in it."

"Yes. Bled a lot, hasn't it, poor thing? Somebody must 'a' been shootin' careless-like. 'Twasn't his grace, nor yet the Captain, poor man. Perhaps it was Mr. Arbuthnot. He shoots a bit wild sometimes. It's a nasty mess, anyway, and it's so hard to clean off, being left so long. I'm sure I wasn't thinking about cleaning nothing the day the poor Captain was killed; and then the Coroner's inquest—'orrid, it was—and his grace being took off like that! Well, there, it upset me. I suppose I'm a bit sensitive. Anyhow, we was all at sixes and sevens for a day or two, and then her ladyship shuts herself up in her room and won't let me go near the wardrobe. 'Ow!' she says, 'do leave that wardrobe door alone. Don't you know it squeaks, and my head's so bad and my nerves so bad I can't stand it,' she says. 'I was only going to brush your skirts, my lady,' I says. 'Bother my skirts,' says her ladyship, 'and do go away, Ellen. I shall scream if I see you fidgeting about there. You get on my nerves,' she says. Well, I didn't see why I should go on, not after being spoken to like that. It's very nice to be a ladyship, and all your tempers coddled and called nervous prostration. I know I was dreadfully cut up about poor Bert, my young man what was killed in the war—nearly cried my eyes out, I did; but, law! Mr. Bunter, I'd be ashamed to go on so. Besides, between you and I and the gate-post, Lady Mary wasn't that fond of the Captain. Never appreciated him, that's what I said to cook at the time, and she agreed with me. He had a way with him, the Captain had. Always quite the gentleman, of course, and never said anything as wasn't his place—I don't mean that—but I mean as it was a pleasure to do anythink for him. Such a handsome man as he was, too, Mr. Bunter."

"Ah!" said Mr. Bunter. "So on the whole her ladyship was a bit more upset than you expected her to be?"

"Well, to tell you the truth, Mr. Bunter, I think it's just temper. She wanted to get married and away from home. Drat this stain! It's regular dried in. She and his grace never could get on, and when she was away in London during the war she had a rare old time, nursing officers, and going about with all kinds of queer people his grace didn't approve of. Then she had some sort of a love-affair with some quite low-down sort of fellow, so cook says; I think he was one of them dirty Russians as wants to blow us all to smithereens—as if there hadn't been enough people blown up in the war already! Anyhow, his grace made a dreadful fuss, and stopped supplies, and sent for her ladyship home, and ever since then she's been just mad to be off with somebody. Full of notions, she is. Makes me tired, I can tell you. Now, I'm sorry for his grace. I can see what he thinks. Poor gentleman! And then to be taken up for murder and put in gaol, just like one of them nasty tramps. Fancy!"

Ellen, having exhausted her breath and finished cleaning off the bloodstains, paused and straightened her back.

"Hard work it is," she said, "rubbing; I quite ache."

"If you would allow me to help you," said Mr. Bunter, appropriating the hot water, the benzene bottle, and the sponge.

He turned up another breadth of the skirt.

"Have you got a brush handy," he asked, "to take this mud off?"

"You're as blind as a bat, Mr. Bunter," said Ellen, giggling. "Can't you see it just in front of you?"

"Ah, yes," said the valet. "But that's not as hard a one as I'd like. Just you run and get me a real hard one, there's a dear good girl, and I'll fix this for you."

"Cheek!" said Ellen. "But," she added, relenting before the admiring gleam in Mr. Bunter's eye, "I'll get the clothes-brush out of the hall for you. That's as hard as a brick-bat, that is."

No sooner was she out of the room than Mr. Bunter produced a pocket-knife and two more pill-boxes. In a twinkling of an eye he had scraped the surface of the skirt in two places and written two fresh labels:

"Gravel from Lady Mary's skirt, about 6 in. from hem."

"Silver sand from hem of Lady Mary's skirt."

He added the date, and had hardly pocketed the boxes when Ellen returned with the clothes-brush. The cleaning process continued for some time, to the accompaniment of desultory conversation. A third stain on the skirt caused Mr. Bunter to stare critically.

"Hullo!" he said. "Her ladyship's been trying her hand at cleaning this herself."

"What?" cried Ellen. She peered closely at the mark, which at one edge was smeared and whitened, and had a slightly greasy appearance.

"Well, I never," she exclaimed, "so she has! Whatever's that for, I wonder? And her pretending to be so ill she couldn't raise her head off the pillow. She's a sly one, she is."

"Couldn't it have been done before?" suggested Mr. Bunter.

"Well, she might have been at it between the day the Captain was killed and the inquest," agreed Ellen, "though you wouldn't think that was a time to choose to begin learning domestic work. *She* ain't much hand at it, anyhow, for all her nursing. I never believed that came to anything."

"She's used soap," said Mr. Bunter, benzening away resolutely. "Can she boil water in her bedroom?"

"Now, whatever should she do that for, Mr. Bunter?" exclaimed Ellen, amazed. "You don't think she keeps a kettle? I bring up her morning tea. Ladyships don't want to boil water."

"No," said Mr. Bunter, "and why didn't she get it from the bathroom?" He scrutinised the stain more carefully still. "Very amateurish," he said; "distinctly amateurish. Interrupted, I fancy. An energetic young lady, but not ingenious."

The last remarks were addressed in confidence to the benzene bottle. Ellen had put her head out of the window to talk to the game-keeper.

.   .   .   .   .

The Police Superintendent at Ripley received Lord Peter at first frigidly, and later, when he found out who he was, with a mixture of the official attitude to private detectives and the official attitude to a Duke's son.

"I've come to you," said Wimsey, "because you can do this combin'-out business a sight better'n an amateur like myself. I suppose your fine organisation's hard at work already, what?"

"Naturally," said the Superintendent, "but it's not altogether easy to trace a motor-cycle without knowing the number. Look at the Bournemouth Murder." He shook his head regretfully and accepted a Villar y Villar.

"We didn't think at first of connecting him with the number-plate business," the Superintendent went on in a careless tone which some-how conveyed to Lord Peter that his own remarks within the last half-hour had established the connection in the official mind for the first time. "Of course, if he'd been seen going through Ripley *without* a number-plate he'd have been noticed and stopped, whereas with Mr. Foulis's he was as safe as—as the Bank of England," he concluded in a burst of originality.

"Obviously," said Wimsey. "Very agitatin' for the parson, poor chap. So early in the mornin', too. I suppose it was just taken to be a practical joke?"

"Just that," agreed the Superintendent, "but, after hearing what you have to tell us, we shall use our best efforts to get the man. I expect his grace won't be any too sorry to hear he's found. You may rely on us, and if we find the man or the number-plates——"

"Lord bless us and save us, man," broke in Lord Peter with unexpected vivacity, "you're not goin' to waste your time lookin' for the number-plates. What d'you s'pose he'd pinch the curate's plates for if he wanted to advertise his own about the neighbourhood? Once you drop on them you've got his name and address; s'long as they're in his trousers pocket you're up a gum-tree. Now, forgive me, Superintendent, for shovin' along with my opinion, but I simply can't bear to think of you takin' all that trouble for nothin'—draggin' ponds an' turnin' over rubbish-heaps to look for number-plates that ain't there. You just scour the railway-stations for a young man six foot one or two with a No. 10 shoe, and dressed in a Burberry that's lost its belt, and with a deep scratch on one of his hands. And look here, here's my address, and I'll be very grateful if you'll let me know anything that turns up. So awkward for my brother, y'know, all this. Sensitive man; feels it keenly. By the way, I'm a very uncertain bird—always hoppin' about; you might wire me any news in duplicate, to Riddlesdale and to town—110 Piccadilly. Always delighted to see you, by the way, if ever you're in town. You'll forgive me slopin' off now, won't you? I've got a lot to do."

.   .   .   .   .

Returning to Riddlesdale, Lord Peter found a new visitor seated at the tea-table. At Peter's entry he rose into towering height, and extended a shapely, expressive hand that would have made an actor's fortune. He was not an actor, but he found this hand useful, nevertheless, in the exploitation of dramatic moments. His magnificent build and the nobility of his head and mask were impressive; his features were flawless; his eyes ruthless. The Dowager Duchess had once remarked: "Sir Impey Biggs is the handsomest man in England, and no woman will ever care twopence for him." He was, in fact, thirty-eight, and a bachelor, and was celebrated for his rhetoric and his suave but pitiless dissection of hostile witnesses. The breeding of canaries was his unexpected hobby, and besides their song he could appreciate no music but revue airs. He answered Wimsey's greeting in his beautiful, resonant, and exquisitely controlled voice. Tragic irony, cutting contempt, or a savage indignation were the emotions by which Sir Impey Biggs swayed court and jury; he prosecuted murderers of the innocent, defended in actions for criminal libel, and, moving others, was himself as stone. Wimsey expressed himself delighted to see him in a voice, by contrast, more husky and hesitant even than usual.

"You just come from Jerry?" he asked. "Fresh toast, please Fleming. How is he? Enjoyin' it? I never knew a fellow like Jerry for gettin' the least possible out of any situation. I'd rather like the experience myself, you know; only I'd hate bein' shut up and watchin' the other idiots bunglin' my case. No reflection on Murbles and you, Biggs. I mean myself—I mean the man who'd be me if I was Jerry. You follow me?"

"I was just saying to Sir Impey," said the Duchess, "that he really must make Gerald say what he was doing in the garden at three in the morning. If only I'd been at Riddlesdale none of this would have happened. Of course, *we* all know that he wasn't doing any harm, but we can't expect the jurymen to understand that. The lower orders are so prejudiced. It is absurd of Gerald not to realise that he must speak out. He has *no* consideration."

"I am doing my very best to persuade him, Duchess," said Sir Impey, "but you must have patience. Lawyers enjoy a little mystery, you know. Why, if everybody came forward and told the truth, the whole truth, and nothing but the truth straight out, we should all retire to the workhouse."

"Captain Cathcart's death is very mysterious," said the Duchess, "though when I think of the things that have come out about him it really seems quite providential, as far as my sister-in-law is concerned."

"I s'pose you couldn't get 'em to bring it in 'Death by the Visitation of God,' could you, Biggs?" suggested Lord Peter. "Sort of judgment for wantin' to marry into our family, what?"

"I have known less reasonable verdicts," returned Biggs dryly. "It's wonderful what you can suggest to a jury if you try. I remember once at the Liverpool Assizes——"

He steered skilfully away into a quiet channel of reminiscence. Lord Peter watched his statuesque profile against the fire; it reminded him of the severe beauty of the charioteer of Delphi and was about as communicative.

. . . . . .

It was not until after dinner that Sir Impey opened his mind to Wimsey. The Duchess had gone to bed, and the two men were alone in the library. Peter, scrupulously in evening dress, had been valeted by Bunter, and had been more than usually rambling and cheerful all evening. He now took a cigar, retired to the largest chair, and effaced himself in a complete silence.

Sir Impey Biggs walked up and down for some half-hour, smoking. Then he came across with determination, brutally switched on a reading-lamp right into Peter's face, sat down opposite to him, and said:

"Now, Wimsey, I want to know all you know."

"Do you, though?" said Peter. He got up, disconnected the reading-lamp, and carried it away to a side-table.

"No bullying of the witness, though," he added, and grinned.

"I don't care so long as you wake up," said Biggs, unperturbed. "Now then."

Lord Peter removed his cigar from his mouth, considered it with his head on one side, turned it carefully over, decided that the ash could hang on to its parent leaf for another minute or two, smoked without speaking until collapse was inevitable, took the cigar out again, deposited the ash entire in the exact centre of the ash-tray, and began his statement, omitting only the matter of the suit-case and Bunter's information obtained from Ellen.

Sir Impey Biggs listened with what Peter irritably described as a cross-examining countenance, putting a sharp question every now and again. He made a few notes, and, when Wimsey had finished, sat tapping his note-book thoughtfully.

"I think we can make a case out of this," he said, "even if the police don't find your mysterious man. Denver's silence is an awkward complication, of course." He hooded his eyes for a moment. "Did you say you'd put the police on to find the fellow?"

"Yes."

"Have you a very poor opinion of the police?"

"Not for that kind of thing. That's in their line; they have all the facilities, and do it well."

"Ah! You expect to find the man, do you?"

"I hope to."

"Ah! What do you think is going to happen to my case if you *do* find him, Wimsey?"

"What do I——"

"See here, Wimsey," said the barrister, "you are not a fool, and it's no use trying to look like a country policeman. You are really trying to find this man?"

"Certainly."

"Just as you like, of course, but my hands are rather tied already. Has it ever occurred to you that perhaps he'd better not be found?"

Wimsey stared at the lawyer with such honest astonishment as actually to disarm him.

"Remember this," said the latter earnestly, "that if once the police get hold of a thing or a person it's no use relying on my, or Murbles's, or anybody's professional discretion. Everything's raked out into the light of common day, and very common it is. Here's Denver accused of murder, and he refuses in the most categorical way to give me the smallest assistance."

"Jerry's an ass. He doesn't realise——"

"Do you suppose," broke in Biggs, "I have not made it my business to *make* him realise? All he says is, 'They can't hang me; I didn't kill the man, though I think it's a jolly good thing he's dead. It's no business of theirs what I was doing in the garden.' Now I ask you, Wimsey, is that a reasonable attitude for a man in Denver's position to take up?"

Peter muttered something about "Never had any sense."

"Had anybody told Denver about this other man?"

"Something vague was said about footsteps at the inquest, I believe."

"That Scotland Yard man is your personal friend, I'm told?"

"Yes."

"So much the better. He can hold his tongue."

"Look here, Biggs, this is all damned impressive and mysterious, but what are you gettin' at? Why shouldn't I lay hold of the beggar if I can?"

"I'll answer that question by another." Sir Impey leaned forward a little. "Why is Denver screening him?"

Sir Impey Biggs was accustomed to boast that no witness could perjure himself in his presence undetected. As he put the question, he released the other's eyes from his, and glanced down with finest cunning at Wimsey's long, flexible mouth and nervous hands. When he glanced up again a second later he met the eyes passing, guarded and inscrutable, through all the changes expressive of surprised enlightenment; but by that time it was too late; he had seen a little line

59

at the corner of the mouth fade out, and the fingers relax ever so slightly. The first movement had been one of relief.

"B'Jove!" said Peter. "I never thought of that. What sleuths you lawyers are. If that's so, I'd better be careful, hadn't I? Always was a bit rash. My mother says——"

"You're a clever devil, Wimsey," said the barrister. "I may be wrong, then. Find your man by all means. There's just one other thing I'd like to ask. Whom are *you* screening?"

"Look here, Biggs," said Wimsey, "you're not paid to ask that kind of question here, you know. You can jolly well wait till you get into court. It's your job to make the best of the stuff we serve up to you, not to give us the third degree. Suppose I murdered Cathcart myself——"

"You didn't."

"I know I didn't, but if I did I'm not goin' to have you askin' questions and lookin' at me in that tone of voice. However, just to oblige you, I don't mind sayin' plainly that I don't know who did away with the fellow. When I do I'll tell you."

"You will?"

"Yes, I will, but not till I'm sure. You people can make such a little circumstantial evidence go such a damn long way, you might hang me while I was only in the early stages of suspectin' myself."

"H'm!" said Biggs. "Meanwhile, I tell you candidly, I am taking the line that they can't make out a case."

"Not proven, eh? Well, anyhow, Biggs, I swear my brother shan't hang for lack of my evidence."

"Of course not," said Biggs, adding inwardly: "but you hope it won't come to that."

A spurt of rain plashed down the wide chimney and sizzled on the logs.

· · · · ·

"Craven Hotel,
"Strand, W.C.,
"*Tuesday.*

"MY DEAR WIMSEY,—A line as I promised, to report progress, but it's precious little. On the journey up I sat next to Mrs. Pettigrew-Robinson, and opened and shut the window for her and looked after her parcels. She mentioned that when your sister roused the household on Thursday morning she went first to Mr. Arbuthnot's room—a circumstance which the lady seemed to think odd, but which is natural enough when you come to think of it, the room being directly opposite the head of the staircase. It was Mr. Arbuthnot who knocked up the Pettigrew-Robinsons, and Mr. P. ran downstairs immediately. Mrs. P. then saw that Lady Mary was looking very faint, and tried to support her. Your sister threw her off—rudely, Mrs. P. says—declined 'in a most savage manner' all offers of assistance, rushed to her own room, and locked herself in. Mrs. Pettigrew-Robinson listened at the door 'to make sure,' as she says, 'that everything was all right,' but, hearing her moving about and slamming cupboards, she concluded that she would have more chance of poking her finger into the pie downstairs, and departed.

"If Mrs. Marchbanks had told me this, I admit I should have thought the episode worth looking into, but I feel strongly that if I were dying I should still lock the door between myself and Mrs. Pettigrew-Robinson. Mrs. P. was quite sure that at no time had Lady Mary anything in her hand. She was dressed as described at the inquest—a long coat over her pyjamas (sleeping suit was Mrs. P.'s expression), stout shoes, and a woolly cap, and she kept these garments on throughout the subsequent visit of the doctor. Another odd little circumstance is that Mrs. Pettigrew-Robinson (who was awake, you remember, from 2 a.m. onwards) is certain that just *before* Lady Mary knocked on Mr. Arbuthnot's door she heard a door slam somewhere in the passage. I don't know what to make of this—perhaps there's nothing in it, but I just mention it.

"I've had a rotten time in town. Your brother-in-law elect was a model of discretion. His room at the Albany is a desert from a detecting point of view; no papers except a few English bills and receipts, and invitations. I looked up a few of his inviters, but they were mostly men who had met him at the club or knew him in the Army, and could tell me nothing about his private life. He is known at several night-clubs. I made the round of them last night —or, rather, this morning. General verdict: generous but impervious. By the way, poker seems to have been his great game. No suggestion of anything crooked. He won pretty consistently on the whole, but never very spectacularly.

"I think the information we want must be in Paris. I have written to the Sûreté and the Crédit Lyonnais to produce his papers, especially his account and cheque-book.

"I'm pretty dead with yesterday's and to-day's work. Dancing all night on top of a journey is a jolly poor joke. Unless you want me, I'll wait here for the papers, or I may run over to Paris myself.

"Cathcart's books here consist of a few modern French novels of the usual kind, and another copy of *Manon* with what the catalogues call 'curious' plates. He must have had a life somewhere, mustn't he?

"The enclosed bill from a beauty specialist in Bond Street may interest you. I called on her. She says he came regularly every week when he was in England.

"I drew quite blank at King's Fenton on Sunday—oh, but I told you that. I don't think the fellow ever went there. I wonder if he slunk off up into the moor. Is it worth rummaging about, do you think? Rather like looking for a needle in a bundle of hay. It's odd about that diamond cat. You've got nothing out of the household, I suppose? It doesn't seem to fit No. 10, somehow—and yet you'd think somebody would have heard about it in the village if it had been lost. Well, so long,

"Yours ever,
"CH. PARKER."

CHAPTER IV

—AND HIS DAUGHTER, MUCH-AFRAID

The women also looked pale and wan.
—The Pilgrim's Progress.

MR. BUNTER BROUGHT Parker's letter up to Lord Peter in bed on the Wednesday morning. The house was almost deserted, everybody having gone to attend the police-court proceedings at Northallerton. The thing would be purely formal, of course, but it seemed only proper that the family should be fully represented. The Dowager Duchess, indeed, was there—she had promptly hastened to her son's side and was living heroically in furnished lodgings, but the younger Duchess thought her mother-in-law more energetic than dignified. There was no knowing what she might do if left to herself. She might even give an interview to a newspaper reporter. Besides, at these moments of crisis a wife's right place is at her husband's side. Lady Mary was ill, and nothing could be said about that, and if Peter chose to stay smoking cigarettes in his pyjamas while his only brother was undergoing public humiliation, that was only what might be expected. Peter took after his mother. How that eccentric strain had got into the family her grace could not imagine, for the Dowager came of a good Hampshire family; there must have been some foreign blood somewhere. Her own duty was clear, and she would do it.

Lord Peter was awake, and looked rather fagged, as though he had been sleuthing in his sleep. Mr. Bunter wrapped him solicitously in a brilliant Oriental robe, and placed the tray on his knees.

"Bunter," said Lord Peter rather fretfully, "your *café au lait* is the one tolerable incident in this beastly place."

"Thank you, my lord. Very chilly again this morning, my lord, but not actually raining."

Lord Peter frowned over his letter.

"Anything in the paper, Bunter?"

"Nothing urgent, my lord. A sale next week at Northbury Hall—Mr. Fleetwhite's library, my lord—a Caxton *Confessio Amantis*——"

"What's the good of tellin' me that when we're stuck up here for God knows how long? I wish to heaven I'd stuck to books and never touched crime. Did you send those specimens up to Lubbock?"

"Yes, my lord," said Bunter gently. Dr. Lubbock was the "analytical gentleman."

"Must have facts," said Lord Peter, "facts. When I was a small boy I always hated facts. Thought of 'em as nasty, hard things, all knobs. Uncompromisin'."

"Yes, my lord. My old mother——"

"Your mother, Bunter? I didn't know you had one. I always imagined you were turned out ready-made, so to speak. 'Scuse me. Infernally rude of me. Beg your pardon, I'm sure."

"Not at all, my lord. My mother lives in Kent, my lord, near Maidstone. Seventy-five, my lord, and an extremely active woman for her years, if you'll excuse my mentioning it. I was one of seven."

"That is an invention, Bunter. I know better. You are unique. But I interrupted you. You were goin' to tell me about your mother."

63

"She always says, my lord, that facts are like cows. If you look them in the face hard enough they generally run away. She is a very courageous woman, my lord."

Lord Peter stretched out his hand impulsively, but Mr. Bunter was too well trained to see it. He had, indeed, already begun to strop a razor. Lord Peter suddenly bundled out of bed with a violent jerk and sped across the landing to the bathroom.

Here he revived sufficiently to lift up his voice in "Come unto these Yellow Sands." Thence, feeling in a Purcellish mood, he passed to "I attempt from Love's Fever to Fly," with such improvement of spirits that, against all custom, he ran several gallons of cold water into the bath and sponged himself vigorously. Wherefore, after a rough towelling, he burst explosively from the bathroom, and caught his shin somewhat violently against the lid of a large oak chest which stood at the head of the staircase—so violently, indeed, that the lid lifted with the shock and shut down with a protesting bang.

Lord Peter stopped to say something expressive and to caress his leg softly with the palm of his hand. Then a thought struck him. He set down his towels, soap, sponge, loofah, bath-brush, and other belongings, and quietly lifted the lid of the chest.

Whether, like the heroine of *Northanger Abbey,* he expected to find anything gruesome inside was not apparent. It is certain that, like her, he beheld nothing more startling than certain sheets and counterpanes neatly folded at the bottom. Unsatisfied, he lifted the top one of these gingerly and inspected it for a few moments in the light of the staircase window. He was just returning it to its place, whistling softly the while, when a little hiss of indrawn breath caused him to look up with a start.

His sister was at his elbow. He had not heard her come, but she stood there in her dressing-gown, her hands clutched together on her breast. Her blue eyes were dilated till they looked almost black, and her skin seemed nearly the colour of her ash-blonde hair. Wimsey stared at her over the sheet he held in his arms, and the terror in her face passed over into his, stamping them suddenly with the mysterious likeness of blood-relationship.

Peter's own impression was that he stared "like a stuck pig" for about a minute. He knew, as a matter of fact, that he had recovered himself in a fraction of a second. He dropped the sheet into the chest and stood up.

"Hullo, Polly, old thing," he said, "where've you been hidin' all this time? First time I've seen you. 'Fraid you've been havin' a pretty thin time of it."

He put his arm round her, and felt her shrink.

"What's the matter?" he demanded. "What's up, old girl? Look here, Mary, we've never seen enough of each other, but I am your brother. Are you in trouble? Can't I——"

"Trouble?" she said. "Why, you silly old Peter, of course I'm in trouble. Don't you know they've killed my man and put my brother in prison? Isn't that enough to be in trouble about?" She laughed, and Peter suddenly thought, "She's talking like somebody in a blood-and-thunder novel." She went on more naturally. "It's all right, Peter, truly—only my head's so bad. I really don't know what I'm doing. What are you after? You made such a noise, I came out. I thought it was a door banging."

"You'd better toddle back to bed," said Lord Peter. "You're gettin' all cold. Why do girls wear such mimsy little pyjimjams in this damn cold climate? There, don't you worry. I'll drop in on you later and we'll have a jolly old pow-wow, what?"

"Not to-day—not to-day, Peter. I'm going mad, I think." ("Sensation fiction again," thought Peter.) "Are they trying Gerald to-day?"

"Not exactly trying," said Peter, urging her gently along to her room. "It's just formal, y'know. The jolly old magistrate bird hears the charge read, and then old Murbles pops up and says please he wants only formal evidence given as he has to instruct counsel. That's Biggy, y'know. Then they hear the evidence of arrest, and Murbles says old Gerald reserves his defence. That's all till the Assizes—evidence before the Grand Jury—a lot of bosh! That'll be early next month, I suppose. You'll have to buck up and be fit by then."

Mary shuddered.

"No—no! Couldn't I get out of it? I couldn't go through it all again. I should be sick. I'm feeling awful. No, don't come in. I don't want you. Ring the bell for Ellen. No, let go; go away! I don't want you, Peter!"

Peter hesitated, a little alarmed.

"Much better not, my lord, if you'll excuse me," said Bunter's voice at his ear. "Only produce hysterics," he added, as he drew his master gently from the door. "Very distressing for both parties, and altogether unproductive of results. Better to wait for the return of her grace, the Dowager."

"Quite right," said Peter. He turned back to pick up his paraphernalia, but was dexterously forestalled. Once again he lifted the lid of the chest and looked in.

"What did you say you found on that skirt, Bunter?"

"Gravel, my lord, and silver sand."

"Silver sand."

.   .   .   .   .

Behind Riddlesdale Lodge the moor stretched starkly away and upward. The heather was brown and wet, and the little streams had no colour in them. It was six o'clock, but there was no sunset. Only a paleness had moved behind the thick sky from east to west all day. Lord Peter, tramping back after a long and fruitless search for tidings of the man with the motor-cycle, voiced the dull suffering of his gregarious spirit. "I wish old Parker was here," he muttered, and squelched down a sheep-track.

He was making, not directly for the Lodge, but for a farmhouse about two and a half miles distant from it, known as Grider's Hole. It lay almost due north of Riddlesdale village, a lonely outpost on the edge of the moor, in a valley of fertile land between two wide swells of heather. The track wound down from the height called Whemmeling Fell, skirted a vile swamp, and crossed the little river Ridd about half a mile before reaching the farm. Peter had small hope of hearing any news at Grider's Hole, but he was filled with a sullen determination to leave no stone unturned. Privately, however, he felt convinced that the motor-cycle had come by the high road, Parker's investigations notwithstanding, and perhaps passed directly through King's Fenton without stopping or attracting attention. Still, he had said he would search the neighbourhood, and Grider's Hole was in the neighbourhood. He paused to relight his pipe, then squelched steadily on. The path was marked with stout white posts at regular intervals, and presently with hurdles. The reason for this was apparent as one came to the bottom of the valley, for only a few yards on the left began the stretch of rough, reedy tussocks, with slobbering black bog between them, in which anything heavier than a water-wagtail would speedily suffer change into a succession of little bubbles. Wimsey stooped for an empty sardine-tin which lay, horridly battered, at his feet, and slung it idly into the quag. It struck the surface with a noise like a wet kiss, and vanished instantly. With that instinct which prompts one, when depressed, to wallow in every circumstance of gloom, Peter leaned sadly upon the hurdles and abandoned himself to a variety of shallow considerations upon (1) The vanity of human wishes; (2) Mutability; (3) First love; (4) The decay of idealism; (5) The aftermath of the Great War; (6) Birth-control; and (7) The fallacy of free-will. This was his nadir, however. Realising that his feet were cold and his stomach empty, and that he had still some miles to go, he crossed the stream on a row of slippery stepping-stones and approached the gate of the farm, which was not an ordinary five-barred one, but solid and uncompromising. A man was leaning over it, sucking a straw. He made no attempt to move at Wimsey's approach. "Good evening," said that nobleman in a sprightly manner, laying his hand on the catch. "Chilly, ain't it?"

The man made no reply, but leaned more heavily, and breathed. He wore a rough coat and breeches, and his leggings were covered with manure.

"Seasonable, of course, what?" said Peter. "Good for the sheep, I daresay. Makes their wool curl, and so on."

The man removed the straw and spat in the direction of Peter's right boot.

"Do you lose many animals in the bog?" went on Peter, carelessly unlatching the gate, and leaning upon it in the opposite direction. "I see you have a good wall all round the house. Must be a bit dangerous in the dark, what, if you're thinkin' of takin' a little evenin' stroll with a friend?"

The man spat again, pulled his hat over his forehead, and said briefly:

"What doost 'a want?"

"Well," said Peter, "I thought of payin' a little friendly call on Mr. —on the owner of this farm, that is to say. Country neighbours, and all that. Lonely kind of country, don't you see. Is he in, d'ye think?"

The man grunted.

"I'm glad to hear it," said Peter; "it's so uncommonly jolly findin' all you Yorkshire people so kind and hospitable, what? Never mind who you are, always a seat at the fireside and that kind of thing. Excuse me, but do you know you're leanin' on the gate so as I can't open it? I'm sure it's a pure oversight, only you mayn't realise that just where you're standin' you get the maximum of leverage. What an awfully charmin' house this is, isn't it? All so jolly stark and grim and all the rest of it. No creepers or little rose-grown porches or anything suburban of that sort. Who lives in it?"

67

The man surveyed him up and down for some moments, and replied, "Mester Grimethorpe."

"No, does he now?" said Lord Peter. "To think of that. Just the fellow I want to see. Model farmer, what? Wherever I go throughout the length and breadth of the North Riding I hear of Mr. Grimethorpe. 'Grimethorpe's butter is the best'; 'Grimethorpe's fleeces Never go to pieces'; 'Grimethorpe's pork Melts on the fork'; 'For Irish stews Take Grimethorpe's ewes'; 'A tummy lined with Grimethorpe's beef, Never, never comes to grief.' It has been my life's ambition to see Mr. Grimethorpe in the flesh. And you no doubt are his sturdy henchman and right-hand man. You leap from bed before the breaking-day, To milk the kine amid the scented hay. You, when the shades of evening gather deep, Home from the mountain lead the mild-eyed sheep. You, by the ingle's red and welcoming blaze, Tell your sweet infants tales of olden days! A wonderful life, though a trifle monotonous p'raps in the winter. Allow me to clasp your honest hand."

Whether the man was moved by this lyric outburst, or whether the failing light was not too dim to strike a pale sheen from the metal in Lord Peter's palm, at any rate he moved a trifle back from the gate.

"Thanks awfully, old bean," said Peter, stepping briskly past him. "I take it I shall find Mr. Grimethorpe in the house?"

The man said nothing till Wimsey had proceeded about a dozen yards up the flagged path, then he hailed him, but without turning round.

"Mester!"

"Yes, old thing?" said Peter affably, returning.

"Happen he'll set dog on tha."

"You don't say so?" said Peter. "The faithful hound welcomes the return of the prodigal. Scene of family rejoicing. 'My own long lost boy!' Sobs and speeches, beer all round for the delighted tenantry. Glees by the old fireside, till the rafters ring and all the smoked hams tumble down to join in the revelry. Good night, sweet Prince, until the cows come home and the dogs eat Jezebel in the portion of Jezreel when the hounds of spring are on winter's traces. I suppose," he added to himself, "they will have finished tea."

As Lord Peter approached the door of the farm his spirits rose. He enjoyed paying this kind of visit. Although he had taken to detecting as he might, with another conscience or constitution, have taken to Indian hemp—for its exhilarating properties—at a moment when life seemed dust and ashes, he had not primarily the detective temperament. He expected next to nothing from inquiries at Grider's Hole, and, if he had, he might probably have extracted all the information he wanted by a judicious display of Treasury notes to the glum man at the gate. Parker would in all likelihood have done so; he was paid to detect and to do nothing else, and neither his natural gifts nor his education (at Barrow-in-Furness Grammar School) prompted him to stray into side-tracks at the beck of an ill-regulated imagination. But to Lord Peter the world presented itself as an entertaining labyrinth of side-issues. He was a respectable scholar in five or six languages, a musician of some skill and more understanding, something of an expert in toxicology, a collector of rare editions, an entertaining man-about-town, and a common sensationalist. He had been seen at half-past twelve on a Sunday morning walking in Hyde Park in a top-hat and frock-coat, reading the *News of the World*. His passion for the unexplored led him to hunt up obscure pamphlets in the British Museum, to unravel the emotional history of income-tax collectors, and to find out where his own drains led to. In this case, the fascinating problem of a Yorkshire farmer who habitually set the dogs on casual visitors imperatively demanded investigation in a personal interview. The result was unexpected.

His first summons was unheeded, and he knocked again. This time there was a movement, and a surly male voice called out:

"Well, let 'un in then, dang 'un—and dang *thee*," emphasised by the sound of something falling or thrown across the room.

The door was opened unexpectedly by a little girl of about seven, very dark and pretty, and rubbing her arm as though the missile had caught her there. She stood defensively, blocking the threshold, till the same voice growled impatiently:

"Well, who is it?"

"Good evening," said Wimsey, removing his hat. "I hope you'll excuse me droppin' in like this. I'm livin' at Riddlesdale Lodge."

"What of it?" demanded the voice. Above the child's head Wimsey saw the outline of a big, thick-set man smoking in the inglenook of an immense fireplace. There was no light but the firelight, for the window was small, and dusk had already fallen. It seemed to be a large room, but a high oak settle on the farther side of the chimney ran out across it, leaving a cavern of impenetrable blackness beyond.

"May I come in?" said Wimsey.

"If tha must," said the man ungraciously. "Shoot door, lass; what art starin' at? Go to thi moother and bid her mend thi manners for thee."

This seemed a case of the pot lecturing the kettle on cleanliness, but the child vanished hurriedly into the blackness behind the settle, and Peter walked in.

"Are you Mr. Grimethorpe?" he asked politely.

"What if I am?" retorted the farmer. "*I've* no call to be ashamed o' my name."

"Rather not," said Lord Peter, "nor of your farm. Delightful place, what? My name's Wimsey, by the way—Lord Peter Wimsey, in fact, the Duke of Denver's brother, y'know. I'm sure I hate interruptin' you—you must be busy with the sheep and all that—but I thought you wouldn't mind if I just ran over in a neighbourly way. Lonely sort of country, ain't it? I like to know the people next door, and all that sort of thing. I'm used to London, you see, where people live pretty thick on the ground. I suppose very few strangers ever pass this way?"

"None," said Mr. Grimethorpe, with decision.

"Well, perhaps it's as well," pursued Lord Peter. "Makes one appreciate one's home circle more, what? Often think one sees too many strangers in town. Nothing like one's family when all's said and done—cosy, don't you know. You a married man, Mr. Grimethorpe?"

"What the hell's that to you?" growled the farmer, rounding on him with such ferocity that Wimsey looked about quite nervously for the dogs before-mentioned.

"Oh, nothin'," he replied, "only I thought that charmin' little girl might be yours."

"And if I thought she weren't," said Mr. Grimethorpe, "I'd strangle the bitch and her mother together. What hast got to say to that?"

As a matter of fact, the remark, considered as a conversational formula, seemed to leave so much to be desired that Wimsey's natural loquacity suffered a severe check. He fell back, however, on the usual resource of the male, and offered Mr. Grimethorpe a cigar, thinking to himself as he did so:

"What a hell of a life the woman must lead."

The farmer declined the cigar with a single word, and was silent. Wimsey lit a cigarette for himself and became meditative, watching his companion. He was a man of about forty-five, apparently, rough, harsh, and weather-beaten, with great ridgy shoulders and short, thick thighs—a bull-terrier with a bad temper. Deciding that delicate hints would be wasted on such an organism, Wimsey adopted a franker method.

"To tell the truth, Mr. Grimethorpe," he said, "I didn't blow in without any excuse at all. Always best to provide oneself with an excuse for a call, what? Though it's so perfectly delightful to see you—I mean, no excuse might appear necessary. But fact is, I'm looking for a young man—a—an acquaintance of mine—who said he'd be roamin' about this neighbourhood some time or other about now. Only I'm afraid I may have missed him. You see, I've only just got over from Corsica—interestin' country and all that, Mr. Grimethorpe, but a trifle out of the way—and from what my friend said I think he must have turned up here about a week ago and found me out. Just my luck. But he didn't leave his card, so I can't be quite sure, you see. You didn't happen to come across him by any chance? Tall fellow with big feet on a motor-cycle with a side-car. I thought he might have come rootin' about here. Hullo! d'you know him?"

The farmer's face had become swollen and almost black with rage.

"What day sayst tha?" he demanded thickly.

"I should think last Wednesday night or Thursday morning," said Peter, with a hand on his heavy malacca cane.

"I knew it," growled Mr. Grimethorpe. "—— the slut, and all these dommed women wi' their dirty ways. Look here, mester. The tyke were a friend o' thine? Well, I wor at Stapley Wednesday and Thursday—tha knew that, didn't tha? And so did thi friend, didn't 'un? An' if I hadn't, it'd 'a' bin the worse for 'un. He'd 'a' been in Peter's Pot if I'd 'a' cot 'un, an' that's where tha'll be thesen in a minute, blast tha! And if I find 'un sneakin' here again, I'll blast every boon in a's body and send 'un to look for thee there."

And with these surprising words he made for Peter's throat like a bull-dog.

"That won't do," said Peter, disengaging himself with an ease which astonished his opponent, and catching his wrist in a grip of mysterious and excruciating agony. "'Tisn't wise, y'know—might murder a fellow like that. Nasty business, murder. Coroner's inquest and all that sort of thing. Counsel for the Prosecution askin' all sorts of inquisitive questions, and a feller puttin' a string round your neck. Besides, your method's a bit primitive. Stand still, you fool, or you'll break your arm. Feelin' better? That's right. Sit down. You'll get into trouble one of these days, behavin' like that when you're asked a civil question."

71

"Get out o' t'house," said Mr. Grimethorpe sullenly.

"Certainly," said Peter. "I have to thank you for a very entertainin' evenin', Mr. Grimethorpe. I'm sorry you can give me no news of my friend——"

Mr. Grimethorpe sprang up with a blasphemous ejaculation, and made for the door, shouting "Jabez!" Lord Peter stared after him for a moment, and then stared round the room.

"Something fishy here," he said. "Fellow knows somethin'. Murderous sort of brute. I wonder——"

He peered round the settle, and came face to face with a woman —a dim patch of whiteness in the thick shadow.

"You?" she said, in a low, hoarse gasp. "You? You are mad to come here. Quick, quick! He has gone for the dogs."

She placed her two hands on his breast, thrusting him urgently back. Then, as the firelight fell upon his face, she uttered a stifled shriek and stood petrified—a Medusa-head of terror.

Medusa was beautiful, says the tale, and so was this woman; a broad white forehead under massed, dusky hair, black eyes glowing under straight brows, a wide, passionate mouth—a shape so wonderful that even in that strenuous moment sixteen generations of feudal privilege stirred in Lord Peter's blood. His hands closed over hers instinctively, but she pulled herself hurriedly away and shrank back.

"Madam," said Wimsey, recovering himself, "I don't quite——"

A thousand questions surged up in his mind, but before he could frame them a long yell, and another, and then another came from the back of the house.

"Run, run!" she said. "The dogs! My God, my God, what will become of me? Go, if you don't want to see me killed. Go, go! Have pity!"

"Look here," said Peter, "can't I stay and protect——"

"You can stay and murder me," said the woman. "Go!"

Peter cast Public School tradition to the winds, caught up his stick, and went. The brutes were at his heels as he fled. He struck the foremost with his stick, and it dropped back, snarling. The man was still leaning on the gate, and Grimethorpe's hoarse voice was heard shouting to him to seize the fugitive. Peter closed with him; there was a scuffle of dogs and men, and suddenly Peter found himself thrown bodily over the gate. As he picked himself up and ran, he heard the farmer cursing the man and the man retorting that he couldn't help it; then the woman's voice, uplifted in a frightened wail. He glanced over his shoulder. The man and the woman and a second man who had now joined the party, were beating the dogs back, and seemed to be persuading Grimethorpe not to let them through. Apparently their remonstrances had some effect, for the farmer turned moodily away, and the second man called the dogs off, with much whip-cracking and noise. The woman said something, and her husband turned furiously upon her and struck her to the ground.

Peter made a movement to go back, but a strong conviction that he could only make matters worse for her arrested him. He stood still, and waited till she had picked herself up and gone in, wiping the blood and dirt from her face with her shawl. The farmer looked round, shook his fist at him, and followed her into the house. Jabez collected the dogs and drove them back, and Peter's friend returned to lean over the gate.

Peter waited till the door had closed upon Mr. and Mrs. Grimethorpe; then he pulled out his handkerchief and, in the half-darkness, signalled cautiously to the man, who slipped through the gate and came slowly down to him.

"Thanks very much," said Wimsey, putting money into his hand. "I'm afraid I've done unintentional mischief."

The man looked at the money and at him.

" 'Tes t' master's way wi' them as cooms t'look at t'missus," he said. "Tha's best keep away if so be tha wutna' have her blood on tha heid."

"See here," said Peter, "did you by any chance meet a young man with a motor-cycle wanderin' round here last Wednesday or thereabouts?"

"Naay. Wednesday? T'wod be day t'mester went to Stapley, Ah reckon, after machines. Naay, Ah seed nowt."

"All right. If you find anybody who did, let me know. Here's my name, and I'm staying at Riddlesdale Lodge. Good night; many thanks."

The man took the card from him and slouched back without a word of farewell.

.   .   .   .   .

Lord Peter walked slowly, his coat collar turned up and his hat pulled over his eyes. This cinematographic episode had troubled his logical faculty. With an effort he sorted out his ideas and arranged them in some kind of order.

"First item," said he, "Mr. Grimethorpe. A gentleman who will stick at nothing. Hefty. Unamiable. Inhospitable. Dominant characteristic—jealousy of his very astonishing wife. Was at Stapley last Wednesday and Thursday buying machinery. (Helpful gentleman at the gate corroborates this, by the way, so that at this stage of the proceedings one may allow it to be a sound alibi.) Did not, therefore, see our mysterious friend with the side-car, *if* he was there. But is disposed to think he *was* there, and has very little doubt about what he came for. Which raises an interestin' point. Why the side-car? Awkward thing to tour about with. Very good. But if our friend came after Mrs. G. he obviously didn't take her. Good again.

"Second item, Mrs. Grimethorpe. Very singular item. By Jove!" He paused meditatively to reconstruct a thrilling moment. "Let us at once admit that if No. 10 came for the purpose suspected he had every excuse for it. Well! Mrs. G. goes in terror of her husband, who thinks nothing of knocking her down on suspicion. I wish to God—but I'd only have made things worse. Only thing you can do for the wife of a brute like that is to keep away from her. Hope there won't be murder done. One's enough at a time. Where was I?

"Yes—well, Mrs. Grimethorpe knows something—and she knows somebody. She took me for somebody who had every reason for not coming to Grider's Hole. Where was she, I wonder, while I was talking to Grimethorpe? She wasn't in the room. Perhaps the child warned her. No, that won't wash; I told the child who I was. Aha! wait a minute. Do I see light? She looked out of the window and saw a bloke in an aged Burberry. No. 10 is a bloke in an aged Burberry. Now, let's suppose for a moment she takes me for No. 10. What does she do? She sensibly keeps out of the way—can't think why I'm such a fool as to turn up. Then, when Grimethorpe runs out shoutin' for the kennel-man, she nips down with her life in her hands to warn her —her—shall we say boldly her lover?—to get away. She finds it isn't her lover, but only a gaping ass of (I fear) a very comin'-on disposition. New compromisin' position. She tells the ass to save himself and herself by clearin' out. Ass clears—not too gracefully. The next instalment of this enthrallin' drama will be shown in this theatre— when? I'd jolly well like to know."

He tramped on for some time.

"All the same," he retorted upon himself, "all this throws no light on what No. 10 was doing at Riddlesdale Lodge."

At the end of his walk he had reached no conclusion.

"Whatever happens," he said to himself, "and if it can be done without danger to her life, I must see Mrs. Grimethorpe again."

CHAPTER V

THE RUE ST. HONORÉ AND THE RUE DE LA PAIX

I think it was the cat.—H.M.S. Pinafore

MR. PARKER SAT DISCONSOLATE in a small *appartement* in the Rue St. Honoré. It was three o'clock in the afternoon. Paris was full of a subdued but cheerful autumn sunlight, but the room faced north, and was depressing, with its plain, dark furniture and its deserted air. It was a man's room, well appointed after the manner of a discreet club; a room that kept its dead owner's counsel imperturbably. Two large saddlebag chairs in crimson leather stood by the cold hearth. On the mantelpiece was a bronze clock, flanked by two polished German shells, a stone tobacco-jar, and an Oriental brass bowl containing a long-cold pipe. There were several excellent engravings in narrow pearwood frames, and the portrait in oils of a rather florid lady of the period of Charles II. The window-curtains were crimson, and the floor covered with a solid Turkey carpet. Opposite the fireplace stood a tall mahogany book-case with glass doors, containing a number of English and French classics, a large collection of books on history and international politics, various French novels, a number of works on military and sporting subjects, and a famous French edition of the *Decameron* with the additional plates. Under the window stood a large bureau.

Parker shook his head, took out a sheet of paper, and began to write a report. He had breakfasted on coffee and rolls at seven; he had made an exhaustive search of the flat; he had interviewed the concierge, the manager of the Crédit Lyonnais, and the Prefect of Police for the Quartier, and the result was very poor indeed.

Information obtained from Captain Cathcart's papers:

Before the war Denis Cathcart had undoubtedly been a rich man. He had considerable investments in Russia and Germany and a large share in a prosperous vineyard in Champagne. After coming into his property at the age of twenty-one he had concluded his three years' residence at Cambridge, and had then travelled a good deal, visiting persons of importance in various countries, and apparently studying with a view to a diplomatic career. During the period from 1913 to 1918 the story told by the books became intensely interesting, baffling, and depressing. At the outbreak of war he had taken a commission in the 15th ——shires. With the help of the cheque-book, Parker reconstructed the whole economic life of a young British officer—clothes, horses, equipment, travelling, wine and dinners when on leave, bridge debts, rent of the flat in the Rue St. Honoré, club subscriptions, and what not. This outlay was strictly moderate and proportioned to his income. Receipted bills, neatly docketed, occupied one drawer of the bureau, and a careful comparison of these with the cheque-book and the returned cheques revealed no discrepancy. But, beyond these, there appeared to have been another heavy drain upon Cathcart's resources. Beginning in 1913, certain large cheques, payable to self, appeared regularly at every quarter, and sometimes at shorter intervals. As to the destination of these sums, the bureau preserved the closest discretion; there were no receipts, no memoranda of their expenditure.

The great crash which in 1914 shook the credits of the world was mirrored in little in the pass-book. The credits from Russian and German sources stopped dead; those from the French shares slumped to a quarter of the original amount, as the tide of war washed over the vineyards and carried the workers away. For the first year or so there were substantial dividends from capital invested in French *rentes;* then came an ominous entry of 20,000 francs on the credit side of the account, and, six months after, another of 30,000 francs. After that the landslide followed fast. Parker could picture those curt notes from the Front, directing the sale of Government securities, as the savings of the past six years whirled away in the maelstrom of rising prices and collapsing currencies. The dividends grew less and less and ceased; then, more ominous still, came a series of debits representing the charges on renewal of promissory notes.

About 1918 the situation had become acute, and several entries showed a desperate attempt to put matters straight by gambling in foreign exchanges. There were purchases, through the bank, of German marks, Russian roubles, and Roumanian lei. Mr. Parker sighed sympathetically, when he saw this, thinking of £12 worth of these delusive specimens of the engraver's art laid up in his own desk at home. He knew them to be waste-paper, yet his tidy mind could not bear the thought of destroying them. Evidently Cathcart had found marks and roubles very broken reeds.

It was about this time that Cathcart's pass-book began to reveal the paying in of various sums in cash, some large, some small, at irregular dates and with no particular consistency. In December, 1919, there had been one of these amounting to as much as 35,000 francs. Parker at first supposed that these sums might represent dividends from some separate securities which Cathcart was handling for himself without passing them through the bank. He made a careful search of the room in the hope of finding either the bonds themselves or at least some memorandum concerning them, but the search was in vain, and he was forced to conclude either that Cathcart had deposited them in some secret place or that the credits in question represented some different source of income.

Cathcart had apparently contrived to be demobilised almost at once (owing, no doubt, to his previous frequentation of distinguished governmental personages), and to have taken a prolonged holiday upon the Riviera. Subsequently a visit to London coincided with the acquisition of £700, which, converted into francs at the then rate of exchange, made a very respectable item in the account. From that time on, the outgoings and receipts presented a similar aspect and were more or less evenly balanced, the cheques to self becoming rather larger and more frequent as time went on, while during 1921 the income from the vineyard began to show signs of recovery.

Mr. Parker noted down all this information in detail, and, leaning back in his chair, looked round the flat. He felt, not for the first time, a distaste for his profession, which cut him off from the great masculine community whose members take each other for granted and respect their privacy. He relighted his pipe, which had gone out, and proceeded with his report.

Information obtained from Monsieur Turgeot, the manager of the Crédit Lyonnais, confirmed the evidence of the pass-book in every particular. Monsieur Cathcart had recently made all his payments in notes, usually in notes of small denominations. Once or twice he had had an overdraft—never very large, and always made up within a few months. He had, of course, suffered a diminution of income, like everybody else, but the account had never given the bank any uneasiness. At the moment it was some 14,000 francs on the right side. Monsieur Cathcart was always very agreeable, but not communicative—*très correct.*

Information obtained from the concierge:

One did not see much of Monsieur Cathcart, but he was *très gentil.* He never failed to say, *"Bon jour, Bourgois,"* when he came in or out. He received visitors sometimes—gentlemen in evening dress. One made card-parties. Monsieur Bourgois had never directed any ladies to his rooms; except once, last February, when he had given a lunch-party to some ladies *très comme il faut* who brought with them his fiancée, *une jolie blonde.* Monsieur Cathcart used the flat as a *pied à terre,* and often he would shut it up and go away for several weeks or months. He was *un jeune homme très rangé.* He had never kept a valet. Madame Leblanc, the cousin of one's late wife, kept his *appartement* clean. Madame Leblanc was very respectable. But certainly monsieur might have Madame Leblanc's address.

Information obtained from Madame Leblanc:

Monsieur Cathcart was a charming young man, and very pleasant to work for. Very generous and took a great interest in the family. Madame Leblanc was desolated to hear that he was dead, and on the eve of his marriage to the daughter of the English milady. Madame Leblanc had seen Mademoiselle last year when she visited Monsieur Cathcart in Paris; she considered the young lady very fortunate. Very few young men were as serious as Monsieur Cathcart, especially when they were so good-looking. Madame Leblanc had had experience of young men, and she could relate many histories if she were disposed, but none of Monsieur Cathcart. He would not always be using his rooms; he had the habit of letting her know when he would be at home, and she then went round to put the flat in order. He kept his things very tidy; he was not like English gentlemen in that respect. Madame Leblanc had known many of them, who kept their affairs *sens dessus dessous.* Monsieur Cathcart was always very well dressed; he was particular about his bath; he was like a woman for his toilet, the poor gentleman. And so he was dead. *Le pauvre garçon!* Really it had taken away Madame Leblanc's appetite.

Information obtained from Monsieur the Prefect of Police:

Absolutely nothing. Monsieur Cathcart had never caught the eye of the police in any way. With regard to the sums of money mentioned by Monsieur Parker, if monsieur would give him the numbers of some of the notes, efforts would be made to trace them.

Where had the money gone? Parker could think only of two destinations—an irregular establishment or a blackmailer. Certainly a handsome man like Cathcart might very well have a woman or two in his life, even without the knowledge of the concierge. Certainly a man who habitually cheated at cards—if he did cheat at cards—might very well have got himself into the power of somebody who knew too much. It was noteworthy that his mysterious receipts in cash began just as his economies were exhausted; it seemed likely that they represented irregular gains from gambling—in the casinos, on the exchange, or, if Denver's story had any truth in it, from crooked play. On the whole, Parker rather inclined to the blackmailing theory. It fitted in with the rest of the business, as he and Lord Peter had reconstructed it at Riddlesdale.

Two or three things, however, still puzzled Parker. Why should the blackmailer have been trailing about the Yorkshire moors with a cycle and side-car? Whose was the green-eyed cat? It was a valuable trinket. Had Cathcart offered it as part of his payment? That seemed somehow foolish. One could only suppose that the blackmailer had tossed it away with contempt. The cat was in Parker's possession, and it occurred to him that it might be worth while to get a jeweller to estimate its value. But the side-car was a difficulty, the cat was a difficulty, and, more than all, Lady Mary was a difficulty.

Why had Lady Mary lied at the inquest? For that she had lied, Parker had no manner of doubt. He disbelieved the whole story of the second shot which had awakened her. What had brought her to the conservatory door at three o'clock in the morning? Whose was the suit-case—if it was a suit-case—that had lain concealed among the cactus-plants? Why this prolonged nervous breakdown, with no particular symptoms, which prevented Lady Mary from giving evidence before the magistrate or answering her brother's inquiries? Could Lady Mary have been present at the interview in the shrubbery? If so, surely Wimsey and he would have found her footprints. Was she in league with the blackmailer? That was an unpleasant thought. Was she endeavouring to help her fiancé? She had an allowance of her own—a generous one, as Parker knew from the Duchess. Could she have tried to assist Cathcart with money? But in that case, why not tell all she knew? The worst about Cathcart—always supposing that card-sharping were the worst—was now matter of public knowledge, and the man himself was dead. If she knew the truth, why did she not come forward and save her brother?

And at this point he was visited by a thought even more unpleasant. If, after all, it had not been Denver whom Mrs. Marchbanks had heard in the library, but someone else—someone who had likewise an appointment with the blackmailer—someone who was on his side as against Cathcart—who knew that there might be danger in the interview. Had he himself paid proper attention to the grass lawn between the house and the thicket? Might Thursday morning perhaps have revealed here and there a trodden blade that rain and sap had since restored to uprightness? Had Peter and he found *all* the footsteps in the wood? Had some more trusted hand fired that shot at close quarters? Once again—*whose was the green-eyed cat?*

Surmises and surmises, each uglier than the last, thronged into Parker's mind. He took up a photograph of Cathcart with which Wimsey had supplied him, and looked at it long and curiously. It was a dark, handsome face; the hair was black, with a slight wave, the nose large and well shaped, the big, dark eyes at once pleasing and arrogant. The mouth was good, though a little thick, with a hint of sensuality in its close curves; the chin showed a cleft. Frankly, Parker confessed to himself, it did not attract him; he would have been inclined to dismiss the man as a "Byronic blighter," but experience told him that this kind of face might be powerful with a woman, either for love or hatred.

Coincidences usually have the air of being practical jokes on the part of Providence. Mr. Parker was shortly to be favoured—if the term is a suitable one—with a special display of this Olympian humour. As a rule, that kind of thing did not happen to him; it was more in Wimsey's line. Parker had made his way from modest beginnings to a respectable appointment in the C.I.D. rather by a combination of hard work, shrewdness, and caution than by spectacular displays of happy guesswork or any knack for taking fortune's tide at the flood. This time, however, he was given a "leading" from above, and it was only part of the nature of things and men that he should have felt distinctly ungrateful for it.

He finished his report, replaced everything tidily in the desk and went round to the police-station to arrange with the Prefect about the keys and the fixing of the seals. It was still early evening and not too cold; he determined, therefore, to banish gloomy thoughts by a *café-cognac* in the Boul' Mich', followed by a stroll through the Paris of the shops. Being of a kindly, domestic nature, indeed, he turned over in his mind the idea of buying something Parisian for his elder sister, who was unmarried and lived a rather depressing life in Barrow-in-Furness. Parker knew that she would take pathetic delight in some filmy scrap of lace underwear which no one but herself would ever see. Mr. Parker was not the kind of man to be deterred by the difficulty of buying ladies' underwear in a foreign language; he was not very imaginative. He remembered that a learned judge had one day asked in court what a camisole was, and recollected that there had seemed to be nothing particularly embarrassing about the garment when explained. He determined that he would find a really Parisian shop, and ask for a camisole. That would give him a start, and then mademoiselle would show him other things without being asked further.

Accordingly, towards six o'clock, he was strolling along the Rue de la Paix with a little carton under his arm. He had spent rather more money than he intended, but he had acquired knowledge. He knew for certain what a camisole was, and he had grasped for the first time in his life that crêpe-de-Chine had no recognisable relation to crape, and was astonishingly expensive for its bulk. The young lady had been charmingly sympathetic, and, without actually insinuating anything, had contrived to make her customer feel just a little bit of a dog. He felt that his French accent was improving. The street was crowded with people, slowly sauntering past the brilliant shop-windows. Mr. Parker stopped and gazed nonchalantly over a gorgeous display of jewellery, as though hesitating between a pearl necklace valued at 80,000 francs and a pendant of diamonds and aquamarines set in platinum.

And there, balefully winking at him from under a label inscribed *"Bonne fortune"* hung a green-eyed cat.

The cat stared at Mr. Parker, and Mr. Parker stared at the cat. It was no ordinary cat. It was a cat with a personality. Its tiny arched body sparkled with diamonds, and its platinum paws, set close together, and its erect and glittering tail were instinct in every line with the sensuous delight of friction against some beloved object. Its head, cocked slightly to one side, seemed to demand a titillating finger under the jaw. It was a minute work of art, by no journeyman hand. Mr. Parker fished in his pocket-book. He looked from the cat in his hand to the cat in the window. They were alike. They were astonishingly alike. They were identical. Mr. Parker marched into the shop.

"I have here," said Mr. Parker to the young man at the counter, "a diamond cat which greatly resembles one which I perceive in your window. Could you have the obligingness to inform me what would be the value of such a cat?"

The young man replied instantly:

"But certainly, monsieur. The price of the cat is 5,000 francs. It is, as you perceive, made of the finest materials. Moreover, it is the work of an artist; it is worth more than the market value of the stones."

"It is, I suppose, a mascot?"

"Yes, monsieur; it brings great good luck, especially at cards. Many ladies buy these little objects. We have here other mascots, but all of this special design are of similar quality and price. Monsieur may rest assured that his cat is a cat of pedigree."

"I suppose that such cats are everywhere obtainable in Paris," said Mr. Parker nonchalantly.

"But no, monsieur. If you desire to match your cat I recommend you to do it quickly. Monsieur Briquet had only a score of these cats to begin with, and there are now only three left, including the one in the window. I believe that he will not make any more. To repeat a thing often is to vulgarise it. There will, of course, be other cats——"

"I don't want another cat," said Mr. Parker, suddenly interested. "Do I understand you to say that cats such as this are only sold by Monsieur Briquet? That my cat originally came from this shop?"

"Undoubtedly, monsieur, it is one of our cats. These little animals are made by a workman of ours—a genius who is responsible for many of our finest articles."

"It would, I imagine, be impossible to find out to whom this cat was originally sold?"

"If it was sold over the counter for cash it would be difficult, but if it was entered in our books it might not be impossible to discover, if monsieur desired it."

"I do desire it very much," said Parker, producing his card. "I am an agent of the British police, and it is of great importance that I should know to whom this cat originally belonged."

"In that case," said the young man, "I shall do better to inform monsieur the proprietor."

He carried away the card into the back premises, and presently emerged with a stout gentleman, whom he introduced as Monsieur Briquet.

In Monsieur Briquet's private office the books of the establishment were brought out and laid on the desk.

"You will understand, monsieur," said Monsieur Briquet, "that I can only inform you of the names and addresses of such purchasers of these cats as have had an account sent them. It is, however, unlikely that an object of such value was paid for in cash. Still, with rich Anglo-Saxons, such an incident may occur. We need not go back further than the beginning of the year, when these cats were made." He ran a podgy finger down the pages of the ledger. "The first purchase was on January 19th."

Mr. Parker noted various names and addresses, and at the end of half an hour Monsieur Briquet said in a final manner:

"That is all, monsieur. How many names have you there?"

"Thirteen," said Parker.

"And there are still three cats in stock—the original number was twenty—so that four must have been sold for cash. If monsieur wishes to verify the matter we can consult the day-book."

The search in the day-book was longer and more tiresome, but eventually four cats were duly found to have been sold; one on January 31st, another on February 6th, the third on May 17th, and the last on August 9th.

Mr. Parker had risen, and embarked upon a long string of compliments and thanks, when a sudden association of ideas and dates prompted him to hand Cathcart's photograph to Monsieur Briquet and ask whether he recognised it.

Monsieur Briquet shook his head.

"I am sure he is not one of our regular customers," he said, "and I have a very good memory for faces. I make a point of knowing anyone who has any considerable account with me. And this gentleman has not everybody's face. But we will ask my assistants."

The majority of the staff failed to recognise the photograph, and Parker was on the point of putting it back in his pocket-book when a young lady, who had just finished selling an engagement-ring to an obese and elderly Jew, arrived, and said, without any hesitation:

"Mais oui, je l'ai vu, ce monsieur-là. It is the Englishman who bought a diamond cat for the *jolie blonde."*

"Mademoiselle," said Parker eagerly, "I beseech you to do me the favour to remember all about it."

"Parfaitement," said she. "It is not the face one would forget, especially when one is a woman. The gentleman bought a diamond cat

83

and paid for it—no, I am wrong. It was the lady who bought it, and I remember now to have been surprised that she should pay like that at once in money, because ladies do not usually carry such large sums. The gentleman bought too. He bought a diamond and tortoiseshell comb for the lady to wear, and then she said she must give him something *pour porter bonheur,* and asked me for a mascot that was good for cards. I showed her some jewels more suitable for a gentleman, but she saw these cats and fell in love with them, and said he should have a cat and nothing else; she was sure it would bring him good hands. She asked me if it was not so, and I said, 'Undoubtedly, and monsieur must be sure never to play without it,' and he laughed very much, and promised always to have it upon him when he was playing."

"And how was she, this lady?"

"Blonde, monsieur, and very pretty; rather tall and svelte, and very well dressed. A big hat and dark blue costume. *Quoi encore? Voyons*—yes, she was a foreigner."

"English?"

"I do not know. She spoke French very, very well, almost like a French person, but she had just the little suspicion of accent."

"What language did she speak with the gentleman?"

"French, monsieur. You see, we were speaking together, and they both appealed to me continually, and so all the talk was in French. The gentleman spoke French *à merveille*, it was only by his clothes and a *je ne sais quoi* in his appearance that I guessed he was English. The lady spoke equally fluently, but one remarked just the accent from time to time. Of course, I went away from them once or twice to get goods from the window, and they talked then; I do not know in what language."

"Now, mademoiselle, can you tell me how long ago this was?"

"*Ah, mon Dieu, ça c'est plus difficile. Monsieur sait que les jours se suivent et se ressemblent. Voyons.*"

"We can see by the day-book," put in Monsieur Briquet, "on what occasion a diamond comb was sold with a diamond cat."

"Of course," said Parker hastily. "Let us go back."

They went back and turned to the January volume, where they found no help. But on February 6th they read:

Peigne en écaille et diamants . . . f.7,500
Chat en diamants (Dessin C-5) . . f.5,000

"That settles it," said Parker gloomily.

"Monsieur does not appear content," suggested the jeweller.

"Monsieur," said Parker, "I am more grateful than I can say for your very great kindness, but I will frankly confess that, of all the twelve months in the year, I had rather it had been any other."

Parker found this whole episode so annoying to his feelings that he bought two comic papers and, carrying them away to Boudet's at the corner of the Rue Auguste Léopold, read them solemnly through over his dinner, by way of settling his mind. Then, returning to his modest hotel, he ordered a drink, and sat down to compose a letter to Lord Peter. It was a slow job, and he did not appear to relish it very much. His concluding paragraph was as follows:

"I have put all these things down for you without any comment. You will be able to draw your own inferences as well as I can—better, I hope, for my own are perplexing and worrying me no end. They may be all rubbish—I hope they are; I daresay something will turn up at your end to put quite a different interpretation upon the facts. But I do feel that they must be cleared up. I would offer to hand over the job, but another man might jump at conclusions even faster than I do, and make a mess of it. But of course, if you say so, I will be taken suddenly ill at any moment. Let me know. If you think I'd better go on grubbing about over here, can you get hold of a photograph of Lady Mary Wimsey, and find out if possible about the diamond comb and the green-eyed cat—also at exactly what date Lady Mary was in Paris in February. Does she speak French as well as you do? Let me know how you are getting on.

"Yours ever,
"CHARLES PARKER."

He re-read the letter and report carefully and sealed them up. Then he wrote to his sister, did up his parcel neatly, and rang for the valet de chambre.

"I want this letter sent off at once, registered," he said, "and the parcel is to go to-morrow as a *colis postal*."

After which he went to bed, and read himself to sleep with a commentary on the Epistle to the Hebrews.

·   ·   ·   ·   ·

Lord Peter's reply arrived by return:

"DEAR CHARLES,—Don't worry. I don't like the look of things myself frightfully, but I'd rather you tackled the business than anyone else. As you say, the ordinary police bloke doesn't mind whom he arrests, provided he arrests someone, and is altogether a most damnable fellow to have poking into one's affairs. I'm putting my mind to getting my brother cleared—that *is* the first consideration, after all, and really anything else would be better than having Jerry hanged for a crime he didn't commit. Whoever did it, it's better the right person should suffer than the wrong. So go ahead.

"I enclose two photographs—all I can lay hands on for the moment. The one in nursing-kit is rather rotten, and the other's all smothered up in a big hat.

"I had a damn' queer little adventure here on Wednesday, which I'll tell you about when we meet. I've found a woman who obviously knows more than she ought, and a most promising ruffian—only I'm afraid he's got an alibi. Also I've got a faint suggestion of a clue about No. 10. Nothing much happened at Northallerton, except that Jerry was of course committed for trial. My mother is here, thank God! and I'm hoping she'll get some sense out of Mary, but she's been worse the last two days—Mary, I mean, not my mother—beastly sick and all that sort of thing. Dr. Thingummy—who is an ass—can't make it out. Mother says it's as clear as noonday, and she'll stop it if I have patience a day or two. I made her ask about the comb and the cat. M. denies the cat altogether, but admits to a diamond comb bought in Paris—says she bought it herself. It's in town—I'll get it and send it on. She says she can't remember where she bought it, has lost the bill, but it didn't cost anything like 7,500 francs. She was in Paris from February 2nd to February 20th. My chief business now is to see Lubbock and clear up a little matter concerning silver sand.

"The Assizes will be the first week in November—in fact, the end of next week. This rushes things a bit, but it doesn't matter, because they can't try him there; nothing will matter but the Grand Jury, who are bound to find a true bill on the face of it. After that we can hang matters up as long as we like. It's going to be a deuce of a business, Parliament sitting and all. Old Biggs is fearfully perturbed under that marble outside of his. I hadn't really grasped what a fuss it was to try peers. It's only happened about once in every sixty years, and the procedure's about as old as Queen Elizabeth. They have to appoint a Lord High Steward for the occasion, and God knows what. They have to make it frightfully clear in the Commission that it *is* only for the occasion, because, somewhere about Richard III's time, the L.H.S. was such a terrifically big pot that he got to ruling the roost. So when Henry IV came to the throne, and the office came into the hands of the Crown, he jolly well kept it there, and now they only appoint a man *pro tem.* for the Coronation and shows like Jerry's. The King always pretends not to know there isn't a L.H.S. till the time comes, and is no end surprised at having to think of somebody to take on the job. Did you know all this? I didn't. I got it out of Biggy.

"Cheer up. Pretend you don't know that any of these people are relations of mine. My mother sends you her kindest regards and what not, and hopes she'll see you again soon. Bunter sends something correct and respectful; I forget what.

"Yours in the brotherhood of detection,

"P.W."

It may as well be said at once that the evidence from the photographs was wholly inconclusive.

CHAPTER VI

MARY QUITE CONTRARY

I am striving to take into public life what any man gets from his mother.—Lady Astor.

ON THE OPENING DAY of the York Assizes, the Grand Jury brought in a true bill, against Gerald, Duke of Denver, for murder. Gerald, Duke of Denver, being accordingly produced in the court, the Judge affected to discover—what, indeed, every newspaper in the country had been announcing to the world for the last fortnight—that he, being but a common or garden judge with a plebeian jury, was incompetent to try a peer of the realm. He added, however, that he would make it his business to inform the Lord Chancellor (who also, for the last fortnight, had been secretly calculating the accommodation in the

Royal Gallery and choosing lords to form the Select Committee).
Order being taken accordingly, the noble prisoner was led away.

.   .   .   .   .

A day or two later, in the gloom of a London afternoon, Mr.
Charles Parker rang the bell of a second-floor flat at No. 110 Piccadilly. The door was opened by Bunter, who informed him with a gracious smile that Lord Peter had stepped out for a few minutes but
was expecting him, and would he kindly come in and wait.

"We only came up this morning," added the valet, "and are not
quite straight yet, sir, if you will excuse us. Would you feel inclined
for a cup of tea?"

Parker accepted the offer, and sank luxuriously into a corner of the
Chesterfield. After the extraordinary discomfort of French furniture
there was solace in the enervating springiness beneath him, the cushions behind his head, and Wimsey's excellent cigarettes. What Bunter
had meant by saying that things were "not quite straight yet" he could
not divine. A leaping wood fire was merrily reflected in the spotless
surface of the black baby grand; the mellow calf bindings of Lord
Peter's rare editions glowed softly against the black and primrose
walls; the vases were filled with tawny chrysanthemums; the latest
editions of all the papers were on the table—as though the owner had
never been absent.

Over his tea Mr. Parker drew out the photographs of Lady Mary
and Denis Cathcart from his breast pocket. He stood them up against
the teapot and stared at them, looking from one to the other as if
trying to force a meaning from their faintly smirking, self-conscious
gaze. He referred again to his Paris notes, ticking off various points
with a pencil. "Damn!" said Mr. Parker, gazing at Lady Mary. "Damn
—damn—damn——"

The train of thought he was pursuing was an extraordinarily interesting one. Image after image, each rich in suggestion, crowded
into his mind. Of course, one couldn't think properly in Paris—it was
so uncomfortable and the houses were central heated. Here, where
so many problems had been unravelled, there was a good fire. Cathcart had been sitting before the fire. Of course, he wanted to think
out a problem. When cats sat staring into the fire they were thinking
out problems. It was odd he should not have thought of that before.
When the green-eyed cat sat before the fire one sank right down into

a sort of rich, black, velvety suggestiveness which was most important. It was luxurious to be able to think so lucidly as this, because otherwise it would be a pity to exceed the speed limit—and the black moors were reeling by so fast. But now he had really got the formula he wouldn't forget it again. The connection was just there—close, thick, richly coherent.

"The glass-blower's cat is bompstable," said Mr. Parker aloud and distinctly.

"I'm charmed to hear it," replied Lord Peter, with a friendly grin. "Had a good nap, old man?"

"I—what?" said Mr. Parker. "Hullo! Watcher mean, nap? I had got hold of a most important train of thought, and you've put it out of my head. What was it? Cat—cat—cat——" He groped wildly.

"You *said* 'The glass-blower's cat is bompstable,'" retorted Lord Peter. "It's a perfectly rippin' word, but I don't know what you mean by it."

"Bompstable?" said Mr. Parker, blushing slightly. "Bomp—oh, well, perhaps you're right—I may have dozed off. But, you know, I thought I'd just got the clue to the whole thing. I attached the greatest importance to that phrase. Even now—— No, now I come to think of it, my train of thought doesn't seem quite to hold together. What a pity. I thought it was so lucid."

"Never mind," said Lord Peter. "Just back?"

"Crossed last night. Any news?"

"Lots."

"Good?"

"No."

Parker's eyes wandered to the photographs.

"I don't believe it," he said obstinately. "I'm damned if I'm going to believe a word of it."

"A word of what?"

"Of whatever it is."

"You'll have to believe it, Charles, as far as it goes," said his friend softly, filling his pipe with decided little digs of the fingers. "I don't say"—dig—"that Mary"—dig—"shot Cathcart"—dig, dig—"but she has lied"—dig—"again and again."—Dig, dig—"She knows who did it"—dig—"she was prepared for it"—dig—"she's malingering and lying to keep the fellow shielded"—dig—"and we shall have to make her speak." Here he struck a match and lit the pipe in a series of angry little puffs.

"If you can think," said Mr. Parker, with some heat, "that that woman"—he indicated the photographs—"had any hand in murdering Cathcart, I don't care what your evidence is, you—hang it all, Wimsey, she's your own sister."

"Gerald is my brother," said Wimsey quietly. "You don't suppose I'm exactly enjoying this business, do you? But I think we shall get along very much better if we try to keep our tempers."

"I'm awfully sorry," said Parker. "Can't think why I said that—rotten bad form—beg pardon, old man."

"The best thing we can do," said Wimsey, "is to look the evidence in the face, however ugly. And I don't mind admittin' that some of it's a positive gargoyle.

"My mother turned up at Riddlesdale on Friday. She marched upstairs at once and took possession of Mary, while I drooped about in the hall and teased the cat, and generally made a nuisance of myself. *You* know. Presently old Dr. Thorpe called. I went and sat on the chest on the landing. Presently the bell rings and Ellen comes upstairs. Mother and Thorpe popped out and caught her just outside Mary's room, and they jibber-jabbered a lot, and presently mother came barging down the passage to the bathroom with her heels tapping and her earrings simply dancing with irritation. I sneaked after 'em to the bathroom door, but I couldn't see anything, because they were blocking the doorway, but I heard mother say, 'There, now, what did I tell you'; and Ellen said, 'Lawks! your grace, who'd 'a' thought it?'; and my mother said, 'All I can say is, if I had to depend on you people to save me from being murdered with arsenic or that other stuff with the name like anemones*—you know what I mean—that that very attractive-looking man with the preposterous beard used to make away with his wife and mother-in-law (who was vastly the more attractive of the two, poor thing), I might be being cut up and analysed by Dr. Spilsbury now—such a horrid, distasteful job he must have of it, poor man, and the poor little rabbits, too.'" Wimsey paused for breath, and Parker laughed in spite of his anxiety.

"I won't vouch for the exact words," said Wimsey, "but it was to that effect—you know my mother's style. Old Thorpe tried to look dignified, but mother ruffled up like a little hen and said, looking beadily at him: 'In *my* day we called that kind of thing hysterics and naughtiness. *We* didn't let girls pull the wool over our eyes like that.

* Antimony? The Duchess appears to have had Dr. Pritchard's case in mind.

90

I suppose *you* call it a neurosis, or a suppressed desire, or a reflex, and coddle it. You might have let that silly child make herself really ill. You are all perfectly ridiculous, and no more fit to take care of yourselves than a lot of babies—not but what there are plenty of poor little things in the slums that look after whole families and show more sense than the lot of you put together. I am very angry with Mary, advertising herself in this way, and she's not to be pitied.' You know," said Wimsey, "I think there's often a great deal in what one's mother says."

"I believe you," said Parker.

"Well, I got hold of mother afterwards and asked her what it was all about. She said Mary wouldn't tell her anything about herself or her illness; just asked to be let alone. Then Thorpe came along and talked about nervous shock—said he couldn't understand these fits of sickness, or the way Mary's temperature hopped about. Mother listened, and told him to go and see what the temperature was now. Which he did, and in the middle mother called him away to the dressing-table. But, bein' a wily old bird, you see, she kept her eyes on the looking-glass, and nipped round just in time to catch Mary stimulatin' the thermometer to terrific leaps on the hot-water bottle."

"Well, I'm damned!" said Parker.

"So was Thorpe. All mother said was, that if he wasn't too old a bird yet to be taken in by that hoary trick he'd no business to be gettin' himself up as a grey-haired family practitioner. So then she asked the girl about the sick fits—when they happened, and how often, and was it after meals or before, and so on, and at last she got out of them that it generally happened a bit after breakfast and occasionally at other times. Mother said she couldn't make it out at first, because she'd hunted all over the room for bottles and things, till at last she asked who made the bed, thinkin', you see, Mary might have hidden something under the mattress. So Ellen said she usually made it while Mary had her bath. 'When's that?' says mother. 'Just before her breakfast,' bleats the girl. 'God forgive you all for a set of nincompoops,' says my mother. 'Why didn't you say so before?' So away they all trailed to the bathroom, and there, sittin' up quietly on the bathroom shelf among the bath salts and the Elliman's embrocation and the Kruschen feelings and the toothbrushes and things, was the family bottle of ipecacuanha—three-quarters empty! Mother said—well, I told you what she said. By the way, how do you spell ipecacuanha?"

Mr. Parker spelt it.

"Damn you!" said Lord Peter. "I *did* think I'd stumped you that time. I believe you went and looked it up beforehand. *No* decent-minded person would know how to spell ipecacuanha out of his own head. Anyway, as you were saying, it's easy to see which side of the family has the detective instinct."

"I didn't say so——"

"I know. Why didn't you? I think my mother's talents deserve a little acknowledgment. I said so to her, as a matter of fact, and she replied in these memorable words: 'My dear child, you can give it a long name if you like, but I'm an old-fashioned woman and I call it mother-wit, and it's so rare for a man to have it that if he does you write a book about him and call him Sherlock Holmes.' However, apart from all that, I said to mother (in private, of course), 'It's all very well, but I can't believe that Mary has been going to all this trouble to make herself horribly sick and frighten us all just to show off. Surely she isn't that sort.' Mother looked at me as steady as an owl, and quoted a whole lot of examples of hysteria, ending up with the servant-girl who threw paraffin about all over somebody's house to make them think it was haunted, and finished up—that if all these new-fangled doctors went out of their way to invent subconsciousness and kleptomania, and complexes and other fancy descriptions to explain away when people had done naughty things, she thought one might just as well take advantage of the fact."

"Wimsey," said Parker, much excited, "did she mean she suspected something?"

"My dear old chap," replied Lord Peter, "whatever can be known about Mary by putting two and two together my mother knows. I told her all *we* knew up to that point, and she took it all in, in her funny way, you know, never answering anything directly, and then she put her head on one side and said: 'If Mary had listened to me, and done something useful instead of that V.A.D. work, which never came to much, if you ask me—not that I have anything against V.A.D.'s in a general way, but that silly woman Mary worked under was the most terrible snob on God's earth—and there were very much more sensible things which Mary might really have done well, only that she was so crazy to get to London—I shall always say it was the fault of that ridiculous club—what could you expect of a place where you ate such horrible food, all packed into an underground cellar painted pink and talking away at the tops of their voices, and never any evening dress —only Soviet jumpers and side-whiskers. Anyhow, I've told that silly old man what to say about it, and they'll never be able to think of a better explanation for themselves.' Indeed, you know," said Peter, "I think if any of them start getting inquisitive, they'll have mother down on them like a ton of bricks."

"What do you really think yourself?" asked Parker.

"I haven't come yet to the unpleasantest bit of the lot," said Peter. "I've only just heard it, and it did give me a nasty jar, I'll admit. Yesterday I got a letter from Lubbock saying he would like to see me, so I trotted up here and dropped in on him this morning. You remember I sent him a stain off one of Mary's skirts which Bunter had cut out for me? I had taken a squint at it myself, and didn't like the look of it, so I sent it up to Lubbock, *ex abundantia cautelæ;* and I'm sorry to say he confirms me. It's human blood, Charles, and I'm afraid it's Cathcart's."

"But—I've lost the thread of this a bit."

"Well, the skirt must have got stained the day Cathcart—died, as that was the last day on which the party was out on the moors, and if it had been there earlier Ellen would have cleaned it off. Afterwards Mary strenuously resisted Ellen's efforts to take the skirt away, and made an amateurish effort to tidy it up herself with soap. So I think we may conclude that Mary knew the stains were there, and wanted to avoid discovery. She told Ellen that the blood was from a grouse —which must have been a deliberate untruth."

"Perhaps," said Parker, struggling against hope to make out a case for Lady Mary, "she only said, 'Oh! one of the birds must have bled,' or something like that."

"I don't believe," said Peter, "that one could get a great patch of human blood on one's clothes like that and not know what it was. She must have knelt right in it. It was three or four inches across."

Parker shook his head dismally, and consoled himself by making a note.

"Well, now," went on Peter, "on Wednesday night everybody comes in and dines and goes to bed except Cathcart, who rushes out and stays out. At 11.50 the gamekeeper, Hardraw, hears a shot which may very well have been fired in the clearing where the—well, let's say the accident—took place. The time also agrees with the medical evidence about Cathcart having already been dead three or four hours when he was examined at 4.30. Very well. At 3 a.m. Jerry comes home from somewhere or other and finds the body. As he is bending over it, Mary arrives in the most apropos manner from the house in her coat and cap and walking shoes. Now what is her story? She says that at three o'clock she was awakened by a shot. Now nobody else heard that shot, and we have the evidence of Mrs. Pettigrew-Robinson, who slept in the next room to Mary, with her window open according to her immemorial custom, that she lay broad awake from 2 a.m. till a little after 3 a.m., when the alarm was given, and heard no shot. According to Mary, the shot was loud enough to waken her on the other side of the building. It's odd, isn't it, that the person already awake should swear so positively that she heard nothing of a noise loud enough to waken a healthy young sleeper next door? And, in any case, *if* that was the shot that killed Cathcart, he can barely have been dead when my brother found him—and again, in that case, how was there time for him to be carried up from the shrubbery to the conservatory?"

"We've been over all this ground," said Parker, with an expression of distaste. "We agreed that we couldn't attach any importance to the story of the shot."

"I'm afraid we've got to attach a great deal of importance to it," said Lord Peter gravely. "Now, what does Mary do? Either she thought the shot——"

"There was no shot."

"I know that. But I'm examining the discrepancies of her story. She said she did not give the alarm because she thought it was probably only poachers. But, if it was poachers, it would be absurd to go down and investigate. So she explains that she thought it might be burglars. Now how does she dress to go and look for burglars? What would you or I have done? I think we would have taken a dressing-gown, a stealthy kind of pair of slippers, and perhaps a poker or a stout stick—not a pair of walking shoes, a coat, and a cap, of all things!"

"It was a wet night," mumbled Parker.

"My dear chap, if it's burglars you're looking for you don't expect to go and hunt them round the garden. Your first thought is that they're getting into the house, and your idea is to slip down quietly and survey them from the staircase or behind the dining-room door. Anyhow, fancy a present-day girl, who rushes about bare-headed in all weathers, stopping to embellish herself in a cap for a burglar-hunt—damn it all, Charles, it won't wash, you know! And she walks straight off to the conservatory and comes upon the corpse, exactly as if she knew where to look for it beforehand."

Parker shook his head again.

"Well, now. She sees Gerald stooping over Cathcart's body. What does she say? Does she ask what's the matter? Does she ask who it is? She exclaims: 'O God! Gerald, you've killed him,' and *then* she says, as if on second thoughts, 'Oh, it's Denis! What has happened? Has there been an accident?' Now, does that strike you as natural?"

"No. But it rather suggests to me that it wasn't Cathcart she expected to see there, but somebody else."

"Does it? It rather sounds to me as if she was pretending not to know who it was. First she says, 'You've killed him!' and then, recollecting that she isn't supposed to know who 'he' is, she says, 'Why, it's Denis!'"

"In any case, then, if her first exclamation was genuine, she didn't expect to find the man dead."

"No—no—we must remember that. The death *was* a surprise. Very well. Then Gerald sends Mary up for help. And here's where a little bit of evidence comes in that you picked up and sent along. Do you remember what Mrs. Pettigrew-Robinson said to you in the train?"

"About the door slamming on the landing, do you mean?"

"Yes. Now I'll tell you something that happened to me the other morning. I was burstin' out of the bathroom in my usual breezy way when I caught myself a hell of a whack on that old chest on the landin', and the lid lifted up and shut down, *plonk!* That gave me an idea, and I thought I'd have a squint inside. I'd got the lid up and was lookin' at some sheets and stuff that were folded up at the bottom, when I heard a sort of gasp, and there was Mary, starin' at me, as white as a ghost. She gave me a turn, by Jove, but nothin' like the turn I'd given her. Well, she wouldn't say anything to me, and got hysterical, and I hauled her back to her room. But I'd seen something on those sheets."

"What?"

"Silver sand."

"Silver——"

"D'you remember those cacti in the greenhouse, and the place where somebody'd put a suit-case or something down?"

"Yes."

"Well, there was a lot of silver sand scattered about—the sort people stick round some kinds of bulbs and things."

"And that was inside the chest too?"

"Yes. Wait a moment. After the noise Mrs. Pettigrew-Robinson heard, Mary woke up Freddy and then the Pettigrew-Robinsons—and then what?"

"She locked herself into her room."

"Yes. And shortly afterwards she came down and joined the others in the conservatory, and it was at this point everybody remembered noticing that she was wearing a cap and coat and walking shoes over pyjamas and bare feet."

"You are suggesting," said Parker, "that Lady Mary was already awake and dressed at three o'clock, that she went out by the conservatory door with her suit-case, expecting to meet the—the murderer of her—damn it, Wimsey!"

"We needn't go so far as that," said Peter; "we decided that she *didn't* expect to find Cathcart dead."

"No. Well, she went, presumably to meet somebody."

"Shall we say, *pro tem.,* she went to meet No. 10?" suggested Wimsey softly.

"I suppose we may as well say so. When she turned on the torch and saw the Duke stooping over Cathcart she thought—by Jove, Wimsey, I was right after all! When she said, 'You've killed him!' she meant No. 10—she thought it was No. 10's body."

"Of course!" cried Wimsey. "I'm a fool! Yes. Then she said, 'It's Denis—what has happened?' That's quite clear. And, meanwhile, what did she do with the suit-case?"

"I see it all now," cried Parker. "When she saw that the body wasn't the body of No. 10 she realised that No. 10 must be the murderer. So her game was to prevent anybody knowing that No. 10 had been there. So she shoved the suit-case behind the cacti. Then, when she went upstairs, she pulled it out again, and hid it in the oak chest on the landing. She couldn't take it to her room, of course, because if anybody'd heard her come upstairs it would seem odd that she should run to her room before calling the others. Then she knocked up Arbuthnot and the Pettigrew-Robinsons—she'd be in the dark, and they'd be flustered and wouldn't see exactly what she had on. Then she escaped from Mrs. P., ran into her room, took off the skirt in which she had knelt by Cathcart's side, and the rest of her clothes, and put on her pyjamas and the cap, which someone might have noticed, and the coat, which they *must* have noticed, and the shoes, which had probably left footmarks already. Then she could go down and show herself. Meantime she'd concocted the burglar story for the Coroner's benefit."

"That's about it," said Peter. "I suppose she was so desperately anxious to throw us off the scent of No. 10 that it never occurred to her that her story was going to help implicate her brother."

"She realised it at the inquest," said Parker eagerly. "Don't you remember how hastily she grasped at the suicide theory?"

"And when she found that she was simply saving her—well, No. 10 —in order to hang her brother, she lost her head, took to her bed, and refused to give any evidence at all. Seems to me there's an extra allowance of fools in my family," said Peter gloomily.

"Well, what could she have done, poor girl?" asked Parker. He had been growing almost cheerful again. "Anyway, she's cleared——"

"After a fashion," said Peter, "but we're not out of the wood yet by a long way. Why is she hand-in-glove with No. 10 who is at least a blackmailer if not a murderer? How did Gerald's revolver come on the scene? And the green-eyed cat? How much did Mary know of that meeting between No. 10 and Denis Cathcart? And if she was seeing and meeting the man she might have put the revolver into his hands any time."

"No, no," said Parker. "Wimsey, don't think such ugly things as that."

"Hell!" cried Peter, exploding. "I'll have the truth of this beastly business if we all go to the gallows together!"

At this moment Bunter entered with a telegram addressed to Wimsey. Lord Peter read as follows:

"Party traced London; seen Marylebone Friday. Further information from Scotland Yard.—POLICE-SUPERINTENDENT GOSLING, Ripley."

"Good egg!" cried Wimsey. "Now we're gettin' down to it. Stay here, there's a good man, in case anything turns up. I'll run round to the Yard now. They'll send you up dinner, and tell Bunter to give you a bottle of the Chateau Yquem—it's rather decent. So long."

He leapt out of the flat, and a moment later his taxi buzzed away up Piccadilly.

CHAPTER VII

THE CLUB AND THE BULLET

He is dead, and by my hand. It were better that I were dead myself, for the guilty wretch I am.—Adventures of Sexton Blake.

HOUR AFTER HOUR Mr. Parker sat waiting for his friend's return. Again and again he went over the Riddlesdale Case, checking his notes here, amplifying them there, involving his tired brain in speculations of the most fantastic kind. He wandered about the room, taking down here and there a book from the shelves, strumming a few unskilful bars upon the piano, glancing through the weeklies, fidgeting restlessly. At length he selected a volume from the criminological section of the bookshelves, and forced himself to read with attention that most fascinating and dramatic of poison trials—the Seddon Case. Gradually the mystery gripped him, as it invariably did, and it was with a start of astonishment that he looked up at a long and vigorous whirring of the door-bell, to find that it was already long past midnight.

His first thought was that Wimsey must have left his latchkey behind, and he was preparing a facetious greeting when the door opened—exactly as in the beginning of a Sherlock Holmes story—to admit a tall and beautiful young woman, in an extreme state of nervous agitation, with halo of golden hair, violet-blue eyes, and disordered apparel all complete; for as she threw back her heavy travelling-coat he observed that she wore evening dress, with light green silk stockings and heavy brogue shoes thickly covered with mud.

"His lordship has not yet returned, my lady," said Mr. Bunter, "but Mr. Parker is here waiting for him, and we are expecting him at any minute now. Will your ladyship take anything?"

"No, no," said the vision hastily, "nothing, thanks. I'll wait. Good evening, Mr. Parker. Where's Peter?"

"He has been called out, Lady Mary," said Parker. "I can't think why he isn't back yet. Do sit down."

"Where did he go?"

"To Scotland Yard—but that was about six o'clock. I can't imagine——"

Lady Mary made a gesture of despair.

"I knew it. Oh, Mr. Parker, what am I to do?"

Mr. Parker was speechless.

"I *must* see Peter," cried Lady Mary. "It's a matter of life and death. Can't you send for him?"

"But I don't know where he is," said Parker. "Please, Lady Mary——"

"He's doing something dreadful—he's all *wrong*," cried the young woman, wringing her hands with desperate vehemence. "I must see him—tell him—— Oh! did anybody ever get into such dreadful trouble! I—oh!——"

Here the lady laughed loudly and burst into tears.

"Lady Mary—I beg you—please don't," cried Mr. Parker anxiously, with a strong feeling that he was being incompetent and rather ridiculous. "Please sit down. Drink a glass of wine. You'll be ill if you cry like that. If it is crying," he added dubiously to himself. "It *sounds* like hiccups. Bunter!"

Mr. Bunter was not far off. In fact, he was just outside the door with a small tray. With a respectful "Allow me, sir," he stepped forward to the writhing Lady Mary and presented a small phial to her nose. The effect was startling. The patient gave two or three fearful whoops, and sat up, erect and furious.

"How *dare* you, Bunter!" said Lady Mary. "Go away at once!"

"Your ladyship had better take a drop of brandy," said Mr. Bunter, replacing the stopper in the smelling-bottle, but not before Parker had caught the pungent reek of ammonia. "This is the 1800 Napoleon brandy my lady. Please don't snort so, if I may make the suggestion. His lordship would be greatly distressed to think that any of it should be wasted. Did your ladyship dine on the way up? No? Most unwise, my lady, to undertake a long journey on a vacant interior. I will take the liberty of sending in an omelette for your ladyship. Perhaps you would like a little snack of something yourself, sir, as it is getting late?"

"Anything you like," said Mr. Parker, waving him off hurriedly. "Now, Lady Mary, you're feeling better, aren't you? Let me help you off with your coat."

No more of an exciting nature was said until the omelette was disposed of, and Lady Mary comfortably settled on the Chesterfield.

She had by now recovered her poise. Looking at her, Parker noticed how her recent illness (however produced) had left its mark upon her. Her complexion had nothing of the brilliance which he remembered; she looked strained and white, with purple hollows under her eyes.

"I am sorry I was so foolish just now, Mr. Parker," she said, looking into his eyes with a charming frankness and confidence, "but I was dreadfully distressed, and I came up from Riddlesdale so hurriedly."

"Not at all," said Parker meaninglessly. "Is there anything I can do in your brother's absence?"

"I suppose you and Peter do everything together?"

"I think I may say that neither of us knows anything about this investigation which he has not communicated to the other."

"If I tell you, it's the same thing?"

"Exactly the same thing. If you can bring yourself to honour me with your confidence——"

"Wait a minute, Mr. Parker. I'm in a difficult position. I don't quite know what I ought—— Can you tell me just how far you've got—what you have discovered?"

Mr. Parker was a little taken aback. Although the face of Lady Mary had been haunting his imagination ever since the inquest, and although the agitation of his feelings had risen to boiling-point during this romantic interview, the official instinct of caution had not wholly deserted him. Holding, as he did, proofs of Lady Mary's complicity in the crime, whatever it was, he was not so far gone as to fling all his cards on the table.

"I'm afraid," he said, "that I can't quite tell you that. You see, so much of what we've got is only suspicion as yet. I might accidentally do great mischief to an innocent person."

"Ah! You definitely suspect somebody, then?"

"*In*definitely would be a better word for it," said Mr. Parker with a smile. "But if you have anything to tell us which may throw light on the matter, I beg you to speak. We may be suspecting a totally wrong person."

"I shouldn't be surprised," said Lady Mary, with a sharp, nervous little laugh. Her hand strayed to the table and began pleating the orange envelope into folds. "What do you want to know?" she asked suddenly, with a change of tone. Parker was conscious of a new hardness in her manner—a something braced and rigid.

100

He opened his note-book, and as he began his questioning his nervousness left him; the official reasserted himself.

"You were in Paris last February?"

Lady Mary assented.

"Do you recollect going with Captain Cathcart—oh! by the way, you speak French, I presume?"

"Yes, very fluently."

"As well as your brother—practically without accent?"

"Quite as well. We always had French governesses as children, and mother was very particular about it."

"I see. Well, now, do you remember going with Captain Cathcart on February 6th to a jeweller's in the Rue de la Paix and buying, or his buying for you, a tortoiseshell comb set with diamonds and a diamond and platinum cat with emerald eyes?"

He saw a lurking awareness come into the girl's eyes.

"Is that the cat you have been making inquiries about in Riddlesdale?" she demanded.

It being never worth while to deny the obvious, Parker replied, "Yes."

"It was found in the shrubbery, wasn't it?"

"Had you lost it? Or was it Cathcart's?"

"If I said it was his——"

"I should be ready to believe you. *Was* it his?"

"No"—a long breath—"it was mine."

"When did you lose it?"

"That night."

"Where?"

"I suppose in the shrubbery. Wherever you found it. I didn't miss it till later."

"Is it the one you bought in Paris?"

"Yes."

"Why did you say before that it was not yours?"

"I was afraid."

"And now?"

"I am going to speak the truth."

Parker looked at her again. She met his eye frankly, but there was a tenseness in her manner which showed that it had cost her something to make her mind up.

"Very well," said Parker, "we shall all be glad of that, for I think there were one or two points at the inquest on which you didn't tell the truth, weren't there?"

"Yes."

"Do believe," said Parker, "that I am sorry to have to ask these questions. The terrible position in which your brother is placed——"

"In which I helped to place him."

"I don't say that."

"I do. I helped to put him in gaol. Don't say I didn't, because I did."

"Well," said Parker, "don't worry. There's plenty of time to put it all right again. Shall I go on?"

"Yes."

"Well, now, Lady Mary, it wasn't true about hearing that shot at three o'clock, was it?"

"No."

"Did you hear the shot at all?"

"Yes."

"When?"

"At 11.50."

"What was it, then, Lady Mary, you hid behind the plants in the conservatory?"

"I hid nothing there."

"And in the oak chest on the landing?"

"My skirt."

"You went out—why?—to meet Cathcart?"

"Yes."

"Who was the other man?"

"What other man?"

"The other man who was in the shrubbery. A tall, fair man dressed in a Burberry?"

"There was no other man."

"Oh, pardon me, Lady Mary. We saw his footmarks all the way up from the shrubbery to the conservatory."

"It must have been some tramp. I know nothing about him."

"But we have proof that he was there—of what he did, and how he escaped. For heaven's sake, and your brother's sake, Lady Mary, tell us the truth—for that man in the Burberry was the man who shot Cathcart."

"No," said the girl, with a white face, "that is impossible."

"Why impossible?"

"I shot Denis Cathcart myself."

·   ·   ·   ·   ·

"So that's how the matter stands, you see, Lord Peter," said the Chief of Scotland Yard, rising from his desk with a friendly gesture of dismissal. "The man was undoubtedly seen at Marylebone on the Friday morning, and, though we have unfortunately lost him again for the moment, I have no doubt whatever that we shall lay hands on him before long. The delay has been due to the unfortunate illness of the porter Morrison, whose evidence has been so material. But we are wasting no time now."

"I'm sure I may leave it to you with every confidence, Sir Andrew," replied Wimsey, cordially shaking hands. "I'm diggin' away too; between us we ought to get somethin'—you in your small corner and I in mine, as the hymn says—or is it a hymn? I remember readin' it in a book about missionaries when I was small. Did you want to be a missionary in your youth? I did. I think most kids do some time or another, which is odd, seein' how unsatisfactory most of us turn out."

"Meanwhile," said Sir Andrew Mackenzie, "if you run across the man yourself, let us know. I would never deny your extraordinary good fortune, or it may be good judgment, in running across the criminals we may be wanting."

"If I catch the bloke," said Lord Peter, "I'll come and shriek under your windows till you let me in, if it's the middle of the night and you in your little night-shirt. And talking of night-shirts reminds me that we hope to see you down at Denver one of these days, as soon as this business is over. Mother sends kind regards, of course."

"Thanks very much," replied Sir Andrew. "I hope you feel that all is going well. I had Parker in here this morning to report, and he seemed a little dissatisfied."

"He's been doing a lot of ungrateful routine work," said Wimsey, "and being altogether the fine, sound man he always is. He's been a damn good friend to me, Sir Andrew, and it's a real privilege to be allowed to work with him. Well, so long, Chief."

He found that his interview with Sir Andrew Mackenzie had taken up a couple of hours, and that it was nearly eight o'clock. He was just trying to make up his mind where to dine when he was accosted by a cheerful young woman with bobbed red hair, dressed in a short checked skirt, brilliant jumper, corduroy jacket, and a rakish green velvet tam-o'-shanter.

"Surely," said the young woman, extending a shapely, ungloved hand, "it's Lord Peter Wimsey. How're you? And how's Mary?"

"B'Jove!" said Wimsey gallantly, "it's Miss Tarrant. How perfectly rippin' to see you again. Absolutely delightful. Thanks, Mary ain't as fit as she might be—worryin' about this murder business, y'know. You've heard that we're what the poor so kindly and tactfully call 'in trouble,' I expect, what?"

"Yes, of course," replied Miss Tarrant eagerly, "and, of course, as a good Socialist, I can't help rejoicing rather when a peer gets taken up, because it does make him look so silly, you know, and the House of Lords is silly, isn't it? But, really, I'd rather it was anybody else's brother. Mary and I were such great friends, you know, and, of course, *you* do investigate things, don't you, not just live on your estates in the country and shoot birds? So I suppose that makes a difference."

"That's very kind of you," said Peter. "If you can prevail upon yourself to overlook the misfortune of my birth and my other deficiencies, p'raps you would honour me by comin' along and havin' a bit of dinner somewhere, what?"

"Oh, I'd have *loved* to," cried Miss Tarrant, with enormous energy, "but I've promised to be at the club to-night. There's a meeting at nine. Mr. Coke—the Labour leader, you know—is going to make a speech about converting the Army and Navy to Communism. We expect to be raided, and there's going to be a grand hunt for spies before we begin. But look here, do come along and dine with me there, and, if you like, I'll try to smuggle you in to the meeting, and you'll be seized and turned out. I suppose I oughtn't to have told you anything about it, because you ought to be a deadly enemy, but I can't really believe you're dangerous."

"I'm just an ordinary capitalist, I expect," said Lord Peter, "highly obnoxious."

"Well, come to dinner, anyhow. I *do* so want to hear all the news."

Peter reflected that the dinner at the Soviet Club would be worse than execrable, and was just preparing an excuse when it occurred to him that Miss Tarrant might be able to tell him a good many of the things that he didn't know, and really ought to know, about his own sister. Accordingly, he altered his polite refusal into a polite acceptance, and, plunging after Miss Tarrant, was led at a reckless pace and by a series of grimy short cuts into Gerrard Street, where an orange door, flanked by windows with magenta curtains, sufficiently indicated the Soviet Club.

The Soviet Club, being founded to accommodate free thinking rather than high living, had that curious amateur air which pervades all worldly institutions planned by unworldly people. Exactly why it made Lord Peter instantly think of mission teas he could not say, unless it was that all the members looked as though they cherished a purpose in life, and that the staff seemed rather sketchily trained and strongly in evidence. Wimsey reminded himself that in so democratic an institution one could hardly expect the assistants to assume that air of superiority which marks the servants in a West End club. For one thing, they would not be such capitalists. In the dining-room below the resemblance to a mission tea was increased by the exceedingly heated atmosphere, the babel of conversation, and the curious inequalities of the cutlery. Miss Tarrant secured seats at a rather crumby table near the serving-hatch, and Peter wedged himself in with some difficulty next to a very large, curly-haired man in a velvet coat, who was earnestly conversing with a thin, eager young woman in a Russian blouse, Venetian beads, a Hungarian shawl and a Spanish comb, looking like a personification of the United Front of the "Internationale."

Lord Peter endeavoured to please his hostess by a question about the great Mr. Coke, but was checked by an agitated "Hush!"

"*Please* don't shout about it," said Miss Tarrant, leaning across till her auburn mop positively tickled his eyebrows. "It's *so* secret."

"I'm awfully sorry," said Wimsey apologetically. "I say, d'you know you're dipping those jolly little beads of yours in the soup?"

"Oh, am I?" cried Miss Tarrant, withdrawing hastily. "Oh, thank you so much. Especially as the colour runs. I hope it isn't arsenic or anything." Then, leaning forward again, she whispered hoarsely:

"The girl next me is Erica Heath-Warburton—the writer, you know."

Wimsey looked with a new respect at the lady in the Russian blouse. Few books were capable of calling up a blush to his cheek, but he remembered that one of Miss Heath-Warburton's had done it. The authoress was just saying impressively to her companion:

"—ever know a sincere emotion to express itself in a subordinate clause?"

"Joyce has freed us from the superstition of syntax," agreed the curly man.

"Scenes which make emotional history," said Miss Heath-Warburton, "should ideally be expressed in a series of animal squeals."

"The D. H. Lawrence formula," said the other.

"Or even Dada," said the authoress.

"We need a new notation," said the curly-haired man, putting both elbows on the table and knocking Wimsey's bread on to the floor. "Have you heard Robert Snoates recite his own verse to the tom-tom and the penny whistle?"

Lord Peter with difficulty detached his attention from this fascinating discussion to find that Miss Tarrant was saying something about Mary.

"One misses your sister very much," she said. "Her wonderful enthusiasm. She spoke so well at meetings. She had such a *real* sympathy with the worker."

"It seems astonishing to me," said Wimsey, "seeing Mary's never had to do a stroke of work in her life."

"Oh," cried Miss Tarrant, "but she *did* work. She worked for us. Wonderfully! She was secretary to our Propaganda Society for nearly six months. And then she worked so hard for Mr. Goyles. To say nothing of her nursing in the war. Of course, I don't approve of England's attitude in the war, but nobody would say the work wasn't hard."

"Who is Mr. Goyles?"

"Oh, one of our leading speakers—quite young, but the Government are really afraid of him. I expect he'll be here to-night. He has been lecturing in the North, but I believe he's back now."

"I say, do look out," said Peter. "Your beads are in your plate again."

"Are they? Well, perhaps they'll flavour the mutton. I'm afraid the cooking isn't very good here, but the subscription's so small, you see. I wonder Mary never told you about Mr. Goyles. They were so *very* friendly, you know, some time ago. Everybody thought she was going to marry him—but it seemed to fall through. And then your sister left town. Do you know about it?"

"That was the fellow, was it? Yes—well, my people didn't altogether see it, you know. Thought Mr. Goyles wasn't quite the son-in-law they'd take to. Family row and so on. Wasn't there myself; besides, Mary'd never listen to *me*. Still, that's what I gathered."

"Another instance of the absurd, old-fashioned tyranny of parents," said Miss Tarrant warmly. "You wouldn't think it could still be possible—in post-war times."

"I don't know," said Wimsey, "that you could exactly call it that. Not parents exactly. My mother's a remarkable woman. I don't think she interfered. Fact, I fancy she wanted to ask Mr. Goyles to Denver. But my brother put his foot down."

"Oh, well, what can you expect?" said Miss Tarrant scornfully. "But I don't see what business it was of his."

"Oh, none," agreed Wimsey. "Only, owin' to my late father's circumscribed ideas of what was owin' to women, my brother has the handlin' of Mary's money till she marries with his consent. I don't say it's a good plan—I think it's a rotten plan. But there it is."

"Monstrous!" said Miss Tarrant, shaking her head so angrily that she looked like shock-headed Peter. "Barbarous! Simply feudal, you know. But, after all, what's money?"

"Nothing, of course," said Peter. "But if you've been brought up to havin' it it's a bit awkward to drop it suddenly. Like baths, you know."

"I can't understand how it could have made any difference to Mary," persisted Miss Tarrant mournfully. "She liked being a worker. We once tried living in a workman's cottage for eight weeks, five of us, on eighteen shillings a week. It was a *marvellous* experience—on the very *edge* of the New Forest."

"In the winter?"

"Well, no—we thought we'd better not *begin* with winter. But we had nine wet days, and the kitchen chimney smoked all the time. You see, the wood came out of the forest, so it was all damp."

"I see. It must have been uncommonly interestin'."

"It was an experience I shall *never* forget," said Miss Tarrant. "One felt so *close* to the earth and the primitive things. If only we could abolish industrialism. I'm afraid, though, we shall never get it put right without a 'bloody revolution,' you know. It's very terrible, of course, but salutary and inevitable. Shall we have coffee? We shall have to carry it upstairs ourselves, if you don't mind. The maids don't bring it up after dinner."

Miss Tarrant settled her bill and returned, thrusting a cup of coffee into his hand. It had already overflowed into the saucer, and as he groped his way round a screen and up a steep and twisted staircase it overflowed quite an amount more.

Emerging from the basement, they almost ran into a young man with fair hair who was hunting for letters in a dark little row of pigeon-holes. Finding nothing, he retreated into the lounge. Miss Tarrant uttered an exclamation of pleasure.

"Why, there *is* Mr. Goyles," she cried.

Wimsey glanced across, and at the sight of the tall, slightly stooping figure with the untidy fair hair and the gloved right hand he gave an irrepressible little gasp.

"Won't you introduce me?" he said.

"I'll fetch him," said Miss Tarrant. She made off across the lounge and addressed the young agitator, who started, looked across at Wimsey, shook his head, appeared to apologise, gave a hurried glance at his watch, and darted out by the entrance. Wimsey sprang forward in pursuit.

"Extraordinary," cried Miss Tarrant, with a blank face. "He says he has an appointment—but he can't surely be missing the——"

"Excuse me," said Peter. He dashed out, in time to perceive a dark figure retreating across the street. He gave chase. The man took to his heels, and seemed to plunge into the dark little alley which leads into the Charing Cross Road. Hurrying in pursuit, Wimsey was almost blinded by a sudden flash and smoke nearly in his face. A crashing blow on the left shoulder and a deafening report whirled his surroundings away. He staggered violently, and collapsed on to a second-hand brass bedstead.

CHAPTER VIII

MR. PARKER TAKES NOTES

A man was taken to the Zoo and shown the giraffe. After gazing at it a little in silence: "I don't believe it," he said.

PARKER'S FIRST IMPULSE was to doubt his own sanity; his next, to doubt Lady Mary's. Then, as the clouds rolled away from his brain, he decided that she was merely not speaking the truth.

"Come, Lady Mary," he said encouragingly, but with an accent of reprimand as to an over-imaginative child, "you can't expect us to believe that, you know."

"But you must," said the girl gravely; "it's a fact. I shot him. I did, really. I didn't exactly mean to do it; it was a—well, a sort of accident."

Mr. Parker got up and paced about the room.

"You have put me in a terrible position, Lady Mary," he said. "You see, I'm a police-officer. I never imagined——"

"It doesn't matter," said Lady Mary. "Of course you'll have to arrest me, or detain me, or whatever you call it. That's what I came for. I'm quite ready to go quietly—that's the right expression, isn't it? I'd like to explain about it, though, first. Of course I ought to have done it long ago, but I'm afraid I lost my head. I didn't realise that Gerald would get blamed. I hoped they'd bring it in suicide. Do I make a statement to you now? Or do I do it at the police-station?"

Parker groaned.

"They won't—they won't punish me so badly if it was an accident, will they?" There was a quiver in the voice.

"No, of course not—of course not. But if only you had spoken earlier! No," said Parker, stopping suddenly short in his distracted pacing and sitting down beside her. "It's impossible—absurd." He caught the girl's hand suddenly in his own. "Nothing will convince me," he said. "It's absurd. It's not like you."

"But an accident——"

"I don't mean that—you know I don't mean that. But that you should keep silence——"

"I was afraid. I'm telling you now."

"No, no, no," cried the detective. "You're lying to me. Nobly, I know; but it's not worth it. No man could be worth it. Let him go, I implore you. Tell the truth. Don't shield this man. If he murdered Denis Cathcart——"

"*No!*" The girl sprang to her feet, wrenching her hand away. "There was no other man. How dare you say it or think it! I killed Denis Cathcart, I tell you, and you *shall* believe it. I swear to you that there was no other man."

Parker pulled himself together.

"Sit down, please. Lady Mary, you are determined to make this statement?"

"Yes."

"Knowing that I have no choice but to act upon it?"

"If you will not hear it I shall go straight to the police."

Parker pulled out his note-book. "Go on," he said.

With no other sign of emotion than a nervous fidgeting with her gloves, Lady Mary began her confession in a clear, hard voice, as though she were reciting it by heart.

"On the evening of Wednesday, October 13th, I went upstairs at half-past nine. I sat up writing a letter. At a quarter past ten I heard my brother and Denis quarrelling in the passage. I heard my brother call Denis a cheat, and tell him that he was never to speak to me again. I heard Denis run out. I listened for some time, but did not hear him return. At half-past eleven I became alarmed. I changed my dress and went out to try and find Denis and bring him in. I feared he might do something desperate. After some time I found him in the shrubbery. I begged him to come in. He refused, and he told me about my brother's accusation and the quarrel. I was very much horrified, of course. He said where was the good of denying anything, as Gerald was determined to ruin him, and asked me to go away and marry him and live abroad. I said I was surprised that he should suggest such a thing in the circumstances. We both became very angry. I said 'Come in now. To-morrow you can leave by the first train.' He seemed almost crazy. He pulled out a pistol and said that he'd come to the end of things, that his life was ruined, that we were a lot of hypocrites, and that I had never cared for him, or I shouldn't have minded what he'd done. Anyway, he said, if I wouldn't come with him it was all over, and he might as well be hanged for a sheep as a lamb—he'd shoot me and himself. I think he was quite out of his mind. He pulled out a revolver; I caught his hand; we struggled; I got the muzzle right up against his chest, and—either I pulled the trigger or it went off of itself—I'm not clear which. It was all in such a whirl."

She paused. Parker's pen took down the words, and his face showed growing concern. Lady Mary went on:

"He wasn't quite dead. I helped him up. We struggled back nearly to the house. He fell once——"

"Why," asked Parker, "did you not leave him and run into the house to fetch help?"

Lady Mary hesitated.

"It didn't occur to me. It was a nightmare. I could only think of getting him along. I think—*I think I wanted him to die.*"

There was a dreadful pause.

"He did die. He died at the door. I went into the conservatory and sat down. I sat for hours and tried to think. I hated him for being a cheat and a scoundrel. I'd been taken in, you see—made a fool of by a common sharper. I was glad he was dead. I must have sat there for hours without a coherent thought. It wasn't till my brother came along that I realised what I'd done, and that I might be suspected of murdering him. I was simply terrified. I made up my mind all in a moment that I'd pretend I knew nothing—that I'd heard a shot and come down. You know what I did."

"Why, Lady Mary," said Parker, in a perfectly toneless voice, "why did you say to your brother 'Good God, Gerald, you've killed him'?"

Another hesitant pause.

"I never said that. I said, 'Good God, Gerald, he's killed, then.' I never meant to suggest anything but suicide."

"You admitted to those words at the inquest?"

"Yes——" Her hands knotted the gloves into all manner of shapes. "By that time I had decided on a burglar story, you see."

The telephone bell rang, and Parker went to the instrument. A voice came thinly over the wire:

"Is that 110 Piccadilly? This is Charing Cross Hospital. A man was brought in to-night who says he is Lord Peter Wimsey. He was shot in the shoulder, and struck his head in falling. He has only just recovered consciousness. He was brought in at 9.15. No, he will probably do very well now. Yes, come round by all means."

"Peter has been shot," said Parker. "Will you come round with me to Charing Cross Hospital? They say he is in no danger; still——"

"Oh, quick!" cried Lady Mary.

Gathering up Mr. Bunter as they hurried through the hall, detective and self-accused rushed hurriedly out into Pall Mall, and, picking up a belated taxi at Hyde Park Corner, drove madly away through the deserted streets.

CHAPTER IX

GOYLES

"—and the moral of that is——" said the Duchess.
—Alice's Adventures in Wonderland.

A PARTY OF FOUR were assembled next morning at a very late breakfast, or very early lunch, in Lord Peter's flat. Its most cheerful member, despite a throbbing shoulder and a splitting headache, was
undoubtedly Lord Peter himself, who lay upon the Chesterfield surrounded with cushions and carousing upon tea and toast. Having
been brought home in an ambulance, he had instantly fallen into a
healing sleep, and had woken at nine o'clock aggressively clear and
active in mind. In consequence, Mr. Parker had been dispatched in a
hurry, half-fed and burdened with the secret memory of last night's
disclosures, to Scotland Yard. Here he had set in motion the proper
machinery for catching Lord Peter's assassin. "Only don't you say
anything about the attack on me," said his lordship. "Tell 'em he's to
be detained in connection with the Riddlesdale case. That's good
enough for them." It was now eleven, and Mr. Parker had returned,
gloomy and hungry, and was consuming a belated omelette and a
glass of claret.

Lady Mary Wimsey was hunched up in the window-seat. Her
bobbed golden hair made a little blur of light about her in the pale
autumn sunshine. She had made an attempt to breakfast earlier, and
now sat gazing out into Piccadilly. Her first appearance that morning
had been made in Lord Peter's dressing-gown, but she now wore a
serge skirt and jade-green jumper, which had been brought to town
for her by the fourth member of the party, now composedly eating
a mixed grill and sharing the decanter with Parker.

This was a rather short, rather plump, very brisk elderly lady, with
bright black eyes like a bird's, and very handsome white hair exquisitely dressed. Far from looking as though she had just taken a
long night journey, she was easily the most composed and trim of the
four. She was, however, annoyed, and said so at considerable length.
This was the Dowager Duchess of Denver.

"It is not so much, Mary, that you went off so abruptly last night—just before dinner, too—inconveniencing and alarming us very much —indeed, poor Helen was totally unable to eat her dinner, which was extremely distressing to her feelings, because, you know, she always makes such a point of never being upset about anything—I really don't know why, for some of the greatest men have not minded showing their feelings, I don't mean Southerners necessarily, but, as Mr. Chesterton very rightly points out—Nelson, too, who was certainly English if he wasn't Irish or Scotch, I forget, but United Kingdom, anyway (if that means anything nowadays with a Free State—such a ridiculous title, especially as it always makes one think of the Orange Free State, and I'm sure they wouldn't care to be mixed up with that, being so very green themselves). And going off without even proper clothes, and taking the car, so that I had to wait till the 1.15 from Northallerton—a ridiculous time to start, and such a bad train, too, not getting up till 10.30. Besides, if you *must* run off to town, why do it in that unfinished manner? If you had only looked up the trains before starting you would have seen you would have half an hour's wait at Northallerton, and you could quite easily have packed a bag. It's so much better to do things neatly and thoroughly—even stupid things. And it was very stupid of you indeed to dash off like that, to embarrass and bore poor Mr. Parker with a lot of twaddle—though I suppose it was Peter you meant to see. You know, Peter, if you will haunt low places full of Russians and sucking Socialists taking themselves seriously, you ought to know better than to encourage them by running after them, however futile, and given to drinking coffee and writing poems with no shape to them, and generally ruining their nerves. And, in any case, it makes not the slightest difference; I could have told Peter all about it myself, if he doesn't know already, as he probably does."

Lady Mary turned very white at this and glanced at Parker, who replied rather to her than to the Dowager:

"No, Lord Peter and I haven't had time to discuss anything yet."

"Lest it should ruin my shattered nerves and bring a fever to my aching brow," added that nobleman amiably. "You're a kind, thoughtful soul, Charles, and I don't know what I should do without you. I wish that rotten old second-hand dealer had been a bit brisker about takin' in his stock-in-trade for the night, though. Perfectly 'straor'nary number of knobs there are on a brass bedstead. Saw it comin', y'know, an' couldn't stop myself. However, what's a mere brass bedstead? The great detective, though at first stunned and dizzy from his brutal treatment by the fifteen veiled assassins all armed with meat-choppers, soon regained his senses, thanks to his sound constitution and healthy manner of life. Despite the severe gassing he had endured in the underground room—eh? A telegram? Oh, thanks, Bunter."

Lord Peter appeared to read the message with great inward satisfaction, for his long lips twitched at the corners, and he tucked the slip of paper away in his pocket-book with a little sigh of satisfaction. He called to Bunter to take away the breakfast-tray and to renew the cooling bandage about his brow. This done, Lord Peter leaned back among his cushions, and with an air of malicious enjoyment launched at Mr. Parker the inquiry:

"Well, now, how did you and Mary get on last night? Polly, did you tell him you'd done the murder?"

Few things are more irritating than to discover, after you have been at great pains to spare a person some painful intelligence, that he has known it all along and is not nearly so much affected by it as he properly should be. Mr. Parker quite simply and suddenly lost his temper. He bounded to his feet, and exclaimed, without the least reason: "Oh, it's perfectly hopeless trying to do anything!"

Lady Mary sprang from the window-seat.

"Yes, I did," she said. "It's quite true. Your precious case is finished, Peter."

The Dowager said, without the least discomposure: "You must allow your brother to be the best judge of his own affairs, my dear."

"As a matter of fact," replied his lordship, "I rather fancy Polly's right. Hope so, I'm sure. Anyway, we've got the fellow, so now we shall know."

Lady Mary gave a sort of gasp, and stepped forward with her chin up and her hands tightly clenched. It caught at Parker's heart to see overwhelming catastrophe so bravely faced. The official side of him was thoroughly bewildered, but the human part ranged itself instantly in support of that gallant defiance.

"Whom have they got?" he demanded, in a voice quite unlike his own.

"The Goyles person," said Lord Peter carelessly. "Uncommon quick work, what? But since he'd no more original idea than to take the boat-train to Folkestone they didn't have much difficulty."

"It isn't true," said Lady Mary. She stamped. "It's a lie. He wasn't there. He's innocent. I killed Denis."

"Fine," thought Parker, "fine! Damn Goyles, anyway, what's he done to deserve it?"

Lord Peter said: "Mary, don't be an ass."

"Yes," said the Dowager placidly. "I was going to suggest to you, Peter, that this Mr. Goyles—such a terrible name, Mary dear, I can't say I ever cared for it, even if there had been nothing else against him—especially as he would sign himself Geo. Goyles—G. e. o. you know, Mr. Parker, for George, and I never *could* help reading it as Gargoyles—I very nearly wrote to you, my dear, mentioning Mr. Goyles, and asking if you could see him in town, because there was something, when I came to think of it, about that ipecacuanha business that made me feel he might have something to do with it."

"Yes," said Peter, with a grin, "you always did find him a bit sickenin', didn't you?"

"How can you, Wimsey?" growled Parker reproachfully, with his eyes on Mary's face.

"Never mind him," said the girl. "If you can't be a gentleman, Peter——"

"Damn it all!" cried the invalid explosively. "Here's a fellow who, without the slightest provocation, plugs a bullet into my shoulder, breaks my collar-bone, brings me up head foremost on a knobbly second-hand brass bedstead and vamooses, and when, in what seems to me jolly mild, parliamentary language, I call him a sickenin' feller my own sister says I'm no gentleman. Look at me! In my own house, forced to sit here with a perfectly beastly headache, and lap up toast and tea, while you people distend and bloat yourselves on mixed grills and omelettes and a damn good vintage claret——"

"Silly boy," said the Duchess, "don't get so excited. And it's time for your medicine. Mr. Parker, kindly touch the bell."

Mr. Parker obeyed in silence. Lady Mary came slowly across, and stood looking at her brother.

"Peter," she said, "what makes you say that *he* did it?"

"Did what?"

"Shot—you?" The words were only a whisper.

The entrance of Mr. Bunter at this moment with a cooling draught dissipated the tense atmosphere. Lord Peter quaffed his potion, had his pillows re-arranged, submitted to have his temperature taken and his pulse counted, asked if he might not have an egg for his lunch, and lit a cigarette. Mr. Bunter retired, people distributed themselves into more comfortable chairs, and felt happier.

"Now, Polly, old girl," said Peter, "cut out the sob-stuff. I accidentally ran into this Goyles chap last night at your Soviet Club. I asked that Miss Tarrant to introduce me, but the minute Goyles heard my name, he made tracks. I rushed out after him, only meanin' to have a word with him, when the idiot stopped at the corner of Newport Court, potted me, and bunked. Silly-ass thing to do. I knew who he was. He couldn't help gettin' caught."

"Peter——" said Mary in a ghastly voice.

"Look here, Polly," said Wimsey. "I did think of you. Honest injun, I did. I haven't had the man arrested. I've made no charge at all—have I, Parker? What did you tell 'em to do when you were down at the Yard this morning?"

"To detain Goyles pending inquiries, because he was wanted as a witness in the Riddlesdale case," said Parker slowly.

"He knows nothing about it," said Mary, doggedly now. "He wasn't anywhere near. He is innocent of *that!*"

"Do you think so?" said Lord Peter gravely. "If you know he is innocent, why tell all these lies to screen him? It won't do, Mary. You know he was there—and you think he is guilty."

"No!"

"Yes," said Wimsey, grasping her with his sound hand as she shrank away. "Mary, have you thought what you are doing? You are perjuring yourself and putting Gerald in peril of his life, in order to shield from justice a man whom you suspect of murdering your lover and who has most certainly tried to murder me."

"Oh," cried Parker, in an agony, "all this interrogation is horribly irregular."

"Never mind him," said Peter. "Do you really think you're doing the right thing, Mary?"

The girl looked helplessly at her brother for a minute or two. Peter cocked up a whimsical, appealing eye from under his bandages. The defiance melted out of her face.

"I'll tell the truth," said Lady Mary.

"Good egg," said Peter, extending a hand. "I'm sorry. I know you like the fellow, and we appreciate your decision enormously. Truly, we do. Now, sail ahead, old thing, and you take it down, Parker."

"Well, it really all started years ago with George. You were at the

116

Front then, Peter, but I suppose they told you about it—and put everything in the worst possible light."

"I wouldn't say that, dear," put in the Duchess. "I think I told Peter that your brother and I were not altogether pleased with what we had seen of the young man—which was not very much, if you remember. He invited himself down one week-end when the house was very full, and he seemed to make a point of consulting nobody's convenience but his own. And you know, dear, you even said yourself you thought he was unnecessarily rude to poor old Lord Mountweazle."

"He said what he thought," said Mary. "Of course, Lord Mountweazle, poor dear, doesn't understand that the present generation is accustomed to discuss things with its elders, not just kow-tow to them. When George gave his opinion, he thought he was just contradicting."

"To be sure," said the Dowager, "when you flatly deny everything a person says it does sound like contradiction to the uninitiated. But all I remember saying to Peter was that Mr. Goyles's manners seemed to me to lack polish, and that he showed a lack of independence in his opinions."

"A lack of independence?" said Mary, wide-eyed.

"Well, dear, I thought so. What oft was thought and frequently much better expressed, as Pope says—or was it somebody else? But the worse you express yourself these days the more profound people think you—though that's nothing new. Like Browning and those quaint metaphysical people, when you never know whether they really mean their mistress or the Established Church, so bridegroomy and biblical—to say nothing of dear S. Augustine—the Hippo man, I mean, not the one who missionised over here, though I daresay he was delightful too, and in those days I suppose they didn't have annual sales of work and tea in the parish room, so it doesn't seem quite like what we mean nowadays by missionaries—he knew all about it—you remember about that mandrake—or is that the thing you had to get a big black dog for? Manichee, that's the word. What was his name? Was it Faustus? Or am I mixing him up with the old man in the opera?"

"Well, anyway," said Mary, without stopping to disentangle the Duchess's sequence of ideas, "George was the only person I really cared about—he still is. Only it did seem so hopeless. Perhaps you didn't say much about him, mother, but Gerald said *lots*—dreadful things!"

"Yes," said the Duchess, "he said what he thought. The present generation does, you know. To the uninitiated, I admit, dear, it does sound a little rude."

Peter grinned, but Mary went on unheeding.

"George had simply *no* money. He'd really given everything he had to the Labour Party one way and another, and he'd lost his job in the Ministry of Information: they found he had too much sympathy with the Socialists abroad. It was awfully unfair. Anyhow, one couldn't be a burden on him; and Gerald was a beast, and said he'd absolutely stop my allowance if I didn't send George away. So I did, but of course it didn't make a bit of difference to the way we both felt. I will say for mother she was a bit more decent. She said she'd help us if George got a job; but, as I pointed out, if George got a job we shouldn't *need* helping!"

"But, my dear, I could hardly insult Mr. Goyles by suggesting that he should live on his mother-in-law," said the Dowager.

"Why not?" said Mary. "George doesn't believe in those old-fashioned ideas about property. Besides, if you'd given it to me, it would be *my* money. We believe in men and women being equal. Why should the one always be the bread-winner more than the other?"

"I can't imagine, dear," said the Dowager. "Still, I could hardly expect poor Mr. Goyles to live on unearned increment when he didn't believe in inherited property."

"That's a fallacy," said Mary, rather vaguely. "Anyhow," she added hastily, "that's what happened. Then, after the war, George went to Germany to study Socialism and Labour questions there, and nothing seemed any good. So when Denis Cathcart turned up, I said I'd marry him."

"Why?" asked Peter. "He never sounded to me a bit the kind of bloke for you. I mean, as far as I could make out, he was Tory and diplomatic and—well, quite crusted old tawny, so to speak, I shouldn't have thought you had an idea in common."

"No; but then he didn't care twopence whether I had any ideas or not. I made him promise he wouldn't bother me with diplomats and people, and he said no, I could do as I liked, provided I didn't compromise him. And we were to live in Paris and go our own ways and not bother. And anything was better than staying here, and marrying somebody in one's own set, and opening bazaars and watching polo and meeting the Prince of Wales. So I said I'd marry Denis, because I didn't care about him, and I'm pretty sure he didn't care a halfpenny about me, and we should have left each other alone. I did so want to be left alone!"

"Was Jerry all right about your money?" inquired Peter.

"Oh, yes. He said Denis was no great catch—I do wish Gerald wasn't so vulgar, in that flat, early-Victorian way—but he said that, after George, he could only thank his stars it wasn't worse."

"Make a note of that, Charles," said Wimsey.

"Well, it seemed all right at first, but, as things went on, I got more and more depressed. Do you know, there was something a little alarming about Denis. He was so extraordinarily reserved. I know I wanted to be left alone, but—well, it was uncanny! He was correct. Even when he went off the deep end and was passionate—which didn't often happen—he was correct about it. Extraordinary. Like one of those odd French novels, you know, Peter: frightfully hot stuff, but absolutely impersonal."

"Charles, old man!" said Lord Peter.

"M'm?"

"That's important. You realise the bearing of that?"

"No."

"Never mind. Drive on, Polly."

"Aren't I making your head ache?"

"Damnably; but I like it. Do go on. I'm not sprouting a lily with anguish moist and fever-dew, or anything like that. I'm getting really thrilled. What you've just said is more illuminating than anything I've struck for a week."

"Really!" Mary stared at Peter with every trace of hostility vanished. "I thought you'd never understand that part."

"Lord!" said Peter. "Why not?"

Mary shook her head. "Well, I'd been corresponding all the time with George, and suddenly he wrote to me at the beginning of this month to say he'd come back from Germany, and had got a job on the *Thunderclap*—the Socialist weekly, you know—at a beginning screw of £4 a week, and wouldn't I chuck these capitalists and so on, and come and be an honest working woman with him. He could get me a secretarial job on the paper. I was to type and so on for him, and help him get his articles together. And he thought between us we should make £6 or £7 a week, which would be heaps to live on. And

I was getting more frightened of Denis every day. So I said I would. But I knew there'd be an awful row with Gerald. And really I was rather ashamed—the engagement had been announced and there'd be a ghastly lot of talk and people trying to persuade me. And Denis might have made things horribly uncomfortable for Gerald—he was rather that sort. So we decided the best thing to do would be just to run away and get married first, and escape the wrangling."

"Quite so," said Peter. "Besides, it would look rather well in the paper, wouldn't it? 'PEER'S DAUGHTER WEDS SOCIALIST—ROMANTIC SIDE-CAR ELOPEMENT—"£6 A WEEK PLENTY," SAYS HER LADY-SHIP.'"

"Pig!" said Lady Mary.

"Very good," said Peter, "I get you! So it was arranged that the romantic Goyles should fetch you away from Riddlesdale—why Riddlesdale? It would be twice as easy from London or Denver."

"No. For one thing he had to be up North. And everybody knows one in town, and—anyhow, we didn't want to wait."

"Besides, one would miss the Young Lochinvar touch. Well, then, why at the unearthly hour of 3 a.m.?"

"He had a meeting on Wednesday night at Northallerton. He was going to come straight on and pick me up, and run me down to town to be married by special license. We allowed ample time. George had to be at the office next day."

"I see. Well, I'll go on now, and you stop me if I'm wrong. You went up at 9.30 on Wednesday night. You packed a suit-case. You—did you think of writing any sort of letter to comfort your sorrowing friends and relations?"

"Yes, I wrote one. But I——"

"Of course. Then you went to bed, I fancy, or, at any rate, turned the clothes back and lay down."

"Yes. I lay down. It was a good thing I did, as it happened——"

"True, you wouldn't have had much time to make the bed look probable in the morning, and we should have heard about it. By the way, Parker, when Mary confessed her sins to you last night, did you make any notes?"

"Yes," said Parker, "if you can read my shorthand."

"Quite so," said Peter. "Well, the rumpled bed disposes of your story about never having gone to bed at all, doesn't it?"

"And I thought it was such a good story!"

"Want of practice," replied her brother kindly.

"You'll do better, next time. It's just as well, really that it's so hard to tell a long, consistent lie. *Did* you, as a matter of fact, hear Gerald go out at 11.30, as Pettigrew-Robinson (damn his ears!) said?"

"I fancy I did hear somebody moving about," said Mary, "but I didn't think much about it."

"Quite right," said Peter, "when I hear people movin' about the house at night, I'm much too delicate-minded to think anything at all."

"Of course," interposed the Duchess, "particularly in England, where it is so oddly improper to think. I will say for Peter that, if he can put a continental interpretation on anything, he will—so considerate of you, dear, as soon as you took to doing it in silence and not mentioning it, as you so intelligently did as a child. You were really a very observant little boy, dear."

"And still is," said Mary, smiling at Peter with surprising friendliness.

"Old bad habits die hard," said Wimsey. "To proceed. At three o'clock you went down to meet Goyles. Why did he come all the way up to the house? It would have been safer to meet him in the lane."

"I knew I couldn't get out of the lodge-gate without waking Hardraw, and so I'd have to get over the palings somewhere. I might have managed alone, but not with a heavy suit-case. So, as George would have to climb over, anyhow, we thought he'd better come and help carry the suit-case. And then we couldn't miss each other by the conservatory door. I sent him a little plan of the path."

"Was Goyles there when you got downstairs?"

"No—at least—no, I didn't see him. But there was poor Denis's body, and Gerald bending over it. My first idea was that Gerald had killed George. That's why I said, 'Oh, God! you've killed him!'" (Peter glanced across at Parker and nodded.) "Then Gerald turned him over, and I saw it was Denis—and then I'm sure I heard something moving a long way off in the shrubbery—a noise like twigs snapping—and it suddenly came over me, where was George? Oh, Peter, I saw everything then, so clearly. I saw that Denis must have come on George waiting there, and attacked him—I'm sure Denis must have attacked him. Probably he thought it was a burglar. Or he found out who he was and tried to drive him away. And in the struggle George must have shot him. It was awful!"

Peter patted his sister on the shoulder. "Poor kid," he said.

"I didn't know what to do," went on the girl. "I'd so awfully little time, you see. My one idea was that nobody must suspect anybody had been there. So I had quickly to invent an excuse for being there myself. I shoved my suit-case behind the cactus-plants to start with. Jerry was taken up with the body and didn't notice—you know, Jerry never *does* notice things till you shove them under his nose. But I knew if there'd been a shot Freddy and the Marchbankses must have heard it. So I pretended I'd heard it too, and rushed down to look for burglars. It was a bit lame, but the best thing I could think of. Gerald sent me up to alarm the house, and I had the story all ready by the time I reached the landing. Oh, and I was quite proud of myself for not forgetting the suit-case!"

"You dumped it into the chest," said Peter.

"Yes. I had a horrible shock the other morning when I found you looking in."

"Nothing like the shock I had when I found the silver sand there."

"Silver sand?"

"Out of the conservatory."

"Good gracious!" said Mary.

"Well, go on. You knocked up Freddy and the Pettigrew-Robinsons. Then you had to bolt into your room to destroy your farewell letter and take your clothes off."

"Yes. I'm afraid I didn't do that very naturally. But I couldn't expect anybody to believe that I went burglar-hunting in a complete set of silk undies and a carefully knotted tie with a gold safety-pin."

"No. I see your difficulty."

"It turned out quite well, too, because they were all quite ready to believe that I wanted to escape from Mrs. Pettigrew-Robinson—except Mrs. P. herself, of course."

"Yes; even Parker swallowed that, didn't you, old man?"

"Oh, quite, quite so," said Parker gloomily.

"I made a dreadful mistake about that shot," resumed Lady Mary. "You see, I explained it all so elaborately—and then I found that nobody had heard a shot at all. And afterwards they discovered that it had all happened in the shrubbery—and the time wasn't right, either. Then at the inquest I *had* to stick to my story—and it got to look worse and worse—and then they put the blame on Gerald. In my wildest moments I'd never thought of that. Of course, I see now how my wretched evidence helped."

"Hence the ipecacuanha," said Peter.

"I'd got into such a frightful tangle," said poor Lady Mary, "I thought I had better shut up altogether for fear of making things still worse."

"And did you still think Goyles had done it?"

"I—I didn't know what to think," said the girl. "I don't now. Peter, who else *could* have done it?"

"Honestly, old thing," said his lordship, "if he didn't do it, I don't know who did."

"He ran away, you see," said Lady Mary.

"He seems rather good at shootin' and runnin' away," said Peter grimly.

"If he hadn't done that to you," said Mary slowly, "I'd never have told you. I'd have died first. But of course, with his revolutionary doctrines—and when you think of red Russia and all the blood spilt in riots and insurrections and things—I suppose it does teach a contempt for human life."

"My dear," said the Duchess, "it seems to me that Mr. Goyles shows no especial contempt for his own life. You must try to look at the thing fairly. Shooting people and running away is not very heroic —according to *our* standards."

"The thing I don't understand," struck in Wimsey hurriedly, "is how Gerald's revolver got into the shrubbery."

"The thing I should like to know about," said the Duchess, "is, was Denis really a card-sharper?"

"The thing *I* should like to know about," said Parker, "is the green-eyed cat."

"Denis *never* gave me a cat," said Mary. "That was a tarradiddle."

"Were you ever in a jeweller's with him in the Rue de la Paix?"

"Oh, yes; heaps of times. And he gave me a diamond and tortoise-shell comb. But never a cat."

"Then we may disregard the whole of last night's elaborate confession," said Lord Peter, looking through Parker's notes, with a smile. "It's really not bad, Polly, not bad at all. You've quite a talent for romantic fiction—no, I mean it! Just here and there you need more attention to detail. For instance, you *couldn't* have dragged that badly wounded man all up the path to the house without getting blood all over your coat, you know. By the way, did Goyles know Cathcart at all?"

"Not to my knowledge."

"Because Parker and I had an alternative theory, which would clear Goyles from the worst part of the charge, anyhow. Tell her, old man; it was your idea."

Thus urged, Parker outlined the blackmail and suicide theory.

"That sounds plausible," said Mary—"academically speaking, I mean; but it isn't a bit like George—I mean, blackmail is so *beastly,* isn't it?"

"Well," said Peter, "I think the best thing is to go and see Goyles. Whatever the key to Wednesday night's riddle is, he holds it. Parker, old man, we're nearing the end of the chase."

CHAPTER X

NOTHING ABIDES AT THE NOON

"Alas!" said Hiya, "the sentiments which this person expressed with irreproachable honourableness, when the sun was high in the heavens and the probability of secretly leaving an undoubtedly well-appointed home was engagingly remote, seem to have an entirely different significance when recalled by night in a damp orchard, and on the eve of their fulfillment."—The Wallet of Kai-Lung.

And his short minute, after noon, is night.—Donne.

MR. GOYLES WAS INTERVIEWED the next day at the police-station. Mr. Murbles was present, and Mary insisted on coming. The young man began by blustering a little, but the solicitor's dry manner made its impression.

"Lord Peter Wimsey identifies you," said Mr. Murbles, "as the man who made a murderous attack upon him last night. With remarkable generosity, he has forborne to press the charge. Now we know further that you were present at Riddlesdale Lodge on the night when Captain Cathcart was shot. You will no doubt be called as a witness in the case. But you would greatly assist justice by making a statement to us now. This is a purely friendly and private interview, Mr. Goyles. As you see, no representative of the police is present. We simply ask for your help. I ought, however, to warn you that, whereas it is, of course, fully competent for you to refuse to an-swer any of our questions, a refusal might lay you open to the gravest imputations."

"In fact," said Goyles, "it's a threat. If I don't tell you, you'll have me arrested on suspicion of murder."

"Dear me, no, Mr. Goyles," returned the solicitor. "We should merely place what information we hold in the hands of the police, who would then act as they thought fit. God bless my soul, no—any-thing like a threat would be highly irregular. In the matter of the as-sault upon Lord Peter, his lordship will, of course, use his own discretion."

"Well," said Goyles sullenly, "it's a threat, call it what you like. However, I don't mind speaking—especially as you'll be jolly well disappointed. I suppose you gave me away, Mary."

Mary flushed indignantly.

"My sister has been extraordinarily loyal to you, Mr. Goyles," said Lord Peter. "I may tell you, indeed, that she put herself into a position of grave personal inconvenience—not to say danger—on your behalf. You were traced to London in consequence of your having left unequivocal traces in your exceedingly hasty retreat. When my sister accidentally opened a telegram addressed to me at Riddlesdale by my family name she hurried immediately to town, to shield you if she could, at any cost to herself. Fortunately I had already received a duplicate wire at my flat. Even then I was not certain of your identity when I accidentally ran across you at the Soviet Club. Your own energetic efforts, however, to avoid an interview gave me complete certainty, together with an excellent excuse for detaining you. In fact, I'm uncommonly obliged to you for your assistance."

Mr. Goyles looked resentful.

"I don't know how you could think, George——" said Mary.

"Never mind what I think," said the young man, roughly. "I gather you've told 'em all about it now, anyhow. Well, I'll tell you my story as shortly as I can, and you'll see I know damn all about it. If you don't believe me I can't help it. I came along at about a quarter to three, and parked the 'bus in the lane."

"Where were you at 11.50?"

"On the road from Northallerton. My meeting didn't finish till 10.45. I can bring a hundred witnesses to prove it."

Wimsey made a note of the address where the meeting had been held, and nodded to Goyles to proceed.

"I climbed over the wall and walked through the shrubbery."

"You saw no person, and no body?"

"Nobody, alive or dead."

"Did you notice any blood or footprints on the path?"

"No. I didn't like to use my torch, for fear of being seen from the house. There was just light enough to see the path. I came to the door of the conservatory just before three. As I came up I stumbled over something. I felt it, and it was like a body. I was alarmed. I thought it might be Mary—ill or fainted or something. I ventured to turn on my light. Then I saw it was Cathcart, dead."

"You are sure he was dead?"

"Stone dead."

"One moment," interposed the solicitor. "You say you saw that it was Cathcart. Had you known Cathcart previously?"

"No, never. I meant that I saw it was a dead man, and learnt afterwards that it was Cathcart."

"In fact, you do not, now, know of your own knowledge, that it was Cathcart?"

"Yes—at least, I recognised the photographs in the papers afterwards."

"It is very necessary to be accurate in making a statement, Mr. Goyles. A remark such as you made just now might give a most unfortunate impression to the police or to a jury."

So saying, Mr. Murbles blew his nose, and resettled his pince-nez.

"What next?" inquired Peter.

"I fancied I heard somebody coming up the path. I did not think it wise to be found there with the corpse, so I cleared out."

"Oh," said Peter, with an indescribable expression, "that was a very simple solution. You left the girl you were going to marry to make for herself the unpleasant discovery that there was a dead man in the garden and that her gallant wooer had made tracks. What did you expect *her* to think?"

"Well, I thought she'd keep quiet for her own sake. As a matter of fact, I didn't think very clearly about anything. I knew I'd broken in where I had no business, and that if I was found with a murdered man it might look jolly queer for me."

"In fact," said Mr. Murbles, "you lost your head, young man, and ran away in a very foolish and cowardly manner."

"You needn't put it that way," retorted Mr. Goyles. "I was in a very awkward and stupid situation to start with."

"Yes," said Lord Peter ironically, "and 3 a.m. is a nasty, chilly time of day. Next time you arrange an elopement, make it for six o'clock in the evening, or twelve o'clock at night. You seem better at framing conspiracies than carrying them out. A little thing upsets your nerves, Mr. Goyles. I don't really think, you know, that a person of your temperament should carry fire-arms. What in the world, you blitherin' young ass, made you loose off that pop-gun at me last night? You *would* have been in a damned awkward situation then, if you'd accidentally hit me in the head or the heart or anywhere that mattered. If you're so frightened of a dead body, why go about shootin' at people? Why, why, why? That's what beats me. If you're tellin' the truth now, you never stood in the slightest danger. Lord! and to think of the time and trouble we've had to waste catchin' you—you ass! And poor old Mary, workin' away and half killin' herself, because she thought at least you wouldn't have run away unless there was somethin' to run from!"

"You must make allowance for a nervous temperament," said Mary in a hard voice.

"If you knew what it felt like to be shadowed and followed and badgered——" began Mr. Goyles.

"But I thought you Soviet Club people enjoyed being suspected of things," said Lord Peter. "Why, it ought to be the proudest moment of your life when you're really looked on as a dangerous fellow."

"It's the sneering of men like you," said Goyles passionately, "that does more to breed hatred between class and class——"

"Never mind about that," interposed Mr. Murbles. "The law's the law for everybody, and you have managed to put yourself in a very awkward position, young man." He touched a bell on the table, and Parker entered with a constable. "We shall be obliged to you," said Mr. Murbles, "if you will kindly have this young man kept under observation. We make no charge against him so long as he behaves himself, but he must not attempt to abscond before the Riddlesdale case comes up for trial."

"Certainly not, sir," said Mr. Parker.

"One moment," said Mary. "Mr. Goyles, here is the ring you gave me. Good-bye. When next you make a public speech calling for decisive action I will come and applaud it. You speak so well about that sort of thing. But otherwise, I think we had better not meet again."

"Of course," said the young man bitterly, "your people have forced me into this position, and you turn round and sneer at me too."

127

"I didn't mind thinking you were a murderer," said Lady Mary spitefully, "but I *do* mind your being such an ass."

Before Mr. Goyles could reply, Mr. Parker, bewildered but not wholly displeased, manœuvred his charge out of the room. Mary walked over to the window, and stood biting her lips.

Presently Lord Peter came across to her. "I say, Polly, old Murbles has asked us to lunch. Would you like to come? Sir Impey Biggs will be there."

"I don't want to meet him to-day. It's very kind of Mr. Murbles——"

"Oh, come along, old thing. Biggs is some celebrity, you know, and perfectly toppin' to look at, in a marbly kind of way. He'll tell you all about his canaries——"

Mary giggled through her obstinate tears.

"It's perfectly sweet of you, Peter, to try and amuse the baby. But I can't. I'd make a fool of myself. I've been made enough of a fool of for one day."

"Bosh," said Peter. "Of course, Goyles didn't show up very well this morning, but, then, he was in an awfully difficult position. *Do* come."

"I hope Lady Mary consents to adorn my bachelor establishment," said the solicitor, coming up. "I shall esteem it a very great honour. I really do not think I have entertained a lady in my chambers for twenty years—dear me, twenty years indeed it must be."

"In that case," said Lady Mary, "I simply *can't* refuse."

Mr. Murbles inhabited a delightful old set of rooms in Staple Inn, with windows looking out upon the formal garden, with its odd little flower-beds and tinkling fountain. The chambers kept up to a miracle the old-fashioned law atmosphere which hung about his own prim person. His dining-room was furnished in mahogany, with a Turkey carpet and crimson curtains. On his sideboard stood some pieces of handsome Sheffield plate and a number of decanters with engraved silver labels round their necks. There was a bookcase full of large volumes bound in law calf, and an oil-painting of a harsh-featured judge over the mantelpiece. Lady Mary felt a sudden gratitude for this discreet and solid Victorianism.

"I fear we may have to wait a few moments for Sir Impey," said Mr. Murbles, consulting his watch. "He is engaged in Quangle & Hamper v. *Truth,* but they expect to be through this morning—in fact, Sir Impey fancied that midday would see the end of it. Brilliant man, Sir Impey. He is defending *Truth."*

"Astonishin' position for a lawyer, what?" said Peter.

"The newspaper," said Mr. Murbles, acknowledging the pleasantry with a slight unbending of the lips, "against these people who profess to cure fifty-nine different diseases with the same pill. Quangle & Hamper produced some of their patients in court to testify to the benefits they'd enjoyed from the cure. To hear Sir Impey handling them was an intellectual treat. His kindly manner goes a long way with old ladies. When he suggested that one of them should show her leg to the Bench the sensation in court was really phenomenal."

"And did she show it?" inquired Lord Peter.

"Panting for the opportunity, my dear Lord Peter, panting for the opportunity."

"I wonder they had the nerve to call her."

"Nerve?" said Mr. Murbles. "The nerve of men like Quangle & Hamper has not its fellow in the universe, to adopt the expression of the great Shakespeare. But Sir Impey is not the man to take liberties with. We are really extremely fortunate to have secured his help.— Ah, I think I hear him!"

A hurried footstep on the stair indeed announced learned counsel, who burst in, still in wig and gown, and full of apology.

"Extremely sorry, Murbles," said Sir Impey. "We became excessively tedious at the end, I regret to say. I really did my best, but dear old Dowson is getting as deaf as a post, you know, and terribly fumbling in his movements.—And how are you, Wimsey? You look as if you'd been in the wars. Can we bring an action for assault against anybody?"

"Much better than that," put in Mr. Murbles; "attempted murder, if you please."

"Excellent, excellent," said Sir Impey.

"Ah, but we've decided not to prosecute," said Mr. Murbles, shaking his head.

"Really! Oh, my dear Wimsey, this will never do. Lawyers have to live, you know. Your sister? I hadn't the pleasure of meeting you at Riddlesdale, Lady Mary. I trust you are fully recovered."

"Entirely, thank you," said Mary with emphasis.

"Mr. Parker—of course your name is very familiar. Wimsey, here, can't do a thing without you, I know. Murbles, are these gentlemen full of valuable information? I am immensely interested in this case."

"Not just this moment, though," put in the solicitor.

"Indeed, no. Nothing but that excellent saddle of mutton has the slightest attraction for me just now. Forgive my greed."

"Well, well," said Mr. Murbles, beaming mildly, "let's make a start. I fear, my dear young people, I am old-fashioned enough not to have adopted the modern practice of cocktail-drinking."

"Quite right too," said Wimsey emphatically. "Ruins the palate and spoils the digestion. Not an English custom—rank sacrilege in this old Inn. Came from America—result, prohibition. That's what happens to people, who don't understand how to drink. God bless me, sir, why you're giving us the famous claret. It's a sin so much as to mention a cocktail in its presence."

"Yes," said Mr. Murbles, "yes, that's the Lafite '75. It's very seldom, very seldom, I bring it out for anybody under fifty years of age —but you, Lord Peter, have a discrimination which would do honour to one of twice your years."

"Thanks very much, sir; that's a testimonial I deeply appreciate. May I circulate the bottle, sir?"

"Do, do—we will wait on ourselves, Simpson, thank you. After lunch," continued Mr. Murbles, "I will ask you to try something really curious. An odd old client of mine died the other day, and left me a dozen of '47 port."

"Gad!" said Peter. " '47! It'll hardly be drinkable, will it, sir?"

"I very greatly fear," replied Mr. Murbles, "that it will not. A great pity. But I feel that some kind of homage should be paid to so notable an antiquity."

"It would be something to say that one had tasted it," said Peter. "Like goin' to see the divine Sarah, you know. Voice gone, bloom gone, savour gone—but still a classic."

"Ah," said Mr. Murbles. "I remember her in her great days. We old fellows have the compensation of some very wonderful memories."

"Quite right, sir," said Peter, "and you'll pile up plenty more yet. But what was this old gentleman doing to let a vintage like that get past its prime?"

"Mr. Featherstone was a very singular man," said Mr. Murbles. "And yet—I don't know. He may have been profoundly wise. He had the reputation for extreme avarice. Never bought a new suit, never took a holiday, never married, lived all his life in the same dark, narrow chambers he occupied as a briefless barrister. Yet he inherited a huge income from his father, all of which he left to accumulate. The port was laid down by the old man, who died in 1860, when my client was thirty-four. He—the son, I mean—was ninety-six when he deceased. He said no pleasure ever came up to the anticipation, and so he lived like a hermit—doing nothing, but planning all the things he might have done. He wrote an elaborate diary, containing, day by day, the record of this visionary existence which he had never dared put to the test of actuality. The diary described minutely a blissful wedded life with the woman of his dreams. Every Christmas and Easter Day a bottle of the '47 was solemnly set upon his table and solemnly removed, unopened, at the close of his frugal meal. An earnest Christian, he anticipated great happiness after death, but, as you see, he put the pleasure off as long as possible. He died with the words, 'He is faithful that promised'—feeling to the end the need of assurance. A very singular man, very singular indeed—far removed from the adventurous spirit of the present generation."

"How curious and pathetic," said Mary.

"Perhaps he had at some time set his heart on something unattainable," said Parker.

"Well, I don't know," said Mr. Murbles. "People used to say that the dream-lady had not always been a dream, but that he never could bring himself to propose."

"Ah," said Sir Impey briskly, "the more I see and hear in the courts the more I am inclined to feel that Mr. Featherstone chose the better part."

"And are determined to follow his example—in that respect at any rate? Eh, Sir Impey!" replied Mr. Murbles, with a mild chuckle.

Mr. Parker glanced towards the window. It was beginning to rain.

Truly enough the '47 port was a dead thing; the merest ghost of its old flame and flavour hung about it. Lord Peter held his glass poised a moment.

"It is like the taste of a passion that has passed its noon and turned to weariness," he said, with sudden gravity. "The only thing to do is to recognise bravely that it is dead, and put it away." With a determined movement, he flung the remainder of the wine into the fire. The mocking smile came back to his face:

> "What I like about Clive
> Is that he is no longer alive—
> There is a great deal to be said
> For being dead.

What classic pith and brevity in those four lines!—However, in the matter of this case, we've a good deal to tell you, sir."

With the assistance of Parker, he laid before the two men of law the whole train of the investigation up to date, Lady Mary coming loyally up to the scratch with her version of the night's proceedings.

"In fact, you see," said Peter, "this Mr. Goyles has lost a lot by *not* being a murderer. We feel he would have cut a fine, sinister figure as a midnight assassin. But things bein' as they are, you see, we must make what we can of him as a witness, what?"

"Well, Lord Peter," said Mr. Murbles slowly, "I congratulate you and Mr. Parker on a great deal of industry and ingenuity in working the matter out."

"I think we may say we have made some progress," said Parker.

"If only negatively," added Peter.

"Exactly," said Sir Impey turning on him with staggering abruptness. "Very negatively indeed. And, having seriously hampered the case for the defence, what are you going to do next?"

"That's a nice thing to say," cried Peter indignantly, "when we've cleared up such a lot of points for you!"

"I daresay," said the barrister, "but they're the sorts of points which are much better left muffled up."

"Damn it all, we want to get at the truth!"

"Do you?" said Sir Impey drily. "I don't. I don't care twopence about the truth. I want a case. It doesn't matter to me who killed Cathcart, provided I can prove it wasn't Denver. It's really enough if I can throw reasonable doubt on its being Denver. Here's a client comes to me with a story of a quarrel, a suspicious revolver, a refusal to produce evidence of his statements, and a totally inadequate and idiotic alibi. I arrange to obfuscate the jury with mysterious footprints, a discrepancy as to time, a young woman with a secret, and a general vague suggestion of something between a burglary and a *crime passionel*. And here you come explaining the footprints, exculpating the unknown man, abolishing the discrepancies, clearing up the motives of the young woman, and most carefully throwing back suspicion to where it rested in the first place. What *do* you expect?"

"I've always said," growled Peter, "that the professional advocate was the most immoral fellow on the face of the earth, and now I know for certain."

"Well, well," said Mr. Murbles, "all this just means that we mustn't rest upon our oars. You must go on, my dear boy, and get more evidence of a positive kind. If this Mr. Goyles did not kill Cathcart we must be able to find the person who did."

"Anyhow," said Biggs, "there's one thing to be thankful for—and that is, that you were still too unwell to go before the Grand Jury last Thursday, Lady Mary"—Lady Mary blushed—"and the prosecution will be building their case on a shot fired at three a.m. Don't answer any questions if you can help it, and we'll spring it on 'em."

"But will they believe anything she says at the trial after that?" asked Peter dubiously.

"All the better if they don't. She'll be their witness. You'll get a nasty heckling, Lady Mary, but you mustn't mind that. It's all in the game. Just stick to your story and we'll deliver the goods. See!" Sir Impey wagged a menacing finger.

"I see," said Mary. "And I'll be heckled like anything. Just go on stubbornly saying, 'I am telling the truth now.' That's the idea, isn't it?"

"Exactly so," said Biggs. "By the way, Denver still refuses to explain his movements, I suppose?"

"Cat-e-gori-cally," replied the solicitor. "The Wimseys are a very determined family," he added, "and I fear that, for the present, it is useless to pursue that line of investigation. If we could discover the truth in some other way, and confront the Duke with it, he might then be persuaded to add his confirmation."

"Well, now," said Parker, "we have, as it seems to me, still three lines to go upon. First, we must try to establish the Duke's alibi from external sources. Secondly, we can examine the evidence afresh with a view to finding the real murderer. And thirdly, the Paris police may give us some light upon Cathcart's past history."

"And I fancy I know where to go next for information on the second point," said Wimsey suddenly. "Grider's Hole."

"Whew-w!" Parker whistled. "I was forgetting that. That's where that bloodthirsty farmer fellow lives, isn't it, who set the dogs on you?"

"With the remarkable wife. Yes. See here, how does this strike you? This fellow is ferociously jealous of his wife, and inclined to suspect every man who comes near her. When I went up there that day, and mentioned that a friend of mine might have been hanging about there the previous week, he got frightfully excited and threatened to have the fellow's blood. Seemed to know who I was referrin'

to. Now, of course, with my mind full of No. 10—Goyles, you know
—I never thought but what he was the man. But supposin' it was
Cathcart? You see, we know now, Goyles hadn't even been in the
neighbourhood till the Wednesday, so you wouldn't expect what's-
his-name—Grimethorpe—to know about him, but Cathcart might have
wandered over to Grider's Hole any day and been seen. And look
here! Here's another thing that fits in. When I went up there Mrs.
Grimethorpe evidently mistook me for somebody she knew, and hurried down to warn me off. Well, of course, I've been thinkin' all the
time she must have seen my old cap and Burberry from the window
and mistaken me for Goyles, but, now I come to think of it, I told
the kid who came to the door that I was from Riddlesdale Lodge.
If the child told her mother, she must have thought it was Cathcart."

"No, no, Wimsey, that won't do," put in Parker; "she must have
known Cathcart was dead by that time."

"Oh, damn it! Yes, I suppose she must. Unless that surly old devil
kept the news from her. By Jove! that's just what he would do if he'd
killed Cathcart himself. He'd never say a word to her—and I don't
suppose he would let her look at a paper, even if they take one in.
It's a primitive sort of place."

"But didn't you say Grimethorpe had an alibi?"

"Yes, but we didn't really test it."

"And how d'you suppose he knew Cathcart was going to be in the
thicket that night?"

Peter considered.

"Perhaps he sent for him," suggested Mary.

"That's right, that's right," cried Peter eagerly. "You remember
we thought Cathcart must somehow or other have heard from
Goyles, making an appointment—but suppose the message was from
Grimethorpe, threatening to split on Cathcart to Jerry."

"You are suggesting, Lord Peter," said Mr. Murbles, in a tone
calculated to chill Peter's blithe impetuosity, "that, at the very time
Mr. Cathcart was betrothed to your sister, he was carrying on a disgraceful intrigue with a married woman very much his social inferior."

"I beg your pardon, Polly," said Wimsey.

"It's all right," said Mary, "I—as a matter of fact, it wouldn't surprise me frightfully. Denis was always—I mean, he had rather Continental ideas about marriage and that sort of thing. I don't think he'd
have thought that mattered very much. He'd probably have said there
was a time and place for everything."

"One of those watertight compartment minds," said Wimsey thoughtfully. Mr. Parker, despite his long acquaintance with the seamy side of things in London, had his brows set in a gloomy frown of as fierce a provincial disapproval as ever came from Barrow-in-Furness.

"If you can upset this Grimethorpe's alibi," said Sir Impey, fitting his right-hand finger-tips neatly between the fingers of his left hand, "we might make some sort of a case of it. What do you think, Murbles?"

"After all," said the solicitor, "Grimethorpe and the servant both admit that he, Grimethorpe, was not at Grider's Hole on Wednesday night. If he can't prove he was at Stapley he may have been at Riddlesdale."

"By Jove!" cried Wimsey; "driven off alone, stopped somewhere, left the gee, sneaked back, met Cathcart, done him in, and toddled home next day with a tale about machinery."

"Or he may even have been to Stapley," put in Parker; "left early or gone late, and put in the murder on the way. We shall have to check the precise times very carefully."

"Hurray!" cried Wimsey. "I think I'll be gettin' back to Riddlesdale."

"I'd better stay here," said Parker. "There may be something from Paris."

"Right you are. Let me know the minute anything comes through. I say, old thing!"

"Yes?"

"Does it occur to you that what's the matter with this case is that there are too many clues? Dozens of people with secrets and elopements bargin' about all over the place——"

"I hate you, Peter," said Lady Mary.

CHAPTER XI

MERIBAH

Oh-ho, my friend! You are gotten into Lob's pond.
                                        —Jack the Giant-killer.

LORD PETER BROKE HIS JOURNEY north at York, whither the Duke of Denver had been transferred after the Assizes, owing to the imminent closing-down of Northallerton Gaol. By dint of judicious persuasion, Peter contrived to obtain an interview with his brother. He found him looking ill at ease, and pulled down by the prison atmosphere, but still unquenchably defiant.

"Bad luck, old man," said Peter, "but you're keepin' your tail up fine. Beastly slow business, all this legal stuff, what? But it gives us time, an' that's all to the good."

"It's a confounded nuisance," said his grace. "And I'd like to know what Murbles means. Comes down and tries to bully me—damned impudence! Anybody'd think he suspected me."

"Look here, Jerry," said his brother earnestly, "why can't you let up on that alibi of yours? It'd help no end, you know. After all, if a fellow won't say what he's been doin'——"

"It ain't my business to prove anything," retorted his grace, with dignity. "They've got to show I was there, murderin' the fellow. I'm not bound to say where I was. I'm presumed innocent, aren't I, till they prove me guilty? I call it a disgrace. Here's a murder committed, and they aren't taking the slightest trouble to find the real criminal. I give 'em my word of honour, to say nothin' of an oath, that I didn't kill Cathcart—though, mind you, the swine deserved it—but they pay no attention. Meanwhile, the real man's escapin' at his confounded leisure. If I were only free, I'd make a fuss about it."

"Well, why the devil don't you cut it short, then?" urged Peter. "I don't mean here and now to me"—with a glance at the warder, within earshot—"but to Murbles. Then we could get to work."

"I wish you'd jolly well keep out of it," grunted the Duke. "Isn't it all damnable enough for Helen, poor girl, and mother, and everyone, without you makin' it an opportunity to play Sherlock Holmes?

I'd have thought you'd have had the decency to keep quiet, for the family's sake. I may be in a damned rotten position, but I ain't makin' a public spectacle of myself, by Jove!"

"Hell!" said Lord Peter, with such vehemence that the wooden-faced warder actually jumped. "It's you that's makin' the spectacle! It need never have started, but for you. Do you think *I* like havin' my brother and sister dragged through the Courts, and reporters swarmin' over the place, and paragraphs and news-bills with your name starin' at me from every corner, and all this ghastly business, endin' up in a great show in the House of Lords, with a lot of people togged up in scarlet and ermine, and all the rest of the damn-fool jiggery-pokery? People are beginnin' to look oddly at me in the Club, and I can jolly well hear 'em whisperin' that 'Denver's attitude looks jolly fishy, b'gad!' Cut it out, Jerry."

"Well, we're in for it now," said his brother, "and thank heaven there are still a few decent fellows left in the peerage who'll know how to take a gentleman's word, even if my own brother can't see beyond his rotten legal evidence."

As they stared angrily at one another, that mysterious sympathy of the flesh which we call family likeness sprang out from its hiding-place, stamping their totally dissimilar features with an elfish effect of mutual caricature. It was as though each saw himself in a distorting mirror, while the voices might have been one voice with its echo.

"Look here, old chap," said Peter, recovering himself, "I'm fright-fully sorry. I didn't mean to let myself go like that. If you won't say anything, you won't. Anyhow, we're all working like blazes, and we're sure to find the right man before very long."

"You'd better leave it to the police," said Denver. "I know you like playin' at detectives, but I do think you might draw the line some-where."

"That's a nasty one," said Wimsey. "But I don't look on this as a game, and I can't say I'll keep out of it, because I know I'm doin' valuable work. Still, I can—honestly, I can—see your point of view. I'm jolly sorry you find me such an irritatin' sort of person. I suppose it's hard for you to believe I feel anything. But I do, and I'm goin' to get you out of this, if Bunter and I both perish in the attempt. Well, so long—that warder's just wakin' up to say, 'Time, gentlemen.' Cheer-oh, old thing! Good luck!"

He rejoined Bunter outside.

"Bunter," he said, as they walked through the streets of the old city, "is my manner *really* offensive, when I don't mean it to be?"

"It is possible, my lord, if your lordship will excuse my saying so, that the liveliness of your lordship's manner may be misleading to persons of limited——"

"Be careful, Bunter!"

"Limited imagination, my lord."

"Well-bred English people never have imagination, Bunter."

"Certainly not, my lord. I meant nothing disparaging."

"Well, Bunter—oh, lord! there's a reporter! Hide me, quick!"

"In here, my lord."

Mr. Bunter whisked his master into the cool emptiness of the Cathedral.

"I venture to suggest, my lord," he urged in a hurried whisper, "that we adopt the attitude and external appearance of prayer, if your lordship will excuse me."

Peeping through his fingers, Lord Peter saw a verger hastening towards them, rebuke depicted on his face. At that moment, however, the reporter entered in headlong pursuit, tugging a note-book from his pocket. The verger leapt swiftly on this new prey.

"The winder h'under which we stand," he began in a reverential monotone, "is called the Seven Sisters of York. They say——"

Master and man stole quietly out.

.   .   .   .   .

For his visit to the market town of Stapley Lord Peter attired himself in an aged Norfolk suit, stockings with sober tops, an ancient hat turned down all round, stout shoes, and carried a heavy ashplant. It was with regret that he abandoned his favourite stick—a handsome malacca, marked off in inches for detective convenience, and concealing a sword in its belly and a compass in its head. He decided, however, that it would prejudice the natives against him, as having a town-bred, not to say supercilious, air about it. The sequel to this commendable devotion to his art forcibly illustrated the truth of Gertrude Rhead's observation, "All this self-sacrifice is a sad mistake."

The little town was sleepy enough as he drove into it in one of the Riddlesdale dog-carts, Bunter beside him, and the under-gardener on the back seat. For choice, he would have come on a market-day, in the hope of meeting Grimethorpe himself, but things were moving fast now, and he dared not lose a day. It was a raw, cold morning, inclined to rain.

"Which is the best inn to put up at, Wilkes?"

"There's t' 'Bricklayers' Arms,' my lord—a fine, well-thought-of place, or t' 'Bridge and Bottle,' i' t' square, or t' 'Rose and Crown,' t'other side o' square."

"Where do the folks usually put up on market-days?"

"Mebbe 'Rose and Crown' is most popular, so to say—Tim Watchett, t' landlord, is a rare gossip. Now Greg Smith ower t'way at 'Bridge and Bottle,' he's nobbut a grimly, surly man, but he keeps good drink."

"H'm—I fancy, Bunter, our man will be more attracted by surliness and good drink than by a genial host. The 'Bridge and Bottle' for us, I fancy, and, if we draw blank there, we'll toddle over to the 'Rose and Crown,' and pump the garrulous Watchett."

Accordingly they turned into the yard of a large, stony-faced house, whose long-unpainted sign bore the dim outline of a "Bridge Embattled," which local etymology had (by a natural association of ideas) transmogrified into the "Bridge and Bottle." To the grumpy ostler who took the horse Peter, with his most companionable manner, addressed himself:

"Nasty raw morning, isn't it?"

"Eea."

"Give him a good feed. I may be here some time."

"Ugh!"

"Not many people about to-day, what?"

"Ugh!"

"But I expect you're busy enough market-days."

"Eea."

"People come in from a long way round, I suppose."

"Co-oop!" said the ostler. The horse walked three steps forward.

"Wo!" said the ostler. The horse stopped, with the shafts free of the tugs; the man lowered the shafts, to grate viciously on the gravel.

"Coom on oop!" said the ostler, and walked calmly off into the stable, leaving the affable Lord Peter as thoroughly snubbed as that young sprig of the nobility had ever found himself.

"I am more and more convinced," said his lordship, "that this is Farmer Grimethorpe's usual house of call. Let's try the bar. Wilkes, I shan't want you for a bit. Get yourself lunch if necessary. I don't know how long we shall be."

"Very good, my lord."

In the bar of the "Bridge and Bottle" they found Mr. Greg Smith gloomily checking a long invoice. Lord Peter ordered drinks for Bunter and himself. The landlord appeared to resent this as a liberty, and jerked his head towards the barmaid. It was only right and proper that Bunter, after respectfully returning thanks to his master for his half-pint, should fall into conversation with the girl, while Lord Peter paid his respects to Mr. Smith.

"Ah!" said his lordship, "good stuff, that, Mr. Smith. I was told to come here for real good beer, and, by Jove! I've been sent to the right place."

"Ugh!" said Mr. Smith, "'tisn't what it was. Nowt's good these times."

"Well, I don't want better. By the way, is Mr. Grimethorpe here to-day?"

"Eh?"

"Is Mr. Grimethorpe in Stapley this morning, d'you know?"

"How'd I know?"

"I thought he always put up here."

"Ah!"

"Perhaps I mistook the name. But I fancied he'd be the man to go where the best beer is."

"Ay?"

"Oh, well, if you haven't seen him, I don't suppose he's come over to-day."

"Coom where?"

"Into Stapley."

"Doosn't 'e live here? He can go and coom without my knowing."

"Oh, of course!" Wimsey staggered under the shock, and then grasped the misunderstanding. "I don't mean Mr. Grimethorpe of Stapley, but Mr. Grimethorpe of Grider's Hole."

"Why didn't tha say so? Oh, him? Ay."

"He's here to-day?"

"Nay, I knaw nowt about 'un."

"He comes in on market-days, I expect."

"Sometimes."

"It's a longish way. One can put up for the night, I suppose?"

"Doosta want t'stay t'night?"

"Well, no, I don't think so. I was thinking about my friend Mr. Grimethorpe. I daresay he often has to stay the night."

"Happen a does."

"Doesn't he stay here, then?"

"Naay."

"Oh!" said Wimsey, and thought impatiently: "If all these natives are as oyster-like I *shall* have to stay the night. . . . Well, well," he added aloud, "next time he drops in say I asked after him."

"And who mought tha be?" inquired Mr. Smith in a hostile manner.

"Oh, only Brooks of Sheffield," said Lord Peter, with a happy grin. "Good morning. I won't forget to recommend your beer."

Mr. Smith grunted. Lord Peter strolled slowly out, and before long Mr. Bunter joined him, coming out with a brisk step and the lingering remains of what, in anyone else, might have been taken for a smirk.

"Well?" inquired his lordship. "I hope the young lady was more communicative than that fellow."

"I found the young person" ("Snubbed again," muttered Lord Peter) "perfectly amiable, my lord, but unhappily ill-informed. Mr. Grimethorpe is not unknown to her, but he does not stay here. She has sometimes seen him in company with a man called Zedekiah Bone."

"Well," said his lordship, "suppose you look for Bone, and come and report progress to me in a couple of hours' time. I'll try the 'Rose and Crown.' We'll meet at noon under that thing."

"That thing," was a tall erection in pink granite, neatly tooled to represent a craggy rock, and guarded by two petrified infantry-men in trench helmets. A thin stream of water gushed from a bronze knob half-way up, a roll of honour was engraved on the octagonal base, and four gas-lamps on cast-iron standards put the finishing touch to a very monument of incongruity. Mr. Bunter looked carefully at it, to be sure of recognising it again, and moved respectfully away. Lord Peter walked ten brisk steps in the direction of the "Rose and Crown," then a thought struck him.

"Bunter!"

Mr. Bunter hurried back to his side.

"Oh, nothing!" said his lordship. "Only I've just thought of a name for it."

"For——"

"That memorial," said Lord Peter. "I choose to call it 'Meribah.' "

"Yes, my lord. The waters of strife. Exceedingly apt, my lord.

Nothing harmonious about it, if I may say so. Will there be anything further, my lord?"

"No, that's all."

.   .   .   .   .

Mr. Timothy Watchett of the "Rose and Crown" was certainly a contrast to Mr. Greg Smith. He was a small, spare, sharp-eyed man of about fifty-five, with so twinkling and humorous an eye and so alert a cock of the head that Lord Peter summed up his origin the moment he set eyes on him.

"Morning, landlord," said he genially, "and when did *you* last see Piccadilly Circus?"

"'Ard to say, sir. Gettin' on for thirty-five year, I reckon. Many's the time I said to my wife, 'Liz, I'll tike you ter see the 'Olborn Empire afore I die.' But, with one thing and another, time slips aw'y. One day's so like another—blowed if I ever remember 'ow old I'm gettin', sir."

"Oh, well, you've lots of time yet," said Lord Peter.

"I 'ope so, sir. I ain't never wot you may call got used ter these Northerners. That slow, they are, sir—it fair giv' me the 'ump when I first come. And the w'y they speak—that took some gettin' used to. Call that English, I useter say, give me the Frenchies in the Chantycleer Restaurong, I ses. But there, sir, custom's everything. Blowed if I didn't ketch myself a-syin' 'yon side the square' the other day. Me!"

"I don't think there's much fear of your turning into a Yorkshire man," said Lord Peter, "didn't I know you the minute I set eyes on you? In Mr. Watchett's bar I said to myself, 'My foot is on my native paving-stones.'"

"That's raight, sir. And, bein' there, sir, what can I 'ave the pleasure of offerin' you? . . . Excuse me, sir, but 'aven't I seen your fice somewhere?"

"I don't think so," said Peter; "but that reminds me. Do you know one, Mr. Grimethorpe?"

"I know five Mr. Grimethorpes. W'ich of 'em was you meanin', sir?"

"Mr. Grimethorpe of Grider's Hole."

The landlord's cheerful face darkened.

"Friend of yours, sir?"

"Not exactly. An acquaintance."

"There naow!" cried Mr. Watchett, smacking his hand down upon the counter. "I knowed as I knowed your fice! Don't you live over at Riddlesdale, sir?"

"I'm stayin' there."

"I knowed it," retorted Mr. Watchett triumphantly. He dived behind the counter and brought up a bundle of newspapers, turning over the sheets excitedly with a well-licked thumb. "There! Riddlesdale! That's it, of course."

He smacked open a *Daily Mirror* of a fortnight or so ago. The front page bore a heavy block headline: THE RIDDLESDALE MYSTERY. And beneath was a lifelike snapshot entitled, *"Lord Peter Wimsey, the Sherlock Holmes of the West End, who is devoting all his time and energies to proving the innocence of his brother, the Duke of Denver."* Mr. Watchett gloated.

"You won't mind my syin' 'ow proud I am to 'ave you in my bar, my lord.—'Ere, Jem, you attend ter them gentlemen; don't you see they're wytin'?—Follered all yer caises I 'ave, my lord, in the pipers —jest like a book they are. An' ter think——"

"Look here, old thing," said Lord Peter, "d'you mind not talkin' quite so loud. Seein' dear old Felix is out of the bag, so to speak, do you think you could give me some information and keep your mouth shut, what?"

"Come be'ind into the bar-parlour, my lord. Nobody'll 'ear us there," said Mr. Watchett eagerly, lifting up the flap. "Jem, 'ere! Bring a bottle of—what'll you 'ave, my lord?"

"Well, I don't know how many places I may have to visit," said his lordship dubiously.

"Jem, bring a quart of the old ale.—It's special, that's wot it is, my lord. I ain't never found none like it, except it might be once at Oxford. Thanks, Jem. Naow you get along sharp and attend to the customers. Now, my lord."

Mr. Watchett's information amounted to this. That Mr. Grimethorpe used to come to the "Rose and Crown" pretty often, especially on market-days. About ten days previously he had come in lateish, very drunk and quarrelsome, with his wife, who seemed, as usual, terrified of him. Grimethorpe had demanded spirits, but Mr. Watchett had refused to serve him. There had been a row, and Mrs. Grimethorpe had endeavoured to get her husband away. Grimethorpe had promptly knocked her down, with epithets reflecting upon her virtue, and Mr. Watchett had at once called upon the potmen to turn Grimethorpe out, refusing to have him in the house again. He had heard it said on all sides that Grimethorpe's temper, always notoriously bad, had become positively diabolical of late.

"Could you hazard, so to speak, a calculation as to how long, or since when?"

"Well, my lord, come to think of it, especially since the middle of last month—p'r'aps a bit earlier."

"M'm!"

"Not that I'd go for to insinuate anythink, nor your lordship, neither, of course," said Mr. Watchett quickly.

"Certainly not," said Lord Peter. "What about?"

"Ah!" said Mr. Watchett, "there it is, wot abaht?"

"Tell me," said Lord Peter, "do you recollect Grimethorpe comin' into Stapley on October 13th—a Wednesday, it was."

"That would be the day of the—ah! to be sure! Yes, I do recollect it, for I remember thinking it was odd him comin' here except on a market-day. Said he 'ad ter look at some machinery—drills and such, that's raight. 'E was 'ere raight enough."

"Do you remember what time he came in?"

"Well, naow, I've a fancy 'e was 'ere ter lunch. The waitress'd know. 'Ere, Bet!" he called through the side door, "d'yer 'appen to recollect whether Mr. Grimethorpe lunched 'ere October the 13th—Wednesday it were, the d'y the pore gent was murdered over at Riddlesdale?"

"Grimethorpe o' Grider's Hole?" said the girl, a well-grown young Yorkshire woman. "Yes! 'E took loonch, and coom back to sleep. Ah'm not mistook, for ah waited on 'un, an' took up 'is watter i' t'morning, and 'e only gied me tuppence."

"Monstrous!" said Lord Peter. "Look here, Miss Elizabeth, you're sure it was the thirteenth? Because I've got a bet on it with a friend, and I don't want to lose the money if I can help it. You're positive it was Wednesday night he slept here? I could have sworn it was Thursday."

"Naay, sir, t'wor Wednesday for I remember hearing the men talking o' t'murder i' t'bar, an' telling Mester Grimethorpe next daay."

144

"Sounds conclusive. What did Mr. Grimethorpe say about it?"

"There now," cried the young woman, "'tis queer you should ask that; everyone noticed how strange he acted. He turned all white like a sheet, and looked at both his hands, one after the other, and then he pushes 'es hair off 's forehead—dazed-like. We reckoned he hadn't got over the drink. He's more often drunk than not. Ah wouldn't be his wife for five hundred pounds."

"I should think not," said Peter; "you can do a lot better than that. Well, I suppose I've lost my money, then. By the way, what time did Mr. Grimethorpe come in to bed?"

"Close on two i' t'morning," said the girl, tossing her head. "He were locked oot, an' Jem had to go down and let 'un in."

"That so?" said Peter. "Well, I might try to get out on a technicality, eh, Mr. Watchett? Two o'clock is Thursday, isn't it? I'll work that for all it's worth. Thanks frightfully. That's all I want to know."

Bet grinned and giggled herself away, comparing the generosity of the strange gentleman with the stinginess of Mr. Grimethorpe. Peter rose.

"I'm no end obliged, Mr. Watchett," he said. "I'll just have a word with Jem. Don't say anything, by the way."

"Not me," said Mr. Watchett; "I knows wot's wot. Good luck, my lord."

Jem corroborated Bet. Grimethorpe had returned at about 1.50 a.m. on October 14th, drunk, and plastered with mud. He had muttered something about having run up against a man called Watson.

The ostler was next interrogated. He did not think that anybody could get a horse and trap out of the stable at night without his knowing it. He knew Watson. He was a carrier by trade, and lived in Windon Street. Lord Peter rewarded his informant suitably, and set out for Windon Street.

But the recital of his quest would be tedious. At a quarter-past noon he joined Bunter at the Meribah memorial.

"Any luck?"

"I have secured certain information, my lord, which I have duly noted. Total expenditure on beer for self and witnesses 7s. 2d., my lord."

Lord Peter paid the 7s. 2d. without a word, and they adjourned to the "Rose and Crown." Being accommodated in a private parlour, and having ordered lunch, they proceeded to draw up the following schedule:

GRIMETHORPE'S MOVEMENTS. *Wednesday, October* 13*th* to *Thursday, October* 14*th.*

October 13*th:*

12.30 p.m.	Arrives "Rose and Crown."
1.0 p.m.	Lunches.
3.0 p.m.	Orders two drills from man called Gooch in Trimmer's Lane.
4.30 p.m.	Drink with Gooch to clinch bargain.
5.0 p.m.	Calls at house of John Watson carrier, about delivering some dog-food. Watson absent. Mrs. Watson says W. expected back that night. G. says will call again.
5.30 p.m.	Calls on Mark Dolby, grocer, to complain about some tinned salmon.
5.45 p.m.	Calls on Mr. Hewitt, optician, to pay bill for spectacles and dispute the amount.
6.0 p.m.	Drinks with Zedekiah Bone at "Bridge and Bottle."
6.45 p.m.	Calls again on Mrs. Watson. Watson not yet home.
7.0 p.m.	Seen by Constable Z15 drinking with several men at "Pig and Whistle." Heard to use threatening language with regard to some person unknown.
7.20 p.m.	Seen to leave "Pig and Whistle" with two men (not yet identified).

October 14*th:*

1.15 a.m.	Picked up by Watson, carrier, about a mile out on road to Riddlesdale, very dirty and ill-tempered, and not quite sober.
1.45 a.m.	Let into "Rose and Crown" by James Johnson, potman.
9.0 a.m.	Called by Elizabeth Dobbin.
9.30 a.m.	In Bar of "Rose and Crown." Hears of man murdered at Riddlesdale. Behaves suspiciously.
10.15 a.m.	Cashes cheque £129 17s. 8d. at Lloyds Bank.
10.30 a.m.	Pays Gooch for drills.
11.5 a.m.	Leaves "Rose and Crown" for Grider's Hole.

Lord Peter looked at this for a few minutes, and put his finger on the great gap of six hours after 7.20.

"How far to Riddlesdale, Bunter?"

"About thirteen and three-quarter miles, my lord."

"And the shot was heard at 11.50. It couldn't be done on foot. Did Watson explain why he didn't get back from his round till two in the morning?"

"Yes, my lord. He says he reckons to be back about eleven, but his horse cast a shoe between King's Fenton and Riddlesdale. He had to walk him quietly into Riddlesdale—about 3½ miles—getting

146

there about ten, and knock up the blacksmith. He turned in to the 'Lord in Glory' till closing time, and then went home with a friend and had a few more. At 12.40 he started off home, and picked Grimethorpe up a mile or so out, near the cross roads."

"Sounds circumstantial. The blacksmith and the friend ought to be able to substantiate it. But we simply must find those men at the 'Pig and Whistle.'"

"Yes, my lord. I will try again after lunch."

It was a good lunch. But that seemed to exhaust their luck for the day, for by three o'clock the men had not been identified, and the scent seemed cold.

Wilkes, the groom, however, had his own contribution to the inquiry. He had met a man from King's Fenton at lunch, and they had, naturally, got to talking over the mysterious murder at the Lodge, and the man had said that he knew an old man living in a hut on the Fell, who said that on the night of the murder he'd seen a man walking over Whemmeling Fell in the middle of the night. "And it coom to me, all of a sooden, it mought be his grace," said Wilkes brightly.

Further inquiries elicited that the old man's name was Groot, and that Wilkes could easily drop Lord Peter and Bunter at the beginning of the sheep-path which led up to his hut.

Now, had Lord Peter taken his brother's advice, and paid more attention to English country sports than to incunabula and criminals in London—or had Bunter been brought up on the moors, rather than in a Kentish village—or had Wilkes (who was a Yorkshire man bred and born, and ought to have known better) not been so outrageously puffed up with the sense of his own importance in suggesting a clue, and with impatience to have that clue followed up without delay—or had any one of the three exercised common sense—this preposterous suggestion would never have been made, much less carried out, on a November day in the North Riding. As it was, however, Lord Peter and Bunter left the trap at the foot of the moor-path at ten minutes to four, and, dismissing Wilkes, climbed steadily up to the wee hut on the edge of the Fell.

.   .   .   .   .

The old man was extremely deaf, and, after half an hour of interrogation, his story did not amount to much. On a night in October, which he thought might be the night of the murder, he had been sitting by his peat fire when—about midnight, as he guessed—a tall man had loomed up out of the darkness. He spoke like a Southerner, and said he had got lost on the moor. Old Groot had come to his door and pointed out the track down towards Riddlesdale. The stranger had then vanished, leaving a shilling in his hand. He could not describe the stranger's dress more particularly than that he wore a soft hat and an overcoat, and, he thought, leggings. He was pretty near sure it was the night of the murder, because afterwards he had turned it over in his mind and made out that it might have been one of yon folk at the Lodge—possibly the Duke. He had only arrived at this result by a slow process of thought, and had not "come forward," not knowing whom or where to come to.

With this the inquirers had to be content, and, presenting Groot with half a crown, they emerged upon the moor at something after five o'clock.

"Bunter," said Lord Peter through the dusk, "I am abso-bally-lutely positive that the answer to all this business is at Grider's Hole."

"Very possibly, my lord."

Lord Peter extended his finger in a south-easterly direction. "That is Grider's Hole," he said. "Let's go."

"Very good, my lord."

So, like two Cockney innocents, Lord Peter and Bunter set forth at a brisk pace down the narrow moor-track towards Grider's Hole, with never a glance behind them for the great white menace rolling silently down through the November dusk from the wide loneliness of Whemmeling Fell.

. . . . .

"Bunter!"

"Here, my lord!"

The voice was close at his ear.

"Thank God! I thought you'd disappeared for good. I say, we ought to have known."

"Yes, my lord."

It had come on them from behind, in a single stride, thick, cold, choking—blotting each from the other, though they were only a yard or two apart.

"I'm a fool, Bunter," said Lord Peter.

"Not at all, my lord."

"Don't move; go on speaking."

"Yes, my lord."

Peter groped to the right and clutched the other's sleeve.

"Ah! Now what are we to do?"

"I couldn't say, my lord, having no experience. Has the—er—phenomenon any habits, my lord?"

"No regular habits, I believe. Sometimes it moves. Other times it stays in one place for days. We can wait all night, and see if it lifts at daybreak."

"Yes, my lord. It is unhappily somewhat damp."

"Somewhat—as you say," agreed his lordship, with a short laugh. Bunter sneezed, and begged pardon politely.

"If we go on going south-east," said his lordship, "we shall get to Grider's Hole all right, and they'll jolly well *have* to put us up for the night—or give us an escort. I've got my torch in my pocket, and we can go by compass—oh, hell!"

"My lord?"

"I've got the wrong stick. This beastly ash! No compass, Bunter—we're done in."

"Couldn't we keep on going downhill, my lord?"

Lord Peter hesitated. Recollections of what he had heard and read surged up in his mind to tell him that uphill or downhill seems much the same thing in a fog. But man walks in a vain shadow. It is hard to believe that one is really helpless. The cold was icy. "We might try," he said weakly.

"I have heard it said, my lord, that in a fog one always walked round in a circle," said Mr. Bunter, seized with a tardy diffidence.

"Not on a slope, surely," said Lord Peter, beginning to feel bold out of sheer contrariness.

Bunter, being out of his element, had, for once, no good counsel to offer.

"Well, we can't be much worse off than we are," said Lord Peter. "We'll try it, and keep on shouting."

He grasped Bunter's hand, and they strode gingerly forward into the thick coldness of the fog.

How long that nightmare lasted neither could have said. The world might have died about them. Their own shouts terrified them; when they stopped shouting the dead silence was more terrifying still. They stumbled over tufts of thick heather. It was amazing how, deprived of sight, they exaggerated the inequalities of the ground. It was with very little confidence that they could distinguish uphill from downhill. They were shrammed through with cold, yet the sweat was running from their faces with strain and terror.

Suddenly—from directly before them as it seemed, and only a few yards away—there rose a long, horrible shriek—and another—and another.

"My God! What's that?"

"It's a horse, my lord."

"Of course." They remembered having heard horses scream like that. There had been a burning stable near Poperinghe——

"Poor devil," said Peter. He started off impulsively in the direction of the sound, dropping Bunter's hand.

"Come back, my lord," cried the man in a sudden agony. And then, with a frightened burst of enlightenment:

"For God's sake stop, my lord—the bog!"

A sharp shout in the utter blackness.

"Keep away there—don't move—it's got me!"

And a dreadful sucking noise.

CHAPTER XII

THE ALIBI

When actually in the embrace of a voracious and powerful wild animal, the desirability of leaving a limb is not a matter to be subjected to lengthy consideration.—The Wallet of Kai-Lung.

"I TRIPPED RIGHT INTO IT," said Wimsey's voice steadily, out of the blackness. "One sinks very fast. You'd better not come near, or you'll go too. We'll yell a bit. I don't think we can be very far from Grider's Hole."

"If your lordship will keep shouting," returned Mr. Bunter, "I think—I can—get to you," he panted, untying with his teeth the hard knot of a coil of string.

"Oy!" cried Lord Peter obediently. "Help! Oy! Oy!"

150

Mr. Bunter groped towards the voice, feeling cautiously before him with his walking-stick.

"Wish you'd keep away, Bunter," said Lord Peter peevishly. "Where's the sense of both of us——?" He squelched and floundered again.

"Don't do that, my lord," cried the man entreatingly. "You'll sink farther in."

"I'm up to my thighs now," said Lord Peter.

"I'm coming," said Bunter. "Go on shouting. Ah, here's where it gets soggy."

He felt the ground carefully, selected a tussocky bit which seemed reasonably firm, and drove his stick well into it.

"Oy! Hi! Help!" said Lord Peter, shouting lustily.

Mr. Bunter tied one end of the string to the walking-stick, belted his Burberry tightly about him, and, laying himself cautiously down upon his belly, advanced, clue in hand, like a very Gothic Theseus of a late and degenerate school.

The bog heaved horribly as he crawled over it, and slimy water squelched up into his face. He felt with his hands for tussocks of grass, and got support from them when he could.

"Call out again, my lord!"

"Here!" The voice was fainter and came from the right. Bunter had lost his line a little, hunting for tussocks. "I daren't come faster," he explained. He felt as though he had been crawling for years.

"Get out while there's time," said Peter. "I'm up to my waist. Lord! this is rather a beastly way to peg out."

"You won't peg out," grunted Bunter. His voice was suddenly quite close. "Your hands now."

For a few agonising minutes two pairs of hands groped over the invisible slime. Then:

"Keep yours still," said Bunter. He made a slow, circling movement. It was hard work keeping his face out of the mud. His hands slithered over the slobbery surface—and suddenly closed on an arm.

"Thank God!" said Bunter. "Hang on here, my lord."

He felt forward. The arms were perilously close to the sucking mud. The hands crawled clingingly up his arms and rested on his shoulders. He grasped Wimsey beneath the armpits and heaved. The exertion drove his own knees deep into the bog. He straightened himself hurriedly. Without using his knees he could get no purchase, but to use them meant certain death. They could only hang on desperately till help came—or till the strain became too great. He could not even shout; it was almost more than he could do to keep his mouth free of water. The dragging strain on his shoulders was intolerable; the mere effort to breathe meant an agonising crick in the neck.

"You must go on shouting, my lord."

Wimsey shouted. His voice was breaking and fading.

"Bunter, old thing," said Lord Peter, "I'm simply beastly sorry to have let you in for this."

"Don't mention it, my lord," said Bunter, with his mouth in the slime. A thought struck him.

"What became of your stick, my lord?"

"I dropped it. It should be somewhere near, if it hasn't sunk in."

Bunter cautiously released his left hand and felt about.

"Hi! Hi! Help!"

Bunter's hand closed over the stick, which, by a happy accident, had fallen across a stable tuft of grass. He pulled it over to him, and laid it across his arms, so that he could just rest his chin upon it. The relief to his neck was momentarily so enormous that his courage was renewed. He felt he could hang on for ever.

"Help!"

. . . . .

Minutes passed like hours.

. . . . .

"See that?"

A faint, flickering gleam somewhere away to the right. With desperate energy both shouted together.

"Help! Help! Oy! Oy! Help!"

An answering yell. The light swayed—came nearer—a spreading blur in the fog.

"We *must* keep it up," panted Wimsey. They yelled again.

"Where be?"

"Here!"

"Hello!" A pause. Then:

"Here be stick," said a voice, suddenly near.

"Follow the string!" yelled Bunter. They heard two voices, apparently arguing. Then the string was twitched.

"Here! Here! Two of us! Make haste!"

More consultation.

"Hang on, canst a?"

"Yes, if you're quick."

"Fetchin' hurdle. Two on 'ee, sayst a?"

"Yes."

"Deep in?"

"One of us."

"Aw reet. Jem's comin'."

A splattering noise marked the arrival of Jem with a hurdle. Then came an endless wait. Then another hurdle, the string twitching, and the blur of the lantern bobbing violently about. Then a third hurdle was flung down, and the light came suddenly out of the mist. A hand caught Bunter by the ankle.

"Where's t'other?"

"Here—nearly up to his neck. Have you a rope?"

"Aye, sure. Jem! T'rope!"

The rope came snaking out of the fog. Bunter grasped it, and passed it round his master's body.

"Now—coom tha back and heave."

Bunter crawled cautiously backwards upon the hurdle. All three set hands upon the rope. It was like trying to heave the earth out of her course.

"'Fraid I'm rooted to Australia," panted Peter apologetically. Bunter sweated and sobbed.

"It's aw reet—he's coomin'!"

With slow heavings the rope began to come towards them. Their muscles cracked.

Suddenly, with a great *plop!* the bog let go its hold. The three at the rope were hurled head over heels upon the hurdles. Something unrecognisable in slime lay flat, heaving helplessly. They dragged at him in a kind of frenzy, as though he might be snatched back from them again. The evil bog stench rose thickly round them. They crossed the first hurdle—the second—the third—and rose staggeringly to their feet on firm ground.

"What a beastly place," said Lord Peter faintly. " 'Pologise, stupid of me to have forgotten—what'sy name?"

"Well, tha's loocky," said one of their rescuers. "We thowt we heerd someun a-shouting. There be few folks as cooms oot o' Peter's Pot dead or alive, I reckon."

"Well, it was nearly potted Peter that time," said his lordship, and fainted.

.   .   .   .   .

To Lord Peter the memory of his entry that night into the farmhouse at Grider's Hole always brought with it a sensation of nightmare. The coils of fog rolled in with them as the door opened, and through them the firelight leapt steamily. A hanging lamp made a blur. The Medusa-head of Mrs. Grimethorpe, terribly white against her black hair, peered over him. A hairy paw caught her by the shoulder and wrenched her aside.

"Shameless! A mon—ony mon—that's a' tha thinks on. Bide till tha's wanted. What's this?"

Voices—voices—ever so many fierce faces peering down all round.

"Peter's Pot? An' what were 'ee a-wanting on t'moor this time night? No good. Nobbody but a fool or a thief 'ud coom oop 'ere i' t'fog."

One of the men, a farm labourer with wry shoulders and a thin, malicious face, suddenly burst into tuneless song:

"I been a-courtin' Mary Jane
On Ilkla' Moor bar t'at."

"Howd toong!" yelled Grimethorpe, in a fury. "Doost want Ah should break ivery bwoan i' thi body?" He turned on Bunter. "Tak thesen off, Ah tell tha. Tha'rt here for no good."

"But, William——" began his wife. He snapped round at her like a dog, and she shrank back.

"Naay now, naay now," said a man, whom Wimsey dimly recognised as the fellow who had befriended him on his previous visit, "tha mun' taak them in for t'night, racken, or there'll be trouble wi' t' folk down yonder at t' Lodge, lat aloan what police 'ull saay. Ef t' fellow 'm coom to do harm, 'ee's doon it already—to 'unself. Woan't do no more to-night—look at 'un. Bring 'un to fire, mon," he added to Bunter, and then, turning to the farmer again, "'Tes tha'll be in Queer Street ef 'e wor to goo an' die on us wi' noomony or rhoomaticks."

This reasoning seemed partly to convince Grimethorpe. He made way, grumbling, and the two chilled and exhausted men were brought near the fire. Somebody brought two large, steaming tumblers of spirits. Wimsey's brain seemed to clear, then swim again drowsily, drunkenly.

.   .   .   .   .

Presently he became aware that he was being carried upstairs and put to bed. A big, old-fashioned room, with a fire on the hearth and a huge, grim four-poster. Bunter was helping him out of soaked clothes; rubbing him. Another man appeared from time to time to help him. From below came the bellowing sound of Grimethorpe's voice, blasphemously uplifted. Then the harsh, brassy singing of the wry-shouldered man:

> "Then woorms will coom an' ate thee oop
> On Ilkla' Moor bar t'at . . . .
>
> Then doocks will coom an' ate oop woorms
> On Ilkla' Moor . . . ."

Lord Peter rolled into bed.

"Bunter—where—you all right? Never said thank you—dunno what I'm doing—anywhere to sleep—what?"

He drifted away into oblivion. The old song came up mockingly, and wound its horrible fancies into his dreams:

> "Then we shall coom an' ate oop doocks
> On Ilkla' Moor bar t'at . . . .
>
> An' that is how—an' that is how—is how . . . ."

.   .   .   .   .

When Wimsey next opened his eyes a pale November sun was struggling in at the window. It seemed that the fog had fulfilled its mission and departed. For some time he lay, vaguely unaware of how he came to be where he was; then the outlines of recollection straightened themselves, the drifting outposts of dreams were called back, the burden of his preoccupation settled down as usual. He became aware of an extreme bodily lassitude, and of the dragging pain of wrenched shoulder muscles. Examining himself perfunctorily, he found a bruised and tender zone beneath the armpits and round his chest and back, where the rescuing rope had hauled at him. It was painful to move, so he lay back and closed his eyes once more.

Presently the door opened to admit Bunter, neatly clothed and bearing a tray from which rose a most excellent odour of ham and eggs.

"Hullo, Bunter!"

"Good morning, my lord! I trust your lordship has rested."

"Feel as fit as a fiddle, thanks—come to think of it, why fiddle?— except for a general feeling of havin' been violently massaged by some fellow with cast-iron fingers and knobbly joints. How about you?"

"The arms are a trifle fatigued, thank you, my lord; otherwise, I am happy to say, I feel no trace of the misadventure. Allow me, my lord."

He set the tray tenderly upon Lord Peter's ready knees.

"They must be jolly well dragged out of their sockets," said his lordship, "holdin' me up all that ghastly long time. I'm so beastly deep in debt to you already, Bunter, it's not a bit of use tryin' to repay it. You know I won't forget, anyhow, don't you? All right, I won't be embarrassin' or anything—thanks awfully, anyhow. That's that. What? Did they give you anywhere decent to sleep? I didn't seem to be able to sit up an' take notice last night."

"I slept excellently, I thank your lordship." Mr. Bunter indicated a kind of truckle-bed in a corner of the room. "They would have given me another room, my lord, but in the circumstances, I preferred to remain with your lordship, trusting you would excuse the liberty. I told them that I feared the effects of prolonged immersion upon your lordship's health. I was uneasy, besides, about the intention of Grime-thorpe. I feared he might not feel altogether hospitably disposed, and that he might be led into some hasty action if we were not together."

"I shouldn't wonder. Most murderous-lookin' fellow I ever set eyes on. I'll have to talk to him this morning—or to Mrs. Grimethorpe. I'd take my oath she could tell us something, what?"

"I should say there was very little doubt of it, my lord."

"Trouble is," pursued Wimsey, with his mouth full of egg, "I don't know how to get at her. That jolly husband of hers seems to cherish the most unpleasant suspicions of anything that comes this way in trousers. If he found out we'd been talkin' to her, what you may call privately, he might, as you say, be hurried by his feelin's into doin' something regrettable."

"Just so, my lord."

"Still, the fellow must go an' look after his bally old farm some

156

time, and then, p'raps, we'll be able to tackle her. Queer sort of woman—damn fine one, what? Wonder what she made of Cathcart?" he added musingly.

Mr. Bunter volunteered no opinion on this delicate point.

"Well, Bunter, I think I'll get up. I don't suppose we're altogether welcome here. I didn't fancy the look in our host's eye last night."

"No, my lord. He made a deal of opposition about having your lordship conveyed to this room."

"Why, whose room is it?"

"His own and Mrs. Grimethorpe's, my lord. It appeared most suitable, there being a fireplace, and the bed already made up. Mrs. Grimethorpe showed great kindness, my lord, and the man Jake pointed out to Grimethorpe that it would doubtless be to his pecuniary advantage to treat your lordship with consideration."

"H'm. Nice, graspin' character, ain't he? Well, it's up and away for me. O Lord! I *am* stiff. I say, Bunter, have I any clothes to put on?"

"I have dried and brushed your lordship's suit to the best of my ability, my lord. It is not as I should wish to see it, but I think your lordship will be able to wear it to Riddlesdale."

"Well, I don't suppose the streets will be precisely crowded," retorted his lordship. "I *do* so want a hot bath. How about shavin' water?"

"I can procure that from the kitchen, my lord."

Bunter padded away, and Lord Peter, having pulled on a shirt and trousers with many grunts and groans, roamed over to the window. As usual with hardy country dwellers, it was tightly shut, and a thick wedge of paper had been rammed in to keep the sash from rattling. He removed this and flung up the sash. The wind rollicked in, laden with peaty moor scents. He drank it in gladly. It was good to see the jolly old sun after all—he would have hated to die a sticky death in Peter's Pot. For a few minutes he stood there, returning thanks vaguely in his mind for the benefits of existence. Then he withdrew to finish dressing. The wad of paper was still in his hand, and he was about to fling it into the fire, when a word caught his eye. He unrolled the paper. As he read it his eyebrows went up and his mouth pursed itself into an indescribable expression of whimsical enlightenment. Bunter, returning with the hot water, found his master transfixed, the paper in one hand, and his socks in the other, and whistling a complicated passage of Bach under his breath.

"Bunter," said his lordship, "I am, without exception, the biggest ass in Christendom. When a thing is close under my nose I can't see it. I get a telescope, and look for the explanation in Stapley. I deserve to be crucified upside-down, as a cure for anæmia of the brain. Jerry! Jerry! But, naturally, of course, you rotten ass, isn't it obvious? Silly old blighter. Why couldn't he tell Murbles or me?"

Mr. Bunter advanced, the picture of respectful inquiry.

"Look at it—look at it!" said Wimsey, with a hysterical squeak of laughter. "O Lord! O Lord! Stuck into the window-frame for anybody to find. *Just* like Jerry. Signs his name to the business in letters a foot long, leaves it conspicuously about, and then goes away and is chivalrously silent."

Mr. Bunter put the jug down upon the washstand in case of accident, and took the paper.

It was the missing letter from Tommy Freeborn.

No doubt about it. There it was—the evidence which established the truth of Denver's evidence. More—which established his alibi for the night of the 13th.

Not Cathcart—Denver.

Denver suggesting that the shooting party should return in October to Riddlesdale, where they had opened the grouse season in August. Denver sneaking hurriedly out at 11.30 to walk two miles across the fields on a night when Farmer Grimethorpe had gone to buy machinery. Denver carelessly plugging a rattling sash on a stormy night with an important letter bearing his title on it for all to see. Denver padding back at three in the morning like a homing tom-cat, to fall over his guest's dead body by the conservatory. Denver, with his kind, stupid, English-gentleman ideas about honour, going obstinately off to prison, rather than tell his solicitor where he had been. Denver misleading them all into the wildest and most ingenious solutions of a mystery which now stood out clear as seven sunbeams. Denver, whose voice the woman had thought she recognised on the memorable day when she flung herself into the arms of his brother. Denver calmly setting in motion the enormous, creaking machinery of a trial by his noble peers in order to safeguard a woman's reputation.

This very day, probably, a Select Committee of lords was sitting "to inspect the Journals of this House upon former trials of peers in criminal cases, in order to bring the Duke of Denver to a speedy trial, and to report to the House what they should think proper thereupon." There they were: moving that an address be presented to His

Majesty by the lords with white staves, to acquaint His Majesty of the date proposed for the trial; arranging for fitting up the Royal Gallery at Westminster; humbly requesting the attendance of a sufficient police force to keep clear the approaches leading to the House; petitioning His Majesty graciously to appoint a Lord High Steward; ordering, in sheeplike accordance with precedent, that all lords be summoned to attend in their robes; that every lord, in giving judgment, disclose his opinion upon his honour, laying his right hand upon his heart; that the Sergeant-at-Arms be within the House to make proclamations in the King's name for keeping silence—and so on, and on, unendingly. And there, jammed in the window-sash, was the dirty little bit of paper which, discovered earlier, would have made the whole monstrous ceremonial unnecessary.

Wimsey's adventure in the bog had unsettled his nerves. He sat down on the bed and laughed, with the tears streaming down his face.

Mr. Bunter was speechless. Speechlessly he produced a razor—and to the end of his days Wimsey never knew how or from whom he had so adequately procured it—and began to strop it thoughtfully upon the palm of his hand.

Presently Wimsey pulled himself together and staggered to the window for a little cooling draught of moor air. As he did so, a loud hullabaloo smote his ear, and he perceived, in the courtyard below, Farmer Grimethorpe striding among his dogs; when they howled he struck at them with a whip, and they howled again. Suddenly he glanced up at the window, with an expression of such livid hatred that Wimsey stepped hurriedly back as though struck.

While Bunter shaved him he was silent.

.   .   .   .   .

The interview before Lord Peter was a delicate one; the situation, however one looked at it, unpleasant. He was under a considerable debt of gratitude to his hostess; on the other hand, Denver's position was such that minor considerations really had to go to the wall. His lordship had, nevertheless, never felt quite such a cad as he did while descending the staircase at Grider's Hole.

In the big farm kitchen he found a stout country-woman, stirring a pot of stew. He asked for Mr. Grimethorpe, and was told that he had gone out.

"Can I speak to Mrs. Grimethorpe, please?"

The woman looked doubtfully at him, wiped her hands on her apron, and, going into the scullery, shouted, "Mrs. Grimethorpe!" A voice replied from somewhere outside.

"Gentleman wants see tha."

"Where is Mrs. Grimethorpe?" broke in Peter hurriedly.

"I' t'dairy, recken."

"I'll go to her there," said Wimsey, stepping briskly out. He passed through a stone-paved scullery, and across a yard, in time to see Mrs. Grimethorpe emerging from a dark doorway opposite.

Framed there, the cold sunlight just lighting upon her still, dead-white face and heavy, dark hair, she was more wonderful than ever. There was no trace of Yorkshire descent in the long, dark eyes and curled mouth. The curve of nose and cheekbones vouched for an origin immensely remote; coming out of the darkness, she might have just risen from her far tomb in the Pyramids, dropping the dry and perfumed grave-bands from her fingers.

Lord Peter pulled himself together.

"Foreign," he said to himself matter-of-factly. "Touch of Jew perhaps, or Spanish, is it? Remarkable type. Don't blame Jerry. Couldn't live with Helen myself. Now for it."

He advanced quickly.

"Good morning," she said, "are you better?"

"Perfectly all right, thank you—thanks to your kindness, which I do not know how to repay."

"You will repay any kindness best by going at once," she answered in her remote voice. "My husband does not care for strangers, and 'twas unfortunate the way you met before."

"I will go directly. But I must first beg for the favour of a word with you." He peered past her into the dimness of the dairy. "In here, perhaps?"

"What do you want with me?"

She stepped back, however, and allowed him to follow her in.

"Mrs. Grimethorpe, I am placed in a most painful position. You know that my brother, the Duke of Denver, is in prison, awaiting his trial for a murder which took place on the night of October 13th?"

Her face did not change. "I have heard so."

"He has, in the most decided manner, refused to state where he was between eleven and three on that night. His refusal has brought him into great danger of his life."

She looked at him steadily.

160

"He feels bound in honour not to disclose his whereabouts, though I know that, if he chose to speak, he could bring a witness to clear him."

"He seems to be a very honourable man." The cold voice wavered a trifle, then steadied again.

"Yes. Undoubtedly, from his point of view, he is doing the right thing. You will understand, however, that, as his brother, I am naturally anxious to have the matter put in its proper light."

"I don't understand why you are telling me all this. I suppose, if the thing is disgraceful, he doesn't want it known."

"Obviously. But to us—to his wife and young son, and to his sister and myself—his life and safety are matters of the first importance."

"Of more importance than his honour?"

"The secret is a disgraceful one in a sense, and will give pain to his family. But it would be an infinitely greater disgrace that he should be executed for murder. The stigma in that case would involve all those who bear his name. The shame of the truth will, I fear, in this very unjust society of ours, rest more upon the witness to his alibi than upon himself."

"Can you in that case expect the witness to come forward?"

"To prevent the condemnation of an innocent man? Yes, I think I may venture to expect even that."

"I repeat—why are you telling me all this?"

"Because, Mrs. Grimethorpe, you know, even better than I, how innocent my brother is of this murder. Believe me, I am deeply distressed at having to say these things to you."

"I know nothing about your brother."

"Forgive me, that is not true."

"I know nothing. And surely, if the Duke will not speak, you should respect his reasons."

"I am not bound in any way."

"I am afraid I cannot help you. You are wasting time. If you cannot produce your missing witness, why do you not set about finding the real murderer? If you do so you surely need not trouble about this alibi. Your brother's movements are his own business."

"I could wish," said Wimsey, "you had not taken up this attitude. Believe me, I would have done all I could to spare you. I have been working hard to find, as you say, the real murderer, but with no success. The trial will probably take place at the end of the month."

Her lips twitched a little at that, but she said nothing.

"I had hoped that with your help we might agree on some explanation—less than the truth, perhaps, but sufficient to clear my brother. As it is, I fear I shall have to produce the proof I hold, and let matters take their course."

That, at last, struck under her guard. A dull flush crept up her cheeks; one hand tightened upon the handle of the churn, where she had rested it.

"What do you mean by proof?"

"I can prove that on the night of the 13th my brother slept in the room I occupied last night," said Wimsey, with calculated brutality.

She winced. "It is a lie. You cannot prove it. He will deny it. I shall deny it."

"He was not there?"

"No."

"Then how did this come to be wedged in the sash of the bedroom window?"

At sight of the letter she broke down, crumpling up in a heap against the table. The set lines of her face distorted themselves into a mere caricature of terror.

"No, no, no! It is a lie! God help me!"

"Hush!" said Wimsey peremptorily. "Someone will hear you." He dragged her to her feet. "Tell the truth, and we will see if we can find a way out. It is true—he was here that night?"

"You know it."

"When did he come?"

"At a quarter past twelve."

"Who let him in?"

"He had the keys."

"When did he leave you?"

"A little after two."

"Yes, that fits in all right. Three quarters of an hour to go and three quarters to come back. He stuck this into the window, I suppose, to keep it from rattling?"

"There was a high wind—I was nervous. I thought every sound was my husband coming back."

"Where was your husband?"

"At Stapley."

"Had he suspected this?"

"Yes, for some time."

"Since my brother was here in August?"

162

"Yes. But he could get no proof. If he had had proof he would have killed me. You have seen him. He is a devil."

"M'm."

Wimsey was silent. The woman glanced fearfully at his face and seemed to read some hope there, for she clutched him by the arm.

"If you call me to give evidence," she said, "he will know. He *will* kill me. For God's sake, have pity. That letter is my death-warrant. Oh, for the mother that bore you, have mercy upon me. My life is a hell, and when I die I shall go to hell for my sin. Find some other way—you can—you must."

Wimsey gently released himself.

"Don't do that, Mrs. Grimethorpe. We might be seen. I am deeply sorry for you, and, if I can get my brother out of this without bringing you in, I promise you I will. But you see the difficulty. Why don't you leave this man? He is openly brutal to you."

She laughed.

"Do you think he'd leave me alive while the law was slowly releasing me? Knowing him, do you think so?"

Wimsey really did not think so.

"I will promise you this, Mrs. Grimethorpe. I will do all I can to avoid having to use your evidence. But if there should be no other way, I will see that you have police protection from the moment that the subpœna is served on you."

"And for the rest of my life?"

"When you are once in London we will see about freeing you from this man."

"No. If you call upon me, I am a lost woman. But you will find another way?"

"I will try, but I can promise nothing. I will do everything that is possible to protect you. If you care at all for my brother——"

"I don't know. I am so horribly afraid. He was kind and good to me. He was—so different. But I am afraid—I'm afraid."

Wimsey turned. Her terrified eyes had seen the shadow cross the threshold. Grimethorpe was at the door, glowering in upon them.

"Ah, Mr. Grimethorpe," exclaimed Wimsey cheerfully, "there you are. Awfully pleased to see you and thank you, don'tcherknow, for puttin' me up. I was just saying so to Mrs. Grimethorpe, an' asking her to say good-bye to you for me. Must be off now, I'm afraid. Bunter and I are ever so grateful to you both for all your kindness. Oh, and I say, could you find me the stout fellows who hauled us out of that Pot of yours last night—if it is yours. Nasty, damp thing to keep outside the front door, what? I'd like to thank 'em."

"Dom good thing for unwelcome guests," said the man ferociously. "An' tha'd better be off afore Ah throws thee out."

"I'm just off," said Peter. "Good-bye again, Mrs. Grimethorpe, and a thousand thanks."

He collected Bunter, rewarded his rescuers suitably, took an affectionate farewell of the enraged farmer, and departed, sore in body and desperately confused in mind.

CHAPTER XIII

MANON

"That one word, my dear Watson, should have told me the whole story, had I been the ideal reasoner which you are so fond of depicting."—Memoirs of Sherlock Holmes.

"THANK GOD," said Parker. "Well, that settles it."

"It does—and yet again, it doesn't," retorted Lord Peter. He leaned back against the fat silk cushion in the sofa corner meditatively.

"Of course, it's disagreeable having to give this woman away," said Parker sensibly and pleasantly, "but these things have to be done."

"I know. It's all simply awfully nice and all that. And Jerry, who's got the poor woman into this mess, has to be considered first. I know. And if we don't restrain Grimethorpe quite successfully, and he cuts her throat for her, it'll be simply rippin' for Jerry to think of all his life. . . . Jerry! I say, you know, what frightful idiots we were not to see the truth right off! I mean—of course, my sister-in-law is an awfully good woman, and all that, but Mrs. Grimethorpe—whew! I told you about the time she mistook me for Jerry. One crowded, split second of glorious all-overishness. I ought to have known then. Our voices are alike, of course, and she couldn't see in that dark kitchen. I don't believe there's an ounce of any feeling left in the woman except sheer terror—but, ye gods! what eyes and skin! Well, never mind. Some undeserving fellows have all the luck. Have you got

164

any really good stories? No? Well, I'll tell you some—enlarge your mind and all that. Do you know the rhyme about the young man at the War Office?"

Mr. Parker endured five stories with commendable patience, and then suddenly broke down.

"Hurray!" said Wimsey. "Splendid man! I love to see you melt into a refined snigger from time to time. I'll spare you the really outrageous one about the young housewife and the traveller in bicycle-pumps. You know, Charles, I really *should* like to know who did Cathcart in. Legally, it's enough to prove Jerry innocent, but, Mrs. Grimethorpe or no Mrs. Grimethorpe, it doesn't do us credit in a professional capacity. 'The father weakens, but the governor is firm'; that is, as a brother I am satisfied—I may say light-hearted—but as a sleuth I am cast down, humiliated, thrown back upon myself, a lodge in a garden of cucumbers. Besides, of all defences an alibi is the most awkward to establish, unless a number of independent and disinterested witnesses combine to make it thoroughly air-tight. If Jerry sticks to his denial, the most they can be sure of is that *either* he *or* Mrs. Grimethorpe is being chivalrous."

"But you've got the letter."

"Yes. But how are we going to prove that it came that evening? The envelope is destroyed. Fleming remembers nothing about it. Jerry might have received it days earlier. Or it might be a complete fake. Who is to say that I didn't put it in the window myself and pretend to find it. After all, I'm hardly what you would call disinterested."

"Bunter saw you find it."

"He didn't, Charles. At that precise moment he was out of the room fetching shaving-water."

"Oh, was he?"

"Moreover, only Mrs. Grimethorpe can swear to what is really the important point—the moment of Jerry's arrival and departure. Unless he was at Grider's Hole before 12.30 at least, it's immaterial whether he was there or not."

"Well," said Parker, "can't we keep Mrs. Grimethorpe up our sleeve, so to speak——"

"Sounds a bit abandoned," said Lord Peter, "but we will keep her with pleasure if you like."

"—and meanwhile," pursued Mr. Parker, unheeding, "do our best to find the actual criminal?"

"Oh, yes," said Lord Peter, "and that reminds me. I made a discovery at the Lodge—at least, I think so. Did you notice that somebody had been forcing one of the study windows?"

"No, really?"

"Yes; I found distinct marks. Of course, it was a long time after the murder, but there were scratches on the catch all right—the sort of thing a penknife would leave."

"What fools we were not to make an examination at the time!"

"Come to think of it, why should you have? Anyhow, I asked Fleming about it, and he said he did remember, now he came to think of it, that on the Thursday morning he'd found the window open, and couldn't account for it. And here's another thing. I've had a letter from my friend Tim Watchett. Here it is:

"My Lord.—About our conversation. I have found a Man who was with the Party in question at the 'Pig and Whistle' on the night of the 13th ult. and he tells me that the Party borrowed his bicycle, and same was found afterwards in the ditch where Party was picked up with the Handlebars bent and wheels buckled.

"Trusting to the Continuance of your esteemed favour.

"Timothy Watchett."

"What do you think of that?"

"Good enough to go on," said Parker. "At least, we are no longer hampered with horrible doubts."

"No. And, though she's my sister, I must say that of all the blithering she-asses Mary is the blitheringest. Taking up with that awful bounder to start with——"

"She was jolly fine about it," said Mr. Parker, getting rather red in the face. "It's just because she's your sister that you can't appreciate what a fine thing she did. How should a big, chivalrous nature like hers see through a man like that? She's so sincere and thorough herself, she judges everyone by the same standard. She wouldn't believe anybody could be so thin and wobbly-minded as Goyles till it was *proved* to her. And even then she couldn't bring herself to think ill of him till he'd given himself away out of his own mouth. It was wonderful, the way she fought for him. Think what it must have meant to such a splendid, straight-forward woman to——"

"All right, all right," cried Peter, who had been staring at his friend, transfixed with astonishment. "Don't get worked up. I believe you. Spare me. I'm only a brother. All brothers are fools. All lovers are lunatics—Shakespeare says so. Do you want Mary, old man? You surprise me, but I believe brothers always are surprised. Bless you, dear children!"

"Damn it all, Wimsey," said Parker, very angry, "you've no right to talk like that. I only said how greatly I admired your sister—everyone must admire such pluck and staunchness. You needn't be insulting. I know she's Lady Mary Wimsey and damnably rich, and I'm only a common police official with nothing a year and a pension to look forward to, but there's no need to sneer about it."

"I'm not sneering," retorted Peter indignantly. "I can't imagine why anybody should want to marry my sister, but you're a friend of mine and a damn good sort, and you've my good word for what it's worth. Besides—dash it all, man!—to put it on the lowest grounds, do look what it might have been! A Socialist Conchy of neither bowels nor breeding, or a card-sharping dark horse with a mysterious past! Mother and Jerry must have got to the point when they'd welcome a decent, God-fearing plumber, let alone a policeman. Only thing I'm afraid of is that Mary, havin' such beastly bad taste in blokes, won't know how to appreciate a really decent fellow like you, old son."

Mr. Parker begged his friend's pardon for his unworthy suspicions, and they sat a little time in silence. Parker sipped his port, and saw unimaginable visions warmly glowing in its rosy depths. Wimsey pulled out his pocket-book, and began idly turning over its contents, throwing old letters into the fire, unfolding and refolding memoranda, and reviewing a miscellaneous series of other people's visiting-cards. He came at length to the slip of blotting-paper from the study at Riddlesdale, to whose fragmentary markings he had since given scarcely a thought.

Presently Mr. Parker, finishing his port and recalling his mind with an effort, remembered that he had been meaning to tell Peter something before the name of Lady Mary had driven all other thoughts out of his head. He turned to his host, open-mouthed for speech, but his remark never got beyond a preliminary click like that of a clock about to strike, for, even as he turned, Lord Peter brought his fist down on the little table with a bang that made the decanters ring, and cried out in the loud voice of complete and sudden enlightenment:

"*Manon Lescaut!*"

"Eh?" said Mr. Parker.

"Boil my brains!" said Lord Peter. "Boil 'em and mash 'em and serve 'em up with butter as a dish of turnips, for it's damn well all they're fit for! Look at me!" (Mr. Parker scarcely needed this exhortation.) "Here we've been worryin' over Jerry, an' worryin' over Mary, an' huntin' for Goyleses an' Grimethorpes and God knows who —and all the time I'd got this little bit of paper tucked away in my pocket. The blot upon the paper's rim a blotted paper was to him, and it was nothing more. But Manon, Manon! Charles, if I'd had the grey matter of a woodlouse that book ought to have told me the whole story. And think what we'd have been saved!"

"I wish you wouldn't be so excited," said Parker. "I'm sure it's perfectly splendid for you to see your way so clearly, but I never read *Manon Lescaut,* and you haven't shown me the blotting-paper, and I haven't the foggiest idea what you've discovered."

Lord Peter passed the relic over without comment.

"I observe," said Parker, "that the paper is rather crumpled and dirty, and smells powerfully of tobacco and Russian leather, and deduce that you have been keeping it in your pocket-book."

"No!" said Wimsey incredulously. "And when you actually saw me take it out! Holmes, how do you do it?"

"At one corner," pursued Parker, "I see two blots, one rather larger than the other. I think someone must have shaken a pen there. Is there anything sinister about the blot?"

"I haven't noticed anything."

"Some way below the blots the Duke has signed his name two or three times—or, rather, his title. The inference is that his letters were not to intimates."

"The inference is justifiable, I fancy."

"Colonel Marchbanks has a neat signature."

"He can hardly mean mischief," said Peter. "He signs his name like an honest man! Proceed."

"There's a sprawly message about five something of fine something. Do you see anything occult there?"

"The number five may have a cabalistic meaning, but I admit I don't know what it is. There are five senses, five fingers, five great Chinese precepts, five books of Moses, to say nothing of the mysterious entities hymned in the Dilly Song—'Five are the flamboys under the pole.' I must admit that I have always panted to know what the five flamboys were. But, not knowing, I get no help from it in this case."

"Well, that's all, except a fragment consisting of 'oe' on one line, and 'is fou—' below it."

"What do you make of that?"

" 'Is found,' I suppose."

"Do you?"

"That seems the simplest interpretation. Or possibly 'his foul'— there seems to have been a sudden rush of ink to the pen just there. Do you think it is 'his foul'? Was the Duke writing about Cathcart's foul play? Is that what you mean?"

"No, I don't make that of it. Besides, I don't think it's Jerry's writing."

"Whose is it?"

"I don't know, but I can guess."

"And it leads somewhere?"

"It tells the whole story."

"Oh, cough it up, Wimsey. Even Dr. Watson would lose patience."

"Tut, tut! Try the line above."

"Well, there's only 'oe.' "

"Yes, well?"

"Well, I don't know. Poet, poem, manœuvre, Loeb edition, Citroen—it might be anything."

"Dunno about that. There aren't lashings of English words with 'oe' in them—and it's written so close it almost looks like a diphthong at that."

"Perhaps it isn't an English word."

"Exactly; perhaps it isn't."

"Oh! Oh, I see. French?"

"Ah, you're gettin' warm."

"*Sœur—œuvre—œuf—bœuf*——"

"No, no. You were nearer the first time."

"*Sœur—cœur!*"

"*Cœur*. Hold on a moment. Look at the scratch in front of that."

"Wait a bit—*er—cer*——"

"How about *percer?*"

"I believe you're right. '*Percer le cœur*.' "

"Yes. Or '*perceras le cœur*.' "

"That's better. It seems to need another letter or two."

"And now your 'is found' line."

"*Fou!*"

"Who?"

"I didn't say 'who'; I said '*fou.*' "

"I know you did. I said who?"

"Who?"

"Who's *fou?*"

"Oh, *is.* By Jove, '*suis*'! '*Je suis fou.*' "

"*A la bonne heure!* And I suggest that the next words are '*de douleur,*' or something like it."

"They might be."

"Cautious beast! I say they are."

"Well, and suppose they are?"

"It tells us everything."

"Nothing!"

"Everything, I say. Think. This was written on the day Cathcart died. Now who in the house would be likely to write these words, '*perceras le cœur . . . je suis fou de douleur*'? Take everybody. I know it isn't Jerry's fist, and he wouldn't use those expressions. Colonel or Mrs. Marchbanks? Not Pygmalion likely! Freddy? Couldn't write passionate letters in French to save his life."

"No, of course not. It would have to be either Cathcart or—Lady Mary."

"Rot! It couldn't be Mary."

"Why not?"

"Not unless she changed her sex, you know."

"Of course not. It would have to be '*je suis folle.*' Then Cathcart——"

"Of course. He lived in France all his life. Consider his bank-book. Consider——"

"Lord! Wimsey, we've been blind."

"Yes."

"And listen! I was going to tell you. The Sûreté write me that they've traced one of Cathcart's bank-notes."

"Where to?"

"To a Mr. François who owns a lot of house property near the Etoile."

"And lets it out in *appartements!*"

"No doubt."

"When's the next train? Bunter!"

"My lord!"

Mr. Bunter hurried to the door at the call.

"The next boat-train for Paris?"

"Eight-twenty, my lord, from Waterloo."

"We're going by it. How long?"

"Twenty minutes, my lord."

"Pack my toothbrush and call a taxi."

"Certainly, my lord."

"But, Wimsey, what light does it throw on Cathcart's murder? Did this woman——"

"I've no time," said Wimsey hurriedly. "But I'll be back in a day or two. Meanwhile——"

He hunted hastily in the bookshelf.

"Read this."

He flung the book at his friend and plunged into his bedroom.

At eleven o'clock, as a gap of dirty water disfigured with oil and bits of paper widened between the *Normannia* and the quay; while hardened passengers fortified their sea-stomachs with cold ham and pickles, and the more nervous studied the Boddy jackets in their cabins; while the harbour lights winked and swam right and left, and Lord Peter scraped acquaintance with a second-rate cinema actor in the bar, Charles Parker sat, with a puzzled frown, before the fire at 110 Piccadilly, making his first acquaintance with the delicate master-piece of the Abbé Prévost.

CHAPTER XIV

THE EDGE OF THE AXE TOWARDS HIM

Scene I. *Westminster Hall. Enter as to the Parliament, Bolingbroke, Aumerle, Northumberland, Percy, Fitz-water, Surrey, the Bishop of Carlisle, the Abbot of Westminster, and another Lord, Herald, Officers, and Bagot.*

BOLINGBROKE: Call forth Bagot.
Now, Bagot, freely speak thy mind;
What thou dost know of noble Gloucester's death;
Who wrought it with the king, and who performed
The bloody office of his timeless end.

BAGOT: Then set before my face the Lord Aumerle.
King Richard II.

THE HISTORIC TRIAL of the Duke of Denver for murder opened as soon as Parliament reassembled after the Christmas vacation. The papers had leaderettes on "Trial by his Peers," by a Woman Barrister, and "The Privilege of Peers: should it be abolished?" by a Student of History. The *Evening Banner* got into trouble for contempt by publishing an article entitled "The Silken Rope" (by an Antiquarian), which was deemed to be prejudicial, and the *Daily Trumpet*—the Labour organ—inquired sarcastically why, when a peer was tried, the fun of seeing the show should be reserved to the few influential persons who could wangle tickets for the Royal Gallery.

Mr. Murbles and Detective Inspector Parker, in close consultation, went about with preoccupied faces, while Sir Impey Biggs retired into a complete eclipse for three days, revolved about by Mr. Glibbery, K.C., Mr. Brownrigg-Fortescue, K.C., and a number of lesser satellites. The schemes of the Defence were kept dark indeed

172

—the more so that they found themselves on the eve of the struggle deprived of their principal witness, and wholly ignorant whether or not he would be forthcoming with his testimony.

Lord Peter had returned from Paris at the end of four days, and had burst in like a cyclone at Great Ormond Street. "I've got it," he said, "but it's touch and go. Listen!"

For an hour Parker had listened, feverishly taking notes.

"You can work on that," said Wimsey. "Tell Murbles. I'm off."

His next appearance was at the American Embassy. The Ambassador, however, was not there, having received a royal mandate to dine. Wimsey damned the dinner, abandoned the polite, horn-rimmed secretaries, and leapt back into his taxi with a demand to be driven to Buckingham Palace. Here a great deal of insistence with scandalised officials produced first a higher official, then a very high official, and, finally, the American Ambassador and a Royal Personage while the meat was yet in their mouths.

"Oh, yes," said the Ambassador, "of course it can be done——"

"Surely, surely," said the Personage genially, "we mustn't have any delay. Might cause an international misunderstanding, and a lot of paragraphs about Ellis Island. Terrible nuisance to have to adjourn the trial—dreadful fuss, isn't it? Our secretaries are everlastingly bringing things along to our place to sign about extra policemen and seating accommodation. Good luck to you, Wimsey! Come and have something while they get your papers through. When does your boat go?"

"To-morrow morning, sir. I'm catching the Liverpool train in an hour—if I can."

"You surely will," said the Ambassador cordially, signing a note. "And they say the English can't hustle."

So, with his papers all in order, his lordship set sail from Liverpool the next morning, leaving his legal representatives to draw up alternative schemes of defence.

.   .   .   .   .

"Then the peers, two by two, in their order, beginning with the youngest baron."

Garter King-of-Arms, very hot and bothered, fussed unhappily around the three hundred or so British peers who were sheepishly struggling into their robes, while the heralds did their best to line up the assembly and keep them from wandering away when once arranged.

"Of all the farces!" grumbled Lord Attenbury irritably. He was a very short, stout gentleman of a choleric countenance, and was annoyed to find himself next to the Earl of Strathgillan and Begg, an extremely tall, lean nobleman, with pronounced views on Prohibition and the Legitimation question.

"I say, Attenbury," said a kindly, brick-red peer, with five rows of ermine on his shoulder, "is it true that Wimsey hasn't come back? My daughter tells me she heard he'd gone to collect evidence in the States. Why the States?"

"Dunno," said Attenbury; "but Wimsey's a dashed clever fellow. When he found those emeralds of mine, you know, I said——"

"Your grace, your grace," cried Rouge Dragon desperately, diving in, "your grace is out of line again."

"Eh, what?" said the brick-faced peer. "Oh, damme! Must obey orders, I suppose, what?" And was towed away from the mere earls and pushed into position next to the Duke of Wiltshire, who was deaf, and a distant connection of Denver's on the distaff side.

The Royal Gallery was packed. In the seats reserved below the Bar for peeresses sat the Dowager Duchess of Denver, beautifully dressed and defiant. She suffered much from the adjacent presence of her daughter-in-law, whose misfortune it was to become disagreeable when she was unhappy—perhaps the heaviest curse that can be laid on man, who is born to sorrow.

Behind the imposing array of Counsel in full-bottomed wigs in the body of the hall were seats reserved for witnesses, and here Mr. Bunter was accommodated—to be called if the defence should find it necessary to establish the alibi—the majority of the witnesses being pent up in the King's Robing-Room, gnawing their fingers and glaring at one another. On either side, above the Bar, were the benches for the peers—each in his own right a judge both of fact and law—while on the high dais the great chair of state stood ready for the Lord High Steward.

The reporters at their little table were beginning to fidget and look at their watches. Muffled by the walls and the buzz of talk, Big Ben dropped eleven slow notes into the suspense. A door opened. The reporters started to their feet; Counsel rose; everybody rose; the Dowager Duchess whispered irrepressibly to her neighbour that it reminded her of the Voice that breathed o'er Eden; and the procession streamed slowly in, lit by a shaft of wintry sunshine from the tall windows.

The proceedings were opened by a Proclamation of Silence from the Sergeant-at-Arms, after which the Clerk of the Crown in Chancery, kneeling at the foot of the throne, presented the Commission under the Great Seal to the Lord High Steward,* who, finding no use for it, returned it with great solemnity to the Clerk of the Crown. The latter accordingly proceeded to read it at dismal and wearisome length, affording the assembly an opportunity of judging just how bad the acoustics of the chamber were. The Sergeant-at-Arms retorted with great emphasis, "God Save the King," whereupon Garter King-of-Arms and the Gentleman Usher of the Black Rod, kneeling again, handed the Lord High Steward his staff of office. ("So picturesque, isn't it?" said the Dowager—"quite High Church, you know.")

The Certiorari and Return followed in a long, sonorous rigmarole, which, starting with George the Fifth by the Grace of God, called upon all the Justices and Judges of the Old Bailey, enumerated the Lord Mayor of London, the Recorder, and a quantity of assorted aldermen and justices, skipped back to our Lord the King, roamed about the City of London, Counties of London and Middlesex, Essex, Kent, and Surrey, mentioned our late Sovereign Lord King William the Fourth, branched off to the Local Government Act one thousand eight hundred and eighty-eight, lost its way in a list of all treasons, murders, felonies, and misdemeanours by whomsoever and in what manner soever done, committed or perpetrated and by whom or to whom, when, how and after what manner and of all other articles and circumstances concerning the premises and every one of them and any of them in any manner whatsoever, and at last, triumphantly, after reciting the names of the whole Grand Jury, came to the presentation of the indictment with a sudden, brutal brevity.

"The Jurors for our Lord the King upon their oaths present that the most noble and puissant prince Gerald Christian Wimsey, Viscount St. George, Duke of Denver, a Peer of the United Kingdom of Great Britain and Ireland, on the thirteenth day of October in the year of Our Lord one thousand nine hundred and twenty—in the Parish of Riddlesdale in the County of Yorkshire did kill and murder Denis Cathcart."

* The Lord Chancellor held the appointment on this occasion as usual.

"After which, Proclamation* was made by the Sergeant-at-Arms for the Gentleman Usher of the Black Rod to call in Gerald Christian Wimsey, Viscount St. George, Duke of Denver, to appear at the Bar to answer his indictment, who, being come to the Bar, kneeled until the Lord High Steward acquainted him that he might rise."

The Duke of Denver looked very small and pink and lonely in his blue serge suit, the only head uncovered among all his peers, but he was not without a certain dignity as he was conducted to the "Stool placed within the Bar," which is deemed appropriate to noble prisoners, and he listened to the Lord High Steward's rehearsal of the charge with a simple gravity which became him very well.

"Then the said Duke of Denver was arraigned by the Clerk of the Parliaments in the usual manner and asked whether he was Guilty or Not Guilty, to which he pleaded Not Guilty."

Whereupon Sir Wigmore Wrinching, the Attorney-General, rose to open the case for the Crown.

After the usual preliminaries to the effect that the case was a very painful one and the occasion a very solemn one, Sir Wigmore proceeded to unfold the story from the beginning: the quarrel, the shot at 3 a.m., the pistol, the finding of the body, the disappearance of the letter, and the rest of the familiar tale. He hinted, moreover, that evidence would be called to show that the quarrel between Denver and Cathcart had motives other than those alleged by the prisoner, and that the latter would turn out to have had "good reason to fear exposure at Cathcart's hands." At which point the accused was observed to glance uneasily at his solicitor. The exposition took only a short time, and Sir Wigmore proceeded to call witnesses.

The prosecution being unable to call the Duke of Denver, the first important witness was Lady Mary Wimsey. After telling about her relations with the murdered man, and describing the quarrel, "At three o'clock," she proceeded, "I got up and went downstairs."

"In consequence of what did you do so?" inquired Sir Wigmore, looking round the Court with the air of a man about to produce his great effect.

"In consequence of an appointment I had made to meet a friend."

All the reporters looked up suddenly, like dogs expecting a piece of biscuit, and Sir Wigmore started so violently that he knocked his

* For Report of the procedure see House of Lords Journal for the dates in question.

brief over upon the head of the Clerk to the House of Lords sitting below him.

"Indeed! Now, witness, remember you are on your oath, and be very careful. What was it caused you to wake at three o'clock?"

"I was not asleep. I was waiting for my appointment."

"And while you were waiting did you hear anything?"

"Nothing at all."

"Now, Lady Mary, I have here your deposition sworn before the Coroner. I will read it to you. Please listen very carefully. You say, 'At three o'clock I was wakened by a shot. I thought it might be poachers. It sounded very loud, close to the house. I went down to find out what it was.' Do you remember making that statement?"

"Yes, but it was not true."

"Not true?"

"No."

"In the face of that statement, you still say that you heard nothing at three o'clock?"

"I heard nothing at all. I went down because I had an appointment."

"My lords," said Sir Wigmore, with a very red face. "I must ask leave to treat this witness as a hostile witness."

Sir Wigmore's fiercest onslaught, however, produced no effect, except a reiteration of the statement that no shot had been heard at any time. With regard to the finding of the body, Lady Mary explained that when she said, "Oh, God! Gerald, you've killed him," she was under the impression that the body was that of the friend who had made the appointment. Here a fierce wrangle ensued as to whether the story of the appointment was relevant. The Lords decided that on the whole it was relevant; and the entire Goyles story came out, together with the intimation that Mr. Goyles was in court and could be produced. Eventually, with a loud snort, Sir Wigmore Wrinching gave up the witness to Sir Impey Biggs, who, rising suavely and looking extremely handsome, brought back the discussion to a point long previous.

"Forgive the nature of the question," said Sir Impey, bowing blandly, "but will you tell us whether, in your opinion, the late Captain Cathcart was deeply in love with you?"

"No, I am sure he was not; it was an arrangement for our mutual convenience."

"From your knowledge of his character, do you suppose he was capable of a very deep affection?"

"I think he might have been, for the right woman. I should say he had a very passionate nature."

"Thank you. You have told us that you met Captain Cathcart several times when you were staying in Paris last February. Do you remember going with him to a jeweller's—Monsieur Briquet's in the Rue de la Paix?"

"I may have done; I cannot exactly remember."

"The date to which I should like to draw your attention is the sixth."

"I could not say."

"Do you recognise this trinket?"

Here the green-eyed cat was handed to witness.

"No; I have never seen it before."

"Did Captain Cathcart ever give you one like it?"

"Never."

"Did you ever possess such a jewel?"

"I am quite positive I never did."

"My lords, I put in this diamond and platinum cat. Thank you, Lady Mary."

James Fleming, being questioned closely as to the delivery of the post, continued to be vague and forgetful, leaving the Court, on the whole, with the impression that no letter had ever been delivered to the Duke. Sir Wigmore, whose opening speech had contained sinister allusions to an attempt to blacken the character of the victim, smiled disagreeably, and handed the witness over to Sir Impey. The latter contented himself with extracting an admission that witness could not swear positively one way or the other, and passed on immediately to another point.

"Do you recollect whether any letters came by the same post for any of the other members of the party?"

"Yes; I took three or four into the billiard-room."

"Can you say to whom they were addressed?"

"There were several for Colonel Marchbanks and one for Captain Cathcart."

"Did Captain Cathcart open his letter there and then?"

"I couldn't say, sir. I left the room immediately to take his grace's letters to the study."

"Now will you tell us how the letters are collected for the post in the morning at the Lodge?"

"They are put into the post-bag, which is locked. His grace keeps one key and the post-office has the other. The letters are put in through a slit in the top."

"On the morning after Captain Cathcart's death were the letters taken to the post as usual?"

"Yes, sir."

"By whom?"

"I took the bag down myself, sir."

"Had you an opportunity of seeing what letters were in it?"

"I saw there was two or three when the postmistress took 'em out of the bag, but I couldn't say who they was addressed to or anythink of that."

"Thank you."

Sir Wigmore Wrinching here bounced up like a very irritable jack-in-the-box.

"Is this the first time you have mentioned this letter which you say you delivered to Captain Cathcart on the night of his murder?"

"My lords," cried Sir Impey. "I protest against this language. We have as yet had no proof that any murder was committed."

This was the first indication of the line of defence which Sir Impey proposed to take, and caused a little rustle of excitement.

"My lords," went on Counsel, replying to a question of the Lord High Steward, "I submit that so far there has been no attempt to prove murder, and that, until the prosecution have established the murder, such a word cannot properly be put into the mouth of a witness."

"Perhaps, Sir Wigmore, it would be better to use some other word."

"It makes no difference to our case, my lord; I bow to your lordships' decision. Heaven knows that I would not seek, even by the lightest or most trivial word, to hamper the defence on so serious a charge."

"My lords," interjected Sir Impey, "if the learned Attorney-General considers the word murder to be a triviality, it would be interesting to know to what words he does attach importance."

"The learned Attorney-General has agreed to substitute another word," said the Lord High Steward soothingly, and nodding to Sir Wigmore to proceed.

Sir Impey, having achieved his purpose of robbing the Attorney-General's onslaught on the witness of some of its original impetus, sat down, and Sir Wigmore repeated his question.

"I mentioned it first to Mr. Murbles about three weeks ago."

"Mr. Murbles is the solicitor for the accused, I believe."

"Yes, sir."

"And how was it," inquired Sir Wigmore ferociously, settling his pince-nez on his rather prominent nose, and glowering at the witness, "that you did not mention this letter at the inquest or at the earlier proceedings in the case?"

"I wasn't asked about it, sir."

"What made you suddenly decide to go and tell Mr. Murbles about it?"

"He asked me, sir."

"Oh, he asked you; and you conveniently remembered it when it was suggested to you?"

"No, sir. I remembered it all the time. That is to say, I hadn't given any special thought to it, sir."

"Oh, you remembered it all the time, though you hadn't given any thought to it. Now I put it to you that you had not remembered about it at all till it was suggested to you by Mr. Murbles."

"Mr. Murbles didn't suggest nothing, sir. He asked me whether any other letters came by that post, and then I remembered it."

"Exactly. When it was suggested to you, you remembered it, and not before."

"No, sir. That is, if I'd been asked before I should have remembered it and mentioned it, but, not being asked, I didn't think it would be of any importance, sir."

"You didn't think it of any importance that this man received a letter a few hours before his—decease?"

"No, sir. I reckoned if it had been of any importance the police would have asked about it, sir."

"Now, James Fleming, I put it to you again that it never occurred to you that Captain Cathcart might have received a letter the night he died till the idea was put into your head by the defence."

The witness, baffled by this interrogative negative, made a confused reply, and Sir Wigmore, glancing round the house as much as to say, "You see this shifty fellow," proceeded:

"I suppose it didn't occur to you either to mention to the police about the letters in the post-bag?"

"No, sir."

"Why not?"

"I didn't think it was my place, sir."

"Did you think about it at all?"

"No, sir."

"Do you ever think?"

"No, sir—I mean, yes, sir."

"Then will you please think what you are saying now."

"Yes, sir."

"You say that you took all these important letters out of the house without authority and without acquainting the police?"

"I had my orders, sir."

"From whom?"

"They was his grace's orders, sir."

"Ah! His grace's orders. When did you get that order?"

"It was part of my regular duty, sir, to take the bag to the post each morning."

"And did it not occur to you that in a case like this the proper information of the police might be more important than your orders?"

"No, sir."

Sir Wigmore sat down with a disgusted look; and Sir Impey took the witness in hand again.

"Did the thought of this letter delivered to Captain Cathcart never pass through your mind between the day of the death and the day when Mr. Murbles spoke to you about it?"

"Well, it did pass through my mind, in a manner of speaking, sir."

"When was that?"

"Before the Grand Jury, sir."

"And how was it you didn't speak about it then?"

"The gentleman said I was to confine myself to the questions, and not say nothing on my own, sir."

"Who was this very peremptory gentleman?"

"The lawyer that came down to ask questions for the Crown, sir."

"Thank you," said Sir Impey smoothly, sitting down, and leaning over to say something, apparently of an amusing nature, to Mr. Glibbery.

The question of the letter was further pursued in the examination of the Hon. Freddy. Sir Wigmore Wrinching laid great stress upon this witness's assertion that deceased had been in excellent health and spirits when retiring to bed on the Wednesday evening, and had spoken of his approaching marriage. "He seemed particularly cheerio, you know," said the Hon. Freddy.

"Particularly what?" inquired the Lord High Steward.

"Cheerio, my lord," said Sir Wigmore, with a deprecatory bow.

"I do not know whether that is a dictionary word," said his lordship, entering it upon his notes with meticulous exactness, "but I take it to be synonymous with cheerful."

The Hon. Freddy, appealed to, said he thought he meant more than just cheerful, more merry and bright, you know.

"May we take it that he was in exceptionally lively spirits?" suggested Counsel.

"Take it in any spirit you like," muttered the witness, adding, more happily, "Take a peg of John Begg."

"The deceased was particularly lively and merry when he went to bed," said Sir Wigmore, frowning horribly, "and looking forward to his marriage in the near future. Would that be a fair statement of his condition?"

The Hon. Freddy agreed to this.

Sir Impey did not cross-examine as to witness's account of the quarrel, but went straight to his point.

"Do you recollect anything about the letters that were brought in the night of the death?"

"Yes; I had one from my aunt. The Colonel had some, I fancy, and there was one for Cathcart."

"Did Captain Cathcart read his letter there and then?"

"No, I'm sure he didn't. You see, I opened mine, and then I saw he was shoving his away in his pocket, and I thought——"

"Never mind what you thought," said Sir Impey. "What did you do?"

"I said, 'Excuse me, you don't mind, do you?' And he said, 'Not at all'; but he didn't read his; and I remember thinking——"

"We can't have that, you know," said the Lord High Steward.

"But that's why I'm so sure he didn't open it," said the Hon. Freddy, hurt. "You see, I said to myself at the time what a secretive fellow he was, and that's how I know."

Sir Wigmore, who had bounced up with his mouth open, sat down again.

"Thank you, Mr. Arbuthnot," said Sir Impey, smiling.

Colonel and Mrs. Marchbanks testified to having heard movements in the Duke's study at 11.30. They had heard no shot or other noise. There was no cross-examination.

Mr. Pettigrew-Robinson gave a vivid account of the quarrel, and asserted very positively that there could be no mistaking the sound of the Duke's bedroom door.

"We were then called up by Mr. Arbuthnot at a little after 3 a.m.," proceeded witness, "and went down to the conservatory, where I saw the accused and Mr. Arbuthnot washing the face of the deceased. I pointed out to them what an unwise thing it was to do this, as they might be destroying valuable evidence for the police. They paid no attention to me. There were a number of footmarks round about the door which I wanted to examine, because it was my theory that——"

"My lords," cried Sir Impey, "we really cannot have this witness's theory."

"Certainly not!" said the Lord High Steward. "Answer the questions, please, and don't add anything on your own account."

"Of course," said Mr. Pettigrew-Robinson. "I don't mean to imply that there was anything wrong about it, but I considered——"

"Never mind what you considered. Attend to me, please. When you first saw the body, how was it lying?"

"On its back, with Denver and Arbuthnot washing its face. It had evidently been turned over, because——"

"Sir Wigmore," interposed the Lord High Steward, "you really must control your witness."

"Kindly confine yourself to the evidence," said Sir Wigmore, rather heated. "We do not want your deductions from it. You say that when you saw the body it was lying on its back. Is that correct?"

"And Denver and Arbuthnot were washing it."

"Yes. Now I want to pass to another point. Do you remember an occasion when you lunched at the Royal Automobile Club?"

"I do. I lunched there one day in the middle of last August—I think it was about the sixteenth or seventeenth."

"Will you tell us what happened on that occasion?"

"I had gone into the smoke-room after lunch, and was reading in a high-backed armchair, when I saw the prisoner at the Bar come in with the late Captain Cathcart. That is to say, I saw them in the big mirror over the mantelpiece. They did not notice there was anyone there, or they would have been a little more careful what they said, I fancy. They sat down near me and started talking, and presently Cathcart leaned over and said something in a low tone which I couldn't catch. The prisoner leapt up with a horrified face, exclaiming, 'For God's sake, don't give me away, Cathcart—there'd be the devil to pay.' Cathcart said something reassuring—I didn't hear what, he had a furtive sort of voice—and the prisoner replied, "Well, don't, that's all. I couldn't afford to let anybody get hold of it.' The prisoner seemed greatly alarmed. Captain Cathcart was laughing. They dropped their voices again, and that was all I heard."

"Thank you."

Sir Impey took over the witness with a Belial-like politeness.

"You are gifted with very excellent powers of observation and deduction, Mr. Pettigrew-Robinson," he began, "and no doubt you like to exercise your sympathetic imagination in a scrutiny of people's motives and characters?"

"I think I may call myself a student of human nature," replied Mr. Pettigrew-Robinson, much mollified.

"Doubtless, people are inclined to confide in you?"

"Certainly. I may say I am a great repository of human documents."

"On the night of Captain Cathcart's death your wide knowledge of the world was doubtless of great comfort and assistance to the family?"

"They did not avail themselves of my experience, sir," said Mr. Pettigrew-Robinson, exploding suddenly. "I was ignored completely. If only my advice had been taken at the time——"

"Thank you, thank you," said Sir Impey, cutting short an impatient exclamation from the Attorney-General, who thereupon rose and demanded:

"If Captain Cathcart had had any secret or trouble of any kind in his life, you would have expected him to tell you about it?"

"From any right-minded young man I might certainly have expected it," said Mr. Pettigrew-Robinson blusteringly; "but Captain Cathcart was disagreeably secretive. On the only occasion when I showed a friendly interest in his affairs he was very rude indeed. He called me——"

"That'll do," interposed Sir Impey hastily, the answer to the question not having turned out as he expected. "What the deceased called you is immaterial."

Mr. Pettigrew-Robinson retired, leaving behind him the impression of a man with a grudge—an impression which seemed to please Mr. Glibbery and Mr. Brownrigg-Fortescue extremely, for they chuckled continuously through the evidence of the next two witnesses.

Mrs. Pettigrew-Robinson had little to add to her previous evidence at the inquest. Miss Cathcart was asked by Sir Impey about Cathcart's parentage, and explained, with deep disapproval in her voice, that her brother, when an all-too-experienced and middle-aged man of the world, had nevertheless "been entangled by" an Italian singer of nineteen, who had "contrived" to make him marry her. Eighteen years later both parents had died. "No wonder," said Miss Cathcart, "with the rackety life they led," and the boy had been left to her care. She explained how Denis had always chafed at her influence, gone about with men she disapproved of, and eventually gone to Paris to make a diplomatic career for himself, since which time she had hardly seen him.

An interesting point was raised in the cross-examination of Inspector Craikes. A penknife being shown him, he identified it as the one found on Cathcart's body.

By Mr. Glibbery: "Do you observe any marks on the blade?"

"Yes, there is a slight notch near the handle."

"Might the mark have been caused by forcing back the catch of a window?"

Inspector Craikes agreed that it might, but doubted whether so small a knife would have been adequate for such a purpose. The revolver was produced, and the question of ownership raised.

"My lords," put in Sir Impey, "we do not dispute the Duke's ownership of the revolver."

The Court looked surprised, and, after Hardraw, the gamekeeper, had given evidence of the shot heard at 11.50, the medical evidence was taken.

Sir Impey Biggs: "Could the wound have been self-inflicted?"

"It could, certainly."

"Would it have been instantly fatal?"

"No. From the amount of blood found upon the path it was obviously not immediately fatal."

"Are the marks found, in your opinion, consistent with deceased having crawled towards the house?"

"Yes, quite. He might have had sufficient strength to do so."

"Would such a wound cause fever?"

"It is quite possible. He might have lost consciousness for some time, and contracted a chill and fever by lying in the wet."

"Are the appearances consistent with his having lived for some hours after being wounded?"

"They strongly suggest it."

Re-examining, Sir Wigmore Wrinching established that the wound and general appearance of the ground were equally consistent with the theory that deceased had been shot by another hand at very close quarters, and dragged to the house before life was extinct.

"In your experience is it more usual for a person committing suicide to shoot himself in the chest or in the head?"

"In the head is perhaps more usual."

"So much as almost to create a presumption of murder when the wound is in the chest?"

"I would not go so far as that."

"But, other things being equal, you would say that a wound in the head is more suggestive of suicide than a body-wound?"

"That is so."

Sir Impey Biggs: "But suicide by shooting in the heart is not by any means impossible?"

"Oh, dear, no."

"There have been such cases?"

"Oh, certainly; many such."

"There is nothing in the medical evidence before you to exclude the idea of suicide?"

"Nothing whatever."

This closed the case for the Crown.

CHAPTER XV

BAR FALLING

Copyright by Reuter, Press Association Exchange Telegraph, and Central News.

WHEN SIR IMPEY BIGGS ROSE to make his opening speech for the defence on the second day, it was observed that he looked somewhat worried—a thing very unusual in him. His remarks were very brief, yet in those few words he sent a thrill through the great assembly.

"My lords, in rising to open this defence I find myself in a more than usually anxious position. Not that I have any doubt of your lordships' verdict. Never perhaps has it been possible so clearly to prove the innocence of any accused person as in the case of my noble client. But I will explain to your lordships at once that I may be obliged to ask for an adjournment, since we are at present without an important witness and a decisive piece of evidence. My lords, I hold here in my hand a cablegram from this witness—I will tell you his name; it is Lord Peter Wimsey, the brother of the accused. It was handed in yesterday at New York. I will read it to you. He says: 'Evidence secured. Leaving to-night with Air Pilot Grant. Sworn copy and depositions follow by S.S. *Lucarnia* in case accident. Hope arrive Thursday.' My lords, at this moment this all-important witness is cleaving the air high above the wide Atlantic. In this wintry weather he is braving a peril which would appal any heart but his own and that of the world-famous aviator whose help he has enlisted, so that no moment may be lost in freeing his noble brother from this terrible charge. My lords, the barometer is falling."

An immense hush, like the stillness of a black frost, had fallen over the glittering benches. The lords in their scarlet and ermine, the peeresses in their rich furs, counsel in their full-bottomed wigs and billowing gowns, the Lord High Steward upon his high seat, the ushers and the heralds and the gaudy kings-of-arms, rested rigid in their places. Only the prisoner looked across at his counsel and back to the Lord High Steward in a kind of bewilderment, and the reporters scribbled wildly and desperately stop-press announcements—lurid headlines, picturesque epithets, and alarming weather predictions, to halt hurrying London on its way: "PEER'S SON FLIES ATLANTIC"; "BROTHER'S DEVOTION"; "WILL WIMSEY BE IN TIME?"; "RIDDLESDALE MURDER CHARGE: AMAZING DEVELOPMENT." This was news. A million tape-machines ticked it out in offices and clubs, where clerks and messenger-boys gloated over it and laid wagers on the result; the thousands of monster printing-presses sucked it in, boiled it into lead, champed it into slugs, engulfed it in their huge maws, digested it to paper, and flapped it forth again with clutching talons; and a blue-nosed, ragged veteran of Vimy Ridge, who had once assisted to dig Major Wimsey out of a shell-hole, muttered: "Gawd 'elp 'im, 'e's a real decent little blighter," as he tucked his newspapers into the iron grille of a tree in Kingsway and displayed his placard to the best advantage.

After a brief statement that he intended, not merely to prove his noble client's innocence but (as a work of supererogation) to make clear every detail of the tragedy, Sir Impey Biggs proceeded without further delay to call his witnesses.

Among the first was Mr. Goyles, who testified that he had found

Cathcart already dead at 3 a.m., with his head close to the water-trough which stood near the well. Ellen, the maid-servant, next confirmed James Fleming's evidence with regard to the post-bag, and explained how she changed the blotting-paper in the study every day.

The evidence of Detective-Inspector Parker aroused more interest and some bewilderment. His description of the discovery of the green-eyed cat was eagerly listened to. He also gave a minute account of the footprints and marks of dragging, especially the imprint of a hand in the flower-bed. The piece of blotting-paper was then produced, and photographs of it circulated among the peers. A long discussion ensued on both these points, Sir Impey Biggs endeavouring to show that the imprint on the flower-bed was such as would have been caused by a man endeavouring to lift himself from a prone position, Sir Wigmore Wrinching doing his best to force an admission that it might have been made by deceased in trying to prevent himself from being dragged along.

"The position of the fingers being towards the house appears, does it not, to negative the suggestion of dragging?" suggested Sir Impey.

Sir Wigmore, however, put it to the witness that the wounded man might have been dragged head foremost.

"If, now," said Sir Wigmore, "I were to drag you by the coat-collar —my lords will grasp my contention——"

"It appears," observed the Lord High Steward, "to be a case for *solvitur ambulando*." (Laughter.) "I suggest that when the House rises for lunch, some of us should make the experiment, choosing a member of similar height and weight to the deceased." (All the noble lords looked round at one another to see which unfortunate might be chosen for the part.)

Inspector Parker then mentioned the marks of forcing on the study window.

"In your opinion, could the catch have been forced back by the knife found on the body of the deceased?"

"I know it could, for I made the experiment myself with a knife of exactly similar pattern."

After this the message on the blotting-paper was read backwards and forwards and interpreted in every possible way, the defence insisting that the language was French and the words *"Je suis fou de douleur,"* the prosecution scouting the suggestion as far-fetched, and offering an English interpretation, such as "is found" or "his foul." A handwriting expert was then called, who compared the handwriting with that of an authentic letter of Cathcart's, and was subsequently severely handled by the prosecution.

These knotty points being left for the consideration of the noble lords, the defence then called a tedious series of witnesses: the manager of Cox's and Monsieur Turgeot of the Crédit Lyonnais, who went with much detail into Cathcart's financial affairs; the concierge and Madame Leblanc from the Rue St. Honoré; and the noble lords began to yawn, with the exception of a few of the soap and pickles lords, who suddenly started to make computations in their notebooks, and exchanged looks of intelligence as from one financier to another.

Then came Monsieur Briquet, the jeweller from the Rue de la Paix, and the girl from his shop, who told the story of the tall, fair, foreign lady and the purchase of the green-eyed cat—whereat everybody woke up. After reminding the assembly that this incident took place in February, when Cathcart's fiancée was in Paris, Sir Impey invited the jeweller's assistant to look round the house and tell them if she saw the foreign lady. This proved a lengthy business, but the answer was finally in the negative.

"I do not want there to be any doubt about this," said Sir Impey, "and, with the learned Attorney-General's permission, I am now going to confront this witness with Lady Mary Wimsey."

Lady Mary was accordingly placed before the witness, who replied immediately and positively: "No, this is not the lady; I have never seen this lady in my life. There is the resemblance of height and colour and the hair bobbed, but there is nothing else at all—not the least in the world. It is not the same type at all. Mademoiselle is a charming English lady, and the man who marries her will be very happy, but the other was *belle à se suicider*—a woman to kill, suicide one's self, or send all to the devil for, and believe me, gentlemen" (with a wide smile to her distinguished audience), "we have the opportunity to see them in my business."

There was a profound sensation as this witness took her departure, and Sir Impey scribbled a note and passed it down to Mr. Murbles. It contained the one word, "Magnificent!" Mr. Murbles scribbled back:

"Never said a word to her. Can you beat it?" and leaned back in his seat smirking like a very neat little grotesque from a Gothic corbel.

The witness who followed was Professor Hébert, a distinguished exponent of international law, who described Cathcart's promising career as a rising young diplomat in Paris before the war. He was followed by a number of officers who testified to the excellent war record of the deceased. Then came a witness who gave the aristocratic name of du Bois-Gobey Houdin, who perfectly recollected a very uncomfortable dispute on a certain occasion when playing cards with le Capitaine Cathcart, and having subsequently mentioned the matter to Monsieur Thomas Freeborn, the distinguished English engineer. It was Parker's diligence that had unearthed this witness, and he looked across with an undisguised grin at the discomfited Sir Wigmore Wrinching. When Mr. Glibbery had dealt with all these the afternoon was well advanced, and the Lord High Steward accordingly asked the lords if it was their pleasure that the House be adjourned till the next day at 10.30 of the clock in the forenoon, and the lords replying "Aye" in a most exemplary chorus, the House was accordingly adjourned.

A scurry of swift black clouds with ragged edges was driving bleakly westward as they streamed out into Parliament Square, and the seagulls screeched and wheeled inwards from the river. Charles Parker wrapped his ancient Burberry closely about him as he scrambled on to a 'bus to get home to Great Ormond Street. It was only one more drop in his cup of discomfort that the conductor greeted him with "Outside only!" and rang the bell before he could get off again. He climbed to the top and sat there holding his hat on. Mr. Bunter returned sadly to 110 Piccadilly, and wandered restlessly about the flat till seven o'clock, when he came into the sitting-room and switched on the loud speaker.

"London calling," said the unseen voice impartially. "2LO calling. Here is the weather forecast. A deep depression is crossing the Atlantic, and a secondary is stationary over the British Isles. Storms, with heavy rain and sleet, will be prevalent, rising to a gale in the south and south-west. . . ."

"You never know," said Bunter. "I suppose I'd better light a fire in his bedroom."

"Further outlook similar."

CHAPTER XVI

THE SECOND STRING

O, whan he came to broken briggs
He bent his bow and swam,
And whan he came to the green grass growin'
He slacked his shoone and ran.

O, whan he came to Lord William's gates
He baed na to chap na ca',
But set his bent bow till his breast,
An' lightly lap the wa'.

—Ballad of Lady Maisry.

LORD PETER PEERED OUT through the cold scurry of cloud. The thin struts of steel, incredibly fragile, swung slowly across the gleam and glint far below, where the wide country dizzied out and spread like a revolving map. In front the sleek leather back of his companion humped stubbornly, sheeted with rain. He hoped that Grant was feeling confident. The roar of the engine drowned the occasional shout he threw to his passenger as they lurched from gust to gust.

He withdrew his mind from present discomforts and went over that last, strange, hurried scene. Fragments of conversation spun through his head.

"Mademoiselle, I have scoured two continents in search of you."

"*Voyons*, then, it is urgent. But be quick for the big bear may come in and be grumpy, and I do not like *des histoires*."

There had been a lamp on a low table; he remembered the gleam through the haze of short gold hair. She was a tall girl, but slender, looking up at him from the huge black-and-gold cushions.

"Mademoiselle, it is incredible to me that you should ever—dine or dance—with a person called Van Humperdinck."

Now what had possessed him to say that—when there was so little time, and Jerry's affairs were of such importance?

191

"Monsieur van Humperdinck does not dance. Did you seek me through two continents to say that?"

"No, I am serious."

"Eh bien, sit down."

She had been quite frank about it.

"Yes, poor soul. But life was very expensive since the war. I refused several good things. But always *des histoires.* And so little money. You see, one must be sensible. There is one's old age. It is necessary to be provident, *hein?"*

"Assuredly." She had a little accent—very familiar. At first he could not place it. Then it came to him—Vienna before the war, that capital of incredible follies.

"Yes, yes, I wrote. I was very kind, very sensible. I said, '*Je ne suis pas femme à supporter de gros ennuis.' Cela se comprend, n'est-ce pas?"*

That was readily understood. The 'plane dived sickly into a sudden pocket, the propeller whirring helplessly in the void, then steadied and began to nose up the opposite spiral.

"I saw it in the papers—yes. Poor boy! Why should anybody have shot him?"

"Mademoiselle, it is for that I have come to you. My brother, whom I dearly love, is accused of the murder. He may be hanged."

"Brr!"

"For a murder he did not commit."

"Mon pauvre enfant——"

"Mademoiselle, I implore you to be serious. My brother is accused, and will be standing his trial——"

Once her attention had been caught she had been all sympathy. Her blue eyes had a curious and attractive trick—a full lower lid that shut them into glimmering slits.

"Mademoiselle, I implore you, try to remember what was in his letter."

"But, *mon pauvre ami,* how can I? I did not read it. It was very long, very tedious, full of *histoires.* The thing was finished—I never bother about what cannot be helped, do you?"

But his real agony at this failure had touched her.

"Listen, then; all is perhaps not lost. It is possible the letter is still somewhere about. Or we will ask Adèle. She is my maid. She collects letters to blackmail people—oh, yes, I know! But she is *habile comme tout pour la toilette.* Wait—we will look first."

Tossing out letters, trinkets, endless perfumed rubbish from the little gimcrack secretaire, from drawers full of lingerie ("I am so untidy—I am Adèle's despair") from bags—hundreds of bags—and at last Adèle, thin-lipped and wary-eyed, denying everything till her mistress suddenly slapped her face in a fury, and called her ugly little names in French and German.

"It is useless, then," said Lord Peter. "What a pity that Mademoiselle Adèle cannot find a thing so valuable to me."

The word "valuable" suggested an idea to Adèle. There was Mademoiselle's jewel-case which had not been searched. She would fetch it.

"*C'est cela que cherche monsieur?*"

After that the sudden arrival of Mr. Cornelius van Humperdinck, very rich and stout and suspicious, and the rewarding of Adèle in a tactful, unobtrusive fashion by the elevator shaft.

Grant shouted, but the words flipped feebly away into the blackness and were lost. "What?" bawled Wimsey in his ear. He shouted again, and this time the word "juice" shot into sound and fluttered away. But whether the news was good or bad Lord Peter could not tell.

.   .   .   .

Mr. Murbles was aroused a little after midnight by a thunderous knocking upon his door. Thrusting his head out of the window in some alarm, he saw the porter with his lantern steaming through the rain, and behind him a shapeless figure which for the moment Mr. Murbles could not make out.

"What's the matter?" said the solicitor.

"Young lady askin' urgently for you, sir."

The shapeless figure looked up, and he caught the spangle of gold hair in the lantern-light under the little tight hat.

"Mr. Murbles, please come. Bunter rang me up. There's a woman come to give evidence. Bunter doesn't like to leave her—she's frightened—but he says it's *frightfully* important, and Bunter's always right, you know."

"Did he mention the name?"

"A Mrs. Grimethorpe."

"God bless me! Just a moment, my dear young lady, and I will let you in."

And, indeed, more quickly than might have been expected, Mr. Murbles made his appearance in a Jaeger dressing-gown at the front door.

"Come in, my dear. I will get dressed in a very few minutes. It was quite right of you to come to me. I'm very, very glad you did. What a terrible night! Perkins, would you kindly wake up Mr. Murphy and ask him to oblige me with the use of his telephone?"

Mr. Murphy—a noisy Irish barrister with a hearty manner—needed no waking. He was entertaining a party of friends, and was delighted to be of service.

"Is that you Biggs? Murbles speaking. That alibi——"

"Yes?"

"Has come along of its own accord."

"My God! You don't say so!"

"Can you come round to 110 Piccadilly?"

"Straight away."

It was a strange little party gathered round Lord Peter's fire—the white-faced woman, who started at every sound; the men of law, with their keen, disciplined faces; Lady Mary; Bunter, the efficient. Mrs. Grimethorpe's story was simple enough. She had suffered the torments of knowledge ever since Lord Peter had spoken to her. She had seized an hour when her husband was drunk in the "Lord in Glory," and had harnessed the horse and driven in to Stapley.

"I couldn't keep silence. It's better my man should kill me, for I'm unhappy enough, and maybe I couldn't be any worse off in the Lord's hand—rather than they should hang him for a thing he never done. He was kind, and I was desperate miserable, that's the truth, and I'm hoping his lady won't be hard on him when she knows it all."

"No, no," said Mr. Murbles, clearing his throat. "Excuse me a moment, madam. Sir Impey——"

The lawyers whispered together in the window-seat.

"You see," said Sir Impey, "she has burnt her boats pretty well now by coming at all. The great question for us is, Is it worth the risk? After all, we don't know what Wimsey's evidence amounts to."

"No, that is why I feel inclined—in spite of the risk—to put this evidence in," said Mr. Murbles.

"I am ready to take the risk," interposed Mrs. Grimethorpe starkly.

"We quite appreciate that," replied Sir Impey. "It is the risk to our client we have to consider first of all."

"Risk?" cried Mary. "But surely this clears him!"

"Will you swear absolutely to the time when his grace of Denver arrived at Grider's Hole, Mrs. Grimethorpe?" went on the lawyer, as though he had not heard her.

"It was a quarter past twelve by the kitchen clock—'tis a very good clock."

"And he left you at——"

"About five minutes past two."

"And how long would it take a man, walking quickly, to get back to Riddlesdale Lodge?"

"Oh, wellnigh an hour. It's rough walking, and a steep bank up and down to the beck."

"You mustn't let the other counsel upset you on those points, Mrs. Grimethorpe, because they will try to prove that he had time to kill Cathcart either before he started or after he returned, and by admitting that the Duke had something in his life that he wanted kept secret we shall be supplying the very thing the prosecution lack—*a motive for murdering anyone who might have found him out.*"

There was a stricken silence.

"If I may ask, madam," said Sir Impey, "has any person any suspicion?"

"My husband guessed," she answered hoarsely. "I am sure of it. He has always known. But he couldn't prove it. That very night——"

"What night?"

"The night of the murder—he laid a trap for me. He came back from Stapley in the night, hoping to catch us and do murder. But he drank too much before he started, and spent the night in the ditch, or it might be Gerald's death you'd be inquiring into, and mine, as well as the other."

It gave Mary an odd shock to hear her brother's name spoken like that, by that speaker and in that company. She asked suddenly, apropos of nothing, "Isn't Mr. Parker here?"

"No, my dear," said Mr. Murbles reprovingly, "this is not a police matter."

"The best thing we can do, I think," said Sir Impey, "is to put in the evidence, and, if necessary, arrange for some kind of protection for this lady. In the meantime——"

"She is coming round with me to mother," said Lady Mary determinedly.

"My dear lady," expostulated Mr. Murbles, "that would be very unsuitable in the circumstances. I think you hardly grasp——"

"Mother said so," retorted her ladyship. "Bunter, call a taxi."

Mr. Murbles waved his hands helplessly, but Sir Impey was rather amused. "It's no good, Murbles," he said. "Time and trouble will tame an advanced young woman, but an advanced old woman is uncontrollable by any earthly force."

So it was from the Dowager's town house that Lady Mary rang up Mr. Charles Parker to tell him the news.

CHAPTER XVII

THE ELOQUENT DEAD

Je connaissais Manon: pourquoi m'affliger tant d'un malheur que j'avis dû prévoir.—Manon Lescaut.

THE GALE HAD BLOWN itself out into a wonderful fresh day, with clear spaces of sky, and a high wind rolling boulders of cumulus down the blue slopes of air.

The prisoner had been wrangling for an hour with his advisers when finally they came into court, and even Sir Impey's classical face showed flushed between the wings of his wig.

"I'm not going to say anything," said the Duke obstinately. "Rotten thing to do. I suppose I can't prevent you callin' her if she insists on comin'—damn' good of her—makes me feel no end of a beast."

"Better leave it at that," said Mr. Murbles. "Makes a good impression, you know. Let him go into the box and behave like a perfect gentleman. They'll like it."

Sir Impey, who had sat through the small hours altering his speech, nodded.

The first witness that day came as something of a surprise. She gave her name and address as Eliza Briggs, known as Madame Brigette of New Bond Street, and her occupation as beauty specialist and perfumer. She had a large and aristocratic clientele of both sexes, and a branch in Paris.

Deceased had been a client of hers in both cities for several years. He had massage and manicure. After the war he had come to her about some slight scars caused by grazing with shrapnel. He was extremely particular about his personal appearance, and, if you called that vanity in a man, you might certainly say he was vain. Thank you. Sir Wigmore Wrinching made no attempt to cross-examine the witness, and the noble lords wondered to one another what it was all about.

At this point Sir Impey Biggs leaned forward, and, tapping his brief impressively with his forefinger, began:

"My lords, so strong is our case that we had not thought it necessary to present an alibi——" when an officer of the court rushed up from a little whirlpool of commotion by the door and excitedly thrust a note into his hand. Sir Impey read, coloured, glanced down the hall, put down his brief, folded his hands over it, and said in a sudden, loud voice which penetrated even to the deaf ear of the Duke of Wiltshire:

"My lords, I am happy to say that our missing witness is here. I call Lord Peter Wimsey."

Every neck was at once craned, and every eye focused on the very grubby and oily figure that came amiably trotting up the long room. Sir Impey Biggs passed the note down to Mr. Murbles, and, turning to the witness, who was yawning frightfully in the intervals of grinning at all his acquaintances, demanded that he should be sworn.

The witness's story was as follows:

"I am Lord Peter Wimsey, brother of the accused. I live at 110 Piccadilly. In consequence of what I read on that bit of blotting-paper which I now identify, I went to Paris to look for a certain lady. The name of the lady is Mademoiselle Simone Vonderaa. I found she had left Paris in company with a man named Van Humperdinck. I followed her, and at length came up with her in New York. I asked her to give me the letter Cathcart wrote on the night of his death. (Sensation.) I produce that letter, with Mademoiselle Vonderaa's signature on the corner, so that it can be identified if Wiggy there tries to put it over you. (Joyous sensation, in which the indignant protests of prosecuting counsel were drowned.) And I'm sorry I've given you such short notice of this, old man, but I only got it the day before yesterday. We came as quick as we could, but we had to come down

197

near Whitehaven with engine trouble, and if we had come down half a mile sooner I shouldn't be here now." (Applause, hurriedly checked by the Lord High Steward.)

"My lords," said Sir Impey, "your lordships are witnesses that I have never seen this letter in my life before. I have no idea of its contents; yet so positive am I that it cannot but assist my noble client's case, that I am willing—nay, eager—to put in this document immediately, as it stands, without perusal, to stand or fall by the contents."

"The handwriting must be identified as that of the deceased," interposed the Lord High Steward.

The ravening pencils of the reporters tore along the paper. The lean young man who worked for the *Daily Trumpet* scented a scandal in high life and licked his lips, never knowing what a much bigger one had escaped him by a bare minute or so.

Miss Lydia Cathcart was recalled to identify the handwriting, and the letter was handed to the Lord High Steward, who announced:

"The letter is in French. We shall have to swear an interpreter."

"You will find," said the witness suddenly, "that those bits of words on the blotting-paper come out of the letter. You'll 'scuse my mentioning it."

"Is this person put forward as an expert witness?" inquired Sir Wigmore witheringly.

"Right ho!" said Lord Peter. "Only, you see, it has been rather sprung on Biggy as you might say.

> "Biggy and Wiggy
>> Were two pretty men,
>> They went into court
>> When the clock——"

"Sir Impey, I must really ask you to keep your witness in order."

Lord Peter grinned, and a pause ensued while an interpreter was fetched and sworn. Then, at last, the letter was read, amid a breathless silence:

> "Riddlesdale Lodge,
>> "Stapley,
>>> "N.E. Yorks.
>>> *"le* 13 *Octobre,* 192—
> "SIMONE,—Je viens de recevoir ta lettre. Que dire? Inutiles, les

prières ou les reproches. Tu ne comprendras—tu ne liras même pas.

"N'ai-je pas toujours su, d'ailleurs, que tu devais infailliblement me trahir? Depuis huit ans déjà je souffre tous les torments que puisse infliger la jalousie. Je comprends bien que tu n'as jamais voulu me faire de la peine. C'est tout justement cette insouciance, cette légèreté, cette façon séduisante d'être malhonnête, que j'adorais en toi. J'ai tout su, et je t'ai aimée.

"Ma foi, non, ma chère, jamais je n'ai eu la moindre illusion. Te rappelles-tu cette première rencontre, un soir au Casino? Tu avais dix-sept ans, et tu étais jolie à ravir. Le lendemain tu fus à moi. Tu m'as dit, si gentiment, que tu m'aimais bien, et que j'étais, moi, le premier. Ma pauvre enfant, tu en as menti. Tu riais, toute seule, de ma naiveté—il y avait bien de quoi rire! Dès notre premier baiser, j'ai prévu ce moment.

"Mais écoute, Simone. J'ai la faiblesse de vouloir te montrer exactement ce que tu as fait de moi. Tu regretteras peut-être en peu. Mais, non—si tu pouvais regretter quoi que ce fût, tu ne serais plus Simone.

"Il y a huit ans, la veille de la guerre, j'étais riche—moins riche que ton Américain, mais assez riche pour te donner l'établissement qu'il te fallait. Tu étais moins exigeante avant la guerre, Simone—qui est-ce qui, pendant mon absence, t'a enseigné le goût du luxe? Charmante discrétion de ma part de ne jamais te le demander! Eh bien, une grande partie de ma fortune se trouvant placée en Russie et en Allemagne, j'en ai perdu plus des trois-quarts. Ce que m'en restait en France a beaucoup diminué en valeur. Il est vrai que j'avais mon traitement de capitaine dans l'armée britannique, mais c'est peu de chose, tu sais. Avant même la fin de la guerre, tu m'avais mangé toutes mes économies. C'était idiot, quoi? Un jeune homme qui a perdu les trois-quarts de ses rentes ne se permet plus une maîtresse et un appartement Avenue Kléber. Ou il congédie madame, ou bien il lui demande quelques sacrifices. Je n'ai rien osé demander. Si j'étais venu un jour te dire, 'Simone, je suis pauvre'—que m'aurais-tu répondu?

"Sais-tu ce que j'ai fait? Non—tu n'as jamais pensé à demander d'où venait cet argent. Qu'est-ce que cela pouvait te faire que j'ai tout jeté—fortune, honneur, bonheur—pour te posséder? J'ai joué, désespérément, éperdument—j'ai fait pis: j'ai triché au jeu. Je te vois hausser les épaules—tu ris—tu dis, 'Tiens, c'est malin, ça!' Oui, mais cela ne se fait pas. On m'aurait chassé du régiment. Je devenais le dernier des hommes.

"D'ailleurs, cela ne pouvait durer. Déjà un soir à Paris on m'a fait une scène désagréable, bien qu'on n'ait rien pu prouver. C'est alors que je me suis fiancé avec cette demoiselle dont je t'ai parlé, la fille du duc anglais. Le beau projet, quoi! Entretenir ma maîtresse avec l'argent de ma femme! Et je l'aurais fait—et je le ferais encore demain, si c'était pour te reposséder.

"Mais tu me quittes. Cet Américain est riche—archi-riche. Depuis longtemps tu me répètes que ton appartement est trop petit et que tu t'ennuies à mourir. Cet 'ami bienveillant' t'offre les autos, les diamants, les mille-et-une nuits, la lune! Auprès de ces merveilles, évidemment, que valent l'amour et l'honneur?

"Enfin, le bon duc est d'une stupidité très commode. Il laisse traîner son révolver dans le tiroir de son bureau. D'ailleurs, il vient de me demander une explication à propos de cette histoire de cartes. Tu vois qu'en tout cas la partie était finie. Pourquoi t'en vouloir? On mettra sans doute mon suicide au compte de cet exposé. Tant mieux, je ne veux pas qu'on affiche mon histoire amoureuse dans les journaux.

"Adieu, ma bien-aimée—mon adorée, mon adorée, ma Simone. Sois heureuse avec ton nouvel amant. Ne pense plus à moi. Qu'est-ce tout cela peut bien te faire? Mon Dieu, comme je t'ai aimée—comme je t'aime toujours, malgré moi. Mais c'en est fini. Jamais plus tu ne me perceras le cœur. Oh! J'enrage—je suis fou de douleur! Adieu.

"DENIS CATHCART."

TRANSLATION

"SIMONE,—I have just got your letter. What am I to say? It is useless to entreat or reproach you. You would not understand, or even read the letter.

"Besides, I always knew you must betray me some day. I have suffered a hell of jealousy for the last eight years. I know perfectly well you never meant to hurt me. It was just your utter lightness and carelessness and your attractive way of being dishonest which was so adorable. I knew everything, and loved you all the same.

"Oh, no, my dear, I never had any illusions. You remember our first meeting that night at the Casino. You were seventeen, and heartbreakingly lovely. You came to me the very next day. You told me, very prettily, that you loved me and that I was the first. My poor little girl, that wasn't true. I expect, when you were alone, you laughed to think I was so easily taken in. But there was nothing to laugh at. From our very first kiss I foresaw this moment.

"I'm afraid I'm weak enough, though, to want to tell you just what you have done for me. You may be sorry. But no—if you could regret anything, you wouldn't be Simone any longer.

"Eight years ago, before the war, I was rich—not so rich as your new American, but rich enough to give you what you wanted. You didn't want quite so much before the war, Simone. Who taught you to be so extravagant while I was away? I think it was very nice of me never to ask you. Well, most of my money was in Russian and German securities, and more than three-quarters of it went west. The remainder in France went down considerably in value. I had my captain's pay, of course, but that didn't amount to much. Even before the end of the war you had managed to get through all my savings. Of course, I was a fool. A young man whose income has been reduced by three-quarters can't afford an expensive mistress and a flat in the Avenue Kléber. He ought either to dismiss the lady or to demand a little self-sacrifice. But I didn't dare demand anything. Suppose I had come to you one day and said, 'Simone, I've lost my money'—what would you have said to me?

"What do you think I did? I don't suppose you ever thought about it at all. You didn't care if I was chucking away my money and my honour and my happiness to keep you. I gambled desperately. I did worse, I cheated at cards. I can see you shrug your shoulders and say, 'Good for you!' But it's a rotten thing to do—a rotter's game. If anybody had found out they'd have cashiered me.

"Besides, it couldn't go on for ever. There was one row in Paris, though they couldn't prove anything. So then I got engaged to the English girl I told you about—the duke's daughter. Pretty, wasn't it? I actually brought myself to consider keeping my mistress on my wife's money! But I'd have done it, and I'd do it again, to get you back.

"And now you've chucked me. This American is colossally rich. For a long time you've been dinning into my ears that the flat is too small and that you're bored to death. Your 'good friend' can offer you cars, diamonds—Aladdin's palace—the moon! I admit that love and honour look pretty small by comparison.

"Ah, well, the Duke is most obligingly stupid. He leaves his revolver about in his desk drawer. Besides, he's just been in to ask what about this card-sharping story. So you see the game's up, anyhow. I don't blame you. I suppose they'll put my suicide down to fear of exposure. All the better. I don't want my love-affairs in the Sunday Press.

"Good-bye, my dear—oh, Simone, my darling, my darling, good-bye. Be happy with your new lover. Never mind me—what does it all matter? My God—how I loved you, and how I still love you in spite of myself. It's all done with. You'll never break my heart again. I'm mad—mad with misery! Good-bye."

CHAPTER XVIII

THE SPEECH FOR THE DEFENCE

"Nobody; I myself; farewell"—Othello.

AFTER THE READING of Cathcart's letter even the appearance of the prisoner in the witness-box came as an anti-climax. In the face of the Attorney-General's cross-examination he maintained stoutly that he had wandered on the moor for several hours without meeting anybody, though he was forced to admit that he had gone downstairs at 11.30, and not at 2.30, as he had stated at the inquest. Sir Wigmore Wrinching made a great point of this, and, in a spirited endeavour to suggest that Cathcart was blackmailing Denver, pressed his questions so hard that Sir Impey Biggs, Mr. Murbles, Lady Mary, and Bunter had a nervous feeling that learned counsel's eyes were boring through the walls to the side-room where, apart from the other witnesses, Mrs. Grimethorpe sat waiting. After lunch Sir Impey Biggs rose to make his plea for the defence.

"My lords,—Your lordships have now heard—and I, who have watched and pleaded here for these three anxious days, know with what eager interest and with what ready sympathy you have heard—the evidence brought by my noble client to defend him against this dreadful charge of murder. You have listened while as it were from his narrow grave, the dead man has lifted his voice to tell you the story of that fatal night of the thirteenth of October, and I feel sure you can have no doubt in your hearts that that story is the true one. As your lordships know, I was myself totally ignorant of the contents of that letter until I heard it read in Court just now, and, by the profound impression it made upon my own mind, I can judge how tremendously and how painfully it must have affected your lordships. In my long experience at the criminal bar, I think I have never met with a history more melancholy than that of the unhappy young man whom a fatal passion—for here indeed we may use that well-worn expression in all the fulness of its significance—whom a truly fatal passion thus urged into deep after deep of degradation, and finally to a violent death by his own hand.

"The noble peer at the Bar has been indicted before your lordships of the murder of this young man. That he is wholly innocent of the charge must, in the light of what we have heard, be so plain to your lordships that any words from me might seem altogether superfluous. In the majority of cases of this kind the evidence is confused, contradictory; here, however, the course of events is so clear, so coherent, that had we ourselves been present to see the drama unrolled before us, as before the all-seeing eye of God, we could hardly have a more vivid or a more accurate vision of that night's adventures. Indeed, had the death of Denis Cathcart been the sole event of the night, I will venture to say that the truth could never have been one single moment in doubt. Since, however, by a series of unheard-of coincidences, the threads of Denis Cathcart's story became entangled with so many others, I will venture to tell it once again from the beginning, lest, in the confusion of so great a cloud of witnesses, any point should still remain obscure.

"Let me, then, go back to the beginning. You have heard how Denis Cathcart was born of mixed parentage—from the union of a young and lovely southern girl with an Englishman twenty years older than herself: imperious, passionate, and cynical. Till the age of 18 he lives on the Continent with his parents, travelling from place to place, seeing more of the world even than the average young Frenchman of his age, learning the code of love in a country where the *crime passionel* is understood and forgiven as it never can be over here.

"At the age of 18 a terrible loss befalls him. In a very short space of time he loses both his parents—his beautiful and adored mother and his father, who might, had he lived, have understood how to guide the impetuous nature which he had brought into the world. But the father dies, expressing two last wishes, both of which, natural as they were, turned out in the circumstances to be disastrously ill-advised. He left his son to the care of his sister, whom he had not seen for many years, with the direction that the boy should be sent to his own old University.

"My lords, you have seen Miss Lydia Cathcart, and heard her evidence. You will have realised how uprightly, how conscientiously, with what Christian disregard of self, she performed the duty entrusted to her, and yet how inevitably she failed to establish any real sympathy between herself and her young ward. He, poor lad, missing his parents at every turn, was plunged at Cambridge into the society of young men of totally different upbringing from himself. To a young man of his cosmopolitan experience the youth of Cambridge, with its sports and rags and naïve excursions into philosophy o' nights, must have seemed unbelievably childish. You all, from your own recollections of your Alma Mater, can reconstruct Denis Cathcart's life at Cambridge, its outward gaiety, its inner emptiness.

"Ambitious of embracing a diplomatic career, Cathcart made extensive acquaintances among the sons of rich and influential men. From a worldly point of view he was doing well, and his inheritance of a handsome fortune at the age of twenty-one seemed to open up the path to very great success. Shaking the academic dust of Cambridge from his feet as soon as his Tripos was passed, he went over to France, established himself in Paris, and began, in a quiet, determined kind of way, to carve out a little niche for himself in the world of international politics.

"But now comes into his life that terrible influence which was to rob him of fortune, honour, and life itself. He falls in love with a young woman of that exquisite, irresistible charm and beauty for which the Austrian capital is world-famous. He is enthralled body and soul, as utterly as any Chevalier des Grieux, by Simone Vonderaa.

"Mark that in this matter he follows the strict, continental code: complete devotion, complete discretion. You have heard how quietly he lived, how *rangé* he appeared to be. We have had in evidence his discreet banking-account, with its generous cheques drawn to self, and cashed in notes of moderate denominations, and with its regular accumulation of sufficient 'economies' quarter by quarter. Life has expanded for Denis Cathcart. Rich, ambitious, possessed of a beautiful and complaisant mistress, the world is open before him.

"Then, my lords, across this promising career there falls the thunderbolt of the Great War—ruthlessly smashing through his safeguards, overthrowing the edifice of his ambition, destroying and devastating here, as everywhere, all that made life beautiful and desirable.

"You have heard the story of Denis Cathcart's distinguished army career. On that I need not dwell. Like thousands of other young men, he went gallantly through those five years of strain and disillusionment, to find himself left, in the end, with his life and health indeed, and, so far, happy beyond many of his comrades, but with his life in ruins about him.

"Of his great fortune—all of which had been invested in Russian and German securities—literally nothing is left to him. What, you say, did that matter to a young man so well equipped, with such excellent connections, with so many favourable openings, ready to his hand? He needed only to wait quietly for a few years, to reconstruct much of what he had lost. Alas! my lords, he could not afford to wait. He stood in peril of losing something dearer to him than fortune or ambition; he needed money in quantity, and at once.

"My lords, in that pathetic letter which we have heard read nothing is more touching and terrible than that confession: 'I knew you could not but be unfaithful to me.' All through that time of seeming happiness he knew—none better—that his house was built on sand. 'I was never deceived by you,' he says. From their earliest acquaintance she had lied to him, and he knew it, and that knowledge was yet powerless to loosen the bands of his fatal fascination. If any of you, my lords, have known the power of love exercised in this irresistible —I may say, this predestined manner—let your experience interpret the situation to you better than any poor words of mine can do. One great French poet and one great English poet have summed the matter up in a few words. Racine says of such a fascination:

> *C'est Vénus tout entière à sa proie attachée.*

And Shakespeare has put the lover's despairing obstinacy into two piteous lines:

> If my love swears that she is made of truth
> I will believe her, though I know she lies.

My lords, Denis Cathcart is dead; it is not our place to condemn him, but only to understand and pity him.

"My lords, I need not put before you in detail the shocking shifts to which this soldier and gentleman unhappily condescended. You have heard the story in all its cold, ugly details upon the lips of Monsieur du Bois-Gobey Houdin, and, accompanied by unavailing expressions of shame and remorse, in the last words of the deceased. You know how he gambled, at first honestly—then dishonestly. You know from whence he derived those large sums of money which came at irregular intervals, mysteriously and in cash, to bolster up a bank-account always perilously on the verge of depletion. We need not, my lords, judge too harshly of the woman. According to her own lights, she did not treat him unfairly. She had her interests to consider. While he could pay for her she could give him beauty and passion and good humour and a moderate faithfulness. When he could pay no longer she would find it only reasonable to take another position. This Cathcart understood. Money he must have, by hook or by crook. And so, by an inevitable descent, he found himself reduced to the final deep of dishonour.

"It is at this point, my lords, that Denis Cathcart and his miserable fortunes come into the life of my noble client and of his sister. From this point begin all those complications which led to the tragedy of October 14th, and which we are met in this solemn and historic assembly to unravel.

"About eighteen months ago Cathcart, desperately searching for a secure source of income, met the Duke of Denver, whose father had been a friend of Cathcart's father many years before. The acquaintance prospered, and Cathcart was introduced to Lady Mary Wimsey, at that time (as she has very frankly told us) 'at a loose end,' 'fed up,' and distressed by the dismissal of her fiancé, Mr. Goyles. Lady Mary felt the need of an establishment of her own, and accepted Denis Cathcart, with the proviso that she should be considered a free agent, living her own life in her own way, with the minimum of interference. As to Cathcart's object in all this, we have his own bitter comment, on which no words of mine could improve: 'I actually brought myself to consider keeping my mistress on my wife's money.'

"So matters go on until October of this year. Cathcart is now obliged to pass a good deal of his time in England with his fiancée, leaving Simone Vonderaa unguarded in the Avenue Kléber. He seems to have felt fairly secure so far; the only drawback was that Lady Mary, with a natural reluctance to commit herself to the hands of a man she could not really love, had so far avoided fixing a definite date for the wedding. Money is shorter than it used to be in the Avenue Kléber, and the cost of robes and millinery, amusements and so forth, has not diminished. And, meanwhile, Mr. Cornelius van Humperdinck, the American millionaire, has seen Simone in the Bois, at the races, at the opera, in Denis Cathcart's flat.

"But Lady Mary is becoming more and more uneasy about her engagement. And at this critical moment, Mr. Goyles suddenly sees the prospect of a position, modest but assured, which will enable him to maintain a wife. Lady Mary makes her choice. She consents to elope with Mr. Goyles, and by an extraordinary fatality the day and hour selected are 3 a.m. on the morning of October 14th.

"At about 9.30 on the night of Wednesday, October 13th, the party at Riddlesdale Lodge are just separating to go to bed. The Duke of Denver was in the gun-room, the other men were in the billiard-room, the ladies had already retired, when the manservant, Fleming, came up from the village with the evening post. To the Duke of Denver he brought a letter with news of a startling and very unpleasant kind. To Denis Cathcart he brought another letter—one which we shall never see, but whose contents it is easy enough to guess.

"You have heard the evidence of Mr. Arbuthnot that, before reading this letter, Cathcart had gone upstairs gay and hopeful, mentioning that he hoped soon to get a date fixed for the marriage. At a little after ten, when the Duke of Denver went up to see him, there was a great change. Before his grace could broach the matter in hand Cathcart spoke rudely and harshly, appearing to be all on edge, and entreating to be left alone. Is it very difficult, my lords, in the face of what we have heard to-day—in the face of our knowledge that Mademoiselle Vonderaa crossed to New York on the *Berengaria* on October 15th—to guess what news had reached Denis Cathcart in that interval to change his whole outlook upon life?

"At this unhappy moment, when Cathcart is brought face to face with the stupefying knowledge that his mistress has left him, comes the Duke of Denver with a frightful accusation. He taxes Cathcart with the vile truth—that this man, who has eaten his bread and sheltered under his roof, and who is about to marry his sister, is nothing more nor less than a card-sharper. And when Cathcart refuses to deny the charge—when he, most insolently, as it seems, declares that he is no longer willing to wed the noble lady to whom he is affianced—is it surprising that the Duke should turn upon the impostor and forbid him ever to touch or speak to Lady Mary Wimsey again? I say, my lords, that no man with a spark of honourable feeling would have done otherwise. My client contents himself with directing Cathcart to leave the house next day; and when Cathcart rushes madly out into the storm he calls after him to return, and even takes the trouble to direct the footman to leave open the conservatory door for Cathcart's convenience. It is true that he called Cathcart a dirty scoundrel, and told him he should have been kicked out of his regiment, but he was justified; while the words he shouted from the window—'Come back, you fool,' or even, according to one witness, 'you b—— fool'—have almost an affectionate ring in them. (Laughter.)

"And now I will direct your lordships' attention to the extreme weakness of the case against my noble client from the point of view of motive. It has been suggested that the cause of the quarrel between them was not that mentioned by the Duke of Denver in his evidence, but something even more closely personal to themselves. Of this contention not a jot or tittle, not the slightest shadow of evidence, has been put forward except, indeed, that of the extraordinary witness, Robinson, who appears to bear a grudge against his whole acquaintance, and to have magnified some trifling allusion into a matter of vast importance. Your lordships have seen this person's demeanour in the box, and will judge for yourselves how much weight is to be attached to his observations. While we on our side have been able to show that the alleged cause of complaint was perfectly well founded in fact.

"So Cathcart rushes out into the garden. In the pelting rain he paces heedlessly about, envisaging a future stricken at once suddenly barren of love, wealth, and honour.

"And, meanwhile, a passage door opens, and a stealthy foot creeps down the stair. We know now whose it is—Mrs. Pettigrew-Robinson has not mistaken the creak of the door. It is the Duke of Denver.

"That is admitted. But from this point we join issue with my learned friend for the prosecution. It is suggested that the Duke, on thinking matters over, determines that Cathcart is a danger to society and better dead—or that his insult to the Denver family can only be washed out in blood. And we are invited to believe that the Duke creeps downstairs, fetches his revolver from the study table, and prowls out into the night to find Cathcart and make away with him in cold blood.

"My lords, is it necessary for me to point out the inherent absurdity of this suggestion? What conceivable reason could the Duke of Denver have for killing, in this cold-blooded manner, a man of whom a single word has rid him already and for ever? It has been suggested to you that the injury had grown greater in the Duke's mind by brooding—had assumed gigantic proportions. Of that suggestion, my lords, I can only say that a more flimsy pretext for fixing an impulse to murder upon the shoulders of an innocent man was never devised, even by the ingenuity of an advocate. I will not waste my time or insult you by arguing about it. Again it has been suggested that the cause of quarrel was not what it appeared, and the Duke had reason to fear some disastrous action on Cathcart's part. Of this contention I think we have already disposed; it is an assumption constructed *in vacuo,* to meet a set of circumstances which my learned friend is at a loss to explain in conformity with the known facts. The very number and variety of motives suggested by the prosecution is proof that they are aware of the weakness of their own case. Frantically they cast about for any sort of explanation to give colour to this unreasonable indictment.

"And here I will direct your lordships' attention to the very important evidence of Inspector Parker in the matter of the study window. He has told you that it was forced from outside by the latch being slipped back with a knife. If it was the Duke of Denver, who was in the study at 11.30, what need had he to force the window? He was already inside the house. When, in addition, we find that Cathcart had in his pocket a knife, and that there are scratches upon the blade such as might come from forcing back a metal catch, it surely becomes evident that not the Duke, but Cathcart himself forced the window and crept in for the pistol, not knowing that the conservatory door had been left open for him.

"But there is no need to labour this point—we *know* that Captain Cathcart was in the study at that time, for we have seen in evidence the sheet of blotting-paper on which he blotted his letter to Simone Vonderaa, and Lord Peter Wimsey has told us how he himself removed that sheet from the study blotting-pad a few days after Cathcart's death.

"And let me here draw your attention to the significance of one point in the evidence. The Duke of Denver has told us that he saw the revolver in his drawer a short time before the fatal 13th, when he and Cathcart were together."

The Lord High Steward: "One moment, Sir Impey, that is not quite as I have it in my notes."

Counsel: "I beg your lordship's pardon if I am wrong."

L.H.S.: "I will read what I have. 'I was hunting for an old photograph of Mary to give Cathcart, and that was how I came across it.' There is nothing about Cathcart being there."

Counsel: "If your lordship will read the next sentence——"

L.H.S.: "Certainly. The next sentence is: 'I remember saying at the time how rusty it was getting.'"

Counsel: "And the next?"

L.H.S.: " 'To whom did you make that observation?' Answer: 'I really don't know, but I distinctly remember saying it.' "

Counsel: "I am much obliged to your lordship. When the noble peer made that remark he was looking out some photographs to give to Captain Cathcart. I think we may reasonably infer that the remark was made to the deceased."

L.H.S. (to the House): "My lords, your lordships will, of course, use your own judgment as to the value of this suggestion."

Counsel: "If your lordships can accept that Denis Cathcart may have known of the existence of the revolver, it is immaterial at what exact moment he saw it. As you have heard, the table-drawer was always left with the key in it. He might have seen it himself at any time, when searching for an envelope or sealing-wax or what not. In any case, I contend that the movements heard by Colonel and Mrs. Marchbanks on Wednesday night were those of Denis Cathcart. While he was writing his farewell letter, perhaps with the pistol before him on the table—yes, at that very moment the Duke of Denver slipped down the stairs and out through the conservatory door. Here is the incredible part of this affair—that again and again we find two series of events, wholly unconnected between themselves, converging upon the same point of time, and causing endless confusion. I have used the word 'incredible'—not because any coincidence is incredible, for we see more remarkable examples every day of our lives than any writer of fiction would dare to invent—but merely in order to take it out of the mouth of the learned Attorney-General, who is preparing to make it return, boomerang-fashion, against me. (Laughter.)

"My lords, this is the first of these incredible—I am not afraid of the word—coincidences. At 11.30 the Duke goes downstairs and Cathcart enters the study. The learned Attorney-General, in his cross-examination of my noble client, very justifiably made what capital he could out of the discrepancy between witness's statement at the inquest—which was that he did not leave the house till 2.30—and his present statement—that he left it at half-past eleven. My lords, whatever interpretation you like to place upon the motives of the noble Duke in so doing, I must remind you once more that at the time when that first statement was made everybody supposed that the shot had been fired at three o'clock, and that the misstatement was then useless for the purpose of establishing an alibi.

"Great stress, too, has been laid on the noble Duke's inability to establish this alibi for the hours from 11.30 to 3 a.m. But, my lords, if he is telling the truth in saying that he walked all that time upon the moors without meeting anyone, what alibi could he establish? He is not bound to supply a motive for all his minor actions during the twenty-four hours. No rebutting evidence has been brought to discredit his story. And it is perfectly reasonable that, unable to sleep after the scene with Cathcart, he should go for a walk to calm himself down.

"Meanwhile, Cathcart has finished his letter and tossed it into the post-bag. There is nothing more ironical in the whole of this case than that letter. While the body of a murdered man lay stark upon the threshold, and detectives and doctors searched everywhere for clues, the normal routine of an ordinary English household went, unquestioned, on. That letter, which contained the whole story, lay undisturbed in the post-bag, till it was taken away and put in the post as a matter of course, to be fetched back again, at enormous cost, delay, and risk of life, two months later in vindication of the great English motto: 'Business as usual.'

"Upstairs, Lady Mary Wimsey was packing her suit-case and writing a farewell letter to her people. At length Cathcart signs his name; he takes up the revolver and hurries out into the shrubbery. Still he paces up and down, with what thoughts God alone knows—reviewing the past, no doubt, racked with vain remorse, most of all, bitter against the woman who has ruined him. He bethinks him of the little love-token, the platinum-and-diamond cat which his mistress gave him for good luck! At any rate, he will not die with *that* pressing upon his heart. With a furious gesture he hurls it far from him. He puts the pistol to his head.

"But something arrests him. Not that! Not that! He sees in fancy his own hideously disfigured corpse—the shattered jaw—the burst eyeball—blood and brains horribly splashed about. No. Let the bullet go cleanly to the heart. Not even in death can he bear the thought of looking—*so!*

"He places the revolver against his breast and draws the trigger. With a little moan, he drops to the sodden ground. The weapon falls from his hand; his fingers scrabble a little at his breast.

"The gamekeeper who heard the shot is puzzled that poachers should come so close. Why are they not on the moors? He thinks of the hares in the plantation. He takes his lantern and searches in the thick drizzle. Nothing. Only soggy grass and dripping trees. He is human. He concludes his ears deceived him, and he returns to his warm bed. Midnight passes. One o'clock passes.

"The rain is less heavy now. Look! In the shrubbery—what was that? A movement. The shot man is moving—groaning a little—crawling to his feet. Chilled to the bone, weak from loss of blood, shaking with the fever of his wound, he but dimly remembers his purpose. His groping hands go to the wound in his breast. He pulls out a handkerchief and presses it upon the place. He drags himself up, slipping and stumbling. The handkerchief slides to the ground, and lies there beside the revolver among the fallen leaves.

"Something in his aching brain tells him to crawl back to the house. He is sick, in pain, hot and cold by turns, and horribly thirsty. There someone will take him in and be kind to him—give him things to drink. Swaying and starting, now falling on hands and knees, now reeling to and fro, he makes that terrible nightmare journey to the house. Now he walks, now he crawls, dragging his heavy limbs after him. At last, the conservatory door! Here there will be help. And water for his fever in the trough by the well. He crawls up to it on hands and knees, and strains to lift himself. It is growing very difficult to breathe—a heavy weight seems to be bursting his chest. He lifts himself—a frightful hiccuping cough catches him—the blood rushes from his mouth. He drops down. It is indeed all over.

"Once more the hours pass. Three o'clock, the hour of rendezvous, draws on. Eagerly the young lover leaps the wall and comes hurrying through the shrubbery to greet his bride to be. It is cold and wet, but his happiness gives him no time to think of his surroundings. He passes through the shrubbery without a thought. He reaches the conservatory door, through which in a few moments love and happiness will come to him. And in that moment he stumbles across—the dead body of a man!

"Fear possesses him. He hears a distant footstep. With but one idea—escape from this horror of horrors—he dashes into the shrubbery, just as, fatigued perhaps a little, but with a mind soothed by his little expedition, the Duke of Denver comes briskly up the path, to meet the eager bride over the body of her betrothed.

"My lords, the rest is clear. Lady Mary Wimsey, forced by a horrible appearance of things into suspecting her lover of murder, undertook—with what courage every man amongst you will realise—to conceal that George Goyles ever was upon the scene. Of this ill-considered action of hers came much mystery and perplexity. Yet, my lords, while chivalry holds its own, not one amongst us will breathe one word of blame against that gallant lady. As the old song says:

> God send each man at his end
> Such hawks, such hounds, and such a friend.

"I think, my lords, that there is nothing more for me to say. To you I leave the solemn and joyful task of freeing the noble peer, your companion, from this unjust charge. You are but human, my lords, and some among you will have grumbled, some will have mocked on assuming these mediaeval splendours of scarlet and ermine, so foreign to the taste and habit of a utilitarian age. You know well enough that

> 'Tis not the balm, the sceptre and the ball,
> The sword, the mace, the crown imperial,
> The intertissued robe of gold and pearl,
> The farcèd title, nor the tide of pomp
> That beats upon the high shores of the world

that can add any dignity to noble blood. And yet, to have beheld, day after day, the head of one of the oldest and noblest houses in England standing here, cut off from your fellowship, stripped of his historic honours, robed only in the justice of his cause—this cannot have failed to move your pity and indignation.

"My lords, it is your happy privilege to restore to his grace the Duke of Denver these traditional symbols of his exalted rank. When the clerk of this House shall address to you severally the solemn question: Do you find Gerald, Duke of Denver, Viscount St. George, guilty or not guilty of the dreadful crime of murder, every one of you may, with a confidence unmarred by any shadow of doubt, lay his hand upon his heart and say, 'Not guilty, upon my honour.' "

CHAPTER XIX

WHO GOES HOME?

Drunk as a lord? As a class they are really very sober.
Judge Cluer, in court.

WHILE THE ATTORNEY-GENERAL was engaged in the ungrateful task of trying to obscure what was not only plain, but agreeable to everybody's feelings, Lord Peter hauled Parker off to a Lyons over the way, and listened, over an enormous dish of eggs and bacon, to a brief account of Mrs. Grimethorpe's dash to town, and a long one of Lady Mary's cross-examination.

"What are you grinning about?" snapped the narrator.

"Just natural imbecility," said Lord Peter. "I say, poor old Cathcart. She *was* a girl! For the matter of that, I suppose she still is. I don't know why I should talk as if she'd died away the moment I took my eyes off her."

"Horribly self-centred, you are," grumbled Mr. Parker.

"I know. I always was from a child. But what worries me is that I seem to be gettin' so susceptible. When Barbara turned me down——"

"You're cured," said his friend brutally. "As a matter of fact, I've noticed it for some time."

Lord Peter sighed deeply. "I value your candour, Charles," he said, "but I wish you hadn't such an unkind way of putting things. Besides—— I say, are they coming out?"

The crowd in Parliament Square was beginning to stir and spread. Sparse streams of people began to drift across the street. A splash of scarlet appeared against the grey stone of St. Stephen's. Mr. Murbles's clerk dashed in suddenly at the door.

"All right, my lord—acquitted—unanimously—and will you please come across, my lord?"

They ran out. At sight of Lord Peter some excited bystanders raised a cheer. The great wind tore suddenly through the Square, bellying out the scarlet robes of the emerging peers. Lord Peter was bandied from one to the other, till he reached the centre of the group.

"Excuse me, your grace."

214

It was Bunter. Bunter, miraculously, with his arms full of scarlet and ermine, enveloping the shameful blue serge suit which had been a badge of disgrace.

"Allow me to offer my respectful congratulations, your grace."

"Bunter!" cried Lord Peter. "Great God, the man's gone mad! Damn you, man, take that thing away," he added, plunging at a tall photographer in a made-up tie.

"Too late, my lord," said the offender, jubilantly pushing in the slide.

"Peter," said the Duke. "Er—thanks, old man."

"All right," said his lordship. "Very jolly trip and all that. You're lookin' very fit. Oh, don't shake hands—there, I knew it! I heard that man's confounded shutter go."

They pushed their way through the surging mob to the cars. The two Duchesses got in, and the Duke was following, when a bullet crashed through the glass of the window, missing Denver's head by an inch, and ricocheting from the wind-screen among the crowd.

A rush and a yell. A big bearded man struggled for a moment with three constables; then came a succession of wild shots, and a fierce rush—the crowd parting, then closing in, like hounds on the fox, streaming past the Houses of Parliament, heading for Westminster Bridge.

"He's shot a woman—he's under that 'bus—no, he isn't—hi!—murder!—stop him!" Shrill screams and yells—police whistles blowing—constables darting from every corner—swooping down in taxis—running.

The driver of a taxi spinning across the bridge saw the fierce face just ahead of his bonnet, and jammed on the brakes, as the madman's fingers closed for the last time on the trigger. Shot and tyre exploded almost simultaneously; the taxi slewed giddily over to the right, scooping the fugitive with it, and crashed horribly into a tram standing vacant on the Embankment dead-end.

"I couldn't 'elp it," yelled the taxi-man, "'e fired at me. Ow, Gawd, I couldn't 'elp it."

Lord Peter and Parker arrived together, panting.

"Here, constable," gasped his lordship; "I know this man. He has an unfortunate grudge against my brother. In connection with a poaching matter—up in Yorkshire. Tell the coroner to come to me for information."

"Very good, my lord."

"Don't photograph *that*," said Lord Peter to the man with the reflex, whom he suddenly found at his elbow.

The photographer shook his head.

"They wouldn't like to see that, my lord. Only the scene of the crash and the ambulance-men. Bright, newsy pictures, you know. Nothing gruesome"—with an explanatory jerk of the head at the great dark splotches in the roadway—"it doesn't pay."

A red-haired reporter appeared from nowhere with a note-book.

"Here," said his lordship, "do you want the story? I'll give it you now."

.　　.　　.　　.　　.

There was not, after all, the slightest trouble in the matter of Mrs. Grimethorpe. Seldom, perhaps, has a ducal escapade resolved itself with so little embarrassment. His grace, indeed, who was nothing if not a gentleman, braced himself gallantly for a regretful and sentimental interview. In all his rather stupid affairs he had never run away from a scene, or countered a storm of sobs with that maddening "Well, I'd better be going now" which has led to so many despairs and occasionally to cold shot. But, on this occasion, the whole business fell flat. The lady was not interested.

"I am free now," she said. "I am going back to my own people in Cornwall. I do not want anything, now that he is dead." The Duke's dutiful caress was a most uninteresting failure.

Lord Peter saw her home to a respectable little hotel in Bloomsbury. She liked the taxi, and the large, glittering shops, and the sky-signs. They stopped at Piccadilly Circus to see the Bonzo dog smoke his gasper and the Nestlé's baby consume his bottle of milk. She was amazed to find that the prices of the things in Swan & Edgar's window were, if anything, more reasonable than those current in Stapley.

"I should like one of those blue scarves," she said, "but I'm thinking 'twould not be fitting, and me a widow."

"You could buy it now, and wear it later on," suggested his lordship, "in Cornwall, you know."

"Yes." She glanced at her brown stuff gown. "Could I buy my blacks here? I shall have to get some for the funeral. Just a dress and a hat—and a coat, maybe."

"I should think it would be a very good idea."

"Now?"

"Why not?"

"I have money," she said; "I took it from his desk. It's mine now, I suppose. Not that I'd wish to be beholden to him. But I don't look at it that way."

"I shouldn't think twice about it, if I were you," said Lord Peter. She walked before him into the shop—her own woman at last.

.   .   .   .   .

In the early hours of the morning Inspector Sugg, who happened to be passing Parliament Square, came upon a taxi-man apparently addressing a heated expostulation to the statue of Lord Palmerston. Indignant at this senseless proceeding, Mr. Sugg advanced, and then observed that the statesman was sharing his pedestal with a gentleman in evening dress, who clung precariously with one hand, while with the other he held an empty champagne-bottle to his eye, and surveyed the surrounding streets.

"Hi," said the policeman, "what are you doing there? Come off of it!"

"Hullo!" said the gentleman, losing his balance quite suddenly, and coming down in a jumbled manner. "Have you seen my friend? Very odd thing—damned odd. 'Spec you know where find him, what? When in doubt—tasker pleeshman, what? Friend of mine. Very dignified sort of man 'nopera-hat. Freddy—good ol' Freddy. Alwaysh answersh t'name—jush like jolly ol' bloodhound!" He got to his feet and stood beaming on the officer.

"Why, if it ain't his lordship," said Inspector Sugg, who had met Lord Peter in other circumstances. "Better be gettin' home, my lord. Night air's chilly-like, ain't it? You'll catch a cold or summat o' that. Here's your taxi—just you jump in now."

"No," said Lord Peter. "No. Couldn' do that. Not without frien'. Good ol' Freddy. Never—desert—friend! Dear ol' Sugg. Wouldn't desert Freddy." He attempted an attitude, with one foot poised on the step of the taxi, but, miscalculating his distance, stepped heavily into the gutter, thus entering the vehicle unexpectedly, head first.

Mr. Sugg tried to tuck his legs in and shut him up, but his lordship thwarted this movement with unlooked-for agility, and sat firmly on the step.

"Not my taxi," he explained solemnly. "Freddy's taxi. Not right—run away with frien's taxi. Very odd. Jush went roun' corner to fesh

Fred'sh taxshi—Freddy jush went roun' corner fesh *my* taxi—fesh friend'sh taxshi—friendship sush a beautiful thing—don't you thing-so, Shugg? Can't leave frien'. Beshides—there'sh dear ol' Parker."

"Mr. Parker?" said the Inspector apprehensively. "Where?"

"Hush!" said his lordship. "Don' wake baby, theresh good shoul. Neshle'sh baby—jush shee 'm neshle, don't he neshle nishely?"

Following his lordship's gaze, the horrified Sugg observed his official superior cosily tucked up on the far side of Palmerston and smiling a happy smile in his sleep. With an exclamation of alarm he bent over and shook the sleeper.

"Unkind!" cried Lord Peter in a deep, reproachful tone. "Dishturb poor fellow—poor hardworkin' pleeshman. Never getsh up till alarm goes. . . . 'Stra'or'nary thing," he added, as though struck by a new idea, "why hashn't alarm gone off, Shugg?" He pointed a wavering finger at Big Ben. "They've for-forgotten to wind it up. Dishgrayshful. I'll write to *The T-T-Timesh* about it."

Mr. Sugg wasted no words, but picked up the slumbering Parker and hoisted him into the taxi.

"Never—never—deshert——" began Lord Peter, resisting all efforts to dislodge him from the step, when a second taxi, advancing from Whitehall, drew up, with the Hon. Freddy Arbuthnot cheering loudly at the window.

"Look who's here!" cried the Hon. Freddy. "Jolly, jolly, jolly ol' Sugg. Let'sh all go home together."

"That'sh *my* taxshi," interposed his lordship, with dignity, staggering across to it. The two whirled together for a moment; then the Hon. Freddy was flung into Sugg's arms, while his lordship, with a satisfied air, cried "Home!" to the new taxi-man, and instantly fell asleep in a corner of the vehicle.

Mr. Sugg scratched his head, gave Lord Peter's address, and watched the cab drive off. Then, supporting the Hon. Freddy on his ample bosom, he directed the other man to convey Mr. Parker to 12a Great Ormond Street.

"Take me home," cried the Hon. Freddy, bursting into tears, "they've all gone and left me!"

"You leave it to me, sir," said the Inspector. He glanced over his shoulder at St. Stephen's, whence a group of Commons were just issuing from an all-night sitting.

"Mr. Parker an' all," said Inspector Sugg, adding devoutly, "Thank Gawd there weren't no witnesses."

218

The Unpleasantness
at the Bellona Club

CONTENTS

CHAPTER I

OLD MOSSY-FACE

"WHAT IN THE WORLD, Wimsey, are you doing in this Morgue?" demanded Captain Fentiman, flinging aside the "Evening Banner" with the air of a man released from an irksome duty.

"Oh, I wouldn't call it that," retorted Wimsey, amiably. "Funeral Parlor at the very least. Look at the marble. Look at the furnishings. Look at the palms and the chaste bronze nude in the corner."

"Yes, and look at the corpses. Place always reminds me of that old thing in 'Punch,' you know—'Waiter, take away Lord Whatsisname, he's been dead two days.' Look at Old Ormsby there, snoring like a hippopotamus. Look at my revered grandpa—dodders in here at ten every morning, collects the 'Morning Post' and the armchair by the fire, and becomes part of the furniture till the evening. Poor old devil. Suppose I'll be like that one of these days. I wish to God Jerry had put me out with the rest of 'em. What's the good of coming through for this sort of thing? What'll you have?"

"Dry martini," said Wimsey. "And you? Two dry martinis, Fred, please. Cheer up. All this remembrance-day business gets on your nerves, don't it? It's my belief most of us would be only too pleased to chuck these community hysterics if the beastly newspapers didn't run it for all it's worth. However, it don't do to say so. They'd hoof me out of the Club if I raised my voice beyond a whisper."

"They'd do that anyway, whatever you were saying," said Fentiman, gloomily. "What *are* you doing here?"

"Waitin' for Colonel Marchbanks," said Wimsey. "Bung-ho!"

"Dining with him?"

"Yes."

Fentiman nodded quietly. He knew that young Marchbanks had been killed at Hill 60, and that the Colonel was wont to give a small, informal dinner on Armistice night to his son's intimate friends.

"I don't mind old Marchbanks," he said, after a pause. "He's a dear old boy."

Wimsey assented.

"And how are things going with you?" he asked.

"Oh, rotten as usual. Tummy all wrong and no money. What's the damn good of it, Wimsey? A man goes and fights for his country, gets his inside gassed out, and loses his job, and all they give him is the privilege of marching past the Cenotaph once a year and paying four shillings in the pound income-tax. Sheila's queer too—overwork, poor girl. It's pretty damnable for a man to have to live on his wife's earnings, isn't it? I can't help it, Wimsey. I go sick and have to chuck jobs up. Money—I never thought of money before the War, but I swear nowadays I'd commit any damned crime to get hold of a decent income."

Fentiman's voice had risen in nervous excitement. A shocked veteran, till then invisible in a neighbouring armchair, poked out a lean head like a tortoise and said "Sh!" viperishly.

"Oh, I wouldn't do that," said Wimsey, lightly. "Crime's a skilled occupation, y' know. Even a comparative imbecile like myself can play the giddy sleuth on the amateur Moriarty. If you're thinkin' of puttin' on a false mustache and lammin' a millionaire on the head, don't do it. That disgustin' habit you have of smoking cigarettes down to the last millimeter would betray you anywhere. I'd only have to come on with a magnifyin' glass and a pair of callipers to say 'The criminal is my dear old friend George Fentiman. Arrest that man!' You might not think it, but I am ready to sacrifice my nearest and dearest in order to curry favour with the police and get a par. in the papers."

Fentiman laughed, and ground out the offending cigarette stub on the nearest ash-tray.

"I wonder anybody cares to know you," he said. The strain and bitterness had left his voice and he sounded merely amused.

"They wouldn't," said Wimsey, "only they think I'm too well-off to have any brains. It's like hearing that the Earl of Somewhere is taking a leading part in a play. Everybody takes it for granted he must act rottenly. I'll tell you my secret. All my criminological investigations are done for me by a 'ghost' at £3 a week, while I get the headlines and frivol with well-known journalists at the Savoy."

"I find you refreshing, Wimsey," said Fentiman, languidly. "You're not in the least witty, but you have a kind of obvious facetiousness which reminds me of the less exacting class of music-hall."

"It's the self-defense of the first-class mind against the superior person," said Wimsey. "But, look here, I'm sorry to hear about Sheila. I don't want to be offensive, old man, but why don't you let me——"

"Damned good of you," said Fentiman, "but I don't care to. There's honestly not the faintest chance I could ever pay you, and I haven't quite got to the point yet——"

"Here's Colonel Marchbanks," broke in Wimsey, "we'll talk about it another time. Good evening, Colonel."

"Evening, Peter. Evening, Fentiman. Beautiful day it's been. No—no cocktails, thanks, I'll stick to whisky. So sorry to keep you waiting like this, but I was having a yarn with poor old Grainger upstairs. He's in a baddish way, I'm afraid. Between you and me, Penberthy doesn't think he'll last out the winter. Very sound man, Penberthy—wonderful, really, that he's kept the old man going so long with his lungs in that frail state. Ah, well! it's what we must all come to. Dear me, there's your grandfather, Fentiman. He's another of Penberthy's miracles. He must be ninety, if he's a day. Will you excuse me for a moment? I must just go and speak to him."

Wimsey's eyes followed the alert, elderly figure as it crossed the spacious smoking-room, pausing now and again to exchange greetings with a fellow-member of the Bellona Club. Drawn close to the huge fireplace stood a great chair with ears after the Victorian pattern. A pair of spindle shanks with neatly-buttoned shoes propped on a footstool were all that was visible of General Fentiman.

"Queer, isn't it," muttered his grandson, "to think that for Old Mossy-face there the Crimea is still *the* War, and the Boer business found him too old to go out. He was given his commission at seventeen, you know—was wounded at Majuba—"

He broke off. Wimsey was not paying attention. He was still watching Colonel Marchbanks.

The Colonel came back to them, walking very quietly and precisely. Wimsey rose and went to meet him.

"I say, Peter," said the Colonel, his kind face gravely troubled, "just come over here a moment. I'm afraid something rather unpleasant has happened."

Fentiman looked round, and something in their manner made him get up and follow them over to the fire.

Wimsey bent down over General Fentiman and drew the "Morning Post" gently away from the gnarled old hands, which lay clasped over the thin chest. He touched the shoulder—put his hand under the white head huddled against the side of the chair. The Colonel watched him anxiously. Then, with a quick jerk, Wimsey lifted the quiet figure. It came up all of a piece, stiff as a wooden doll.

Fentiman laughed. Peal after hysterical peal shook his throat. All round the room, scandalized Bellonians creaked to their gouty feet, shocked by the unmannerly noise.

"Take him away!" said Fentiman, "take him away. He's been dead two days! So are you! So am I! We're all dead and we never noticed it!"

CHAPTER II

THE QUEEN IS OUT

IT IS DOUBTFUL which occurrence was more disagreeable to the senior members of the Bellona Club—the grotesque death of General Fentiman in their midst or the indecent neurasthenia of his grandson. Only the younger men felt no sense of outrage; they knew too much. Dick Challoner—known to his intimates as Tin-Tummy Challoner, owing to the fact that he had been fitted with a spare part after the second battle of the Somme—took the gasping Fentiman away into the deserted library for a stiffener. The Club Secretary hurried in, in his dress-shirt and trousers, the half-dried lather still clinging to his jaws. After one glance he sent an agitated waiter to see if Dr. Penberthy was still in the Club. Colonel Marchbanks laid a large silk handkerchief reverently over the rigid face in the arm-chair and remained quietly standing. A little circle formed about the edge of the hearth-rug, not quite certain what to do. From time to time it was swelled by fresh arrivals, whom the news had greeted in the hall as they wandered in. A little group appeared from the bar. "What? old Fentiman?" they said. "Good God, you don't say so. Poor old blighter. Heart gone at last, I suppose"; and they extinguished cigars and cigarettes, and stood by, not liking to go away again.

Dr. Penberthy was just changing for dinner. He came down hurriedly, caught just as he was going out to an Armistice dinner, his silk hat tilted to the back of his head, his coat and muffler pushed loosely open. He was a thin, dark man with the abrupt manner which distinguishes the Army Surgeon from the West-end practitioner. The group by the fire made way for him, except Wimsey, who hung rather foolishly upon the big elbow-chair, gazing in a helpless way at the body.

Penberthy ran practised hands quickly over neck, wrists and knee-joints.

"Dead several hours," he pronounced, sharply. "Rigor well-established—beginning to pass off." He moved the dead man's left leg in illustration; it swung loose at the knee. "I've been expecting this. Heart very weak. Might happen any moment. Any one spoken to him to-day?"

He glanced round interrogatively.

"I saw him here after lunch," volunteered somebody. "I didn't speak."

"I thought he was asleep," said another.

Nobody remembered speaking to him. They were so used to old General Fentiman, slumbering by the fire.

"Ah, well," said the doctor. "What's the time? Seven?" He seemed to make a rapid calculation. "Say five hours for rigor to set in—must have taken place very rapidly—he probably came in at his usual time, sat down and died straight away."

"He always walked from Dover Street," put in an elderly man. "I told him it was too great an exertion at his age. You've heard me say so, Ormsby."

"Yes, yes, quite," said the purple-faced Ormsby. "Dear me, just so."

"Well, there's nothing to be done," said the doctor. "Died in his sleep. Is there an empty bedroom we can take him to, Culyer?"

"Yes, certainly," said the Secretary. "James, fetch the key of number sixteen from my office and tell them to put the bed in order. I suppose, eh, doctor?—when the rigor passes off we shall be able to—eh?"

"Oh, yes, you'll be able to do everything that's required. I'll send the proper people in to lay him out for you. Somebody had better let his people know—only they'd better not show up till we can get him more presentable."

"Captain Fentiman knows already," said Colonel Marchbanks. "And Major Fentiman is staying in the Club—he'll probably be in before long. Then there's a sister, I think."

225

"Yes, old Lady Dormer," said Penberthy, "she lives round in Portman Square. They haven't been on speaking terms for years. Still, she'll have to know."

"I'll ring them up," said the Colonel. "We can't leave it to Captain Fentiman, he's in no fit state to be worried, poor fellow. You'll have to have a look at him, doctor, when you've finished here. An attack of the old trouble—nerves, you know."

"All right. Ah! is the room ready, Culyer? Then we'll move him. Will somebody take his shoulders—no, not you, Culyer" (for the Secretary had only one sound arm), "Lord Peter, yes, thank you—lift carefully."

Wimsey put his long, strong hands under the stiff arms; the doctor gathered up the legs; they moved away. They looked like a dreadful little Guy Fawkes procession, with that humped and unreverend mannikin bobbing and swaying between them.

The door closed after them, and a tension seemed removed. The circle broke up into groups. Somebody lit a cigarette. The planet's tyrant, dotard Death, had held his gray mirror before them for a moment and shown them the image of things to come. But now it was taken away again. The unpleasantness had passed. Fortunate, indeed, that Penberthy was the old man's own doctor. He knew all about it. He could give a certificate. No inquest. Nothing undesirable. The members of the Bellona Club could go to dinner.

Colonel Marchbanks turned to go through the far door towards the library. In a narrow ante-room between the two rooms there was a convenient telephone-cabinet for the use of those members who did not wish to emerge into the semi-publicity of the entrance-hall.

"Hi, colonel! not that one. That instrument's out of order," said a man called Wetheridge, who saw him go. "Disgraceful, I call it. I wanted to use the 'phone this morning, and—oh! hullo! the notice has gone. I suppose it's all right again. They ought to let one know."

Colonel Marchbanks paid little attention to Wetheridge. He was the club grumbler, distinguished even in that fellowship of the dyspeptic and peremptory—always threatening to complain to the Committee, harassing the Secretary and constituting a perennial thorn in the sides of his fellow-members. He retired, murmuring, to his chair and the evening paper, and the Colonel stepped into the telephone-cabinet to call up Lady Dormer's house in Portman Square.

Presently he came out through the library into the entrance-hall, and met Penberthy and Wimsey just descending the staircase.

"Have you broken the news to Lady Dormer?" asked Wimsey.

"Lady Dormer is dead," said the Colonel. "Her maid tells me she passed quietly away at half-past ten this morning."

CHAPTER III

HEARTS COUNT MORE THAN DIAMONDS

ABOUT TEN DAYS after that notable Armistice Day, Lord Peter Wimsey was sitting in his library, reading a rare fourteenth century manuscript of Justinian. It gave him particular pleasure, being embellished with a large number of drawings in sepia, extremely delicate in workmanship, and not always equally so in subject. Beside him on a convenient table stood a long-necked decanter of priceless old port. From time to time he stimulated his interest with a few sips, pursing his lips thoughtfully, and slowly savouring the balmy after-taste.

A ring at the front-door of the flat caused him to exclaim "Oh, hell!" and cock an attentive ear for the intruder's voice. Apparently the result was satisfactory, for he closed the Justinian and had assumed a welcoming smile when the door opened.

"Mr. Murbles, my lord."

The little elderly gentleman who entered was so perfectly the family solicitor as really to have no distinguishing personality at all, beyond a great kindliness of heart and a weakness for soda-mint lozenges.

"I am not disturbing you, I trust, Lord Peter."

"Good lord, no, sir. Always delighted to see you. Bunter, a glass for Mr. Murbles. Very glad you've turned up, sir. The Cockburn '80 always tastes a lot better in company—discernin' company, that is. Once knew a fellow who polluted it with a Trichinopoly. He was not asked again. Eight months later, he committed suicide. I don't say it was on that account. But he was earmarked for a bad end, what?"

"You horrify me," said Mr. Murbles, gravely. "I have seen many men sent to the gallows for crimes with which I could feel much more sympathy. Thank-you, Bunter, thank-you. You are quite well, I trust?"

"I am in excellent health, I am obliged to you, sir."

"That's good. Been doing any photography lately?"

227

"A certain amount, sir. But merely of a pictorial description, if I may venture to call it so. Criminological material, sir, has been distressingly deficient of late."

"Perhaps Mr. Murbles has brought us something," suggested Wimsey.

"No," said Mr. Murbles, holding the Cockburn '80 beneath his nostrils and gently agitating the glass to release the ethers, "no, I can't say I have, precisely. I will not disguise that I have come in the hope of deriving benefit from your trained habits of observation and deduction, but I fear—that is, I trust—in fact, I am confident—that nothing of an undesirable nature is involved. The fact is," he went on, as the door closed upon the retreating Bunter, "a curious question has arisen with regard to the sad death of General Fentiman at the Bellona Club, to which, I understand, you were a witness."

"If you understand that, Murbles," said his lordship, cryptically, "you understand a damn sight more than I do. I did not witness the death—I witnessed the discovery of the death—which is a very different thing, by a long chalk."

"By how long a chalk?" asked Mr. Murbles, eagerly. "That is just what I am trying to find out."

"That's very inquisitive of you," said Wimsey. "I think perhaps it would be better . . ." he lifted his glass and tilted it thoughtfully, watching the wine coil down in thin flower-petallings from rim to stem . . . "if you were to tell me exactly what you want to know . . . and why. After all . . . I'm a member of the Club . . . family associations chiefly, I suppose . . . but there it is."

Mr. Murbles looked up sharply, but Wimsey's attention seemed focussed upon the port.

"Quite so," said the solicitor. "Very well. The facts of the matter are these. General Fentiman had, as you know, a sister Felicity, twelve years younger than himself. She was very beautiful and very wilful as a girl, and ought to have made a very fine match, but for the fact that the Fentimans, though extremely well-descended, were anything but well-off. As usual at that period, all the money there was went to educating the boy, buying him a commission in a crack regiment and supporting him there in the style which was considered indispensable for a Fentiman. Consequently there was nothing left to furnish a marriage-portion for Felicity, and that was rather disastrous for a young woman sixty years ago.

"Well, Felicity got tired of being dragged through the social round in her darned muslins and gloves that had been to the cleaners—and she had the spirit to resent her mother's perpetual strategies in the match-making line. There was a dreadful, decrepit old viscount, eaten up with diseases and dissipations, who would have been delighted to totter to the altar with a handsome young creature of eighteen, and I am sorry to say that the girl's father and mother did everything they could to force her into accepting this disgraceful proposal. In fact, the engagement was announced and the wedding-day fixed, when, to the extreme horror of her family, Felicity calmly informed them one morning that she had gone out before breakfast and actually got married, in the most indecent secrecy and haste, to a middle-aged man called Dormer, very honest and abundantly wealthy, and—horrid to relate—a prosperous manufacturer. Buttons, in fact—made of papier mâché or something, with a patent indestructible shank—were the revolting antecedents to which this headstrong young Victorian had allied herself.

"Naturally there was a terrible scandal, and the parents did their best—seeing that Felicity was a minor—to get the marriage annulled. However, Felicity checkmated their plans pretty effectually by escaping from her bedroom—I fear, indeed, that she actually climbed down a tree in the back-garden, crinoline and all—and running away with her husband. After which, seeing that the worst had happened—indeed, Dormer, a man of prompt action, lost no time in putting his bride in the family way—the old people put the best face they could on it in the grand Victorian manner. That is, they gave their consent to the marriage, forwarded their daughter's belongings to her new home in Manchester, and forbade her to darken their doors again."

"Highly proper," murmured Wimsey. "I'm determined never to be a parent. Modern manners and the break-up of the fine old traditions have simply ruined the business. I shall devote my life and fortune to the endowment of research on the best method of producin' human beings decorously and unobtrusively from eggs. All parental responsibility to devolve upon the incubator."

"I hope not," said Mr. Murbles. "My own profession is largely supported by domestic entanglements. To proceed. Young Arthur Fentiman seems to have shared the family views. He was disgusted at having a brother-in-law in buttons, and the jests of his mess-mates did nothing to sweeten his feelings toward his sister. He became impenetrably military and professional, crusted over before his time, and refused to acknowledge the existence of anybody called Dormer.

Mind you, the old boy was a fine soldier, and absolutely wrapped up in his Army associations. In due course he married—not well, for he had not the means to entitle him to a noble wife, and he would not demean himself by marrying money, like the unspeakable Felicity. He married a suitable gentlewoman with a few thousand pounds. She died (largely, I believe, owing to the military regularity with which her husband ordained that she should perform her maternal functions), leaving a numerous but feeble family of children. Of these, the only one to attain maturity was the father of the two Fentimans you know—Major Robert and Captain George Fentiman."

"I don't know Robert very well," interjected Wimsey. "I've met him. Frightfully hearty and all that—regular army type."

"Yes, he's of the old Fentiman stock. Poor George inherited a weakly strain from his grandmother, I'm afraid."

"Well, nervous, anyhow," said Wimsey, who knew better than the old solicitor the kind of mental and physical strain George Fentiman had undergone. The War pressed hardly upon imaginative men in responsible positions. "And then he was gassed and all that, you know," he added, apologetically.

"Just so," said Mr. Murbles. "Robert, you know, is unmarried and still in the Army. He's not particularly well-off, naturally, for none of the Fentimans ever had a bean, as I believe one says nowadays; but he does very well. George——"

"Poor old George! All right, sir, you needn't tell me about him. Usual story. Decentish job—imprudent marriage—chucks everything to join up in 1914—invalided out—job gone—health gone—no money —heroic wife keeping the home-fires burning—general fed-upness. Don't let's harrow our feelings. Take it as read."

"Yes, I needn't go into that. Their father is dead, of course, and up till ten days ago there were just two surviving Fentimans of the earlier generation. The old General lived on the small fixed income which came to him through his wife and his retired pension. He had a solitary little flat in Dover Street and an elderly man-servant, and he practically lived at the Bellona Club. And there was his sister, Felicity."

"How did she come to be Lady Dormer?"

"Why, that's where we come to the interesting part of the story. Henry Dormer——"

"The button-maker?"

"The button-maker. He became an exceedingly rich man indeed

—so rich, in fact, that he was able to offer financial assistance to certain exalted persons who need not be mentioned and so, in time, and in consideration of valuable services to the nation not very clearly specified in the Honours List, he became Sir Henry Dormer, Bart. His only child—a girl—had died, and there was no prospect of any further family, so there was, of course, no reason why he should not be made a baronet for his trouble."

"Acid man you are," said Wimsey. "No reverence, no simple faith or anything of that kind. Do lawyers ever go to heaven?"

"I have no information on that point," said Mr. Murbles, dryly. "Lady Dormer——"

"Did the marriage turn out well otherwise?" inquired Wimsey.

"I believe it was perfectly happy," replied the lawyer, "an unfortunate circumstance in one way, since it entirely precluded the possibility of any reconciliation with her relatives. Lady Dormer, who was a fine, generous-hearted woman, frequently made overtures of peace, but the General held sternly aloof. So did his son—partly out of respect for the old boy's wishes, but chiefly, I fancy, because he belonged to an Indian regiment and spent most of his time abroad. Robert Fentiman, however, showed the old lady a certain amount of attention, paying occasional visits and so forth, and so did George at one time. Of course they never let the General know a word about it, or he would have had a fit. After the War, George rather dropped his great-aunt—I don't know why."

"I can guess," said Wimsey. "No job—no money, y' know. Didn't want to look pointed. That sort of thing, what?"

"Possibly. Or there may have been some kind of quarrel. I don't know. Anyway, those are the facts. I hope I am not boring you, by the way?"

"I am bearing up," said Wimsey, "waiting for the point where the Money comes in. There's a steely legal glitter in your eye, sir, which suggests that the thrill is not far off."

"Quite correct," said Mr. Murbles. "I now come—thank-you, well, yes—I will take just one more glass. I thank Providence I am not of a gouty constitution. Yes. Ah!—We now come to the melancholy event of November 11th last, and I must ask you to follow me with the closest attention."

"By all means," said Wimsey, politely.

"Lady Dormer," pursued Mr. Murbles, leaning earnestly forward, and punctuating every sentence with sharp little jabs of his gold-mounted eyeglasses, held in his right finger and thumb, "was an old woman, and had been ailing for a very long time. However, she was still the same headstrong and vivacious personality that she had been as a girl, and on the fifth of November she was suddenly seized with a fancy to go out at night and see a display of fireworks at the Crystal Palace or some such place—it may have been Hampstead Heath or the White City—I forget, and it is of no consequence. The important thing is, that it was a raw, cold evening. She insisted on undertaking her little expedition nevertheless, enjoyed the entertainment as heartily as the youngest child, imprudently exposed herself to the night air and caught a severe cold which, in two days' time, turned to pneumonia. On November 10th she was sinking fast, and scarcely expected to live out the night. Accordingly, the young lady who lived with her as her ward—a distant relative, Miss Ann Dorland—sent a message to General Fentiman that if he wished to see his sister alive, he should come immediately. For the sake of our common human nature, I am happy to say that this news broke down the barrier of pride and obstinacy that had kept the old gentleman away so long. He came, found Lady Dormer just conscious, though very feeble, stayed with her about half an hour and departed, still stiff as a ramrod, but visibly softened. This was about four o'clock in the afternoon. Shortly afterwards, Lady Dormer became unconscious, and, indeed, never moved or spoke again, passing peacefully away in her sleep at half-past ten the following morning.

"Presumably the shock and nervous strain of the interview with his long-estranged sister had been too much for the old General's feeble system, for, as you know, he died at the Bellona Club at some time —not yet clearly ascertained—on the same day, the eleventh of November.

"Now then, at last—and you have been very patient with my tedious way of explaining all this—we come to the point at which we want your help."

Mr. Murbles refreshed himself with a sip of port, and, looking a little anxiously at Wimsey, who had closed his eyes and appeared to be nearly asleep, he resumed.

"I have not mentioned, I think, how I come to be involved in this matter myself. My father was the Fentimans' family solicitor, a position to which I naturally succeeded when I took over the business at his death. General Fentiman, though he had little enough to leave, was not the sort of disorderly person who dies without making a proper testamentary disposition. His retired pension, of course, died with him, but his small private estate was properly disposed by will. There was a small legacy—fifty pounds—to his man-servant (a very attached and superior fellow); then one or two trifling bequests to old military friends and the servants at the Bellona Club (rings, medals, weapons and small sums of a few pounds each). Then came the bulk of his estate, about £2,000, invested in sound securities, and bringing in an income of slightly over £100 per annum. These securities, specifically named and enumerated, were left to Captain George Fentiman, the younger grandson, in a very proper clause, which stated that the testator intended no slight in thus passing over the elder one, Major Robert, but that, as George stood in the greater need of monetary help, being disabled, married, and so forth, whereas his brother had his profession and was without ties, George's greater necessity gave him the better claim to such money as there was. Robert was finally named as executor and residuary legatee, thus succeeding to all such personal effects and monies as were not specifically devised elsewhere. Is that clear?"

"Clear as a bell. Was Robert satisfied with that arrangement?"

"Oh dear, yes; perfectly. He knew all about the will beforehand and had agreed that it was quite fair and right."

"Nevertheless," said Wimsey, "it appears to be such a small matter, on the face of it, that you must be concealing something perfectly devastating up your sleeve. Out with it, man, out with it! Whatever the shock may be, I am braced to bear it."

"The shock," said Mr. Murbles, "was inflicted on me, personally, last Friday by Lady Dormer's man of business—Mr. Pritchard of Lincoln's Inn. He wrote to me, asking if I could inform him of the exact hour and minute of General Fentiman's decease. I replied, of course, that, owing to the peculiar circumstances under which the event took place, I was unable to answer his question as precisely as I could have wished, but that I understood Dr. Penberthy to have given it as his opinion that the General had died some time in the forenoon of November 11th. Mr. Pritchard then asked if he might wait upon me without delay, as the matter he had to discuss was of the most urgent importance. Accordingly I appointed a time for the interview on Monday afternoon, and when Mr. Pritchard arrived he informed me of the following particulars.

"A good many years before her death, Lady Dormer—who, as I said before, was an eminently generous-minded woman—made a will.

Her husband and her daughter were then dead. Henry Dormer had few relations, and all of them were fairly wealthy people. By his own will he had sufficiently provided for these persons, and had left the remainder of his property, amounting to something like seven hundred thousand pounds, to his wife, with the express stipulation that she was to consider it as her own, to do what she liked with, without any restriction whatsoever. Accordingly, Lady Dormer's will divided this very handsome fortune—apart from certain charitable and personal bequests with which I need not trouble you—between the people who, for one reason and another, had the greatest claims on her affection. Twelve thousand pounds were to go to Miss Ann Dorland. The whole of the remainder was to pass to her brother, General Fentiman, if he was still living at her death. If, on the other hand, he should pre-decease her, the conditions were reversed. In that case, the bulk of the money came to Miss Dorland, and fifteen thousand pounds were to be equally divided between Major Robert Fentiman and his brother George."

Wimsey whistled softly.

"I quite agree with you," said Mr. Murbles. "It is a most awkward situation. Lady Dormer died at precisely 10:37 A.M. on November 11th. General Fentiman died that same morning at some time, presumably after 10 o'clock, which was his usual hour for arriving at the Club, and certainly before 7 P.M. when his death was discovered. If he died immediately on his arrival, or at any time up to 10:36, then Miss Dorland is an important heiress, and my clients the Fentimans get only seven thousand pounds or so apiece. If, on the other hand, his death occurred even a few seconds after 10:37, Miss Dorland receives only twelve thousand pounds, George Fentiman is left with the small pittance bequeathed to him under his father's will—while Robert Fentiman, the residuary legatee, inherits a very considerable fortune of well over half a million."

"And what," said Wimsey, "do you want me to do about it?"

"Why," replied the lawyer, with a slight cough, "it occurred to me that you, with your—if I may say so—remarkable powers of deduction and analysis might be able to solve the extremely difficult and delicate problem of the precise moment of General Fentiman's decease. You were in the Club when the death was discovered, you saw the body, you know the places and the persons involved, and you are, by your standing and personal character, exceptionally well fitted to carry out the necessary investigations without creating any—ahem!—

234

public agitation or—er—scandal, or, in fact, notoriety, which would, I need hardly say, be extremely painful to all concerned."

"It's awkward," said Wimsey, "uncommonly awkward."

"It is indeed," said the lawyer with some warmth, "for as we are now situated, it is impossible to execute either will or—or in short do anything at all. It is most unfortunate that the circumstances were not fully understood at the time, when the—um—the body of General Fentiman was available for inspection. Naturally, Mr. Pritchard was quite unaware of the anomalous situation, and as I knew nothing about Lady Dormer's will, I had no idea that anything beyond Dr. Penberthy's certificate was, or ever could become, necessary."

"Couldn't you get the parties to come to some agreement?" suggested Wimsey.

"If we are unable to reach any satisfactory conclusion about the time of the death, that will probably be the only way out of the difficulty. But at the moment there are certain obstacles——"

"Somebody's being greedy, eh?—You'd rather not say more definitely, I suppose? No? H'm, well! From a purely detached point of view it's a very pleasin' and pretty little problem, you know."

"You will undertake to solve it for us then, Lord Peter?"

Wimsey's fingers tapped out an intricate fugal passage on the arm of his chair.

"If I were you, Murbles, I'd try again to get a settlement."

"Do you mean," asked Mr. Murbles, "that you think my clients have a losing case?"

"No—I can't say that. By the way, Murbles, who is your client—Robert or George?"

"Well, the Fentiman family in general. I know, naturally, that Robert's gain is George's loss. But none of the parties wishes anything but that the actual facts of the case should be determined."

"I see. You'll put up with anything I happen to dig out?"

"Of course."

"However favourable or unfavourable it may be?"

"I should not lend myself to any other course," said Mr. Murbles, rather stiffly.

"I know that, sir. But—well!—I only mean that—Look here, sir! when you were a boy, did you ever go about pokin' sticks and things into peaceful, mysterious lookin' ponds, just to see what was at the bottom?"

"Frequently," replied Mr. Murbles. "I was extremely fond of natural history and had a quite remarkable collection (if I may say so at this distance of time) of pond fauna."

"Did you ever happen to stir up a deuce of a stink in the course of your researches?"

"My dear Lord Peter—you are making me positively uneasy."

"Oh, I don't know that you need be. I am only giving you a general warning, you know. Of course, if you wish it, I'll investigate this business like a shot."

"It's very good of you," said Mr. Murbles.

"Not at all. *I* shall enjoy it all right. If anything odd comes of it, that's your funeral. You never know, you know."

"If you decide that no satisfactory conclusion can be arrived at," said Mr. Murbles, "we can always fall back on the settlement. I am sure all parties wish to avoid litigation."

"In case the estate vanishes in costs? Very wise. I hope it may be feasible. Have you made any preliminary inquiries?"

"None to speak of. I would rather you undertook the whole investigation from the beginning."

"Very well. I'll start to-morrow and let you know how it gets on.'

The lawyer thanked him and took his departure. Wimsey sat pondering for a short time—then rang the bell for his man-servant.

"A new notebook, please, Bunter. Head it 'Fentiman' and be ready to come round with me to the Bellona Club to-morrow, complete with camera and the rest of the outfit."

"Very good, my lord. I take it your lordship has a new inquiry in hand?"

"Yes, Bunter—quite new."

"May I venture to ask if it is a promising case, my lord?"

"It has its points. So has a porcupine. No matter. Begone, dull care! Be at great pains, Bunter, to cultivate a detached outlook on life. Take example by the bloodhound, who will follow up with equal and impartial zest the trail of a parricide or of a bottle of aniseed."

"I will bear it in mind, my lord."

Wimsey moved slowly across to the little black baby grand that stood in the corner of the library.

"Not Bach this evening," he murmured to himself. "Bach for to-morrow when the gray matter begins to revolve." A melody of Parry's formed itself crooningly under his fingers. "For man worketh in a vain shadow . . . he heapeth up riches and cannot tell who shall gather them." He laughed suddenly, and plunged into an odd, noisy, and painfully inharmonious study by a modern composer in the key of seven sharps.

CHAPTER IV

LORD PETER LEADS A CLUB

"YOU ARE QUITE SURE this suit is all right, Bunter?" said Lord Peter, anxiously.

It was an easy lounge suit, tweedy in texture, and a trifle more pronounced in colour and pattern than Wimsey usually permitted himself. While not unsuitable for town wear, it yet diffused a faint suggestion of hills and the sea.

"I want to look approachable," he went on, "but on no account loud. I can't help wondering whether that stripe of invisible green wouldn't have looked better if it had been a remote purple."

This suggestion seemed to disconcert Bunter. There was a pause while he visualized a remote purple stripe. At length, however, the palpitating balance of his mind seemed to settle definitely down.

"No, my lord," he said firmly, "I do *not* think purple would be an improvement. Interesting—yes; but, if I may so express myself, decidedly less affable."

"Thank goodness," said his lordship, "I'm sure you're right. You always are. And it would have been a bore to get it changed now. You are sure you've removed all the newness, eh? Hate new clothes."

"Positive, my lord. I assure your lordship that the garments have every appearance of being several months old."

"Oh, all right. Well, give me the malacca with the foot-rule marked on it—and where's my lens?"

"Here, my lord." Bunter produced an innocent-looking monocle, which was, in reality, a powerful magnifier. "And the finger-print powder is in your lordship's right-hand coat-pocket."

"Thanks. Well, I think that's all. I'll go on now, and I want you to follow on with the doings in about an hour's time."

The Bellona Club is situated in Piccadilly, not many hundred yards west of Wimsey's own flat, which overlooks the Green Park. The commissionaire greeted him with a pleased smile.

"Mornin', Rogers, how are you?"

"Very well, my lord, I thank you."

"D'you know if Major Fentiman is in the Club, by the way?"

"No, my lord. Major Fentiman is not residing with us at present. I believe he is occupying the late General Fentiman's flat, my lord."

"Ah, yes—very sad business, that."

"Very melancholy, my lord. Not a pleasant thing to happen in the Club. Very shocking, my lord."

"Yes—still, he was a very old man. I suppose it had to be some day. Queer to think of 'em all sittin' round him there and never noticin', eh, what?"

"Yes, my lord. It gave Mrs. Rogers quite a turn when I told her about it."

"Seems almost unbelievable, don't it? Sittin' round all those hours— must have been several hours, I gather, from what the doctor says. I suppose the old boy came in at his usual time, eh?"

"Ah! regular as clock-work, the General was. Always on the stroke of ten. 'Good-morning, Rogers,' he'd say, a bit stiff-like, but very friendly. And then, 'Fine morning,' he'd say, as like as not. And sometimes ask after Mrs. Rogers and the family. A fine old gentleman, my lord. We shall all miss him."

"Did you notice whether he seemed specially feeble or tired that morning at all?" inquired Wimsey, casually, tapping a cigarette on the back of his hand.

"Why, no, my lord. I beg your pardon, I fancied you knew. I wasn't on duty that day, my lord. I was kindly given permission to attend the ceremony at the Cenotaph. Very grand sight, it was, too, my lord. Mrs. Rogers was greatly moved."

"Oh, of course, Rogers—I was forgetting. Naturally, you would be there. So you didn't see the General to say good-bye, as it were. Still, it wouldn't have done to miss the Cenotaph. Matthews took your duty over, I suppose."

"No, my lord. Matthews is laid up with 'flu, I am sorry to say. It was Weston was at the door all morning, my lord."

"Weston? Who's he?"

"He's new, my lord. Took the place of Briggs. You recollect Briggs —his uncle died and left him a fish-shop."

"Of course he did; just so. When does Weston come on parade? I must make his acquaintance."

"He'll be here at one o'clock, when I go to my lunch, my lord."

"Oh, right! I'll probably be about then. Hallo, Penberthy! You're just the man I want to see. Had your morning's inspiration? Or come in to look for it?"

"Just tracking it to its lair. Have it with me."

"Right you are, old chap—half a mo' while I deposit my outer husk. I'll follow you."

He glanced irresolutely at the hall-porter's desk, but seeing the man already engaged with two or three inquiries, plunged abruptly into the cloak-room, where the attendant, a bright cockney with a Sam Weller face and an artificial leg, was ready enough to talk about General Fentiman.

"Well, now, my lord, that's funny you should ask me that," he said, when Wimsey had dexterously worked in an inquiry as to the time of the General's arrival at the Bellona. "Dr. Penberthy was askin' the same question. It's a fair puzzle, that is. I could count on the fingers of one 'and the mornings I've missed seein' the General come in. Wonderful regular, the General was, and him being such a very old gentleman, I'd make a point of being 'andy, to 'elp him off with his overcoat and such. But there! He must a' come in a bit late, that morning, for I never see him, and I thought at lunch-time, 'The General must be ill,' I thinks. And I goes round, and there I see his coat and 'at 'ung up on his usual peg. So I must 'a missed him. There was a lot of gentlemen in and out that morning, my lord, bein' Armistice Day. A number of members come up from the country and wanting their 'ats and boots attended to, my lord, so that's how I come not to notice, I suppose."

"Possibly. Well, he was in before lunch, at any rate."

"Oh, yes, my lord. 'Alf-past twelve I goes off, and his hat and coat were on the peg then, because I see 'em."

"That gives us a terminus ad quem at any rate," said Wimsey, half to himself.

"I beg your lordship's pardon?"

"I was saying, that shows he came in before half-past twelve—and later than ten o'clock, you think."

"Yes, my lord. I couldn't say to a fraction, but I'm sure if 'e'd arrived before a quarter-past ten I should have seen 'im. But after that,

239

I recollect I was very busy, and he must 'a slipped in without me noticing him."

"Ah, yes—poor old boy! Still, no doubt he'd have liked to pass out quietly like that. Not a bad way to go home, Williamson."

"Very good way, my lord. We've seen worse than that. And what's it all come to, after all? They're all sayin' as it's an unpleasant thing for the Club, but *I* say, where's the odds? There ain't many 'ouses what somebody ain't died in, some time or another. We don't think any the worse of the 'ouses, so why think the worse of the Club?"

"You're a philosopher, Williamson." Wimsey climbed the short flight of marble steps and turned into the bar. "It's narrowin' down," he muttered to himself. "Between ten-fifteen and twelve-thirty. Looks as if it was goin' to be a close run for the Dormer stakes. But —dash it all! Let's hear what Penberthy has to say."

The doctor was already standing at the bar with a whisky-and-soda before him. Wimsey demanded a Worthington and dived into his subject without more ado.

"Look here," he said, "I just wanted a word with you about old Fentiman. Frightfully confidential, and all that. But it seems the exact time of the poor old blighter's departure has become an important item. Question of succession. Get me? They don't want a row made. Asked me, as friend of the family and all that, don't y' know, to barge round and ask questions. Obviously, you're the first man to come to. What's your opinion? Medical opinion, apart from anything else?"

Penberthy raised his eyebrows.

"Oh? there's a question, is there? Thought there might be. That lawyer-fellow, what's-his-name, was here the other day, trying to pin me down. Seemed to think one can say to a minute when a man died by looking at his back teeth. I told him it wasn't possible. Once give these birds an opinion, and the next thing is, you find yourself in a witness-box, swearing to it."

"I know. But one gets a general idea."

"Oh, yes. Only you have to check up your ideas by other things— facts, and so on. You can't just theorize."

"Very dangerous things, theories. F'r instance—take this case—I've seen one or two stiff 'uns in my short life, and, if I'd started theorizin' about this business, just from the look of the body, d'you know what I'd have said?"

"God knows what a layman would say about a medical question," retorted the doctor, with a sour little grin.

"Hear, hear!—Well, I should have said he'd been dead a long time."

"That's pretty vague."

"You said yourself that rigour was well advanced. Give it, say, six hours to set in and—when did it pass off?"

"It was passing off then—I remarked upon it at the time."

"So you did. I thought rigour usually lasted twenty-four hours or so."

"It does, sometimes. Sometimes it goes off quickly. Quick come, quick go, as a rule. Still, I agree with you, that in the absence of other evidence, I should have put the death rather earlier than ten o'clock."

"You admit that?"

"I do. But we know he came in not earlier than a quarter past ten."

"You've seen Williamson, then?"

"Oh, yes. I thought it better to check up on the thing as far as possible. So I can only suppose that, what with the death being sudden, and what with the warmth of the room—he was very close to the fire, you know—the whole thing came on and worked itself off very quickly."

"H'm! Of course, you knew the old boy's constitution very well."

"Oh, rather. He was very frail. Heart gets a bit worn-out when you're over the four-score and ten, you know. I should never have been surprised at his dropping down anywhere. And then, he'd had a bit of a shock, you see."

"What was that?"

"Seeing his sister the afternoon before. They told you about that, I imagine, since you seem to know all about the business. He came along to Harley Street afterwards and saw me. I told him to go to bed and keep quiet. Arteries very strained, and pulse erratic. He was excited—naturally. He ought to have taken a complete rest. As I see it, he must have insisted on getting up, in spite of feeling groggy, walked here—he *would* do it—and collapsed straight away."

"That's all right, Penberthy, but when—just when—did it happen?"

"Lord knows. I don't. Have another?"

"No, thanks; not for the moment. I say, I suppose you are perfectly satisfied about it all?"

"Satisfied?" The doctor stared at him. "Yes, of course. If you mean, satisfied as to what he died of—of course I'm satisfied. I shouldn't have given a certificate if I hadn't been satisfied."

"Nothing about the body struck you as queer?"

"What sort of thing?"

"You know what I mean as well as I do," said Wimsey, suddenly turning and looking the other straight in the face. The change in him was almost startling—it was as if a steel blade had whipped suddenly out of its velvet scabbard. Penberthy met his eye, and nodded slowly.

"Yes, I do know what you mean. But not here. We'd better go up to the Library. There won't be anybody there."

CHAPTER V

—AND FINDS THE CLUB SUIT BLOCKED

THERE NEVER WAS anybody in the library at the Bellona. It was a large, quiet, pleasant room, with the bookshelves arranged in bays; each of which contained a writing-table and three or four chairs. Occasionally some one would wander in to consult the Times Atlas, or a work on Strategy and Tactics, or to hunt up an ancient Army list, but for the most part it was deserted. Sitting in the farthest bay, immured by books and silence, confidential conversation could be carried on with all the privacy of the confessional.

"Well, now," said Wimsey, "what about it?"

"About—?" prompted the doctor, with professional caution.

"About that leg?"

"I wonder if anybody else noticed that?" said Penberthy.

"I doubt it. I did, of course. But then, I make that kind of thing my hobby. Not a popular one, perhaps—an ill-favoured thing, but mine own. In fact, I've got rather a turn for corpses. But not knowin' quite what it meant, and seein' you didn't seem to want to call attention to it, I didn't put myself forward."

"No—I wanted to think it over. You see, it suggested, at the first blush, something rather——"

"Unpleasant," said Wimsey. "If you knew how often I'd heard that word in the last two days! Well, let's face it. Let's admit, straight away, that, once rigor sets in, it stays in till it starts to pass off, and that, when it *does* start to go it usually begins with the face and jaw, and not suddenly in one knee-joint. Now Fentiman's jaw and neck

242

were as rigid as wood—I felt 'em. But the left leg swung loose from the knee. Now how do you explain that?"

"It is extremely puzzling. As no doubt you are aware, the obvious explanation would be that the joint had been forcibly loosened by somebody or something, after rigor had set in. In that case of course, it wouldn't stiffen up again. It would remain loose until the whole body relaxed. But how it happened——"

"That's just it. Dead people don't go about jamming their legs into things and forcing their own joints. And surely, if anybody had found the body like that he would have mentioned it. I mean, can you imagine one of the waiter-johnnies, for instance, finding an old gentleman stiff as a poker in the best arm-chair and then just givin' him a dose of knee-jerks and leavin' him there?"

"The only thing I could think of," said Penberthy, "was that a waiter or somebody had found him, and tried to move him—and then got frightened and barged off without saying anything. It sounds absurd. But people do do odd things, especially if they're scared."

"But what was there to be scared of?"

"It might seem alarming to a man in a very nervous state. We have one or two shell-shock cases here that I wouldn't answer for in an emergency. It would be worth considering, perhaps, if any one had shown special signs of agitation or shock that day."

"That's an idea," said Wimsey, slowly. "Suppose—suppose, for instance, there was somebody connected in some way with the General, who was in an unnerved state of mind—and suppose he came suddenly on this stiff corpse. You think he might—possibly—lose his head?"

"It's certainly possible. I can imagine that he might behave hysterically, or even violently, and force the knee-joint back with some unbalanced idea of straightening the body out and making it look more seemly. And then, you know, he might just run away from the thing and pretend it hadn't happened. Mind you, I'm not saying it was so, but I can easily see it happening. And that being so, I thought it better to say nothing about it. It would be a very unpl—— distressing thing to bring to people's notice. And it might do untold harm to the nervous case to question him about it. I'd rather let sleeping dogs lie. There was nothing wrong about the death, that's definite. As for the rest—our duty is to the living; we can't help the dead."

"Quite. Tell you what, though, I'll have a shot at finding out whether—we may as well say what we mean—whether George Fentiman was alone in the smoking-room at any time during the day. One of the servants may have noticed. It seems the only possible explanation. Well, thanks very much for your help. Oh, by the way, you said at the time that the rigor was passing off when we found the body—was that just camouflage, or does it still hold good?"

"It was just beginning to pass off in the face and jaw as a matter of fact. It had passed away completely by midnight."

"Thanks. That's another fact, then. I like facts, and there are annoyin'ly few of them in this case. Won't you have another whisky?"

"No thanks. Due at my surgery. See you another time. Cheerio!"

Wimsey remained for a few moments after he had gone, smoking meditatively. Then he turned his chair to the table, took a sheet of paper from the rack and began to jot down a few notes of the case with his fountain-pen. He had not got far, however, before one of the Club servants entered, peering into all the bays in turn, looking for somebody.

"Want me, Fred?"

"Your lordship's man is here, my lord, and says you may wish to be advised of his arrival."

"Quite right. I'm just coming." Wimsey took up the blotting-pad to blot his notes. Then his face changed. The corner of a sheet of paper protruded slightly. On the principle that nothing is too small to be looked at, Wimsey poked an inquisitive finger between the leaves, and extracted the paper. It bore a few scrawls relating to sums of money, very carelessly and shakily written. Wimsey looked at it attentively for a moment or two, and shook the blotter to see if it held anything further. Then he folded the sheet, handling it with extreme care by the corners, put it in an envelope and filed it away in his note-case. Coming out of the library, he found Bunter waiting in the hall, camera and tripod in hand.

"Ah, here you are, Bunter. Just a minute, while I see the Secretary." He looked in at the office, and found Culyer immersed in some accounts.

"Oh, I say, Culyer—'mornin' and all that—yes, disgustingly healthy, thanks, always am—I say, you recollect old Fentiman poppin' off in that inconsiderate way a little time ago?"

"I'm not likely to forget it," said Culyer, with a wry face. "I've had three notes of complaint from Wetheridge—one, because the servants didn't notice the matter earlier, set of inattentive rascals and all that; two, because the undertaker's men had to take the coffin past his door and disturbed him; three, because somebody's lawyer came along and asked him questions—together with distant allusions to the telephones being out of order and a shortage of soap in the bathroom. Who'd be a secretary?"

"Awfully sorry for you," said Wimsey with a grin. "I'm not here to make trouble. Au contraire, as the man said in the Bay of Biscay when they asked if he'd dined. Fact is, there's a bit of a muddle about the exact minute when the old boy passed out—mind you, this is in strict confidence—and I'm havin' a look into it. Don't want a fuss made, but I'd like a few photographs of the place, just to look at in absence and keep the lie of the land under my hawk-like optic, what? I've got my man here with a camera. D'you mind pretendin' he's the bloke from 'The Twaddler' or the 'Picture News,' or something, and givin' him your official blessin' while he totters round with the doings?"

"Mysterious idiot—of course, if you like. Though how photographs of the place to-day are going to give you a line on the time of a death which happened ten days ago, I don't pretend to understand. But, I say—it's all fair and above-board? We don't want any——"

"Of course not. That's the idea. Strictest confidence—any sum up to £50,000 on your note of hand alone, delivered in plain vans, no reference needed. Trust little Peter."

"Oh, right-ho! What d'you want done?"

"I don't want to go round with Bunter. Give the show away. May he be called in here?"

"Certainly."

A servant was sent to fetch Bunter, who came in looking imperturbably prim and point-device. Wimsey looked him over and shook his head.

"I'm sorry, Bunter, but you don't look in the least like the professional photographer from 'The Twaddler.' That dark-gray suit is all right, but you haven't got quite the air of devil-may-care seediness that marks the giants of Fleet Street. D'you mind stickin' all those dark-slides into one pocket and a few odd lenses and doodahs into the other, and rufflin' your manly locks a trifle? That's better. Why have you no pyro stains on the right thumb and forefinger?"

"I attribute it, my lord, principally to the circumstance that I prefer metol-quinol for the purpose of development."

"Well, you can't expect an outsider to grasp a thing like that. Wait a minute. Culyer, you seem to have a fairly juicy pipe there. Give us a cleaner."

Wimsey thrust the instrument energetically through the stem of the pipe, bringing out a revolting collection of brown, oily matter.

"Nicotine poisoning, Culyer—that's what you'll die of if you aren't jolly careful. Here you are, Bunter. Judiciously smeared upon the finger tips, that should give quite the right effect. Now, look here, Mr. Culyer here will take you round. I want a shot of the smoking-room from the entrance, a close up of the fireplace, showing General Fentiman's usual chair, and another shot from the door of the ante-room that leads into the library. Another shot through the ante-room into the library, and some careful studies of the far bay of the library from all points of view. After that, I want two or three views of the hall, and a shot of the cloak-room; get the attendant there to show you which was General Fentiman's customary peg, and take care that that gets into the picture. That's all for the moment, but you can take anything else that seems necessary for purposes of camou-flage. And I want all the detail you can possibly get in, so stop down to whatever it is and take as long as you like. You'll find me knocking about somewhere when you've finished, and you'd better get some more plates in, because we're going on to another place."

"Very good, my lord."

"Oh, and, Culyer, by the way. Dr. Penberthy sent a female in to lay the General out, didn't he? D'you happen to remember when she arrived?"

"About nine o'clock the next morning, I think."

"Have you got her name, by any chance?"

"I don't think so. But I know she came from Merritt's, the under-takers—round Shepherd's Market way. They'd probably put you on to her."

"Thanks frightfully, Culyer. I'll make myself scarce now. Carry on, Bunter."

Wimsey thought for a moment; then strolled across to the smoking-room, exchanged a mute greeting with one or two of the assembled veterans, picked up the "Morning Post," and looked round for a seat. The great arm-chair with ears still stood before the fire, but some dim feeling of respect for the dead had left it vacant. Wimsey saun-tered over to it, and dropped lazily into its well-sprung depths. A veteran close at hand looked angrily at him and rustled the "Times" loudly. Wimsey ignored these signals, barricading himself behind his paper. The veteran sank back again, muttering something about "young men" and "no decency." Wimsey sat on unmoved, and paid no attention, even when a man from "The Twaddler" came in, escorted by the Secretary, to take photographs of the smoking-room. A few sensitives retired before this attack. Wetheridge waddled away with a grumbling protest into the library. It gave Wimsey considerable satisfaction to see the relentless camera pursue him into that stronghold.

It was half-past twelve before a waiter approached Lord Peter to say that Mr. Culyer would be glad to speak to him for a moment. In the office, Bunter reported his job done, and was despatched to get some lunch and a fresh supply of plates. Wimsey presently went down to the dining-room, where he found Wetheridge already established, getting the first cut off the saddle of mutton, and grumbling at the wine. Wimsey went deliberately over, greeted him heartily, and sat down at the same table.

Wetheridge said it was beastly weather. Wimsey agreed amiably. Wetheridge said it was scandalous, seeing what one paid for one's food in this place, that one couldn't get anything fit to eat. Wimsey, who was adored by chef and waiters alike for his appreciation of good food, and had been sent the choicest cut without having to ask for it, sympathized with this sentiment too. Wetheridge said he had been chased all over the Club that morning by an infernal photographer fellow, and that one got no peace these days with all this confounded publicity. Wimsey said it was all done for advertisement, and that advertisement was the curse of the age. Look at the papers—nothing but advertisements from cover to cover. Wetheridge said that in his time, by gad, a respectable Club would have scorned advertisements, and that he could remember the time when newspapers were run by gentlemen for gentlemen. Wimsey said that nothing was what it had been; he thought it must be due to the War.

"Infernal slackness, that's what it is," said Wetheridge. "The service in this place is a disgrace. That fellow Culyer doesn't know his job. This week it's the soap. Would you believe it, there was none —actually none—in the bathroom yesterday. Had to ring for it. Made me late for dinner. Last week it was the telephone. Wanted to get through to a man down in Norfolk. Brother was a friend of mine— killed on the last day of the War, half an hour before the guns stopped firing—damnable shame—always ring up on Armistice Day, say a few words, don't you know—hr'rm!"

Wetheridge, having unexpectedly displayed this softer side of his character, relapsed into a snorting silence.

"Couldn't you get through, sir?" inquired Wimsey, with feeling. Anything that had happened at the Bellona Club on Armistice Day was of interest to him.

"I got *through* all right," said Wetheridge, morosely. "But, confound it all, I had to go down to the cloak-room to get a call from one of the boxes there. Didn't want to hang about the entrance. Too many imbeciles coming in and out. Exchanging silly anecdotes. Why a solemn national occasion should be an excuse for all these fools meeting and talking rot, I don't know."

"Beastly annoyin'. But why didn't you tell 'em to put the call through to the box by the library?"

"Aren't I telling you? The damned thing was out of order. Damned great notice stuck across it as cool as you please—'Instrument out of order.' Just like that. No apology. Nothing. Sickening, I call it. I told the fellow at the switch-board it was a disgrace. And all he said was, he hadn't put the notice up, but he'd draw attention to the matter."

"It was all right in the evening," said Wimsey, "because I saw Colonel Marchbanks using it."

"I know it was. And then, dashed if we didn't get the fool thing ringing, ringing at intervals all the next morning. Infuriating noise. When I told Fred to stop it, he just said it was the Telephone Company testing the line. They've no business to make a row like that. Why can't they test it quietly, that's what I want to know?"

Wimsey said telephones were an invention of the devil. Wetheridge grumbled his way through to the end of lunch, and departed. Wimsey returned to the entrance-hall, where he found the assistant commissionaire on duty, and introduced himself.

Weston, however, was of no assistance. He had not noticed General Fentiman's arrival on the eleventh. He was not acquainted with many of the members, having only just taken over his new duties. He thought it odd that he should not have noticed so very venerable a gentleman, but the fact remained that he had not. He regretted it extremely. Wimsey gathered that Weston was annoyed at having lost a chance of reflected celebrity. He had missed his scoop, as the reporters say.

Nor was the hall-porter any more helpful. The morning of November 11th had been a busy one. He had been in and out of his little glass pigeonhole continually, shepherding guests into various rooms to find the members they wanted, distributing letters and chatting to country members who visited the Bellona seldom and liked to "have a chat with Piper" when they did. He could not recollect seeing the General. Wimsey began to feel that there must have been a conspiracy to overlook the old gentleman on the last morning of his life.

"You don't think he never was here at all, do you, Bunter?" he suggested. "Walkin' about invisible and tryin' hard to communicate, like the unfortunate ghost in that story of somebody or other's?"

Bunter was inclined to reject the psychic view of the case. "The General must have been here in the body, my lord, because there *was* the body."

"That's true," said Wimsey. "I'm afraid we can't explain away the body. S'pose that means I'll have to question every member of this beastly Club separately. But just at the moment I think we'd better go round to the General's flat and hunt up Robert Fentiman. Weston, get me a taxi, please."

CHAPTER VI

A CARD OF RE-ENTRY

THE DOOR OF THE LITTLE FLAT in Dover Street was opened by an elderly man-servant, whose anxious face bore signs of his grief at his master's death. He informed them that Major Fentiman was at home and would be happy to receive Lord Peter Wimsey. As he spoke, a tall, soldierly man of about forty-five came out from one of the rooms and hailed his visitor cheerily.

"That you, Wimsey? Murbles told me to expect you. Come in. Haven't seen you for a long time. Hear you're turning into a regular Sherlock. Smart bit of work that was you put in over your brother's little trouble. What's all this? Camera? Bless me, you're going to do our little job in the professional manner, eh? Woodward, see that Lord Peter's man has everything he wants. Have you had lunch? Well, you'll have a spot of something, I take it, before you start measuring up the footprints. Come along. We're a bit at sixes and sevens here, but you won't mind."

He led the way into the small, austerely-furnished sitting room.

249

"Thought I might as well camp here for a bit, while I get the old man's belongings settled up. It's going to be a deuce of a job, though, with all this fuss about the will. However, I'm his executor, so all this part of it falls to me in any case. It's very decent of you to lend us a hand. Queer old girl, Great-aunt Dormer. Meant well, you know, but made it damned awkward for everybody. How are you getting along?"

Wimsey explained the failure of his researches at the Bellona.

"Thought I'd better get a line on it at this end," he added. "If we know exactly what time he left here in the morning, we ought to be able to get an idea of the time he got to the Club."

Fentiman screwed his mouth into a whistle.

"But, my dear old egg, didn't Murbles tell you the snag?"

"He told me nothing. Left me to get on with it. What *is* the snag?"

"Why, don't you see, the old boy never came home that night."

"Never came home?—Where was he, then?"

"Dunno. That's the puzzle. All we know is . . . wait a minute, this is Woodward's story; he'd better tell you himself. Woodward!"

"Yes, sir."

"Tell Lord Peter Wimsey the story you told me—about that telephone-call, you know."

"Yes, sir. About nine o'clock . . ."

"Just a moment," said Wimsey, "I do like a story to begin at the beginning. Let's start with the morning—the mornin' of November 10th. Was the General all right that morning? Usual health and spirits and all that?"

"Entirely so, my lord. General Fentiman was accustomed to rise early, my lord, being a light sleeper, as was natural at his great age. He had his breakfast in bed at a quarter to eight—tea and buttered toast, with a hegg lightly boiled, as he did every day in the year. Then he got up, and I helped him to dress—that would be about half-past eight to nine, my lord. Then he took a little rest, after the exertion of dressing, and at a quarter to ten I fetched his hat, overcoat, muffler and stick, and saw him start off to walk to the Club. That was his daily routine. He seemed in very good spirits—and in his usual health. Of course, his heart was always frail, my lord, but he seemed no different from ordinary."

"I see. And in the ordinary way he'd just sit at the Club all day and come home—when, exactly?"

"I was accustomed to have his evening meal ready for him at half-past seven precisely, my lord."

"Did he always turn up to time?"

"Invariably so, my lord. Everything as regular as on parade. That was the General's way. About three o'clock in the afternoon, there was a ring on the telephone. We had the telephone put in, my lord, on account of the General's heart, so that we could always call up a medical man in case of emergency."

"Very right, too," put in Robert Fentiman.

"Yes, sir. General Fentiman was good enough to say, sir, he did not wish me to have the heavy responsibility of looking after him alone in case of illness. He was a very kind, thoughtful gentleman." The man's voice faltered.

"Just so," said Wimsey. "I'm sure you must be very sorry to lose him, Woodward. Still, one couldn't expect otherwise, you know. I'm sure you looked after him splendidly. What was it happened about three o'clock?"

"Why, my lord, they rang up from Lady Dormer's to say as how her ladyship was very ill, and would General Fentiman please come at once if he wanted to see her alive. So I went down to the Club myself. I didn't like to telephone, you see, because General Fentiman was a little hard of hearing—though he had his faculties wonderful well for a gentleman of his age—and he never liked the telephone. Besides, I was afraid of the shock it might be to him, seeing his heart was so weak—which, of course, at his age you couldn't hardly expect otherwise—so that was why I went myself."

"That was very considerate of you."

"Thank you, my lord. Well, I see General Fentiman, and I give him the message—careful-like, and breaking it gently as you might say. I could see he was took aback a bit, but he just sits thinking for a few minutes, and then he says, 'Very well, Woodward, I will go. It is certainly my duty to go.' So I wraps him up careful, and gets him a taxi, and he says, 'You needn't come with me, Woodward. I don't quite know how long I shall stay there. They will see that I get home quite safely.' So I told the man where to take him and came back to the flat. And that, my lord, was the last time I see him."

Wimsey made a sympathetic clucking sound.

"Yes, my lord. When General Fentiman didn't return at his usual time, I thought he was maybe staying to dine at Lady Dormer's, and took no notice of it. However, at half-past eight, I began to be afraid of the night-air for him; it was very cold that day, my lord, if you remember. At nine o'clock, I was just thinking of calling up the household at Lady Dormer's to ask when he was to be expected home, when the 'phone rang."

"At nine exactly?"

"About nine. It might have been a little later, but not more than a quarter-past at latest. It was a gentleman spoke to me. He said: 'Is that General Fentiman's flat?' I said, 'Yes, who is it, please?' And he said, 'Is that Woodward?' giving my name, just like that. And I said 'Yes.' And he said, 'Oh, Woodward, General Fentiman wishes me to tell you not to wait up for him, as he is spending the night with me.' So I said, 'Excuse me, sir, who is it speaking, please?' And he said, 'Mr. Oliver.' So I asked him to repeat the name, not having heard it before, and he said 'Oliver'—it came over very plain, 'Mr. Oliver,' he said, 'I'm an old friend of General Fentiman's, and he is staying to-night with me, as we have some business to talk over.' So I said, 'Does the General require anything, sir?'—thinking, you know, my lord, as he might wish to have his sleeping-suit and his tooth-brush or somethink of that, but the gentleman said no, he had got everything necessary and I was not to trouble myself. Well, of course, my lord, as I explained to Major Fentiman, I didn't like to take upon myself to ask questions, being only in service, my lord; it might seem taking a liberty. But I was very much afraid of the excitement and staying up late being too much for the General, so I went so far as to say I hoped General Fentiman was in good health and not tiring of himself, and Mr. Oliver laughed and said he would take very good care of him and send him to bed straight away. And I was just about to make so bold as to ask him where he lived, when he rang off. And that was all I knew till I heard next day of the General being dead, my lord."

"There now," said Robert Fentiman. "What do you think of that?"

"Odd," said Wimsey, "and most unfortunate as it turns out. Did the General often stay out at night, Woodward?"

"Never, my lord. I don't recollect such a thing happening once in five or six years. In the old days, perhaps, he'd visit friends occasionally, but not of late."

"And you'd never heard of this Mr. Oliver?"

"No, my lord."

"His voice wasn't familiar?"

"I couldn't say but what I might have heard it before, my lord, but

I find it very difficult to recognize voices on the telephone. But I thought at the time it might be one of the gentlemen from the Club."

"Do *you* know anything about the man, Fentiman?"

"Oh, yes—I've met him. At least, I suppose it's the same man. But I know nothing about him. I fancy I ran across him once in some frightful crush or other, a public dinner, or something of that kind, and he said he knew my grandfather. And I've seen him lunching at Gatti's and that sort of thing. But I haven't the remotest idea where he lives or what he does."

"Army man?"

"No—something in the engineering line, I fancy."

"What's he like?"

"Oh, tall, thin, gray hair and spectacles. About sixty-five to look at. He may be older—must be, if he's an old friend of grandfather's. I gathered he was retired from whatever it is he did, and lived in some suburb, but I'm hanged if I can remember which."

"Not very helpful," said Wimsey. "D'you know, occasionally I think there's quite a lot to be said for women."

"What's that got to do with it?"

"Well, I mean, all this easy, uninquisitive way men have of makin' casual acquaintances is very fine and admirable and all that—but look how inconvenient it is! Here you are. You admit you've met this bloke two or three times, and all you know about him is that he is tall and thin and retired into some unspecified suburb. A woman, with the same opportunities, would have found out his address and occupation, whether he was married, how many children he had, with their names and what they did for a living, what his favourite author was, what food he liked best, the name of his tailor, dentist and bootmaker, when he knew your grandfather and what he thought of him—screeds of useful stuff!"

"So she would," said Fentiman, with a grin. "That's why I've never married."

"I quite agree," said Wimsey, "but the fact remains that as a source of information you're simply a wash-out. Do, for goodness' sake, pull yourself together and try to remember something a bit more definite about the fellow. It may mean half a million to you to know what time grand-pa set off in the morning from Tooting Bec or Finchley or wherever it was. If it was a distant suburb, it would account for his arriving rather late at the Club—which is rather in your favour, by the way."

"I suppose it is. I'll do my best to remember. But I'm not sure that I ever knew."

"It's awkward," said Wimsey. "No doubt the police could find the man for us, but it's not a police case. And I don't suppose you particularly want to advertise."

"Well—it may come to that. But naturally, we're not keen on publicity if we can avoid it. If only I could remember exactly what work he said he'd been connected with."

"Yes—or the public dinner or whatever it was where you first met him. One might get hold of a list of the guests."

"My dear Wimsey—that was two or three years ago!"

"Or maybe they know the blighter at Gatti's."

"That's an idea. I've met him there several times. Tell you what, I'll go along there and make inquiries, and if they don't know him, I'll make a point of lunching there pretty regularly. He's almost bound to turn up again."

"Right. You do that. And meanwhile, do you mind if I have a look round the flat?"

"Rather not. D'you want me? Or would you rather have Woodward? He really knows a lot more about things."

"Thanks. I'll have Woodward. Don't mind me. I shall just be fussing about."

"Carry on by all means. I've got one or two drawers full of papers to go through. If I come across anything bearing on the Oliver bloke I'll yell out to you."

"Right."

Wimsey went out, leaving him to it, and joined Woodward and Bunter, who were conversing in the next room. A glance told Wimsey that this was the General's bedroom.

On a table beside the narrow iron bedstead was an old-fashioned writing-desk. Wimsey took it up, weighed it in his hands a moment and then took it to Robert Fentiman in the other room. "Have you opened this?" he asked.

"Yes—only old letters and things."

"You didn't come across Oliver's address, I suppose?"

"No. Of course I looked for that."

"Looked anywhere else? Any drawers? Cupboards? That sort of thing?"

"Not so far," said Fentiman, rather shortly.

"No telephone memorandum or anything—you've tried the telephone-book, I suppose?"

"Well, no—I can't very well ring up perfect strangers and—"

"And sing 'em the Froth-Blowers' Anthem? Good God, man, anybody'd think you were chasing a lost umbrella, not half a million of money. The man rang you up, so he may very well be on the 'phone himself. Better let Bunter tackle the job. He has an excellent manner on the line; people find it a positive pleasure to be tr-r-roubled by him."

Robert Fentiman greeted this feeble pleasantry with an indulgent grin, and produced the telephone directory, to which Bunter immediately applied himself. Finding two-and-a-half columns of Olivers, he removed the receiver and started to work steadily through them in rotation. Wimsey returned to the bedroom. It was in apple-pie order —the bed neatly made, the wash-hand apparatus set in order, as though the occupant might return at any moment, every speck of dust removed—a tribute to Woodward's reverent affection, but a depressing sight for an investigator. Wimsey sat down, and let his eye rove slowly from the hanging wardrobe, with its polished doors, over the orderly line of boots and shoes arranged on their trees on a small shelf, the dressing table, the washstand, the bed and the chest of drawers which, with the small bedside table and a couple of chairs, comprised the furniture.

"Did the General shave himself, Woodward?"

"No, my lord; not latterly. That was my duty, my lord."

"Did he brush his own teeth, or dental plate, or whatever it was?"

"Oh, yes, my lord. General Fentiman had an excellent set of teeth for his age."

Wimsey fixed his powerful monocle into his eye, and carried the tooth-brush over to the window. The result of the scrutiny was unsatisfactory. He looked round again.

"Is that his walking-stick?"

"Yes, my lord."

"May I see it?"

Woodward brought it across, carrying it, after the manner of a well-trained servant, by the middle. Lord Peter took it from him in the same manner, suppressing a slight, excited smile. The stick was a heavy malacca, with a thick crutch-handle of polished ivory, suitable for sustaining the feeble steps of old age. The monocle came into play again, and this time its owner gave a chuckle of pleasure.

"I shall want to take a photograph of this stick presently, Woodward. Will you be very careful to see that it is not touched by anybody beforehand?"

"Certainly, my lord."

Wimsey stood the stick carefully in its corner again, and then, as though it had put a new train of ideas into his mind, walked across to the shoeshelf.

"Which were the shoes General Fentiman was wearing at the time of his death?"

"These, my lord."

"Have they been cleaned since?"

Woodward looked a trifle stricken.

"Not to say cleaned, my lord. I just wiped them over with a duster. They were not very dirty, and somehow—I hadn't the heart—if you'll excuse me, my lord."

"That's very fortunate."

Wimsey turned them over and examined the soles very carefully, both with the lens and with the naked eye. With a small pair of tweezers, taken from his pocket, he delicately removed a small fragment of pile—apparently from a thick carpet—which was clinging to a projecting brad, and stored it carefully away in an envelope. Then, putting the right shoe aside, he subjected the left to a prolonged scrutiny, especially about the inner edge of the sole. Finally he asked for a sheet of paper, and wrapped the shoe up as tenderly as though it had been a piece of priceless Waterford glass.

"I should like to see all the clothes General Fentiman was wearing that day—the outer garments, I mean—hat, suit, overcoat and so on."

The garments were produced, and Wimsey went over every inch of them with the same care and patience, watched by Woodward with flattering attention.

"Have they been brushed?"

"No, my lord—only shaken out." This time Woodward offered no apology, having grasped dimly that polishing and brushing were not acts which called for approval under these unusual circumstances.

"You see," said Wimsey, pausing for a moment to note an infinitesimally small ruffling of the threads on the left-hand trouser leg, "we might be able to get some sort of a clew from the dust on the clothes, if any—to show us where the General spent the night. If—to take a rather unlikely example—we were to find a lot of sawdust, for instance, we might suppose that he had been visiting a carpenter. Or a dead leaf might suggest a garden or a common, or something of that sort. While a cobweb might mean a wine-cellar, or—or a potting-shed —and so on. You see?"

"Yes, my lord" (rather doubtfully).

"You don't happen to remember noticing that little tear—well, it's hardly a tear—just a little roughness. It might have caught on a nail."

"I can't say I recollect it, my lord. But I might have overlooked it."

"Of course. It's probably of no importance. Well—lock the things up carefully. It's just possible I might have to have the dust extracted and analyzed. Just a moment—Has anything been removed from these clothes? The pockets were emptied, I suppose?"

"Yes, my lord."

"There was nothing unusual in them?"

"No, my lord. Nothing but what the General always took out with him. Just his handkerchief, keys, money and cigar-case."

"H'm. How about the money?"

"Well, my lord—I couldn't say exactly as to that. Major Fentiman has got it all. There was two pound notes in his note-case, I remember. I believe he had two pounds ten when he went out, and some loose silver in the trouser pocket. He'd have paid his taxi-fare and his lunch at the Club out of the ten-shilling note."

"That shows he didn't pay for anything unusual, then, in the way of train or taxis backwards and forwards, or dinner, or drinks."

"No, my lord."

"But naturally, this Oliver fellow would see to all that. Did the General have a fountain pen?"

"No, my lord. He did very little writing, my lord. I was accustomed to write any necessary letters to tradesmen, and so on."

"What sort of nib did he use, when he did write?"

"A J pen, my lord. You will find it in the sitting-room. But mostly I believe he wrote his letters at the Club. He had a very small private correspondence—it might be a letter or so to the Bank or to his man of business, my lord."

"I see. Have you his check-book?"

"Major Fentiman has it, my lord."

"Do you remember whether the General had it with him when he last went out?"

"No, my lord. It was kept in his writing desk as a rule. He would write the checks for the household here, my lord, and give them to me. Or occasionally he might take the book down to the Club with him."

"Ah! well, it doesn't look as though the mysterious Mr. Oliver was one of those undesirable blokes who demand money. Right you are, Woodward. You're perfectly certain that you removed nothing whatever from those clothes except what was in the pockets?"

"I am quite positive of that, my lord."

"That's very odd," said Wimsey, half to himself. "I'm not sure that it isn't the oddest thing about the case."

"Indeed, my lord? Might I ask why?"

"Why," said Wimsey, "I should have expected—" he checked himself. Major Fentiman was looking in at the door.

"What's odd, Wimsey?"

"Oh, just a little thing struck me," said Wimsey, vaguely. "I expected to find something among those clothes which isn't there. That's all."

"Impenetrable sleuth," said the major, laughing. "What are you driving at?"

"Work it out for yourself, my dear Watson," said his lordship, grinning like a dog. "You have all the data. Work it out for yourself, and let me know the answer."

Woodward, a trifle pained by this levity, gathered up the garments and put them away in the wardrobe.

"How's Bunter getting on with those calls?"

"No luck, at present."

"Oh!—well, he'd better come in now and do some photographs. We can finish the telephoning at home. Bunter!—Oh, and, I say, Woodward—d'you mind if we take your finger-prints?"

"Finger-prints, my lord?"

"Good God, you're not trying to fasten anything on Woodward?"

"Fasten what?"

"Well—I mean, I thought it was only burglars and people who had finger-prints taken."

"Not exactly. No—I want the General's finger-prints, really, to compare them with some others I got at the Club. There's a very fine set on that walking-stick of his, and I want Woodward's, just to make sure I'm not getting the two sets mixed up. I'd better take yours, too. It's just possible you might have handled the stick without noticing."

"Oh, I get you, Peter. I don't think I've touched the thing, but it's as well to make sure, as you say. Funny sort of business, what? Quite the Scotland Yard touch. How d'you do it?"

"Bunter will show you."

Bunter immediately produced a small inking-pad and roller, and a number of sheets of smooth, white paper. The fingers of the two candidates were carefully wiped with a clean cloth, and pressed first on the pad and then on the paper. The impressions thus obtained were labeled and put away in envelopes, after which the handle of the walking-stick was lightly dusted with gray powder, bringing to light an excellent set of prints of a right-hand set of fingers, superimposed here and there, but quite identifiable. Fentiman and Woodward gazed fascinated at this entertaining miracle.

"Are they all right?"

"Perfectly so, sir; they are quite unlike either of the other two specimens."

"Then presumably they're the General's. Hurry up and get a negative."

Bunter set up the camera and focussed it.

"Unless," observed Major Fentiman, "they are Mr. Oliver's. That would be a good joke, wouldn't it?"

"It would, indeed," said Wimsey, a little taken aback. "A very good joke—on somebody. And for the moment, Fentiman, I'm not sure which of us would do the laughing."

CHAPTER VII

THE CURSE OF SCOTLAND

WHAT WITH TELEPHONE CALLS and the development of photographs, it appeared obvious that Bunter was booked for a busy afternoon. His master, therefore, considerately left him in possession of the flat in Piccadilly, and walked abroad to divert himself in his own peculiar way.

His first visit was to one of those offices which undertake to distribute advertisements to the press. Here he drew up an advertisement addressed to taxi-drivers and arranged for it to appear, at the earliest possible date, in all the papers which men of that profession might be expected to read. Three drivers were requested to communicate with Mr. J. Murbles, Solicitor, of Staple Inn, who would recompense them amply for their time and trouble. First: any driver who remembered taking up an aged gentleman from Lady Dormer's house in Portman Square or the near vicinity on the afternoon of November 10th. Secondly: any driver who recollected taking up an aged gentleman at or near Dr. Penberthy's house in Harley Street at some time in the afternoon or evening of November 10th. And thirdly: any driver who had deposited a similarly aged gentleman at the door of the Bellona Club between 10 and 12.30 in the morning of November 11th.

"Though probably," thought Wimsey, as he footed the bill for the insertions, to run for three days unless cancelled, "Oliver had a car and ran the old boy up himself. Still, it's just worth trying."

He had a parcel under his arm, and his next proceeding was to hail a cab and drive to the residence of Sir James Lubbock, the well-known analyst. Sir James was fortunately at home and delighted to see Lord Peter. He was a square-built man, with a reddish face and strongly-curling gray hair, and received his visitor in his laboratory, where he was occupied in superintending a Marsh's test for arsenic.

"D'ye mind just taking a pew for a moment, while I finish this off?"

Wimsey took the pew and watched, interested, the flame from the Bunsen burner playing steadily upon the glass tube, and the dark brown deposit slowly forming and deepening at the narrow end. From time to time, the analyst poured down the thistle-funnel a small quantity of a highly disagreeable-looking liquid from a stoppered phial; once his assistant came forward to add a few more drops of what Wimsey knew must be hydrochloric acid. Presently, the disagreeable liquid having all been transferred to the flask, and the deposit having deepened almost to black at its densest part, the tube was detached and taken away, and the burner extinguished, and Sir James Lubbock, after writing and signing a brief note, turned round and greeted Wimsey cordially.

"Sure I am not interrupting you, Lubbock?"

"Not a scrap. We've just finished. That was the last mirror. We shall be ready in good time for our appearance in Court. Not that there's much doubt about it. Enough of the stuff to kill an elephant. Considering the obliging care we take in criminal prosecutions to inform the public at large that two or three grains of arsenic will successfully account for an unpopular individual, however tough, it's surprising how wasteful people are with their drugs. You can't teach 'em. An office-boy who was as incompetent as the average murderer would be sacked with a kick in the bottom. Well, now! and what's your little trouble?"

"A small matter," said Wimsey, unrolling his parcel and producing General Fentiman's left boot, "it's cheek to come to you about it. But I want very much to know what this is, and as it's strictly a private matter, I took the liberty of bargin' round to you in a friendly way. Just along the inside of the sole, there—on the edge."

"Blood?" suggested the analyst, grinning.

"Well, no—sorry to disappoint you. More like paint, I fancy."

Sir James looked closely at the deposit with a powerful lens.

"Yes; some sort of brown varnish. Might be off a floor or a piece of furniture. Do you want an analysis?"

"If it's not too much trouble."

"Not at all. I think we'll get Saunders to do it; he has made rather a specialty of this kind of thing. Saunders, would you scrape this off carefully and see what it is? Get a slide of it, and make an analysis of the rest, if you can. How soon is it wanted?"

"Well, I'd like it as soon as possible. I don't mean within the next five minutes."

"Well, stay and have a spot of tea with us, and I dare say we can get something ready for you by then. It doesn't look anything out of the way. Knowing your tastes, I'm still surprised it isn't blood. Have you no blood in prospect?"

"Not that I know of. I'll stay to tea with pleasure, if you're certain I'm not being a bore."

"Never that. Besides, while you're here, you might give me your opinion on those old medical books of mine. I don't suppose they're particularly valuable, but they're quaint. Come along."

Wimsey passed a couple of hours agreeably with Lady Lubbock and crumpets and a dozen or so antiquated anatomical treatises. Presently Saunders returned with his report. The deposit was nothing more nor less than an ordinary brown paint and varnish of a kind well known to joiners and furniture-makers. It was a modern preparation, with nothing unusual about it; one might find it anywhere. It was not a floor-varnish—one would expect to meet it on a door or partition or something of that sort. The chemical formula followed.

"Not very helpful, I'm afraid," said Sir James.

"You never know your luck," replied Wimsey. "Would you be

good enough to label the slide and sign your name to it, and to the analysis, and keep them both by you for reference in case they're wanted?"

"Sure thing. How do you want 'em labeled?"

"Well—put down 'Varnish from General Fentiman's left boot,' and 'Analysis of varnish from General Fentiman's left boot,' and the date, and I'll sign it, and you and Saunders can sign it, and then I think we shall be all right."

"Fentiman? Was that the old boy who died suddenly the other day?"

"It was. But it's no use looking at me with that child-like air of intelligent taking-notice, because I haven't got any gory yarn to spin. It's only a question of where the old man spent the night, if you *must* know."

"Curiouser and curiouser. Never mind, it's nothing to do with me. Perhaps when it's all over, you'll tell me what it's about. Meanwhile the labels shall go on. You, I take it, are ready to witness to the identity of the boot, and I can witness to having seen the varnish on the boot, and Saunders can witness that he removed the varnish from the boot and analyzed it and that this is the varnish he analyzed. All according to Cocker. Here you are. Sign here and here, and that will be eight-and-sixpence, please."

"It might be cheap at eight-and-sixpence," said Wimsey. "It might even turn out to be cheap at eight hundred and sixty quid—or eight thousand and sixty."

Sir James Lubbock looked properly thrilled.

"You're only doing it to annoy, because you know it teases. Well, if you must be sphinx-like, you must. I'll keep these things under lock and key for you. Do you want the boot back?"

"I don't suppose the executor will worry. And a fellow looks such a fool carrying a boot about. Put it away with the other things till called for, there's a good man."

So the boot was put away in a cupboard, and Lord Peter was free to carry on with his afternoon's entertainment.

His first idea was to go on up to Finsbury Park, to see the George Fentimans. He remembered in time, however, that Sheila would not yet be home from her work—she was employed as cashier in a fashionable tea-shop—and further (with a forethought rare in the well-to-do) that if he arrived too early he would have to be asked to supper, and that there would be very little supper and that Sheila would be worried about it and George annoyed. So he turned in to one of his numerous Clubs, and had a Sole Colbert very well cooked, with a bottle of Liebfraumilch; an Apple Charlotte and light savoury to follow, and black coffee and a rare old brandy to top up with—a simple and satisfactory meal which left him in the best of tempers.

The George Fentimans lived in two ground-floor rooms with use of kitchen and bathroom in a semi-detached house with a blue and yellow fanlight over the door and Madras muslin over the windows. They were really furnished apartments, but the landlady always referred to them as a flat, because that meant that tenants had to do their own work and provide their own service. The house felt stuffy as Lord Peter entered it, because somebody was frying fish in oil at no great distance, and a slight unpleasantness was caused at the start by the fact that he had rung only once, thus bringing up the person in the basement, whereas a better-instructed caller would have rung twice, to indicate that he wanted the ground floor.

Hearing explanations in the hall, George put his head out of the dining-room and said, "Oh! hullo!"

"Hullo," said Wimsey, trying to find room for his belongings on an overladen hat-stand, and eventually disposing of them on the handle of a perambulator. "Thought I'd just come and look you up. Hope I'm not in the way."

"Of course not. Jolly good of you to penetrate to this ghastly hole. Come in. Everything's in a beastly muddle as usual, but when you're poor you have to live like pigs. Sheila, here's Lord Peter Wimsey—you have met, haven't you?"

"Yes, of course. How nice of you to come round. Have you had dinner?"

"Yes, thanks."

"Coffee?"

"No, thanks, really—I've only just had some."

"Well," said George, "there's only whisky to offer you."

"Later on, perhaps, thanks, old man. Not just now. I've had a brandy. Never mix grape and grain."

"Wise man," said George, his brow clearing, since as a matter of fact, there was no whisky nearer than the public-house, and acceptance would have meant six-and-six, at least, besides the exertion of fetching it.

Sheila Fentiman drew an armchair forward, and herself sat down on a low pouffe. She was a woman of thirty-five or so, and would have been very good-looking but for an appearance of worry and ill-health that made her look older than her age.

"It's a miserable fire," said George, gloomily, "is this all the coal there is?"

"I'm sorry," said Sheila, "she didn't fill it up properly this morning."

"Well, why can't you see that she does? It's always happening. If the scuttle isn't absolutely empty she seems to think she needn't bother about filling it up."

"I'll get some."

"No, it's all right. I'll go. But you ought to tell her about it."

"I will—I'm always telling her."

"The woman's no more sense than a hen. No—don't you go, Sheila —I won't have you carrying coal."

"Nonsense," said his wife, rather acidly. "What a hypocrite you are, George. It's only because there's somebody here that you're so chivalrous all at once."

"Here, let me," said Wimsey, desperately, "I like fetching coal. Always loved coal as a kid. Anything grubby or noisy. Where is it? Lead me to it!"

Mrs. Fentiman released the scuttle, for which George and Wimsey politely struggled. In the end they all went out together to the inconvenient bin in the back yard, Wimsey quarrying the coal, George receiving it in the scuttle and the lady lighting them with a long candle, insecurely fixed in an enamel candle-stick several sizes too large.

"And tell Mrs. Crickett," said George, irritably sticking to his grievance, "that she must fill that scuttle up properly every day."

"I'll try. But she hates being spoken to. I'm always afraid she'll give warning."

"Well, there are other charwomen, I suppose?"

"Mrs. Crickett is very honest."

"I know; but that's not everything. You could easily find one if you took the trouble."

"Well, I'll see about it. But why don't *you* speak to Mrs. Crickett? I'm generally out before she gets here."

"Oh, yes, I know. You needn't keep on rubbing it in about your having to go out to work. You don't suppose I *enjoy* it, do you? Wimsey can tell you how I feel about it."

"Don't be so silly, George. Why is it, Lord Peter, that men are so cowardly about speaking to servants?"

"It's the woman's job to speak to servants," said George, "no business of mine."

"All right—I'll speak, and you'll have to put up with the consequences."

"There won't *be* any consequences, my dear, if you do it tactfully. I can't think why you want to make all this fuss."

"Right-oh, I'll be as tactful as I can. You don't suffer from charladies, I suppose, Lord Peter?"

"Good lord, no!" interrupted George. "Wimsey lives decently. They don't know the dignified joys of hard-upness in Piccadilly."

"I'm rather lucky," said Wimsey, with that apologetic air which seems forced on anybody accused of too much wealth. "I have an extraordinarily faithful and intelligent man who looks after me like a mother."

"Daresay he knows when he's well off," said George, disagreeably.

"I dunno. I believe Bunter would stick to me whatever happened. He was my N.C.O. during part of the War, and we went through some roughish bits together, and after the whole thing was over I hunted him up and took him on. He was in service before that, of course, but his former master was killed and the family broken up, so he was quite pleased to come along. I don't know what I should do without Bunter now."

"Is that the man who takes the photographs for you when you are on a crime-hunt?" suggested Sheila, hurriedly seizing on this, as she hoped, non-irritant topic.

"Yes. He's a great hand with a camera. Only drawback is that he's occasionally immured in the dark-room and I'm left to forage for myself. I've got a telephone extension through to him. 'Bunter?'—'Yes, my lord!'—'Where are my dress studs?'—'In the middle section of the third small right-hand drawer of the dressing-cabinet, my lord.'—'Bunter!'—'Yes, my lord.'—'Where have I put my cigarette case?'—'I fancy I observed it last on the piano, my lord.'—'Bunter!'—'Yes, my lord!'—'I've got into a muddle with my white tie.'—'Indeed, my lord?'—'Well, can't you do anything about it?'—'Excuse me, my lord, I am engaged in the development of a plate.'—'To hell with the plate!'—'Very good, my lord.'—'Bunter—stop—don't be precipitate—finish the plate and then come and tie my tie.'—'Certainly, my lord.' And then I have to sit about miserably till the infernal plate is fixed, or whatever it is. Perfect slave in my own house—that's what I am."

Sheila laughed.

265

"You look a very happy and well-treated slave. Are you investigating anything just now?"

"Yes. In fact—there you are again—Bunter has retired into photographic life for the evening. I haven't a roof to cover me. I have been wandering round like the what d'you call it bird, which has no feet——"

"I'm sorry you were driven to such desperation as to seek asylum in our poverty-stricken hovel," said George, with a sour laugh.

Wimsey began to wish he had not come. Mrs. Fentiman looked vexed.

"You needn't answer that," she said, with an effort to be light, "there *is* no answer."

"I'll send it to Aunt Judith of 'Rosie's Weekly Bits,'" said Wimsey. "A makes a remark to which there is no answer. What is B to do?"

"Sorry," said George, "my conversation doesn't seem to be up to standard. I'm forgetting all my civilized habits. You'd better go on and pay no attention to me."

"What's the mystery on hand now?" asked Sheila, taking her husband at his word.

"Well, actually it's about this funny business of the old General's will," said Wimsey. "Murbles suggested I should have a look into the question of the survivorship."

"Oh, do you think you can really get it settled?"

"I hope so very much. But it's a very fine-drawn business—may resolve itself into a matter of seconds. By the way, Fentiman, were you in the Bellona smoking-room at all during the morning of Armistice Day?"

"So *that's* what you've come about. Why didn't you say so? No, I wasn't. And what's more, I don't know anything at all about it. And why that infuriating old hag of a Dormer woman couldn't make a decent, sensible will while she was about it, I don't know. Where was the sense of leaving all those wads of money to the old man, when she knew perfectly well he was liable to peg out at any moment. And then, if he did die, handing the whole lot over to the Dorland girl, who hasn't an atom of claim on it? She might have had the decency to think about Robert and us a bit."

"Considering how rude you were to her and Miss Dorland, George, I wonder she even left you the seven thousand."

"What's seven thousand to her? Like a five-pound note to any ordinary person. An insult, I call it. I daresay I was rude to her, but

266

I jolly well wasn't going to have her think I was sucking up to her for her money."

"How inconsistent you are, George. If you didn't want the money, why grumble about not getting it?"

"You're always putting me in the wrong. You know I don't mean that. I *didn't* want the money—but the Dorland girl was always hinting that I did, and I ticked her off. I didn't know anything about the confounded legacy, and I didn't want to. All I mean is, that if she did want to leave anything to Robert and me, she might have made it more than a rotten seven thousand apiece."

"Well! don't grumble at it. It would be uncommonly handy at the moment."

"I know—isn't that exactly what I'm saying? And now the old fool makes such a silly will that I don't know whether I'm to get it or not. I can't even lay hands on the old Governor's two thousand. I've got to sit here and twiddle my thumbs while Wimsey goes round with a tape measure and a tame photographer to see whether I'm entitled to my own grandfather's money!"

"I know it's frightfully trying, darling. But I expect it'll all come right soon. It wouldn't matter if it weren't for Dougal MacStewart."

"Who's Dougal MacStewart?" inquired Wimsey, suddenly alert.

"One of our old Scottish families, by the name. I fancy I have heard of him. Isn't he an obliging, helpful kind of chap, with a wealthy friend in the City?"

"Frightfully obliging," said Sheila, grimly. "He simply forces his acquaintances on one. He——"

"Shut up, Sheila," interrupted her husband, rudely. "Lord Peter doesn't want to know all the sordid details of our private affairs."

"Knowing Dougal," said Wimsey, "I daresay I could give a guess at them. Some time ago you had a kind offer of assistance from our friend MacStewart. You accepted it to the mild tune of—what was it?"

"Five hundred," said Sheila.

"Five hundred. Which turned out to be three-fifty in cash and the rest represented by a little honorarium to his friend in the City who advanced the money in so trustful a manner without security. When was that?"

"Three years ago—when I started that tea-shop in Kensington."

"Ah, yes. And when you couldn't quite manage that sixty per cent per month or whatever it was, owing to trade depression, the friend

267

in the City was obliging enough to add the interest to the principal, at great inconvenience to himself—and so forth. The MacStewart way is familiar to me. What's the demd total now, Fentiman, just out of curiosity?"

"Fifteen hundred by the thirtieth," growled George, "if you must know."

"I warned George—" began Sheila, unwisely.

"Oh, you always know what's best! Anyhow, it was your tea business. I told you there was no money in it, but women always think they can run things on their own nowadays."

"I know, George. But it was MacStewart's interest that swallowed up the profits. You know I wanted you to borrow the money from Lady Dormer."

"Well, I wasn't going to, and that's flat. I told you so at the time."

"Well, but look here," said Wimsey, "you're perfectly all right about MacStewart's fifteen hundred, anyway, whichever way the thing goes. If General Fentiman died before his sister, you get seven thousand; if he died after her, you're certain of his two thousand, by the will. Besides, your brother will no doubt make a reasonable arrangement about sharing the money he gets as residuary legatee. Why worry?"

"Why? Because here's this infernal legal rigamarole tying the thing up and hanging it out till God knows when, and I can't touch anything."

"I know, I know," said Wimsey, patiently, "but all you've got to do is to go to Murbles and get him to advance you the money on your expectations. You can't get away with less than two thousand, whatever happens, so he'll be perfectly ready to do it. In fact, he's more or less bound to settle your just debts for you, if he's asked."

"That's just what I've been telling you, George," said Mrs. Fentiman, eagerly.

"Of course, you *would* be always telling me things. You never make mistakes, do you? And suppose the thing goes into Court and we get let in for thousands of pounds in fees and things, Mrs. Clever, eh?"

"I should leave it to your brother to go into Court, if necessary," said Wimsey, sensibly. "If he wins, he'll have plenty of cash for fees, and if he loses, you'll still have your seven thousand. You go to Murbles—he'll fix you up. Or, tell you what!——I'll get hold of friend Mac-Stewart and see if I can't arrange to get the debt transferred to me.

He won't consent, of course, if he knows it's me, but I can probably do it through Murbles. Then we'll threaten to fight him on the ground of extortionate interest and so on. We'll have some fun with it."

"Dashed good of you, but I'd rather not, thanks."

"Just as you like. But anyway, go to Murbles. He'll get it squared up for you. Anyhow, I don't think there will be any litigation about the will. If we can't get to the bottom of the survivorship question, I should think you and Miss Dorland would be far better advised to come to a settlement out of Court. It would probably be the fairest way in any case. Why don't you?"

"Why? Because the Dorland female wants her pound of flesh. That's why!"

"Does she? What kind of woman is she?"

"One of these modern, Chelsea women. Ugly as sin and hard as nails. Paints things—ugly, skinny prostitutes with green bodies and no clothes on. I suppose she thinks if she can't be a success as a woman she'll be a half-baked intellectual. No wonder a man can't get a decent job these days with these hard-mouthed, cigarette-smoking females all over the place, pretending they're geniuses and business women and all the rest of it."

"Oh, come, George! Miss Dorland isn't doing anybody out of a job; she couldn't just sit there all day being Lady Dormer's companion. What's the harm in her painting things?"

"Why couldn't she be a companion? In the old days, heaps of un-married women were companions, and let me tell you, my dear girl, they had a much better time than they have now, with all this jazzing and short skirts and pretending to have careers. The modern girl hasn't a scrap of decent feeling or sentiment about her. Money—money and notoriety, that's all she's after. That's what we fought the war for—and that's what we've come back to!"

"George, do keep to the point. Miss Dorland doesn't jazz—"

"I am keeping to the point. I'm talking about modern women. I don't say Miss Dorland in particular. But you *will* go taking every-thing personally. That's just like a woman. You can't argue about things in general—you always have to bring it down to some one little personal instance. You will side-track."

"I wasn't side-tracking. We started to talk about Miss Dorland."

"You said a person couldn't just be somebody's companion, and I said that in the old days plenty of nice women were companions and had a jolly good time——"

"I don't know about that."

"Well, I do. They did. And they learned to be decent companions to their husbands, too. Not always flying off to offices and clubs and parties like they are now. And if you think men like that sort of thing, I can tell you candidly, my girl, they don't. They hate it."

"Does it matter? I mean, one doesn't have to bother so much about husband-hunting to-day."

"Oh, no! Husbands don't matter at all, I suppose, to you advanced women. Any man will do, as long as he's got money——"

"Why do you say 'you' advanced women? I didn't say *I* felt that way about it. I don't *want* to go out to work——"

"There you go. Taking everything to yourself. I *know* you don't want to work. I know it's only because of the damned rotten position I'm in. You needn't keep on about it. I know I'm a failure. Thank your stars, Wimsey, that when you marry you'll be able to support your wife."

"George, you've no business to speak like that. I didn't mean that at all. You said——"

"I know what I said, but you took it all the wrong way. You always do. It's no good arguing with a woman. No—that's enough. For God's sake don't start all over again. I want a drink. Wimsey, you'll have a drink. Sheila, tell that girl of Mrs. Munns's to go round for half a bottle of Johnny Walker."

"Couldn't you get it yourself, dear? Mrs. Munns doesn't like us sending her girl. She was frightfully disagreeable last time."

"How can I go? I've taken my boots off. You do make such a fuss about nothing. What does it matter if old Mother Munns does kick up a shindy? She can't eat you."

"No," put in Wimsey. "But think of the corrupting influence of the jug-and-bottle department on Mrs. Munns's girl. I approve of Mrs. Munns. She has a motherly heart. I myself will be the St. George to rescue Mrs. Munns's girl from the Blue Dragon. Nothing shall stop me. No, don't bother to show me the way. I have a peculiar instinct about pubs. I can find one blindfold in a pea-souper with both hands tied behind me."

Mrs. Fentiman followed him to the front door.

"You mustn't mind what George says to-night. His tummy is feeling rotten and it makes him irritable. And it has been so worrying about this wretched money business."

"That's all right," said Wimsey. "I know exactly. You should see me when my tummy's upset. Took a young woman out the other night—lobster mayonnaise, meringues and sweet champagne—her choice—oh, lord!"

He made an eloquent grimace and departed in the direction of the public house.

When he returned, George Fentiman was standing on the doorstep.

"I say, Wimsey—I do apologize for being so bloody rude. It's my filthy temper. Rotten bad form. Sheila's gone up to bed in tears, poor kid. All my fault. If you knew how this damnable situation gets on my nerves—though I know there's no excuse . . ."

" 'S quite all right," said Wimsey. "Cheer up. It'll all come out in the wash."

"My wife—" began George again.

"She's damned fine, old man. But what it is, you both want a holiday."

"We do, badly. Well, never say die. I'll see Murbles, as you suggest, Wimsey."

Bunter received his master that evening with a prim smirk of satisfaction.

"Had a good day, Bunter?"

"Very gratifying indeed, I thank your lordship. The prints on the walking-stick are indubitably identical with those on the sheet of paper you gave me."

"They are, are they? That's something. I'll look at 'em to-morrow, Bunter—I've had a tiring evening."

CHAPTER VIII

LORD PETER LEADS THROUGH STRENGTH

AT ELEVEN O'CLOCK the next morning, Lord Peter Wimsey, unobtrusively attired in a navy-blue suit and dark gray tie, suitable for a house of mourning, presented himself at the late Lady Dormer's house in Portman Square.

"Is Miss Dorland at home?"

"I will inquire, sir."

271

"Kindly give her my card and ask if she can spare me a few moments."

"Certainly, my lord. Will your lordship be good enough to take a seat?"

The man departed, leaving his lordship to cool his heels in a tall, forbidding room, with long crimson curtains, a dark red carpet and mahogany furniture of repellent appearance. After an interval of nearly fifteen minutes, he reappeared, bearing a note upon a salver. It was briefly worded:

"Miss Dorland presents her compliments to Lord Peter Wimsey, and regrets that she is not able to grant him an interview. If, as she supposes, Lord Peter has come to see her as the representative of Major and Captain Fentiman, Miss Dorland requests that he will address himself to Mr. Pritchard, solicitor, of Lincoln's Inn, who is dealing, on her behalf, with all matters connected with the will of the late Lady Dormer."

"Dear me," said Wimsey to himself, "this looks almost like a snub. Very good for me, no doubt. Now I wonder—" He read the note again. "Murbles must have been rather talkative. I suppose he told Pritchard he was putting me on to it. Very indiscreet of Murbles and not like him."

The servant still stood mutely by, with an air of almost violently disassociating himself from all commentary.

"Thank you," said Wimsey. "Would you be good enough to say to Miss Dorland that I am greatly obliged to her for this information."

"Very good, my lord."

"And perhaps you would kindly call me a taxi."

"Certainly, my lord."

Wimsey entered the taxi with all the dignity he could summon, and was taken to Lincoln's Inn.

Mr. Pritchard was nearly as remote and snubbing in his manner as Miss Dorland. He kept Lord Peter waiting for twenty minutes and received him glacially, in the presence of a beady-eyed clerk.

"Oh, good morning," said Wimsey, affably. "Excuse my callin' on you like this. More regular to do it through Murbles, I s'pose—nice old boy, Murbles, isn't he? But I always believe in goin' as direct to the point as may be. Saves time, what?"

Mr. Pritchard bowed his head and asked how he might have the pleasure of serving his lordship.

"Well, it's about this Fentiman business. Survivorship and all that.

Nearly said survival. Appropriate, what? You might call the old General a survival, eh?"

Mr. Pritchard waited without moving.

"I take it Murbles told you I was lookin' into the business, what? Tryin' to check up on the timetable and all that?"

Mr. Pritchard said neither yea nor nay, but placed his fingers together and sat patiently.

"It's a bit of a problem, you know. Mind if I smoke? Have one yourself?"

"I am obliged to you, I never smoke in business hours."

"Very proper. Much more impressive. Puts the wind up the clients, what? Well, now, I just thought I'd let you know that it's likely to be a close-ish thing. Very difficult to tell to a minute or so, don't you know. May turn out one way—may turn out the other—may turn completely bafflin' and all that. You get me?"

"Indeed?"

"Oh, yes, absolutely. P'raps you'd like to hear how far I've got." And Wimsey recounted the history of his researches at the Bellona, in so far as the evidence of the commissionaires and the hall-porter were concerned. He said nothing of his interview with Penberthy, nor of the odd circumstances connected with the unknown Oliver, confining himself to stressing the narrowness of the time-limits between which the General must be presumed to have arrived at the Club. Mr. Pritchard listened without comment. Then he said:

"And what, precisely, have you come to suggest?"

"Well, what I mean to say is, don't you know, wouldn't it be rather a good thing if the parties could be got to come to terms? Give and take, you see—split the doings and share the proceeds? After all, half a million's a goodish bit of money—quite enough for three people to live on in a quiet way, don't you think? And it would save an awful lot of trouble and—ahem—lawyers' fees and things."

"Ah!" said Mr. Pritchard. "I may say that I have been expecting this. A similar suggestion was made to me earlier by Mr. Murbles, and I then told him that my client preferred not to entertain the idea. You will permit me to add, Lord Peter, that the reiteration of this proposal by you, after your employment to investigate the facts of the case in the interests of the other party, has a highly suggestive appearance. You will excuse me, perhaps, if I warn you further that your whole course of conduct in this matter seems to me open to a very undesirable construction."

Wimsey flushed.

"You will perhaps permit *me,* Mr. Pritchard, to inform you that I am not 'employed' by anybody. I have been requested by Mr. Murbles to ascertain the facts. They are rather difficult to ascertain, but I have learned one very important thing from you this afternoon. I am obliged to you for your assistance. Good morning."

The beady-eyed clerk opened the door with immense politeness. "Good morning," said Mr. Pritchard.

"Employed, indeed," muttered his lordship, wrathfully. "Undesirable construction. I'll construct him. That old brute knows something, and if he knows something, that shows there's something to be known. Perhaps he knows Oliver; I shouldn't wonder. Wish I'd thought to spring the name on him and see what he said. Too late now. Never mind, we'll get Oliver. Bunter didn't have any luck with those 'phone calls, apparently. I think I'd better get hold of Charles."

He turned into the nearest telephone-booth and gave the number of Scotland Yard. Presently an official voice replied, of which Wimsey inquired whether Detective-Inspector Parker was available. A series of clicks proclaimed that he was being put through to Mr. Parker, who presently said: "Hullo!"

"Hullo, Charles. This is Peter Wimsey. Look here, I want you to do something for me. It isn't a criminal job, but it's important. A man calling himself Oliver rang up a number in Mayfair at a little after nine on the night of November 10th. Do you think you could get that call traced for me?"

"Probably. What was the number?"

Wimsey gave it.

"Right you are, old chap. I'll have it looked up and let you know. How goes it? Anything doing?"

"Yes—rather a cozy little problem—nothing for you people—as far as I know, that is. Come round one evening and I'll tell you about it, unofficially."

"Thanks very much. Not for a day or two, though. We're run off our feet with this crate business."

"Oh, I know—the gentleman who was sent from Sheffield to Euston in a crate, disguised as York hams. Splendid. Work hard and you will be happy. No, thanks, my child, I don't want another twopenn'orth —I'm spending the money on sweets. Cheerio, Charles!"

The rest of the day Wimsey was obliged to pass in idleness, so far as the Bellona Club affair was concerned. On the following morning he was rung up by Parker.

"I say—that 'phone-call you asked me to trace."

"Yes?"

"It was put through at 9.13 p.m. from a public call-box at Charing Cross Underground Station."

"Oh, hell!—the operator didn't happen to notice the bloke, I suppose?"

"There isn't an operator. It's one of those automatic boxes."

"Oh!—may the fellow who invented them fry in oil. Thanks frightfully, all the same. It gives us a line on the direction, anyhow."

"Sorry I couldn't do better for you. Cheerio!"

"Oh, cheer-damnably-ho!" retorted Wimsey, crossly, slamming the receiver down. "What is it, Bunter?"

"A district messenger, with a note, my lord."

"Ah,—from Mr. Murbles. Good. This may be something. Yes. Tell the boy to wait, there's an answer." He scribbled quickly. "Mr. Murbles has got an answer to that cabman advertisement, Bunter. There are two men turning up at six o'clock, and I'm arranging to go down and interview them."

"Very good, my lord."

"Let's hope that means we get a move on. Get me my hat and coat —I'm running round to Dover Street for a moment."

Robert Fentiman was there when Wimsey called, and welcomed him heartily.

"Any progress?"

"Possibly a little this evening. I've got a line on those cabmen. I just came round to ask if you could let me have a specimen of old Fentiman's fist."

"Certainly. Pick what you like. He hasn't left much about. Not exactly the pen of a ready writer. There are a few interesting notes of his early campaigns, but they're rather antiques by this time."

"I'd rather have something quite recent."

"There's a bundle of cancelled cheques here, if that would do."

"It would do particularly well—I want something with figures in it if possible. Many thanks. I'll take these."

"How on earth is his handwriting going to tell you when he pegged out?"

"That's my secret, dash it all! Have you been down to Gatti's?"

"Yes. They seem to know Oliver fairly well by sight, but that's all.

He lunched there fairly often, say once a week or so, but they don't remember seeing him since the eleventh. Perhaps he's keeping under cover. However, I'll haunt the place a bit and see if he turns up."

"I wish you would. His call came from a public box, so that line of inquiry peters out."

"Oh, bad luck!"

"You've found no mention of him in any of the General's papers?"

"Not a thing, and I've gone through every bit and scrap of writing in the place. By the way, have you seen George lately?"

"Night before last. Why?"

"He seems to me to be in rather a queer state. I went round last night and he complained of being spied on or something."

"Spied on?"

"Followed about. Watched. Like the blighters in the 'tec stories. Afraid all this business is getting on his nerves. I hope he doesn't go off his rocker or anything. It's bad enough for Sheila as it is. Decent little woman."

"Thoroughly decent," agreed Wimsey, "and very fond of him."

"Yes. Works like billy-oh to keep the home together and all that. Tell you the truth, I don't know how she puts up with George. Of course, married couples are always sparring and so on, but he ought to behave before other people. Dashed bad form, being rude to your wife in public. I'd like to give him a piece of my mind."

"He's in a beastly galling position," said Wimsey. "She's his wife and she's got to keep him, and I know he feels it very much."

"Do you think so? Seems to me he takes it rather as a matter of course. And whenever the poor little woman reminds him of it, he thinks she's rubbing it in."

"Naturally, he hates being reminded of it. And I've heard Mrs. Fentiman say one or two sharp things to him."

"I daresay. Trouble with George is, he can't control himself. He never could. A fellow ought to pull himself together and show a bit of gratitude. He seems to think that because Sheila has to work like a man she doesn't want the courtesy and—you know, tenderness and so on—that a woman ought to get."

"It always gives me the pip," said Wimsey, "to see how rude people are when they're married. I suppose it's inevitable. Women are funny. They don't seem to care half so much about a man's being honest and faithful—and I'm sure your brother's all that—as for their opening doors and saying thank-you. I've noticed it lots of times."

"A man ought to be just as courteous after marriage as he was before," declared Robert Fentiman, virtuously.

"So he ought, but he never is. Possibly there's some reason we don't know about," said Wimsey. "I've asked people, you know—my usual inquisitiveness—and they generally just grunt and say that their wives are sensible and take their affection for granted. But I don't believe women ever get sensible, not even through prolonged association with their husbands."

The two bachelors wagged their heads, solemnly.

"Well, I think George is behaving like a sweep," said Robert, "but perhaps I'm hard on him. We never did get on very well. And anyhow, I don't pretend to understand women. Still, this persecution-mania, or whatever it is, is another thing. He ought to see a doctor."

"He certainly ought. We must keep an eye on him. If I see him at the Bellona I'll have a talk to him and try and get out of him what it's all about."

"You won't find him at the Bellona. He's avoided it since all this unpleasantness started. I think he's out hunting for jobs. He said something about one of those motor people in Great Portland Street wanting a salesman. He can handle a car pretty well, you know."

"I hope he gets it. Even if it doesn't pay very well it would do him a world of good to have something to do with himself. Well, I'd better be amblin' off. Many thanks, and let me know if you get hold of Oliver."

"Oh, rather!"

Wimsey considered a few moments on the doorstep, and then drove straight down to New Scotland Yard, where he was soon ushered in to Detective-Inspector Parker's office.

Parker, a square-built man in the late thirties, with the nondescript features which lend themselves so excellently to detective purposes, was possibly Lord Peter's most intimate—in some ways his only intimate friend. The two men had worked out many cases together and each respected the other's qualities, though no two characters could have been more widely different. Wimsey was the Roland of the combination—quick, impulsive, careless and an artistic jack-of-all-trades. Parker was the Oliver—cautious, solid, painstaking, his mind a blank to art and literature and exercising itself, in spare moments, with Evangelical theology. He was the one person who was never irritated by Wimsey's mannerisms, and Wimsey repaid him with a genuine affection foreign to his usually detached nature.

"Well, how goes it?"

"Not so bad. I want you to do something for me."

"Not really?"

"Yes, really, blast your eyes. Did you ever know me when I didn't? I want you to get hold of one of your handwriting experts to tell me if these two fists are the same."

He put on the table, on the one hand the bundle of used cheques, and on the other the sheet of paper he had taken from the library at the Bellona Club.

Parker raised his eyebrows.

"That's a very pretty set of finger-prints you've been pulling up there. What is it? Forgery?"

"No nothing of that sort. I just want to know whether the same bloke who wrote these cheques made the notes too."

Parker rang a bell, and requested the attendance of Mr. Collins.

"Nice fat sums involved, from the looks of it," he went on, scanning the sheet of notes appreciatively. "£150,000 to R., £300,000 to G.—lucky G.—who's G? £20,000 here and £50,000 there. Who's your rich friend, Peter?"

"It's that long story I was going to tell you about when you'd finished your crate problem."

"Oh, is it? Then I'll make a point of solving the crate without delay. As a matter of fact, I'm rather expecting to hear something about it before long. That's why I'm here, dancing attendance on the 'phone. Oh, Collins, this is Lord Peter Wimsey, who wants very much to know whether these two handwritings are the same."

The expert took up the paper and the cheques and looked them over attentively.

"Not a doubt about it, I should say, unless the forgery has been astonishingly well done. Some of the figures, especially, are highly characteristic. The fives, for instance and the threes, and the fours, made all of a piece with the two little loops. It's a very old-fashioned handwriting, and made by a very old man, in not too-good health, especially this sheet of notes. Is that the old Fentiman who died the other day?"

"Well, it is, but you needn't shout about it. It's just a private matter."

"Just so. Well, I should say you need have no doubt about the authenticity of that bit of paper, if that's what you are thinking of."

"Thanks. That's precisely what I do want to know. I don't think there's the slightest question of forgery or anything. In fact, it was just whether we could look on these rough notes as a guide to his wishes. Nothing more."

"Oh, yes, if you rule out forgery, I'd answer for it any day that the same person wrote all these cheques and the notes."

"That's fine. That checks up the results of the finger-print test too. I don't mind telling you, Charles," he added, when Collins had departed, "that this case is getting damned interesting."

At this point the telephone rang, and Parker, after listening for some time, ejaculated "Good work!" and then, turning to Wimsey, "That's our man. They've got him. Excuse me if I rush off. Between you and me, we've pulled this off rather well. It may mean rather a big thing for me. Sure we can't do anything else for you? Because I've got to get to Sheffield. See you to-morrow or next day."

He caught up his coat and hat and was gone. Wimsey made his own way out and sat for a long time at home, with Bunter's photographs of the Bellona Club before him, thinking.

At six o'clock, he presented himself at Mr. Murbles' Chambers in Staple Inn. The two taxi-drivers had already arrived and were seated, well on the edges of their chairs, politely taking old sherry with the solicitor.

"Ah!" said Mr. Murbles, "this is a gentleman who is interested in the inquiry we are making. Perhaps you would have the goodness to repeat to him what you have already told me. I have ascertained enough," he added, turning to Wimsey, "to feel sure that these are the right drivers, but I should like you to put any questions you wish yourself. This gentleman's name is Swain, and his story should come first, I think."

"Well, sir," said Mr. Swain, a stout man of the older type of driver, "you was wanting to know if anybody picked up an old gent in Portman Square the day before Ar*mis*tice Day rahnd abaht the afternoon. Well, sir, I was goin' slow through the Square at 'arf-past four, or it might be a quarter to five on that 'ere day, when a footman comes out of a 'ouse—I couldn't say the number for certain, but it was on the east side of the Square as might be abaht the middle—and 'e makes a sign for me to stop. So I draws up, and presently a very old gent comes out. Very thin, 'e was, an' muffled up, but I see 'is legs and they was very thin and 'e looked abaht a 'undred an' two by 'is face, and walked with a stick. 'E was upright, for such a very old gent, but 'e moved slow and rather feeble. An old milingtary gent, I

279

thought 'e might be—'e 'ad that way of speakin', if you understand me, sir. So the footman tells me to drive 'im to a number in 'Arley Street."

"Do you remember it?"

Swain mentioned a number which Wimsey recognized as Penberthy's.

"So I drives 'im there. And 'e asks me to ring the bell for 'im, and when the young man comes to the door to ask if the doctor could please see General Fenton, or Fennimore or some such name, sir."

"Was it Fentiman, do you think?"

"Well, yes, it might 'ave been Fentiman. I think it was. So the young man comes back and says, yes, certingly, so I 'elps the old gent aht. Very faint, 'e seemed, and a very bad colour, sir, breathin' 'eavy and blue-like abaht the lips. Pore old b . . ., I thinks, beggin' yer pardon, sir, 'e won't be 'ere long, I thinks. So we 'elps him up the steps into the 'ouse and 'e gives me my fare and a shilling for myself, and that's the last I see of 'im, sir."

"That fits in all right with what Penberthy said," agreed Wimsey. "The General felt the strain of his interview with his sister and went straight round to see him. Right. Now how about this other part of the business?"

"Well," said Mr. Murbles, "I think this gentleman, whose name is —let me see—Hinkins—yes. I think Mr. Hinkins picked up the General when he left Harley Street."

"Yes, sir," agreed the other driver, a smartish-looking man with a keen profile and a sharp eye. "A very old gentleman, like what we've 'eard described, took my taxi at this same number in 'Arley Street at 'alf past five. I remember the day very well, sir; November 10th it was, and I remember it because, after I done taking him where I'm telling you, my magneto started to give trouble, and I didn't 'ave the use of the 'bus on Armistice Day, which was a great loss to me, because that's a good day as a rule. Well, this old military gentleman gets in, with his stick and all, just as Swain says, only I didn't notice him looking particular ill, though I see he was pretty old. Maybe the doctor would have given him something to make him better."

"Very likely," said Mr. Murbles.

"Yes, sir. Well, he gets in, and he says, 'Take me to Dover Street,' he says, but if you was to ask me the number, sir, I'm afraid I don't rightly remember, because, you see, we never went there after all."

"Never went there?" cried Wimsey.

"No, sir. Just as we was comin' out into Cavendish Square, the old gentleman puts his head out and says, 'Stop!' So I stops, and I see him wavin' his hand to a gentleman on the pavement. So this other one comes up, and they has a few words together and then the old——"

"One moment. What was this other man like?"

"Dark and thin, sir, and looked about forty. He had on a gray suit and overcoat and a soft hat, with a dark handkerchief round his throat. Oh, yes, and he had a small black mustache. So the old gentleman says, 'Cabman,' he says, just like that, 'cabman, go back up to Regent's Park and drive round till I tell you to stop.' So the other gentleman gets in with him, and I goes back and drives round the Park, quiet-like, because I guessed they wanted to 'ave a bit of a talk. So I goes twice round, and as we was going round the third time, the younger gentleman sticks 'is 'ed out and says, 'Put me down at Gloucester Gate.' So I puts him down there, and the old gentleman says, 'Good-bye, George, bear in mind what I have said.' So the gentleman says, 'I will, sir,' and I see him cross the road, like as if he might be going up Park Street."

Mr. Murbles and Wimsey exchanged glances.

"And then where did you go?"

"Then, sir, the fare says to me, 'Do you know the Bellona Club in Piccadilly?' he says. So I says, 'Yes, sir.'"

"The Bellona Club?"

"Yes, sir."

"What time was that?"

"It might be getting on for half-past six, sir. I'd been driving very slow, as I tells you, sir. So I takes him to the Club, like he said, and in he goes, and that's the last I see of him, sir."

"Thanks very much," said Wimsey. "Did he seem to be at all upset or agitated when he was talking to the man he called George?"

"No, sir, I couldn't say that. But I thought he spoke a bit sharp-like. What you might call telling him off, sir."

"I see. What time did you get to the Bellona?"

"I should reckon it was about twenty minutes to seven, sir, or just a little bit more. There was a tidy bit of traffic about. Between twenty and ten to seven, as near as I can recollect."

"Excellent. Well, you have both been very helpful. That will be all to-day, but I'd like you to leave your names and addresses with

281

Mr. Murbles, in case we might want some sort of a statement from either of you later on. And—er——"

A couple of Treasury notes crackled. Mr. Swain and Mr. Hinkins made suitable acknowledgment and departed, leaving their addresses behind them.

"So he went back to the Bellona Club. I wonder what for?"

"I think I know," said Wimsey. "He was accustomed to do any writing or business there, and I fancy he went back to put down some notes as to what he meant to do with the money his sister was leaving him. Look at this sheet of paper, sir. That's the General's handwriting, as I've proved this afternoon, and those are his finger-prints. And the initials R and G probably stand for Robert and George, and these figures for the various sums he meant to leave them."

"That appears quite probable. Where did you find this?"

"In the end bay of the library at the Bellona, sir, tucked inside the blotting-paper."

"The writing is very weak and straggly."

"Yes—quite tails off, doesn't it. As though he had come over faint and couldn't go on. Or perhaps he was only tired. I must go down and find out if anybody saw him there that evening. But Oliver, curse him! is the man who knows. If only we could get hold of Oliver."

"We've had no answer to our third question in the advertisement. I've had letters from several drivers who took old gentlemen to the Bellona that morning, but none of them corresponds with the General. Some had check overcoats, and some had whiskers and some had bowler hats or beards—whereas the General was never seen without his silk hat and had, of course, his old-fashioned long military mustache."

"I wasn't hoping for very much from that. We might put in another ad. in case anybody picked him up from the Bellona on the evening or night of the 10th, but I've got a feeling that this infernal Oliver probably took him away in his own car. If all else fails, we'll have to get Scotland Yard on to Oliver."

"Make careful inquiries at the Club, Lord Peter. It now becomes more than possible that somebody saw Oliver there and noticed them leaving together."

"Of course. I'll go along there at once. And I'll put the advertisement in as well. I don't think we'll rope in the B.B.C. It is so confoundedly public."

"That," said Mr. Murbles, with a look of horror, "would be *most* undesirable."

Wimsey rose to go. The solicitor caught him at the door.

"Another thing we ought really to know," he said, "is what General Fentiman was saying to Captain George."

"I've not forgotten that," said Wimsey, a little uneasily. "We shall have—oh, yes—certainly—of course, we shall have to know that."

CHAPTER IX

KNAVE HIGH

"LOOK HERE, WIMSEY," said Captain Culyer of the Bellona Club, "aren't you ever going to get finished with this investigation or whatever it is? The members are complaining, really they are, and I can't blame them. They find your everlasting questions an intolerable nuisance, old boy, and I can't stop them from thinking there must be something behind it. People complain that they can't get attention from the porters or the waiters because you're everlastingly there chatting, and if you're not there, you're hanging round the bar, eavesdropping. If this is your way of conducting an inquiry tactfully, I wish you'd do it tactlessly. It's becoming thoroughly unpleasant. And no sooner do you stop it, than the other fellow begins."

"What other fellow?"

"That nasty little skulking bloke who's always turning up at the service door and questioning the staff."

"I don't know anything about *him*," replied Wimsey, "I never heard of him. I'm sorry I'm being a bore and all that, though I swear I couldn't be worse than some of your other choice specimens in that line, but I've hit a snag. This business—quite in your ear, old bean—isn't as straightforward as it looks on the surface. That fellow Oliver whom I mentioned to you——"

"He's not known here, Wimsey."

"No, but he may have been here."

"If nobody saw him, he can't have been here."

"Well, then, where did General Fentiman go to when he left. And when did he leave. That's what I want to know. Dash it all, Culyer,

283

the old boy's a landmark. We know he came back here on the evening of the 10th—the driver brought him to the door, Rogers saw him come in and two members noticed him in the smoking room just before seven. I have a certain amount of evidence that he went into the library. And he can't have stayed long, because he had his outdoor things with him. Somebody *must* have seen him leave. It's ridiculous. The servants aren't all blind. I don't like to say it, Culyer, but I can't help thinking that somebody has been bribed to hold his tongue . . . Of course, I knew that would annoy you, but how can you account for it? Who's this fellow you say has been hangin' round the kitchen?"

"I came across him one morning when I'd been down to see about the wine. By the way, there's a case of Margaux come in which I'd like your opinion on some day. The fellow was talking to Babcock, the wine steward, and I asked him pretty sharply what he wanted. He thanked me, and said he had come from the railway to enquire after a packing-case that had gone astray, but Babcock, who is a very decent fellow, told me afterwards that he had been working the pump-handle about old Fentiman, and I gathered he had been pretty liberal with his cash. I thought you were up to your tricks again."

"Is the fellow a sahib?"

"Good God, no. Looks like an attorney's clerk or something. A nasty little tout."

"Glad you told me. I shouldn't wonder if he's the snag I'm up against. Probably Oliver coverin' his tracks."

"Do you suspect this Oliver of something wrong?"

"Well—I rather think so. But I'm damned if I know quite what. I think he knows something about old Fentiman that we don't. And of course he knows how he spent the night, and that's what I'm after."

"What the devil does it matter how he spent the night? He can't have been very riotous, at his age."

"It might throw some light on the time he arrived in the morning, mightn't it?"

"Oh—Well, all I can say is, I hope to God you'll hurry up and finish with it. This Club's becoming a perfect bear-garden. I'd almost rather have the police in."

"Keep hopin'. You may get 'em yet."

"You don't mean that, seriously?"

"I'm never serious. That's what my friends dislike about me. Honestly, I'll try and make as little row as I can. But if Oliver is sending his minions to corrupt your staff and play old harry with my investigations, it's going to make it damned awkward. I wish you'd let me know if the fellow turns up again. I'd like to cast my eye over him."

"All right, I will. And do clear out now, there's a good fellow."

"I go," said Wimsey, "my tail well tucked down between my legs and a flea in each ear. Oh! by the way——"

"*Well?*" (in an exasperated tone).

"When did you last see George Fentiman?"

"Not for donkey's years. Not since it happened."

"I thought not. Oh, and by the way——"

"*Yes?*"

"Robert Fentiman was actually staying in the Club at the time, wasn't he?"

"Which time?"

"The time it happened, you ass."

"Yes, he was. But he's living at the old man's place now."

"I know, thanks. But I wondered whether—Where does he live when he isn't in town?"

"Out at Richmond, I think. In rooms, or something."

"Oh, does he? Thanks very much. Yes, I really will go. In fact, I've practically gone."

He went. He never stopped going till he came to Finsbury Park. George was out, and so, of course, was Mrs. Fentiman, but the charwoman said she had heard the Captain mention he was going down to Great Portland Street. Wimsey went in pursuit. A couple of hours spent lounging round show-rooms and talking to car-demonstrators, nearly all of whom were, in one manner or another, his dear old pals, resulted in the discovery that George Fentiman was being taken on by the Walmisley-Hubbard outfit for a few weeks to show what he could do.

"Oh, he'll do you all right," said Wimsey, "he's a damn fine driver. Oh, lord, yes! *He's* all right."

"He looks a bit nervy," said the particular dear old pal attached to the Walmisley-Hubbard show. "Wants bucking up, what? That reminds me. What about a quick one?"

Wimsey submitted to a mild quick one and then wandered back to look at a new type of clutch. He spun out this interesting interview till one of the Walmisley-Hubbard "shop 'buses" came in with Fentiman at the wheel.

"Hullo!" said Wimsey, "trying her out?"

"Yes. I've got the hang of her all right."

"Think you could sell her?" asked the old pal.

"Oh, yes. Soon learn to show her off. She's a jolly decent 'bus."

"That's good. Well, I expect you're about ready for a quick one. How about it, Wimsey?"

They had a quick one together. After this, the dear old pal remembered that he must buzz off because he'd promised to hunt up a customer.

"You'll turn up to-morrow, then?" he said to George. "There's an old bird down at Malden wants to have a trial trip. I can't go, so you can have a shot at him. All right?"

"Perfectly."

"Righty-ho! I'll have the 'bus ready for you at eleven. Cheer-most-frightfully-ho! So long."

"Little sunbeam about the house, isn't he?" said Wimsey.

"Rather. Have another?"

"I was thinking, how about lunch? Come along with me if you have nothing better to do."

George accepted and put forward the names of one or two restaurants.

"No," said Wimsey, "I've got a fancy to go to Gatti's to-day, if you don't mind."

"Not at all, that will do splendidly. I've seen Murbles, by the bye, and he's prepared to deal with the MacStewart man. He thinks he can hold him off till it's all settled up—if it ever *is* settled."

"That's good," said Wimsey, rather absently.

"And I'm damned glad about this chance of a job," went on George. "If it turns out any good, it'll make things a lot easier—in more than one way."

Wimsey said heartily that he was sure it would, and then relapsed into a silence unusual with him, which lasted all the way to the Strand.

At Gatti's he left George in a corner while he went to have a chat with the head-waiter, emerging from the interview with a puzzled expression which aroused even George's curiosity, full as he was of his own concerns.

"What's up? Isn't there anything you can bear to eat?"

"It's all right. I was just wondering whether to have *moules marinières* or not."

"Good idea."

Wimsey's face cleared, and for some time they absorbed mussels from the shell with speechless, though not altogether silent, satisfaction.

"By the way," said Wimsey, suddenly, "you never told me that you had seen your grandfather the afternoon before he died."

George flushed. He was struggling with a particularly elastic mussel, firmly rooted to the shell, and could not answer for a moment.

"How on earth?—confound it all, Wimsey, are *you* behind this infernal watch that's being kept on me?"

"Watch?"

"Yes, I said watch. I call it a damn rotten thing to do. I never thought for a moment you had anything to do with it."

"I haven't. Who's keeping a watch on you?"

"There's a fellow following me about. A spy. I'm always seeing him. I don't know whether he's a detective or what. He looks like a criminal. He came down in the 'bus with me from Finsbury Park this morning. He was after me all day yesterday. He's probably about now. I won't have it. If I catch sight of him again I shall knock his dirty little head off. Why should I be followed and spied on? I haven't done anything. And now *you* begin."

"I swear I've nothing to do with anybody following you about. Honestly, I haven't. I wouldn't employ a man, anyway, who'd let a bloke see that he was being followed. No. When I start huntin' you, I shall be as silent and stealthy as a gas-leak. What's this incompetent blood-hound like to look at?"

"Looks like a tout. Small, thin, with his hat pulled down over his eyes and an old rain-coat with the collar turned up. And a very blue chin."

"Sounds like a stage detective. He's a silly ass anyway."

"He gets on my nerves."

"Oh, all right. Next time you see him, punch his head."

"But what does he want?"

"How should I know? What have you been doing?"

"Nothing, of course. I tell you, Wimsey, I believe there's some sort of conspiracy going on to get me into trouble, or do away with me, or something. I can't stand it. It's simply damnable. Suppose this fellow starts hanging round the Walmisley-Hubbard place. Look nice, won't it, for their salesman to have a 'tec on his heels all the time? Just as I hoped things were coming right——"

"Bosh!" said Wimsey. "Don't let yourself get rattled. It's probably all imagination, or just a coincidence."

"It isn't. I wouldn't mind betting he's outside in the street now."

"Well, then, we'll settle his hash when we get outside. Give him in charge for annoying you. Look here, forget him for a bit. Tell me about the old General. How did he seem, that last time you saw him?"

"Oh, he seemed fit enough. Crusty, as usual."

"Crusty, was he? What about?"

"Private matters," said George, sullenly.

Wimsey cursed himself for having started his questions tactlessly. The only thing now was to retrieve the situation as far as possible.

"I'm not at all sure," he said, "that relations shouldn't all be painlessly put away after three-score and ten. Or at any rate segregated. Or have their tongues sterilized, so that they can't be poisonously interferin'."

"I wish they were," growled George. "The old man—damn it all, I know he was in the Crimea, but he's no idea what a real war's like. He thinks things can go on just as they did half a century ago. I daresay he never did behave as I do. Anyway, I know he never had to go to his wife for his pocket-money, let alone having the inside gassed out of him. Coming preaching to me—and I couldn't say anything, because he was so confoundedly old, you know."

"Very trying," murmured Wimsey, sympathetically.

"It's all so damned unfair," said George. "Do you know," he burst out, the sense of grievance suddenly overpowering his wounded vanity, "the old devil actually threatened to cut me out of the miserable little bit of money he had to leave me if I didn't 'reform my domestic behaviour.' That's the way he talked. Just as if I was carrying on with another woman or something. I know I did have an awful row with Sheila one day, but of course I didn't mean half I said. She knows that, but the old man took it all seriously."

"Half a moment," broke in Wimsey, "did he say all this to you in the taxi that day?"

"Yes, he did. A long lecture, all about the purity and courage of a good woman, driving round and round Regent's Park. I had to promise to turn over a new leaf and all that. Like being back at one's prep. school."

"But didn't he mention anything about the money Lady Dormer was leaving to him?"

"Not a word. I don't suppose he knew about it."

"I think he did. He'd just come from seeing her, you know, and I've a very good idea she explained matters to him then."

"Did she? Well, that rather explains it. I thought he was being very pompous and stiff about it. He said what a responsibility money was, you know, and how he would like to feel that anything he left to me was being properly used and all that. And he rubbed it in about my not having been able to make good for myself—that was what got my goat—and about Sheila. Said I ought to appreciate a good woman's love more, my boy, and cherish her and so on. As if I needed him to tell me that. But of course, if he knew he was in the running for this half-million, it makes rather a difference. By jove, yes! I expect he would feel a bit anxious at the idea of leaving it all to a fellow he looked on as a waster."

"I wonder he didn't mention it."

"You didn't know grandfather. I bet he was thinking over in his mind whether it wouldn't be better to give my share to Sheila, and he was sounding me, to see what sort of disposition I'd got. The old fox! Well, I did my best to put myself in a good light, of course, because just at the moment I didn't want to lose my chance of his two thousand. But I don't think he found me satisfactory. I say," went on George, with rather a sheepish laugh, "perhaps it's just as well he popped off when he did. He might have cut me off with a shilling, eh?"

"Your brother would have seen you through in any case."

"I suppose he would. Robert's quite a decent sort, really, though he does get on one's nerves so."

"Does he?"

"He's so thick-skinned; the regular unimaginative Briton. I believe Robert would cheerfully go through another five years of war and think it all a very good rag. Robert was proverbial, you know, for never turning a hair. I remember Robert, at that ghastly hole at Carency, where the whole ground was rotten with corpses—ugh!—potting those swollen great rats for a penny a time, and laughing at them. Rats. Alive and putrid with what they'd been feeding on. Oh, yes. Robert was thought a damn good soldier."

"Very fortunate for him," said Wimsey.

"Yes. He's the same sort as grandfather. They liked each other. Still, grandfather was very decent about me. A beast, as the schoolboy said, but a just beast. And Sheila was a great favourite of his."

"Nobody could help liking her," said Wimsey, politely.

Lunch ended on a more cheerful note than it had begun. As they came out into the street, however, George Fentiman glanced round uneasily. A small man in a buttoned-up overcoat and with a soft hat pulled down over his eyes, was gazing into the window of a shop near at hand.

George strode up to him.

"Look here, you!" he said. "What the devil do you mean by following me about? You clear off, d'you hear?"

"I think you are mistaken, sir," said the man, quietly enough. "I have never seen you before."

"Haven't you, by jove? Well, *I've* seen *you* hanging about, and if you do it any more, I'll give you something to remember me by. D'you hear?"

"Hullo!" said Wimsey, who had stopped to speak to the commissionaire, "what's up?—Here, you, wait a moment!"

But at sight of Wimsey, the man had slipped like an eel among the roaring Strand traffic, and was lost to view.

George Fentiman turned to his companion triumphantly.

"Did you see that? That lousy little beggar! Made off like a shot when I threatened him. That's the fellow who's been dogging me about for three days."

"I'm sorry," said Wimsey, "but it was not your prowess, Fentiman. It was my awful aspect that drove him away. What is it about me? Have I a front like Jove to threaten and command? Or am I wearing a repulsive tie?"

"He's gone, anyway."

"I wish I'd had a better squint at him. Because I've got a sort of idea that I've seen those lovely features before, and not so long ago, either. Was this the face that launched a thousand ships? No, I don't think it was that."

"All I can say is," said George, "that if I see him again, I'll put such a face on him that his mother won't know him."

"Don't do that. You might destroy a clue. I—wait a minute—I've got an idea. I believe it must be the same man who's been haunting the Bellona and asking questions. Oh, hades! and we've let him go. And I'd put him down in my mind as Oliver's minion. If ever you see him again, Fentiman, freeze on to him like grim death. I want to talk to him."

CHAPTER X

LORD PETER FORCES A CARD

"HULLO!"

"Is that you, Wimsey? Hullo! I say, is that Lord Peter Wimsey. Hullo! I must speak to Lord Peter Wimsey. Hullo!"

"All right. I've said hullo. Who're you? And what's the excitement?"

"It's me. Major Fentiman. I say—*is* that Wimsey?"

"Yes. Wimsey speaking. What's up?"

"I can't hear you."

"Of course you can't if you keep on shouting. This is Wimsey. Good morning. Stand three inches from the mouthpiece and speak in an ordinary voice. Do not say hullo! To recall the operator, depress the receiver *gently* two or three times."

"Oh, shut up! don't be an ass. I've seen Oliver."

"Have you, where?"

"Getting into a train at Charing Cross."

"Did you speak to him?"

"No—it's maddening. I was just getting my ticket when I saw him passing the barrier. I tore down after him. Some people got in my way, curse them. There was a Circle train standing at the platform. He bolted in and they clanged the doors. I rushed on, waving and shouting, but the train went out. I cursed like anything."

"I bet you did. How very sickening."

"Yes, wasn't it? I took the next train——"

"What for?"

"Oh, I don't know. I thought I might spot him on a platform somewhere."

"What a hope! You didn't think to ask where he'd booked for?"

"No. Besides, he probably got the ticket from an automatic."

"Probably. Well, it can't be helped, that's all. He'll probably turn up again. You're sure it was he?"

"Oh, dear, yes. I couldn't be mistaken. I'd know him anywhere. I thought I'd just let you know."

"Thanks awfully. It encourages me extremely. Charing Cross

seems to be a haunt of his. He 'phoned from there on the evening of the tenth, you know."

"So he did."

"I'll tell you what we'd better do, Fentiman. The thing is getting rather serious. I propose that you should go and keep an eye on Charing Cross station. I'll get hold of a detective——"

"A police detective?"

"Not necessarily. A private one would do. You and he can go along and keep watch on the station for, say a week. You must describe Oliver to the detective as best you can, and you can watch turn and turn about."

"Hang it all, Wimsey—it'll take a lot of time. I've gone back to my rooms at Richmond. And besides, I've got my own duties to do."

"Yes, well, while you're on duty the detective must keep watch."

"It's a dreadful grind, Wimsey." Fentiman's voice sounded dissatisfied.

"It's half a million of money. Of course, if you're not keen——"

"I *am* keen. But I don't believe anything will come of it."

"Probably not; but it's worth trying. And in the meantime, I'll have another watch kept at Gatti's."

"At Gatti's?"

"Yes. They know him there. I'll send a man down——"

"But he never comes there now."

"Oh, but he may come again. There's no reason why he shouldn't. We know now that he's in town, and not gone out of the country or anything. I'll tell the management that he's wanted for an urgent business matter, so as not to make unpleasantness."

"They won't like it."

"Then they'll have to lump it."

"Well, all right. But, look here—*I'll* do Gatti's."

"That won't do. We want you to identify him at Charing Cross. The waiter or somebody can do the identifying at Gatti's. You say they know him."

"Yes, of course they do. But——"

"But what?—By the way, which waiter is it you spoke to. I had a talk with the head man there yesterday, and he didn't seem to know anything about it."

"No—it wasn't the head waiter. One of the others. The plump, dark one."

"All right. I'll find the right one. Now, will you see to the Charing Cross end?"

"Of course—if you really think it's any good."

"Yes, I do. Right you are. I'll get hold of the 'tec and send him along to you, and you can arrange with him."

"Very well."

"Cheerio!"

Lord Peter rang off and sat for a few moments, grinning to himself. Then he turned to Bunter.

"I don't often prophesy, Bunter, but I'm going to do it now. Your fortune told by hand or cards. Beware of the dark stranger. That sort of thing."

"Indeed, my lord?"

"Cross the gipsy's palm with silver. I see Mr. Oliver. I see him taking a journey in which he will cross water. I see trouble. I see the ace of spades—upside-down, Bunter."

"And what then, my lord?"

"Nothing. I look into the future and I see a blank. The gipsy has spoken."

"I will bear it in mind, my lord."

"Do. If my prediction is not fulfilled, I will give you a new camera. And now I'm going round to see that fellow who calls himself Sleuths Incorporated, and get him to put a good man on to keep watch at Charing Cross. And after that, I'm going down to Chelsea and I don't quite know when I shall be back. You'd better take the afternoon off. Put me out some sandwiches or something, and don't wait up if I'm late."

Wimsey disposed quickly of his business with Sleuths Incorporated, and then made his way to a pleasant little studio overlooking the river at Chelsea. The door, which bore a neat label "Miss Marjorie Phelps," was opened by a pleasant-looking young woman with curly hair and a blue overall heavily smudged with clay.

"Lord Peter! How nice of you. Do come in."

"Shan't I be in the way?"

"Not a scrap. You don't mind if I go on working."

"Rather not."

"You could put the kettle on and find some food if you liked to be really helpful. I just want to finish up this figure."

"That's fine. I took the liberty of bringing a pot of Hybla honey with me."

"What sweet ideas you have! I really think you are one of the nicest people I know. You don't talk rubbish about art, and you don't want your hand held, and your mind always turns on eating and drinking."

"Don't speak too soon. I don't want my hand held, but I did come here with an object."

"Very sensible of you. Most people come without any."

"And stay interminably."

"They do."

Miss Phelps cocked her head on one side and looked critically at the little dancing lady she was modeling. She had made a line of her own in pottery figurines, which sold well and were worth the money.

"That's rather attractive," said Wimsey.

"Rather pretty-pretty. But it's a special order, and one can't afford to be particular. I've done a Christmas present for you, by the way. You'd better have a look at it, and if you think it offensive we'll smash it together. It's in that cupboard."

Wimsey opened the cupboard and extracted a little figure about nine inches high. It represented a young man in a flowing dressing-gown, absorbed in the study of a huge volume held on his knee. The portrait was life-like. He chuckled.

"It's damned good, Marjorie. A very fine bit of modeling. I'd love to have it. You aren't multiplying it too often, I hope? I mean, it won't be on sale at Selfridges?"

"I'll spare you that. I thought of giving one to your mother."

"That'll please her no end. Thanks ever so. I shall look forward to Christmas, for once. Shall I make some toast?"

"Rather!"

Wimsey squatted happily down before the gasfire, while the modeler went on with her work. Tea and figurine were ready almost at the same moment, and Miss Phelps, flinging off her overall, threw herself luxuriously into a battered arm-chair by the hearth.

"And what can I do for you?"

"You can tell me all you know about Miss Ann Dorland."

"Ann Dorland? Great heavens! You haven't fallen for Ann Dorland, have you? I've heard she's coming into a lot of money."

"You have a perfectly disgusting mind, Miss Phelps. Have some more toast. Excuse me licking my fingers. I have not fallen for the lady. If I had, I'd manage my affairs without assistance. I haven't even seen her. What's she like?"

"To look at?"

"Among other things."

"Well, she's rather plain. She has dark, straight hair, cut in a bang across the forehead and bobbed—like a Flemish page. Her forehead is broad and she has a square sort of face and a straight nose—quite good. Also, her eyes are good—gray, with nice heavy eyebrows, not fashionable a bit. But she has a bad skin and rather sticky-out teeth. And she's dumpy."

"She's a painter, isn't she?"

"M'm—well! she paints."

"I see. A well-off amateur with a studio."

"Yes. I will say that old Lady Dormer was very decent to her. Ann Dorland, you know, is some sort of far-away distant cousin on the female side of the Fentiman family, and when Lady Dormer first got to hear of her she was an orphan and incredibly poverty-stricken. The old lady liked to have a bit of young life about the house, so she took charge of her, and the wonderful thing is that she didn't try to monopolize her. She let her have a big place for a studio and bring in any friends she liked and go about as she chose—in reason, of course."

"Lady Dormer suffered a good deal from oppressive relations in her own youth," said Wimsey.

"I know, but most old people seem to forget that. I'm sure Lady Dormer had time enough. She must have been rather unusual. Mind you, I didn't know her very well, and I don't really know a great deal about Ann Dorland. I've been there, of course. She gave parties—rather incompetently. And she comes round to some of our studios from time to time. But she isn't really one of us."

"Probably one has to be really poor and hard-working to be that."

"No. You, for instance, fit in quite well on the rare occasions when we have the pleasure. And it doesn't matter not being able to paint. Look at Bobby Hobart and his ghastly daubs—he's a perfect dear and everybody loves him. I think Ann Dorland must have a complex of some kind. Complexes explain so much, like the blessed word hippopotamus."

Wimsey helped himself lavishly to honey and looked receptive.

"I think really," went on Miss Phelps, "that Ann ought to have been something in the City. She has brains, you know. She'd run anything awfully well. But she isn't creative. And then, of course, so many of our little lot seem to be running love-affairs. And a continual atmosphere of hectic passion is very trying if you haven't got any of your own."

"Has Miss Dorland a mind above hectic passion?"

"Well, no. I daresay she would quite have liked—but nothing ever came of it. Why are you interested in having Ann Dorland analyzed?"

"I'll tell you some day. It isn't just vulgar curiosity."

"No, you're very decent as a rule, or I wouldn't be telling you all this. I think, really, Ann has a sort of fixed idea that she couldn't ever possibly attract any one, and so she's either sentimental and tiresome, or rude and snubbing, and our crowd does hate sentimentality and simply can't bear to be snubbed. Ann's rather pathetic, really. As a matter of fact, I think she's gone off art a bit. Last time I heard about her, she had been telling some one she was going in for social service, or sick-nursing, or something of that kind. I think it's very sensible. She'd probably get along much better with the people who do that sort of thing. They're so much more solid and polite."

"I see. Look here, suppose I ever wanted to run across Miss Dorland accidentally on purpose—where should I be likely to find her?"

"You *do* seem thrilled about her! I think I should try the Rushworths. They go in rather for science and improving the submerged tenth and things like that. Of course, I suppose Ann's in mourning now, but I don't think that would necessarily keep her away from the Rushworths'. Their gatherings aren't precisely frivolous."

"Thanks very much. You're a mine of valuable information. And, for a woman, you don't ask many questions."

"Thank you for those few kind words, Lord Peter."

"I am now free to devote my invaluable attention to *your* concerns. What is the news? And who is in love with whom?"

"Oh, life is a perfect desert. Nobody is in love with me, and the Schlitzers have had a worse row than usual and separated."

"No!"

"Yes. Only, owing to financial considerations, they've got to go on sharing the same studio—you know, that big room over the mews. It must be very awkward having to eat and sleep and work in the same room with somebody you're being separated from. They don't even speak, and it's very awkward when you call on one of them and the other has to pretend not to be able to see or hear you."

"I shouldn't think one could keep it up under those circumstances."

"It's difficult. I'd have had Olga here, only she is so dreadfully bad-tempered. Besides, neither of them will give up the studio to the other."

"I see. But isn't there any third party in the case?"

"Yes—Ulric Fiennes, the sculptor, you know. But he can't have her at his place because his wife's there, and he's really dependent on his wife, because his sculping doesn't pay. And besides, he's at work on that colossal group for the Exhibition and he can't move it; it weighs about twenty tons. And if he went off and took Olga away, his wife would lock him out of the place. It's very inconvenient being a sculptor. It's like playing the double-bass; one's so handicapped by one's baggage."

"True. Whereas, when you run away with me, we'll be able to put all the pottery shepherds and shepherdesses in a handbag."

"Of course. What fun it will be. Where shall we run to?"

"How about starting to-night and getting as far as Oddenino's and going on to a show—if you're not doing anything?"

"You are a loveable man, and I shall call you Peter. Shall we see 'Betwixt and Between'?"

"The thing they had such a job to get past the censor? Yes, if you like. Is it particularly obscene?"

"No, epicene, I fancy."

"Oh, I see. Well, I'm quite agreeable. Only I warn you that I shall make a point of asking you the meaning of all the risky bits in a very audible voice."

"That's your idea of amusement, is it?"

"Yes. It does make them so wild. People say 'Hush!' and giggle, and if I'm lucky I end up with a gorgeous row in the bar."

"Then I won't risk it. No. I'll tell you what I'd really love. We'll go and see 'George Barnwell' at the Elephant and have a fish-and-chips supper afterwards."

This was agreed upon, and was voted in retrospect a most profitable evening. It finished up with grilled kippers at a friend's studio in the early hours. Lord Peter returned home to find a note upon the hall-table.

"My lord,

The person from Sleuths Incorporated rang up to-day that he was inclined to acquiesce in your lordship's opinion, but that he was keeping his eye upon the party and would report further to-morrow. The sandwiches are on the dining-room table, if your lordship should require refreshment.

"Yours obediently,
"M. BUNTER."

"Cross the gipsy's palm with silver," said his lordship, happily, and rolled into bed.

CHAPTER XI

LORD PETER CLEARS TRUMPS

"SLEUTH'S INCORPORATED'S" report, when it came, might be summed up as "Nothing doing and Major Fentiman convinced that there never will be anything doing; opinion shared by Sleuths Incorporated." Lord Peter's reply was: "Keep on watching and something will happen before the week is out."

His lordship was justified. On the fourth evening, "Sleuths Incorporated" reported again by telephone. The particular sleuth in charge of the case had been duly relieved by Major Fentiman at 6 P.M. and had gone to get his dinner. On returning to his post an hour later, he had been presented with a note left for him with the ticket-collector at the stair-head. It ran: "Just seen Oliver getting into taxi. Am following. Will communicate to refreshment-room. Fentiman." The sleuth had perforce to return to the refreshment-room and hang about waiting for a further message. "But all the while, my lord, the second man I put on as instructed by you, my lord, was a-following the Major unbeknownst." Presently a call was put through from Waterloo. "Oliver is on the Southampton train. I am following." The sleuth hurried down to Waterloo, found the train gone and followed on by the next. At Southampton he made inquiries and learned that a gentleman answering to Fentiman's description had made a violent disturbance as the Havre boat was just starting, and had been summarily ejected at the instance of an elderly man whom he appeared to have annoyed or attacked in some way. Further investigation among the Port authorities made it clear that Fentiman had followed this person down, made himself offensive on the train and been warned off by the guard, collared his prey again on the gangway and tried to prevent him from going aboard. The gentleman had produced his passport and pièces d'identité, showing him to be a retired manufacturer of the name of Postlethwaite, living at Kew. Fentiman had insisted that he was, on the contrary, a man called Oliver, address and circumstances unknown, whose testimony was wanted in some family matter. As Fentiman was unprovided with a passport and appeared to have no official authority for stopping and questioning travelers, and as his story seemed vague and his manner agitated, the local police had decided to detain Fentiman. Postlethwaite was allowed to proceed on his way, after leaving his address in England and his destination, which, as he contended, and as he produced papers and correspondence to prove, was Venice.

The sleuth went round to the police-station, where he found Fentiman, apoplectic with fury, threatening proceedings for false imprisonment. He was able to get him released, however, on bearing witness to Fentiman's identity and good faith, and after persuading him to give a promise to keep the peace. He had then reminded Fentiman that private persons were not entitled to assault or arrest peaceable people against whom no charge could be made, pointing out to him that his proper course, when Oliver denied being Oliver, would have been to follow on quietly and keep a watch on him, while communicating with Wimsey or Mr. Murbles or Sleuths Incorporated. He added that he was himself now waiting at Southampton for further instructions from Lord Peter. Should he follow to Venice, or send his subordinate, or should he return to London? In view of the frank behaviour of Mr. Postlethwaite, it seemed probable that a genuine mistake had been made as to identity, but Fentiman insisted that he was not mistaken.

Lord Peter, holding the trunk line, considered for a moment. Then he laughed.

"Where is Major Fentiman?" he asked.

"Returning to town, my lord. I have represented to him that I have now all the necessary information to go upon, and that his presence in Venice would only hamper my movements, now that he has made himself known to the party."

"Quite so. Well, I think you might as well send your man on to Venice, just in case it's a true bill. And listen" . . . He gave some further instructions, ending with: "And ask Major Fentiman to come and see me as soon as he arrives."

"Certainly, my lord."

"What price the gipsy's warning now?" said Lord Peter, as he communicated this piece of intelligence to Bunter.

Major Fentiman came round to the flat that afternoon, in a whirl of apology and indignation.

"I'm sorry, old man. It was damned stupid of me, but I lost my temper. To hear that fellow calmly denying that he had ever seen me or poor old grandfather, and coming out with his bits of evidence so pat, put my bristles up. Of course, I see now that I made a mistake. I quite realize that I ought to have followed him up quietly. But how was I to know that he wouldn't answer to his name?"

"But you ought to have guessed when he didn't, that either you had made a mistake or that he had some very good motive for trying to get away," said Wimsey.

"I wasn't accusing him of anything."

"Of course not, but he seems to have thought you were."

"But why?—I mean, when I first spoke to him, I just said, 'Mr. Oliver, I think?' And he said, 'You are mistaken.' And I said, 'Surely not. My name's Fentiman, and you knew my grandfather, old General Fentiman.' And he said he hadn't the pleasure. So I explained that we wanted to know where the old boy had spent the night before he died, and he looked at me as if I was a lunatic. That annoyed me, and I said I knew he was Oliver, and then he complained to the guard. And when I saw him just trying to hop off like that, without giving us any help, and when I thought about that half-million, it made me so mad I just collared him. 'Oh, no, you don't,' I said—and that was how the fun began, don't you see."

"I see perfectly," said Wimsey. "But don't *you* see, that if he really *is* Oliver and has gone off in that elaborate manner, with false passports and everything, he must have something important to conceal."

Fentiman's jaw dropped.

"You don't mean—you don't mean there's anything funny about the death? Oh! surely not."

"There must be something funny about Oliver, anyway, mustn't there? On your own showing?"

"Well, if you look at it that way, I suppose there must. I tell you what, he's probably got into some bother or other and is clearing out. Debt, or a woman, or something. Of course that must be it. And I was beastly inconvenient popping up like that. So he pushed me off. I see it all now. Well, in that case, we'd better let him rip. We can't get him back, and I daresay he won't be able to tell us anything after all."

"That's possible, of course. But when you bear in mind that he seems to have disappeared from Gatti's, where you used to see him, almost immediately after the General's death, doesn't it look rather as though he was afraid of being connected up with that particular incident?"

Fentiman wriggled uncomfortably.

"Oh, but, hang it all! What could he have to do with the old man's death?"

"I don't know. But I think we might try to find out."

"How?"

"Well, we might apply for an exhumation order."

"Dig him up!" cried Fentiman, scandalized.

"Yes. There was no post-mortem, you know."

"No, but Penberthy knew all about it and gave the certificate."

"Yes; but at that time there was no reason to suppose that anything was wrong."

"And there isn't now."

"There are a number of peculiar circumstances, to say the least."

"There's only Oliver—and I may have been mistaken about him."

"But I thought you were so sure?"

"So I was. But—this is preposterous, Wimsey! Besides, think what a scandal it would make!"

"Why should it? You are the executor. You can make a private application and the whole thing can be done quite privately."

"Yes, but surely the Home Office would never consent, on such flimsy grounds."

"I'll see that they do. They'll know I wouldn't be keen on anything flimsy. Little bits of fluff were never in my line."

"Oh, do be serious. What reason can we give?"

"Quite apart from Oliver, we can give a very good one. We can say that we want to examine the contents of the viscera to see how soon the General died after taking his last meal. That might be of great assistance in solving the question of the survivorship. And the law, generally speaking, is nuts on what they call the orderly devolution of property."

"Hold on! D'you mean to say you can tell when a bloke died just by looking inside his tummy?"

"Not exactly, of course. But one might get an idea. If we found, that is, that he'd only that moment swallowed his brekker, it would show that he'd died not very long after arriving at the Club."

"Good lord!—that would be a poor look-out for me."

"It might be the other way, you know."

"I don't like it, Wimsey. It's very unpleasant. I wish to goodness we could compromise on it."

"But the lady in the case won't compromise. You know that. We've got to get at the facts somehow. I shall certainly get Murbles to suggest the exhumation to Pritchard."

"Oh, lord! What'll *he* do?"

"Pritchard? If he's an honest man and his client's an honest woman, they'll support the application. If they don't, I shall fancy they've something to conceal."

"I wouldn't put it past them. They're a low-down lot. But they can't do anything without my consent, can they?"

"Not exactly—at least, not without a lot of trouble and publicity. But if *you're* an honest man, you'll give your consent. *You've* nothing to conceal, I suppose?"

"Of course not. Still, it seems rather——"

"They suspect us already of some kind of dirty work," persisted Wimsey. "That brute Pritchard as good as told me so. I'm expecting every day to hear that he has suggested exhumation off his own bat. I'd rather we got in first with it."

"If that's the case, I suppose we must do it. But I can't believe it'll do a bit of good, and it's sure to get round and make an upheaval. Isn't there some other way—you're so darned clever——"

"Look here, Fentiman. Do you want to get at the facts? Or are you out to collar the cash by hook or by crook? You may as well tell me frankly which it is."

"Of course I want to get at the facts."

"Very well; I've told you the next step to take."

"Damn it all," said Fentiman, discontentedly; "I suppose it'll have to be done, then. But I don't know whom to apply to or how to do it."

"Sit down, then, and I'll dictate the letter for you."

From this there was no escape, and Robert Fentiman did as he was told, grumbling.

"There's George. I ought to consult him."

"It doesn't concern George, except indirectly. That's right. Now write to Murbles, telling him what you're doing and instructing him to let the other party know."

"Oughtn't we to consult about the whole thing with Murbles first?"

"I've already consulted Murbles, and he agrees it's the thing to do."

"These fellows would agree to anything that means fees and trouble."

"Just so. Still, solicitors are necessary evils. Is that finished?"

"Yes."

"Give the letters to me; I'll see they're posted. Now you needn't worry any more about it. Murbles and I will see to it all, and the detective-wallah is looking after Oliver all right, so you can run away and play."

"You——"

"I'm sure you're going to say how good it is of me to take all this trouble. Delighted, I'm sure. It's of no consequence. A pleasure, in fact. Have a drink."

The disconcerted major refused the drink rather shortly and prepared to depart.

"You mustn't think I'm not grateful, Wimsey, and all that. But it is rather unseemly."

"With all your experience," said Wimsey, "you oughtn't to be so sensitive about corpses. We've seen many things much unseemlier than a nice, quiet little resurrection in a respectable cemetery."

"Oh, I don't care twopence about the corpse," retorted the Major, "but the thing doesn't look well. That's all."

"Think of the money," grinned Wimsey, shutting the door of the flat upon him.

He returned to the library, balancing the two letters in his hand. "There's many a man now walking the streets of London," said he, "through not clearing trumps. Take these letters to the post, Bunter. And Mr. Parker will be dining here with me this evening. We will have a *perdrix aux choux* and a savoury to follow, and you can bring up two bottles of the *Chambertin*."

"Very good, my lord."

Wimsey's next proceeding was to write a little confidential note to an official whom he knew very well at the Home Office. This done, he returned to the telephone and asked for Penberthy's number.

"That you, Penberthy? . . . Wimsey speaking. . . . Look here, old man, you know that Fentiman business? . . . Yes, well, we're applying for an exhumation."

"For a *what?*"

"An exhumation. Nothing to do with your certificate. We know *that's* all right. It's just by way of getting a bit more information about when the beggar died."

He outlined his suggestion.

"Think there's something in it?"

"There might be, of course."

"Glad to hear you say that. I'm a layman in these matters, but it occurred to me as a good idea."

"Very ingenious."

"I always was a bright lad. You'll have to be present, of course."

"Am I to do the autopsy?"

"If you like. Lubbock will do the analysis."

"Analysis of what?"

"Contents of the doings. Whether he had kidneys on toast or eggs and bacon and all that."

"Oh, I see. I doubt if you'll get much from that, after all this time."

"Possibly not, but Lubbock had better have a squint at it."

"Yes, certainly. As I gave the certificate, it's better that my findings should be checked by somebody."

"Exactly, I knew you'd feel that way. You quite understand about it?"

"Perfectly. Of course, if we'd had any idea there was going to be all this uncertainty, I'd have made a post-mortem at the time."

"Naturally you would. Well, it can't be helped. All in the day's work. I'll let you know when it's to be. I suppose the Home Office will send somebody along. I thought I ought just to let you know about it."

"Very good of you. Yes. I'm glad to know. Hope nothing unpleasant will come out."

"Thinking of your certificate?"

"Oh, well—no—I'm not worrying much about that. Though you never know, of course. I was thinking of that rigour, you know. Seen Captain Fentiman lately?"

"Yes. I didn't mention—"

"No. Better not, unless it becomes absolutely necessary. Well, I'll hear from you later, then?"

"That's the idea. Good-bye."

That day was a day of incident.

About four o'clock a messenger arrived, panting, from Mr. Murbles. (Mr. Murbles refused to have his chambers desecrated by a telephone.) Mr. Murbles' compliments, and would Lord Peter be good enough to read this note and let Mr. Murbles have an immediate answer.

The note ran:

"Dear Lord Peter,

In re Fentiman deceased. Mr. Pritchard has called. He informs me that his client is now willing to compromise on a division of the money if the Court will permit. Before I consult my client, Major Fentiman, I should be greatly obliged by your opinion as to how the investigation stands at present.

Yours faithfully,

Jno. Murbles."

Lord Peter replied as follows:

"Dear Mr. Murbles,

Re Fentiman deceased. Too late to compromise now, unless you are willing to be party to a fraud. I warned you, you know. Robert has applied for exhumation. Can you dine with me at 8?

P. W."

Having sent this off, his lordship rang for Bunter.

"Bunter, as you know, I seldom drink champagne. But I am inclined to do so now. Bring a glass for yourself as well."

The cork popped merrily, and Lord Peter rose to his feet.

"Bunter," said he, "I give you a toast. The triumph of Instinct over Reason!"

CHAPTER XII

LORD PETER TURNS A TRICK

DETECTIVE-INSPECTOR PARKER came to dinner encircled in a comfortable little halo of glory. The Crate Mystery had turned out well and the Chief Commissioner had used expressions suggestive of promotion in the immediate future. Parker did justice to his meal and, when the party had adjourned to the library, gave his attention to Lord Peter's account of the Bellona affair with the cheerful appreciation of a connoisseur sampling a vintage port. Mr. Murbles, on the other hand, grew more and more depressed as the story was unfolded.

"And what do you think of it?" inquired Wimsey.

Parker opened his mouth to reply, but Mr. Murbles was beforehand with him.

"This Oliver appears to be a very elusive person," said he.

"Isn't he?" agreed Wimsey, dryly. "Almost as elusive as the famous Mrs. Harris. Would it altogether surprise you to learn that when I asked a few discreet questions at Gatti's, I discovered not only that nobody there had the slightest recollection of Oliver, but that no inquiries about him had ever been made by Major Fentiman?"

"Oh, dear me!" said Mr. Murbles.

"You forced Fentiman's hand very ingeniously by sending him down with your private sleuth to Charing Cross," remarked Parker, approvingly.

"Well, you see, I had a feeling that unless we did something pretty definite, Oliver would keep vanishing and reappearing like the Cheshire Cat, whenever our investigations seemed to be taking an awkward turn."

"You are intimating, if I understand you rightly," said Mr. Murbles, "that this Oliver has no real existence."

"Oliver was the carrot on the donkey's nose," said Peter, "my noble self being cast for the part of the donkey. Not caring for the rôle, I concocted a carrot of my own, in the person of Sleuths Incorporated. No sooner did my trusting sleuth depart to his lunch than, lo and behold! the hue and cry is off again after Oliver. Away goes friend Fentiman—and away goes Sleuth Number Two, who was there all the time, neatly camouflaged, to keep his eye on Fentiman. Why Fentiman should have gone to the length of assaulting a perfect stranger and accuse him of being Oliver, I don't know. I fancy his passion for thoroughness made him over-reach himself a bit there."

"But what exactly has Major Fentiman been doing?" asked Mr. Murbles. "This is a very painful business, Lord Peter. It distresses me beyond words. Do you suspect him of—er—?"

"Well," said Wimsey, "I knew *something* odd had happened, you know, as soon as I saw the General's body—when I pulled the *Morning Post* away so easily from his hands. If he had really died clutching it, the rigour would have made his clutch so tight that one would have had to pry the fingers open to release it. And then, that knee-joint!"

"I didn't quite follow about that."

"Well, you know that when a man dies, rigour begins to set in after a period of some hours, varying according to the cause of death, temperature of the room and a lot of other conditions. It starts in the face and jaw and extends gradually over the body. Usually it lasts about twenty-four hours and then passes off again in the same order in which it started. But if, during the period of rigidity, you loosen one of the joints by main force, then it doesn't stiffen again, but remains loose. Which is why, in a hospital, if the nurses have carelessly let a patient die and stiffen with his knees up, they call in the largest and fattest person on the staff to sit on the corpse's knees and break the joints loose again."

Mr. Murbles shuddered distastefully.

"So that, taking the loose knee-joint and the general condition of the body together, it was obvious from the start that somebody had been tampering with the General. Penberthy knew that too, of course, only, being a doctor, he wasn't going to make any indiscreet uproar if he could avoid it. It doesn't pay, you know."

"I suppose not."

"Well, then, you came round to me, sir, and insisted on making the uproar. I warned you, you know, to let sleeping dogs lie."

"I wish you had spoken more openly."

"If I had, would you have cared to hush the matter up?"

"Well, well," said Mr. Murbles, polishing his eyeglasses.

"Just so. The next step was to try and find out what had actually happened to the General on the night of the 10th, and morning of the 11th. And the moment I got round to his flat I was faced with two entirely contradictory pieces of evidence. First, there was the story about Oliver, which appeared more or less remarkable upon the face of it. And secondly, there was Woodward's evidence about the clothes."

"What about them?"

"I asked him, you remember, whether anything at all had been removed from the clothes after he had fetched them away from the cloak-room at the Bellona, and he said, nothing. His memory as to other points seemed pretty reliable, and I felt sure that he was honest and straightforward. So I was forced to the conclusion that, wherever the General had spent the night, he had certainly never set foot in the street the next morning."

"Why?" asked Mr. Murbles. "What did you expect to find on the clothes?"

"My dear sir, consider what day it was. November 11th. Is it conceivable that, if the old man had been walking in the streets as a free agent on Armistice Day, he would have gone into the Club without his Flanders poppy? A patriotic, military old bird like that? It was really unthinkable."

"Then where was he? And how did he get into the Club? He was there, you know."

"True; he *was* there—in a state of advanced rigour. In fact, according to Penberthy's account, which, by the way, I had checked by the woman who laid out the body later, the rigour was even then beginning to pass off. Making every possible allowance for the warmth of the room and so on, he must have been dead long before ten in the morning, which was his usual time for going to the Club."

"But, my dear lad, bless my soul, that's impossible. He couldn't have been carried in there dead. Somebody would have noticed it."

"So they would. And the odd thing is that nobody ever saw him arrive at all. What is more, nobody saw him leave for the last time on the previous evening. General Fentiman—one of the best-known figures in the Club! And he seems to have become suddenly invisible. That won't do, you know."

"What is your idea, then? That he slept the night in the Club?"

"I think he slept a very peaceful and untroubled sleep that night —in the Club."

"You shock me inexpressibly," said Mr. Murbles. "I understand you to suggest that he died—"

"Some time the previous evening. Yes."

"But he couldn't have sat there all night in the smoking-room. The servants would have been bound to—er—notice him."

"Of course. But it was to somebody's interest to see that they didn't notice. Somebody who wanted it thought that he hadn't died till the following day, after the death of Lady Dormer."

"Robert Fentiman."

"Precisely."

"But how did Robert know about Lady Dormer?"

"Ah! That is a point I'm not altogether happy about. George had an interview with General Fentiman after the old man's visit to his sister. George denies that the General mentioned anything to him about the will, but then, if George was in the plot he naturally would deny it. I am rather concerned about George."

"What had he to gain?"

"Well, if George's information was going to make a difference of half a million to Robert, he would naturally expect to be given a share of the boodle, don't you think?"

Mr. Murbles groaned.

"Look here," broke in Parker, "this is a very pretty theory, Peter, but, allowing that the General died, as you say, on the evening of the tenth, where was the body? As Mr. Murbles says, it would have been a trifle noticeable if left about."

"No, no," said Mr. Murbles, seized with an idea. "Repellent as the whole notion is to me, I see no difficulty about that. Robert Fentiman was at that time living in the Club. No doubt the General died in Robert's bedroom and was concealed there till the next morning!"

Wimsey shook his head. "That won't work. I think the General's hat and coat and things were in Robert's bedroom, but the corpse couldn't have been. Think, sir. Here is a photograph of the entrance-hall, with the big staircase running up in full view of the front door and the desk and the bar-entrance. Would you risk carrying a corpse downstairs in the middle of the morning, with servants and members passing in and out continually? And the service stairs would be even worse. They are right round the other side of the building, with continual kitchen traffic going on all the time. No. The body wasn't in Robert's bedroom."

"Where, then?"

"Yes, where? After all, Peter, we've got to make this story hold water."

Wimsey spread the rest of the photographs out upon the table.

"Look for yourselves," he said. "Here is the end bay of the library, where the General was sitting making notes about the money he was to inherit. A very nice, retired spot, invisible from the doorway, supplied with ink, blotter, writing-paper and every modern convenience, including the works of Charles Dickens elegantly bound in morocco. Here is a shot of the library taken from the smoking-room, clean through the ante-room and down the gangway—again a tribute to the convenience of the Bellona Club. Observe how handily the telephone cabinet is situated, in case—"

"The telephone cabinet?"

"Which, you will remember, was so annoyingly labeled 'Out of Order' when Wetheridge wanted to telephone. I can't find anybody who remembers putting up that notice, by the way."

"Good God, Wimsey. Impossible. Think of the risk."

"What risk? If anybody opened the door, there was old General Fentiman, who had gone in, not seeing the notice, and died of fury at not being able to get his call. Agitation acting on a weak heart and all that. Not *very* risky, really. Unless somebody was to think to inquire about the notice, and probably it wouldn't occur to any one in the excitement of the moment."

"You're an ingenious beast, Wimsey."

"Aren't I? But we can prove it. We're going down to the Bellona Club to prove it now. Half-past eleven. A nice, quiet time. Shall I tell you what we are going to find inside that cabinet?"

"Finger-prints?" suggested Mr. Murbles, eagerly.

"Afraid that's too much to hope for after all this time. What do you say, Charles?"

"I say we shall find a long scratch on the paint," said Parker, "where the foot of the corpse rested and stiffened in that position."

"Holed it in one, Charles. And that, you see, was when the leg had to be bent with violence in order to drag the corpse out."

"And as the body was in a sitting position," pursued Parker, "we shall, of course, find a seat inside the cabinet."

"Yes, and, with luck, we *may* find a projecting nail or something which caught the General's trouser-leg when the body was removed."

"And possibly a bit of carpet."

"To match the fragment of thread I got off the corpse's right boot? I hope so."

"Bless my soul," said Mr. Murbles. "Let us go at once. Really, this is most exciting. That is, I am profoundly grieved. I hope it is not as you say."

They hastened downstairs and stood for a few moments waiting for a taxi to pass. Suddenly Wimsey made a dive into a dark corner by the porch. There was a scuffle, and out into the light came a small man, heavily muffled in an overcoat, with his hat thrust down to his eyebrows in the manner of a stage detective. Wimsey unbonneted him with the air of a conjuror producing a rabbit from a hat.

"So it's you, is it? I thought I knew your face. What the devil do you mean by following people about like this?"

The man ceased struggling and glanced sharply up at him with a pair of dark, beady eyes.

"Do you think it wise, my lord, to use violence?"

"Who is it?" asked Parker.

"Pritchard's clerk. He's been hanging round George Fentiman for days. Now he's hanging round me. He's probably the fellow that's been hanging round the Bellona. If you go on like this, my man, you'll find yourself hanging somewhere else one of these days. Now, see here. Do you want me to give you in charge?"

"That is entirely as your lordship pleases," said the clerk, with a cunning sneer. "There is a policeman just round the corner, if you wish to attract publicity."

Wimsey looked at him for a moment, and then began to laugh.

"When did you last see Mr. Pritchard? Come on, out with it! Yesterday? This morning? Have you seen him since lunch time?"

A shadow of indecision crossed the man's face.

"You haven't? I'm sure you haven't! Have you?"

"And why not, my lord?"

"You go back to Mr. Pritchard," said Wimsey, impressively, and shaking his captive gently by the coat-collar to add force to his words, "and if he doesn't countermand your instructions and call you off this sleuthing business (which, by the way, you do very amateurishly), I'll give you a fiver. See? Now, hop it. I know where to find you and you know where to find me. Good-night and may Morpheus hover over your couch and bless your slumbers. Here's our taxi."

CHAPTER XIII

SPADES ARE TRUMPS

IT WAS CLOSE on one o'clock when the three men emerged from the solemn portals of the Bellona Club. Mr. Murbles was very much subdued. Wimsey and Parker displayed the sober elation of men whose calculations have proved satisfactory. They had found the scratches. They had found the nail in the seat of the chair. They had even found the carpet. Moreover, they had found the origin of Oliver. Reconstructing the crime, they had sat in the end bay of the library,

311

as Robert Fentiman might have sat, casting his eyes around him while he considered how he could best hide and cover up this extremely inopportune decease. They had noticed how the gilt lettering on the back of a volume caught the gleam from the shaded reading lamp. "Oliver Twist." The name, not consciously noted at the time, had yet suggested itself an hour or so later to Fentiman, when, calling up from Charing Cross, he had been obliged to invent a surname on the spur of the moment.

And, finally, placing the light, spare form of the unwilling Mr. Murbles in the telephone cabinet, Parker had demonstrated that a fairly tall and strong man could have extricated the body from the box, carried it into the smoking-room and arranged it in the armchair by the fire, all in something under four minutes.

Mr. Murbles made one last effort on behalf of his client.

"There were people in the smoking-room all morning, my dear Lord Peter. If it were as you suggest, how could Fentiman have made sure of four, or even three minutes secure from observation while he brought the body in?"

"Were people there *all* morning, sir? Are you sure? Wasn't there just one period when one could be certain that everybody would be either out in the street or upstairs on the big balcony that runs along in front of the first-floor windows, looking out—and listening? It was Armistice Day, remember."

Mr. Murbles was horror-struck.

"The two-minutes' silence?—God bless my soul! How abominable! How—how blasphemous! Really, I cannot find words. This is the most disgraceful thing I ever heard of. At the moment when all our thoughts should be concentrated on the brave fellows who laid down their lives for us—to be engaged in perpetrating a fraud—an irreverent crime—"

"Half a million is a good bit of money," said Parker, thoughtfully.

"Horrible!" said Mr. Murbles.

"Meanwhile," said Wimsey, "what do you propose to do about it?"

"Do?" spluttered the old solicitor, indignantly. "Do?—Robert Fentiman will have to confess to this disgraceful plot immediately. Bless my soul! To think that I should be mixed up in a thing like this! He will have to find another man of business in future. We shall have to explain matters to Pritchard and apologize. I really hardly know how to tell him such a thing."

"I rather gather he suspects a good deal of it already," said Parker,

312

mildly. "Else why should he have sent that clerk of his to spy on you and George Fentiman? I daresay he has been keeping tabs on Robert, too."

"I shouldn't wonder," said Wimsey. "He certainly treated me like a conspirator when I called on him. The only thing that puzzles me now is why he should have suddenly offered to compromise."

"Probably Miss Dorland lost patience, or they despaired of proving anything," said Parker. "While Robert stuck to that Oliver story, it would be very hard to prove anything."

"Exactly," said Wimsey. "That is why I had to hang on so long, and press Robert so hard about it. I might suspect Oliver to be non-existent, but one can't prove a negative."

"And suppose he still sticks to the story now?"

"Oh! I think we can put the wind up him all right," said Wimsey. "By the time we've displayed our proofs and told him exactly what he was doing with himself on November 10th and 11th, he'll have no more spirit in him than the Queen of Sheba."

"It must be done at once," said Mr. Murbles. "And of course this exhumation business will have to be stopped. I will go round and see Robert Fentiman to-morrow—this morning, that is."

"Better tell him to trot round to your place," said Wimsey. "I'll bring all the evidence round there, and I'll have the varnish on the cabinet analyzed and shown to correspond with the sample I took from the General's boots. Make it for two o'clock, and then we can all go round and interview Pritchard afterwards."

Parker supported this suggestion. Mr. Murbles was so wrought up that he would gladly have rushed away to confront Robert Fentiman immediately. It being, however, pointed out to him that Fentiman was in Richmond, that an alarm at this ungodly hour might drive him to do something desperate, and also that all three investigators needed repose, the old gentleman gave way and permitted himself to be taken home to Staple Inn.

Wimsey went round to Parker's flat in Great Ormond Street to have a drink before turning in, and the session was prolonged till the small hours had begun to grow into big hours and the early workman was abroad.

.   .   .   .   .

Lord Peter, having set the springe for his woodcock, slept the sleep of the just until close upon eleven o'clock the next morning. He was aroused by voices without, and presently his bedroom door was flung open to admit Mr. Murbles, of all people, in a high state of agitation, followed by Bunter, protesting.

"Hullo, sir!" said his lordship, much amazed. "What's up?"

"We have been outwitted," cried Mr. Murbles, waving his umbrella, "we have been forestalled! We should have gone to Major Fentiman last night. I wished to do so, but permitted myself to be persuaded against my better judgment. It will be a lesson to me."

He sat down, panting a little.

"My dear Mr. Murbles," said Wimsey, pleasantly, "your method of recalling one to the dull business of the day is as delightful as it is unexpected. Anything better calculated to dispel that sluggish feeling I can scarcely imagine. But pardon me—you are somewhat out of breath. Bunter! a whisky-and-soda for Mr. Murbles."

"Indeed no!" ejaculated the solicitor, hurriedly. "I couldn't touch it. Lord Peter—"

"A glass of sherry?" suggested his lordship, helpfully.

"No, no—nothing, thanks. A shocking thing has occurred. We are left—"

"Better and better. A shock is exactly what I feel to need. My *café-au-lait*, Bunter—and you may turn the bath on. Now, sir—out with it. I am fortified against anything."

"Robert Fentiman," announced Mr. Murbles, impressively, "has disappeared."

He thumped his umbrella.

"Good God!" said Wimsey.

"He has gone," repeated the solicitor. "At ten o'clock this morning I attended in person at his rooms in Richmond—in *person*—in order to bring him the more effectually to a sense of his situation. I rang the bell. I asked for him. The maid told me he had left the night before. I asked where he had gone. She said she did not know. He had taken a suit-case with him. I interviewed the landlady. She told me that Major Fentiman had received an urgent message during the evening and had informed her that he was called away. He had not mentioned where he was going nor how soon he would return. I left a note addressed to him, and hastened back to Dover Street. The flat there was shut up and untenanted. The man Woodward was nowhere to be found. I then came immediately to you. And I find you—"

Mr. Murbles waved an expressive hand at Wimsey, who was just taking from Bunter's hands a chaste silver tray, containing a Queen

Anne coffee-pot and milk-jug, a plate of buttered toast, a delicate china coffee-cup and a small pile of correspondence.

"So you do," said Wimsey. "A depraved sight, I am afraid. H'm! It looks very much as though Robert had got wind of trouble and didn't like to face the music."

He sipped his *café-au-lait* delicately, his rather bird-like face cocked sideways. "But why worry? He can't have got very far."

"He may have gone abroad."

"Possibly. All the better. The other party won't want to take proceedings against him over there. Too much bother—however spiteful they may feel. Hallo! Here's a writing I seem to recognize. Yes. It is my sleuth from Sleuths Incorporated. Wonder what *he* wants. I told him to go home and send the bill in.—Whew!"

"What is it?"

"This is the bloke who chased Fentiman to Southampton. Not the one who went on to Venice after the innocent Mr. Postlethwaite; the other. He's writing from Paris. He says:

'My lord,
While making a few inquiries at Southampton pursuant to the investigation with which your lordship entrusted me' (what marvelous English those fellows write, don't they? Nearly as good as the regular police), 'I came, almost accidentally' ('almost' is good) 'upon a trifling clue which led me to suppose that the party whom I was instructed by your lordship to keep under observation had been less in error than we were led to suppose, and had merely been misled by a confusion of identity natural in a gentleman not scientifically instructed in the art of following up suspected persons. In short' (thank God for that!) 'in short, I believe that I have myself come upon the track of O.' (These fellows are amazingly cautious; he might just as well write Oliver and have done with it), 'and have followed the individual in question to this place. I have telegraphed to the gentleman your friend' (I presume that means Fentiman) 'to join me immediately with a view to identifying the party. I will of course duly acquaint your lordship with any further developments in the case, and believe me'—and so forth.

"Well, I'm damned!"

"The man must be mistaken, Lord Peter."

"I jolly well hope so," said Wimsey, rather red in the face. "It'll

315

be a bit galling to have Oliver turning up, just when we've proved so conclusively that he doesn't exist. Paris! I suppose he means that Fentiman spotted the right man at Waterloo and lost him on the train or in the rush for the boat. And got hold of Postlethwaite instead. Funny. Meanwhile, Fentiman's off to France. Probably taken the 10.30 boat from Folkestone. I don't know how we're to get hold of him."

"How very extraordinary," said Mr. Murbles. "Where does that detective person write from?"

"Just 'Paris,' " said Wimsey. "Bad paper and worse ink. And a small stain of *vin ordinaire*. Probably written in some little café yesterday afternoon. Not much hope there. But he's certain to let me know where they get to."

"We must send some one to Paris immediately in search of them," declared Mr. Murbles.

"Why?"

"To fetch Major Fentiman back."

"Yes, but look here, sir. If there really is an Oliver after all, it rather upsets our calculations, doesn't it?"

Mr. Murbles considered this.

"I cannot see that it affects our conclusions as to the hour of the General's death," he said.

"Perhaps not, but it considerably alters our position with regard to Robert Fentiman."

"Ye—es. Yes, that is so. Though," said Mr. Murbles, severely, "I still consider that the story requires close investigation."

"Agreed. Well, look here. I'll run over to Paris myself and see what I can do. And you had better temporize with Pritchard. Tell him you think there will be no need to compromise and that we hope soon to be in possession of the precise facts. That'll show him we don't mean to have any truck with anythin' fishy. I'll learn him to cast nasturtiums at me!"

"And—oh, dear! there's another thing. We must try and get hold of Major Fentiman to stop this exhumation."

"Oh, lord!—Yes. That's a bit awkward. Can't you stop it by yourself?"

"I hardly think I can. Major Fentiman has applied for it as executor, and I cannot quite see what I can do in the matter without his signature. The Home Office would hardly—"

"Yes. I quite see that you can't mess about with the Home Office.

Well, though, that's easy. Robert never was keen on the resurrection idea. Once we've got his address, he'll be only too happy to send you a chit to call the whole thing off. You leave it to me. After all, even if we don't find Robert for a few days and the old boy has to be dug up after all, it won't make things any worse. Will it?"

Mr. Murbles agreed, dubiously.

"Then I'll pull the old carcass together," said Wimsey, brightly, flinging the bedclothes aside and leaping to his feet, "and toddle off to the City of Light. Will you excuse me for a few moments, sir? The bath awaits me. Bunter, put a few things into a suit-case and be ready to come with me to Paris."

.   .   .   .   .

On second thoughts, Wimsey waited till the next day, hoping, as he explained, to hear from the detective. As nothing reached him, however, he started in pursuit, instructing the head office of Sleuths Incorporated to wire any information received to him at the Hôtel Meurice. The next news that arrived from him was a card to Mr. Murbles written on a P.L.M. express, which said simply, "Quarry gone on to Rome. Hard on trail. P.W." The next day came a foreign telegram: "Making for Sicily. Faint but pursuing. P.W."

In reply to this, Mr. Murbles wired: "Exhumation fixed for day after to-morrow. Please make haste."

To which Wimsey replied: "Returning for exhumation. P.W."

He returned alone.

"Where is Robert Fentiman?" demanded Mr. Murbles, agitatedly.

Wimsey, his hair matted damply and his face white from traveling day and night, grinned feebly.

"I rather fancy," he said, in a wan voice, "that Oliver is at his old tricks again."

"Again?" cried Mr. Murbles, aghast. "But the letter from your detective was genuine."

"Oh, yes—that was genuine enough. But even detectives can be bribed. Anyhow, we haven't seen hide or hair of our friends. They've been always a little ahead. Like the Holy Grail, you know. Fainter by day but always in the night blood-red, and sliding down the blackened marsh, blood-red—perfectly bloody, in fact. Well, here we are. When does the ceremony take place? Quietly, I take it? No flowers?"

.   .   .   .   .

317

The "ceremony" took place, as such ceremonies do, under the discreet cover of darkness. George Fentiman, who, in Robert's absence, attended to represent the family, was nervous and depressed. It is trying enough to go to the funeral of one's friends and relations, amid the grotesque pomps of glass hearses, and black horses, and wreaths, and appropriate hymns "beautifully" rendered by well-paid choristers, but, as George irritably remarked, the people who grumble over funerals don't realize their luck. However depressing the thud of earth on the coffin-lid may be, it is music compared to the rattle of gravel and thump of spades which herald a premature and un-reverent resurrection, enveloped in clouds of formalin and without benefit of clergy.

Dr. Penberthy also appeared abstracted and anxious to get the business over. He made the journey to the cemetery ensconced in the farthest corner of the big limousine, and discussed thyroid abnormalities with Dr. Horner, Sir James Lubbock's assistant, who had come to help with the autopsy. Mr. Murbles was, naturally, steeped in gloom. Wimsey devoted himself to his accumulated corre-spondence, out of which one letter only had any bearing on the Fentiman case. It was from Marjorie Phelps, and ran:

"If you want to meet Ann Dorland, would you care to come along to a 'do' at the Rushworths' Wednesday week? It will be very deadly, because Naomi Rushworth's new young man is going to read a paper on ductless glands which nobody knows anything about. However, it appears that ductless glands will be 'news' in next to no time—ever so much more up-to-date than vitamins—so the Rushworths are all over glands—in the social sense, I mean. Ann D. is certain to be there, because as I told you, she is taking to this healthy bodies for all stunt, or whatever it is, so you'd bet-ter come. It will be company for me!—and I've got to go, anyway, as I'm supposed to be a friend of Naomi's. Besides, they say that if one paints or sculps or models, one ought to know all about glands, because of the way they enlarge your jaw and alter your face, or something. Do come, because if you don't I shall be fastened on by some deadly bore or other—and I shall have to hear all Naomi's raptures about the man, which will be too awful."

Wimsey made a note to be present at this enlivening party, and looking round, saw that they were arriving at the Necropolis—so vast, so glittering with crystal-globed wreaths, so towering with skyscraping monuments, that no lesser name would serve it. At the gate they were met by Mr. Pritchard in person (acidulated in his manner and elaborately polite to Mr. Murbles), and by the Home Office representative (suave and bland and disposed to see reporters lurking behind every tombstone). A third person, coming up, proved to be an official from the Cemetery Company, who took charge of the party and guided them along the neat graveled walks to where digging operations were already in process.

The coffin, being at length produced and identified by its brass plate, was then carefully borne to a small outbuilding close at hand, which appeared to be a potting-shed in ordinary life, converted by a board and a couple of trestles into a temporary mortuary. Here a slight halt and confusion was caused by the doctors, demanding in aggressively cheerful and matter-of-fact tones more light and space to work in. The coffin was placed on a bench; somebody produced a mackintosh sheet and spread it on the trestle table; lamps were brought and suitably grouped. After which, the workmen advanced, a little reluctantly, to unscrew the coffin lid, preceded by Dr. Penberthy, scattering formalin from a spray, rather like an infernal thurifer at some particularly unwholesome sacrifice.

"Ah! very nice indeed," said Dr. Horner, appreciatively, as the corpse was disengaged from the coffin and transferred to the table. "Excellent. Not much difficulty over this job. That's the best of getting on to it at once. How long has he been buried, did you say? Three or four weeks? He doesn't look it. Will you make the autopsy or shall I? Just as you like. Very well. Where did I put my bag? Ah! thank you, Mr.–er–er–" (An unpleasantly-occupied pause, during which George Fentiman escaped, murmuring that he thought he'd have a smoke outside.) "Undoubted heart trouble, of course, I don't see any unusual appearances, do you? . . . I suppose we'd better secure the stomach as it stands . . . pass me the gut, would you? Thanks. D'you mind holding while I get this ligature on? Ta." (Snip, snip.) "The jars are just behind you. Thanks. Look out! You'll have it over. Ha! ha! that was a near thing. Reminds me of Palmer, you know— and Cook's stomach—always think that a very funny story, ha, ha!—I won't take all the liver—just a sample—it's only a matter of form—and sections of the rest—yes—better have a look at the brain while we are about it, I suppose. Have you got the large saw?"

"How callous these medical men seem," murmured Mr. Murbles.

"It's nothing to them," said Wimsey. "Horner does this kind of job several times a week."

"Yes, but he need not be so noisy. Dr. Penberthy behaves with decorum."

"Penberthy runs a practice," said Wimsey with a faint grin. "He has to exercise a little restraint over himself. Besides, he knew old Fentiman, and Horner didn't."

At length the relevant portions of General Fentiman's anatomy having been collected into suitable jars and bottles, the body was returned to the coffin and screwed down. Penberthy came across to Wimsey and took his arm.

"We ought to be able to get a pretty good idea of what you want to know," he said. "Decomposition is very little advanced, owing to an exceptionally well-made coffin. By the way" (he dropped his voice) "that leg, you know—did it ever occur to you—or rather, did you ever discover any explanation of that?"

"I *did* have an idea about it," admitted Wimsey, "but I don't yet know whether it was the right one. I shall probably know for certain in a day or two."

"You think the body was interfered with?" said Penberthy, looking him steadily in the face.

"Yes, and so do you," replied Wimsey, returning the gaze.

"I've had my suspicions all the time, of course. I told you so, you know. I wonder whether—you don't think I was wrong to give the certificate, do you?"

"Not unless you suspected anything wrong with the death itself," said Wimsey. "Have you and Horner noticed anything queer?"

"No. But—oh, well! having patients dug up always makes me worried, you know. It's easy to make a mistake and one looks an awful fool in court. I'd hate being made to look a fool just at present," added the doctor with a nervous laugh. "I'm thinking of—great Scott, man! how you startled me!"

Dr. Horner had brought a large, bony hand down on his shoulder. He was a red-faced, jovial man, and he smiled as he held up his bag before them.

"All packed up and ready," he announced. "Got to be getting back now, aha! Got to be getting back."

"Have the witnesses signed the labels?" asked Penberthy, rather shortly.

"Yes, yes, quite all right. Both the solicitor johnnies, so they can't quarrel about *that* in the witness-box," replied Horner. "Come along, please—I've got to get off."

They found George Fentiman outside, seated on a tombstone, and sucking at an empty pipe.

"Is it all over?"

"Yes."

"Have they found anything?"

"Haven't looked yet," broke in Horner, genially. "Not at the part which interests *you,* that is. Leave that for my colleague Lubbock, you know. Soon give you an answer—say, in a week's time."

George passed his handkerchief over his forehead, which was beaded with little drops of sweat.

"I don't like it," he said. "But I suppose it had to be done. What was that? I thought—I'd swear I saw something moving over there."

"A cat, probably," said Penberthy, "there's nothing to be alarmed at."

"No," said George, "but sitting about here, one—fancies things." He hunched his shoulders, squinting round at them with the whites of his eyeballs showing.

"Things," he said, "people—going to and fro . . . and walking up and down. Following one."

CHAPTER XIV

GRAND SLAM IN SPADES

ON THE SEVENTH MORNING after the exhumation—which happened to be a Tuesday—Lord Peter walked briskly into Mr. Murbles' chambers in Staple Inn, with Detective-Inspector Parker at his heels.

"Good morning," said Mr. Murbles, surprised.

"Good morning," said Wimsey. "Hark! hark! the lark at heaven's gate sings. He is coming, my own, my sweet, were it ever so airy a tread. He will be here in a quarter of an hour."

"Who will?" demanded Mr. Murbles, somewhat severely.

"Robert Fentiman."

Mr. Murbles gave a little ejaculation of surprise.

"I had almost given up hope in that direction," he said.

321

"So had not I. I said to myself, he is not lost but gone before. And it was so. Charles, we will lay out the *pièces de conviction* on the table. The boots. The photographs. The microscopic slides showing the various specimens. The paper of notes from the library. The outer garments of the deceased. Just so. And 'Oliver Twist.' Beautiful. Now, as Sherlock Holmes says, we shall look imposing enough to strike terror into the guilty breast, though armed in triple steel."

"Did Fentiman return of his own accord?"

"Not altogether. He was, if I may so express myself, led. Almost, in fact, led on. O'er moor and fen, o'er crag and torrent till, don't you know. What is that noise in the outer room? It is, it is the cannon's opening roar."

It was, indeed, the voice of Robert Fentiman, not in the best of tempers. In a few seconds he was shown in. He nodded curtly to Mr. Murbles, who replied with a stiff bow, and then turned violently upon Wimsey.

"Look here, what's the meaning of all this? Here's that damned detective fellow of yours leading me a devil of a dance all over Europe and home again, and then this morning he suddenly turns round and tells me that you want to see me here with news about Oliver. What the devil do you know about Oliver?"

"Oliver?" said Wimsey. "Oh, yes—he's an elusive personality. Almost as elusive in Rome as he was in London. Wasn't it odd, Fentiman, the way he always seemed to bob up directly your back was turned? Wasn't it funny, the way he managed to disappear from places the moment you set foot in 'em? Almost like the way he used to hang about Gatti's and then give you and me the slip. Did you have a jolly time abroad, old man? I suppose you didn't like to tell your companion that he and you were chasing a will o' the wisp?"

Robert Fentiman's face was passing through phases ranging from fury to bewilderment and back again. Mr. Murbles interrupted.

"Has this detective vouchsafed any explanation of his extraordinary behaviour, in keeping us in the dark for nearly a fortnight as to his movements?"

"I'm afraid I owe you the explanation," said Wimsey, airily. "You see, I thought it was time the carrot was dangled before the other donkey. I knew that if we pretended to find Oliver in Paris, Fentiman would be in honour bound to chase after him. In fact, he was probably only too pleased to get away—weren't you, Fentiman?"

"Do you mean to say that you invented all this story about Oliver, Lord Peter?"

"I did. Not the original Oliver, of course, but the Paris Oliver. I told the sleuth to send a wire from Paris to summon our friend away and keep him away."

"But why?"

"I'll explain that later. And of course you had to go, hadn't you, old man? Because you couldn't very well refuse to go without confessing that there was no such person as Oliver?"

"Damnation!" burst out Fentiman, and then suddenly began to laugh. "You cunning little devil! I began to think there was something fishy about it, you know. When that first wire came, I was delighted. Thought the sleuth-hound fellow had made a perfectly providential floater, don't you know. And the longer we kept tootin' round Europe the better I was pleased. But when the hare started to double back to England, home and beauty, I began to get the idea that somebody was pullin' my leg. By the way, was that why I was able to get all my visas with that uncanny facility at an unearthly hour overnight?"

"It was," said Wimsey, modestly.

"I might have known there was something wrong about it. You devil! Well—what now?—If you've exploded Oliver, I suppose you've spilled all the rest of the beans, eh?"

"If you mean by that expression," said Mr. Murbles, "that we are aware of your fraudulent and disgraceful attempt to conceal the true time of General Fentiman's decease, the answer is, Yes—we do know it. And I may say that it has come as a most painful shock to my feelings."

Fentiman flung himself into a chair, slapping his thigh and roaring with laughter.

"I might have known you'd be on to it," he gasped, "but it was a damn good joke, wasn't it? Good lord! I couldn't help chuckling to myself, you know. To think of all those refrigerated old imbeciles at the Club sittin' solemnly round there, and comin' in and noddin' to the old guv'nor like so many mandarins, when he was as dead as a door-nail all the time. That leg of his was a bit of a slip-up, of course, but that was an accident. Did you ever find out where he was all the time?"

"Oh, yes—pretty conclusively. You left your marks on the cabinet, you know."

"No, did we? Hell!"

"Yes—and when you stuck the old boy's overcoat back in the cloak-room, you forgot to stick a poppy in it."

"Oh, lord! that *was* a bloomer. D'you know, I never thought of that. Oh, well! I suppose I couldn't hope to carry it off with a confounded bloodhound like you on the trail. But it was fun while it lasted. Even now, the thought of old Bunter solemnly callin' up two and a half columns of Olivers makes me shout with joy. It's almost as good as getting the half-million."

"That reminds me," said Wimsey. "The one thing I don't know is how you knew about the half-million. Did Lady Dormer tell you about her will? Or did you hear of it from George?"

"George? Great scott, no! George knew nothing about it. The old boy told me himself."

"General Fentiman?"

"Of course. When he came back to the Club that night, he came straight up to see me."

"And we never thought of that," said Wimsey, crushed. "Too obvious, I suppose."

"You can't be expected to think of everything," said Robert, condescendingly. "I think you did very well, take it all round. Yes—the old boy toddled up to me and told me all about it. He said I wasn't to tell George, because he wasn't quite satisfied with George —about Sheila, you know—and he wanted to think it over and see what was best to be done, in the way of making a new will, you see."

"Just so. And he went down to the library to do it."

"That's right; and I went down and had some grub. Well then, afterwards I thought perhaps I hadn't said quite enough on behalf of old George. I mean, the guv'nor needed to have it pointed out to him that George's queerness was caused a great deal by bein' dependent on Sheila and all that, and if he had some tin of his own he'd be much better-tempered—you get me? So I hopped through to the library to find the guv'—and there he was—dead!"

"What time was that?"

"Somewhere round about eightish, I should think. Well, I was staggered. Of course, my first idea was to call for help, but it wasn't any go. He was quite dead. And then it jolly well came over me all at once how perfectly damnably we had missed the train. Just to think of that awful Dorland woman walking into all those thousands—I tell you, it made me so bally wild, I could have exploded and blown the place up! . . . And then, you know, I began to get a sort of creepy feeling, alone there with the body and nobody in the library at all. We seemed cut off from the world, as the writing fellows say. And then it just seemed to take hold of my mind, why should he have died like that?—I did have a passing hope that the old girl might have pegged out first, and I was just going along to the telephone to find out, when—thinking of the telephone cabinet, you see—the whole thing popped into my head ready-made, as you might say. In three minutes I'd lugged him along and stuck him up on the seat, and then I hopped back to write a label for the door. I say, I thought I was jolly smart to remember not to blot that label on the library blotting-paper."

"Believe me," said Wimsey, "I appreciated that point."

"Good. I'm glad you did. Well, it was pretty plain sailing after that. I got the guv'nor's togs from the cloak-room and took 'em up to my room, and then I thought about old Woodward sittin' up waitin' for him. So I trundled out and went down to Charing Cross—how do you think?"

"By bus?"

"Not quite as bad as that. By Underground. I did realize it wouldn't work to call a taxi."

"You show quite a disposition for fraud, Fentiman."

"Yes, don't I?—Well, all that was easy. I must say, I didn't pass a frightfully good night."

"You'll take it more calmly another time."

"Yes—it was my maiden effort in crime, of course. The next morning——"

"Young man," said Mr. Murbles, in an awful voice, "we will draw a veil over the next morning. I have listened to your shameless statement with a disgust which words cannot express. But I cannot, and I will not sit here and listen while you congratulate yourself, with a cynicism at which you should blush, on having employed those sacred moments when every thought should have been consecrated——"

"Oh, punk!" interrupted Robert, rudely. "My old pals are none the worse because I did a little bit of self-help. I know fraud isn't altogether the clean potato, but, dash it all! surely we have a better right to the old boy's money than that girl. I bet *she* never did anything in the Great War, Daddy. Well, it's all gone bust—but it was a darn good stunt while it lasted."

"I perceive," replied Mr. Murbles, icily, "that any appeal to your better feelings would be waste of time. I imagine, however, you realize that fraud is a penal offence."

"Yes—that's a nuisance, isn't it? What are we going to do about it? Do I have to go and eat humble pie to old Pritchard? Or does Wimsey pretend to have discovered something frightfully abstruse from looking at the body?—Oh, good lord, by the way—what's happened about that confounded exhumation stunt? I never thought a word more about it. I say, Wimsey, was that the idea? Did you know then that I'd been trying to work this stunt and was it your notion you could get me out of it?"

"Partly."

"Damned decent of you. You know, I did tumble to it that you'd got a line on me when you sent me down with that detective fellow to Charing Cross. And, I say, you nearly had me there! I'd made up my mind to pretend to go after Oliver—you know—and then I spotted that second bloodhound of yours on the train with me. That gave me gooseflesh all over. The only thing I could think of—short of chucking up the whole show—was to accuse some harmless old bird of being Oliver—as a proof of good faith, don't you see."

"That was it, was it? I thought you must have some reason."

"Yes—and then, when I got that summons to Paris, I thought I must, somehow, have diddled the lot of you. But I suppose that was all arranged for. I say, Wimsey, why? Did you just want to get your own back, or what? Why did you want me out of England?"

"Yes, indeed, Lord Peter," said Mr. Murbles, gravely. "I think you owe *me* at least some explanation on that point."

"Don't you see," said Wimsey, "Fentiman was his grandfather's executor. If I got him out of the way, you couldn't stop the exhumation."

"Ghoul!" said Robert. "I believe you batten on corpses."

Wimsey laughed, rather excitedly.

"Fentiman," he said, "what would you give at this moment for your chance of that half-million?"

"Chance?" cried Fentiman. "There's no chance at all. What do you mean?"

Wimsey slowly drew a paper from his pocket.

"This came last night," he said. "And, by jove, my lad, it's lucky for you that you had a good bit to lose by the old man's death. This is from Lubbock—

'Dear Lord Peter,

I am sending you a line in advance to let you know the result of the autopsy on General Fentiman. As regards the ostensible reason for the investigation, I may say that there was no food in the stomach and that the last meal had been taken several hours previously. The important point, however, is that, following your own rather obscurely-expressed suggestion, I tested the viscera for poison and discovered traces of a powerful dose of digitalin, swallowed not very long previous to decease. As you know, with a subject whose heart was already in a weak state, the result of such a dose could not but be fatal. The symptoms would be a slowing-down of the heart's action and collapse—practically indistinguishable from a violent heart-attack.

I do not, of course, know what your attitude in this business is, though I congratulate you on the perspicacity which prompted you to suggest an analysis. In the meanwhile, of course, you will realize that I am obliged to communicate the result of the autopsy to the public prosecutor.'"

Mr. Murbles sat petrified.

"My God!" cried Fentiman. And then again, "My God!—Wimsey —if I'd known—if I'd had the faintest idea—I wouldn't have touched the body for twenty millions. Poison! Poor old blighter! What a damned shame! I remember now his saying that night he felt a bit sickish, but I never thought—I say, Wimsey—you do believe, don't you, that I hadn't the foggiest? I say—that awful female—I knew she was a wrong 'un. But poison! that is too thick. Good lord!"

Parker, who had hitherto preserved the detached expression of a friendly spectator, now beamed. "Damn good, old man!" he cried, and smote Peter on the back. Professional enthusiasm overcame him. "It's a real case," he said, "and you've handled it finely, Peter. I didn't know you had it in you to hang on so patiently. Forcing the exhumation on 'em through putting pressure on Major Fentiman was simply masterly! Pretty work! Pretty work!"

"Thank you, Charles," said Wimsey, dryly. "I'm glad somebody appreciates me. Anyhow," he added, viciously, "I bet that's wiped old Pritchard's eye."

And at this remark, even Mr. Murbles showed signs of returning animation.

CHAPTER XV

SHUFFLE THE CARDS AND DEAL AGAIN

A HASTY CONSULTATION with the powers that be at Scotland Yard put Detective-Inspector Parker in charge of the Fentiman case, and he promptly went into consultation with Wimsey.

"What put you on to this poison business?" he asked.

"Aristotle, chiefly," replied Wimsey. "He says, you know, that one should always prefer the probable impossible to the improbable possible. It was possible, of course, that the General should have died off in that neat way at the most confusing moment. But how much nicer and more probable that the whole thing had been stage-managed. Even if it had seemed much more impossible I should have been dead nuts on murder. And there really was nothing impossible about it. Then there was Pritchard and the Dorland woman. Why should they have been so dead against compromise and so suspicious about things unless they had inside information from somewhere. After all, they hadn't seen the body as Penberthy and I did."

"That leads on to the question of who did it. Miss Dorland is the obvious suspect, naturally."

"She's got the biggest motive."

"Yes. Well, let's be methodical. Old Fentiman was apparently as right as rain up till about half past three when he started off for Portman Square, so that the drug must have been given him between then and eightish, when Robert Fentiman found him dead. Now who saw him between those two times?"

"Wait a sec. That's not absolutely accurate. He must have *taken* the stuff between those two times, but it might have been *given* him earlier. Suppose, for instance, somebody had dropped a poisoned pill into his usual bottle of soda-mints or whatever he used to take. That could have been worked at any time."

"Well—not too early on, Peter. Suppose he had died a lot too soon and Lady Dormer had heard about it."

"It wouldn't have made any difference. She wouldn't need to alter her will, or anything. The bequest to Miss Dorland would just stand as before."

"Quite right. I was being stupid. Well, then, we'd better find out if he did take anything of that kind regularly. If he did, who would have had the opportunity to drop the pill in?"

"Penberthy, for one."

"The doctor?—yes, we must stick his name down as a possible, though he wouldn't have had the slightest motive. Still, we'll put him in the column headed Opportunity."

"That's right, Charles. I do like your methodical ways."

"Attraction of opposites," said Parker, ruling a notebook into three columns. "Opportunity. Number 1, Dr. Penberthy. If the tablets or globules or whatever they were, were Penberthy's own prescription, he would have a specially good opportunity. Not so good, though, if they were the kind of things you get ready-made from the chemist in sealed bottles."

"Oh, bosh! he could always have asked to have a squint at 'em to see if they were the right kind. I insist on having Penberthy in. Besides, he was one of the people who saw the General between the critical hours—during what we may call the administration period, so he had an extra amount of opportunity."

"So he had. Well, I've put him down. Though there seems no reason for him——"

"I'm not going to be put off by a trifling objection like that. He had the opportunity, so down he goes. Well, then, Miss Dorland comes next."

"Yes. She goes down under opportunity and also under motive. She certainly had a big interest in polishing off the old man, she saw him during the period of administration and she very likely gave him something to eat or drink while he was in the house. So she is a very likely subject. The only difficulty with her is the difficulty of getting hold of the drug. You can't get digitalin just by asking for it, you know."

"N—no. At least, not by itself. You can get it mixed up with other drugs quite easily. I saw an ad. in the *Daily Views* only this morning, offering a pill with half a grain of digitalin in it."

"Did you? where?—oh, that! Yes, but it's got nux vomica in it too, which is supposed to be an antidote. At any rate, it bucks the heart up by stimulating the nerves, so as to counteract the slowing-down action of the digitalin."

"H'm. Well, put down Miss Dorland under Means with a query-mark. Oh, of course, Penberthy has to go down under Means too.

He is the one person who could get the stuff without any bother."

"Right. Means: No. 1, Dr. Penberthy. Opportunity: No. 1, Dr. Penberthy, No. 2, Miss Dorland. We'll have to put in the servants at Lady Dormer's too, shan't we? Any of them who brought him food or drink, at any rate."

"Put 'em in, by all means. They might have been in collusion with Miss Dorland. And how about Lady Dormer herself?"

"Oh, come, Peter. There wouldn't be any sense in that."

"Why not? She may have been planning revenge on her brother all these years, camouflaging her feelings under a pretense of generosity. It would be rather fun to leave a terrific legacy to somebody you loathed, and then, just when he was feelin' nice and grateful and all over coals of fire, poison him to make sure he didn't get it. We simply must have Lady Dormer. Stick her down under Opportunity and under Motive."

"I refuse to do more than Opportunity and Motive (query?)."

"Have it your own way. Well, now—there are our friends the two taxi-drivers."

"I don't think you can be allowed those. It would be awfully hard work poisoning a fare, you know."

"I'm afraid it would. I say! I've just got a rippin' idea for poisoning a taxi-man, though. You give him a dud half-crown, and when he bites it——"

"He dies of lead poisoning. That one's got whiskers on it."

"Juggins. You poison the half-crown with Prussic acid."

"Splendid! And he falls down foaming at the mouth. That's frightfully brilliant. Do you mind giving your attention to the matter in hand?"

"You think we can leave out the taxi-drivers, then?"

"I think so."

"Right-oh! I'll let you have them. That brings us, I'm sorry to say, to George Fentiman."

"You've got rather a weakness for George Fentiman, haven't you?"

"Yes—I like old George. He's an awful pig in some ways, but I quite like him."

"Well, I don't know George, so I shall firmly put him down. Opportunity No. 3, he is."

"He'll have to go down under Motive, too, then."

"Why? What did he stand to gain by Miss Dorland's getting the legacy?"

"Nothing—if he knew about it. But Robert says emphatically that he didn't know. So does George. And if he didn't, don't you see, the General's death meant that he would immediately step into that two thousand quid which Dougal MacStewart was being so pressing about."

"MacStewart?—oh, yes—the money-lender. That's one up to you, Peter; I'd forgotten him. That certainly does put George on the list of the possibles. He was pretty sore about things too, wasn't he?"

"Very. And I remember his saying one rather unguarded thing at least down at the Club on the very day the murder—or rather, the death—was discovered."

"That's in his favour, if anything," said Parker, cheerfully, "unless he's very reckless indeed."

"It won't be in his favour with the police," grumbled Wimsey.

"My dear man!"

"I beg your pardon. I was forgetting for the moment. I'm afraid you are getting a little above your job, Charles. So much intelligence will spell either a Chief-Commissionership or ostracism if you aren't careful."

"I'll chance that. Come on—get on with it. Who else is there?"

"There's Woodward. Nobody could have a better opportunity of tampering with the General's pill-boxes."

"And I suppose his little legacy might have been a motive."

"Or he may have been in the enemy's pay. Sinister men-servants so often are, you know. Look what a boom there has been lately in criminal butlers and thefts by perfect servants."

"That's a fact. And now, how about the people at the Bellona?"

"There's Wetheridge. He's a disagreeable devil. And he has always cast covetous eyes at the General's chair by the fire. I've seen him."

"Be serious, Peter."

"I'm perfectly serious. I don't like Wetheridge. He annoys me. And then we mustn't forget to put down Robert."

"Robert? Why, he's the one person we can definitely cross off. He knew it was to his interest to keep the old man alive. Look at the pains he took to cover up the death."

"Exactly. He is the Most Unlikely Person, and that is why Sherlock Holmes would suspect him at once. He was, by his own admission, the last person to see General Fentiman alive. Suppose he had a row with the old man and killed him, and then discovered, afterwards, about the legacy."

"You're scintillating with good plots to-day, Peter. If they'd quarreled, he might possibly have knocked his grandfather down—though I don't think he'd do such a rotten and unsportsmanlike thing —but he surely wouldn't have poisoned him."

Wimsey sighed.

"There's something in what you say," he admitted. "Still, you never know. Now then, is there any name we've thought of which appears in all three columns of our list?"

"No, not one. But several appear in two."

"We'd better start on those, then. Miss Dorland is the most obvious, naturally, and after her, George, don't you think?"

"Yes. I'll have a round-up among all the chemists who may possibly have supplied her with the digitalin. Who's her family doctor?"

"Dunno. That's your pigeon. By the way, I'm supposed to be meeting the girl at a cocoa-party or something of the sort to-morrow. Don't pinch her before then if you can help it."

"No; but it looks to me as though we might need to put a few questions. And I'd like to have a look round Lady Dormer's house."

"For heaven's sake, don't be flat-footed about it, Charles. Use tact."

"You can trust your father. And, I say, you might take me down to the Bellona in a tactful way. I'd like to ask a question or two there."

Wimsey groaned.

"I shall be asked to resign if this goes on. Not that it's much loss. But it would please Wetheridge so much to see the back of me. Never mind. I'll make a Martha of myself. Come on."

The entrance of the Bellona Club was filled with an unseemly confusion. Culyer was arguing heatedly with a number of men and three or four members of the committee stood beside him with brows as black as thunder. As Wimsey entered, one of the intruders caught sight of him with a yelp of joy.

"Wimsey—Wimsey, old man! Here, be a sport and get us in on this. We've got to have the story some day. You probably know all about it, you old blighter."

It was Salcombe Hardy of the *Daily Yell,* large and untidy and slightly drunk as usual. He gazed at Wimsey with child-like blue eyes. Barton of the *Banner,* red-haired and pugnacious, faced round promptly.

"Ah, Wimsey, that's fine. Give us a line on this, can't you? Do explain that if we get a story we'll be good and go."

"Good lord," said Wimsey, "how do these things get into the papers?"

"I think it's rather obvious," said Culyer, acidly.

"It wasn't me," said Wimsey.

"No, no," put in Hardy. "You mustn't think that. It was my stunt. In fact, I saw the whole show up at the Necropolis. I was on a family vault, pretending to be a recording angel."

"You would be," said Wimsey. "Just a moment, Culyer." He drew the secretary aside. "See here, I'm damned annoyed about this, but it can't be helped. You can't stop these boys when they're after a story. And anyway, it's all got to come out. It's a police affair now. This is Detective-Inspector Parker of Scotland Yard."

"But what's the matter?" demanded Culyer.

"Murder's the matter, I'm afraid."

"Oh, hell!"

"Sorry and all that. But you'd better grin and bear it. Charles, give these fellows as much story as you think they ought to have and get on with it. And, Salcombe, if you'll call off your tripe-hounds, we'll let you have an interview and a set of photographs."

"That's the stuff," said Hardy.

"I'm sure," agreed Parker, pleasantly, "that you lads don't want to get in the way, and I'll tell you all that's advisable. Show us a room, Captain Culyer, and I'll send out a statement and then you'll let us get to work."

This was agreed, and, a suitable paragraph having been provided by Parker, the Fleet Street gang departed, bearing Wimsey away with them like a captured Sabine maiden to drink in the nearest bar, in the hope of acquiring picturesque detail.

"But I wish you'd kept out of it, Sally," mourned Peter.

"Oh, God," said Salcombe, "nobody loves us. It's a forsaken thing to be a poor bloody reporter." He tossed a lank black lock of hair back from his forehead and wept.

.   .   .   .   .

Parker's first and most obvious move was to interview Penberthy, whom he caught at Harley Street, after surgery hours.

"Now I'm not going to worry you about that certificate, doctor," he began, pleasantly. "We're all liable to make mistakes, and I understand that a death resulting from an over-dose of digitalin would look very like a death from heart-failure."

"It would *be* a death from heart-failure," corrected the doctor, patiently. Doctors are weary of explaining that heart-failure is not a specific disease, like mumps or housemaid's knee. It is this incompatibility of outlook between the medical and the lay mind which involves counsel and medical witnesses in a fog of misunderstanding and mutual irritation.

"Just so," said Parker. "Now, General Fentiman had got heart disease already, hadn't he? Is digitalin a thing one takes for heart disease?"

"Yes; in certain forms of heart disease, digitalin is a very valuable stimulant."

"Stimulant? I thought it was a depressant."

"It acts as a stimulant at first; in later stages it depresses the heart's action."

"Oh, I see." Parker did not see very well, since, like most people, he had a vague idea that each drug has one simple effect appropriate to it, and is, specifically, a cure for something or the other. "It first speeds up the heart and then slows it down."

"Not exactly. It strengthens the heart's action by retarding the beat, so that the cavities can be more completely emptied and the pressure is relieved. We give it in certain cases of valvular disease—under proper safeguards, of course."

"Were you giving it to General Fentiman?"

"I had given it him from time to time."

"On the afternoon of November 10th,—you remember that he came to you in consequence of a heart attack. Did you give him digitalin then?"

Dr. Penberthy appeared to hesitate painfully for a moment. Then he turned to his desk and extracted a large book.

"I had better be perfectly frank with you," he said. "I did. When he came to me, the feebleness of the heart's action and the extreme difficulty in breathing suggested the urgent necessity of a cardiac stimulant. I gave him a prescription containing a small quantity of digitalin to relieve this condition. Here is the prescription. I will write it out for you."

"A small quantity?" repeated Parker.

"Quite small, combined with other drugs to counteract the depressing after-effects."

"It was not as large as the dose afterwards found in the body?"

"Good heavens, no—nothing like. In a case like General Fentiman's, digitalin is a drug to be administered with the greatest caution."

"It would not be possible, I suppose, for you to have made a mistake in dispensing? To have given an overdose by error?"

"That possibility occurred to me at once, but as soon as I heard Sir James Lubbock's figures, I realized that it was quite out of the question. The dose given was enormous; nearly two grains. But, to make quite certain, I have had my supply of the drug carefully checked, and it is all accounted for."

"Who did that for you?"

"My trained nurse. I will let you have the books and chemists' receipts."

"Thank you. Did your nurse make up the dose for General Fentiman?"

"Oh, no; it is a prescription I always keep by me, ready made up. If you'd like to see her, she will show it to you."

"Thanks very much. Now, when General Fentiman came to see you, he had just had an attack. Could that have been caused by digitalin?"

"You mean, had he been poisoned before he came to me? Well, of course, digitalin is rather an uncertain drug."

"How long would a big dose like that take to act?"

"I should expect it to take effect fairly quickly. In the ordinary way it would cause sickness and vertigo. But with a powerful cardiac stimulant like digitalin, the chief danger is that any sudden movement, such as springing suddenly to one's feet from a position of repose, is liable to cause sudden syncope and death. I should say that this was what occurred in General Fentiman's case."

"And that might have happened at any time after the administration of the dose?"

"Just so."

"Well, I'm very much obliged to you, Dr. Penberthy. I will just see your nurse and take copies of the entries in your books, if I may."

This done, Parker made his way to Portman Square, still a little hazy in his mind as to the habits of the common foxglove when applied internally—a haziness which was in no way improved by a subsequent consultation of the Materia Medica, the Pharmacopœia, Dixon Mann, Taylor, Glaister, and others of those writers who have so kindly and helpfully published their conclusions on toxicology.

CHAPTER XVI

QUADRILLE

"MRS. RUSHWORTH, this is Lord Peter Wimsey. Naomi, this is Lord Peter. He's fearfully keen on glands and things, so I've brought him along. And Naomi, do tell me all about your news. Who is it? Do I know him?"

Mrs. Rushworth was a long, untidy woman, with long, untidy hair wound into bell-pushes over her ears. She beamed short-sightedly at Peter.

"So glad to see you. So very wonderful about glands, isn't it? Dr. Voronoff, you know, and those marvelous old sheep. Such a hope for all of us. Not that dear Walter is specially interested in rejuvenation. Perhaps life is long and difficult enough as it is, don't you think —so full of problems of one kind and another. And the insurance companies have quite set their faces against it, or so I understand. That's natural, isn't it, when you come to think of it. But the effect on character is so interesting, you know. Are you devoted to young criminals by any chance?"

Wimsey said that they presented a very perplexing problem.

"How very true. So perplexing. And just to think that we have been quite wrong about them all these thousands of years. Flogging and bread-and-water, you know, and Holy Communion, when what they really needed was a little bit of rabbit-gland or something to make them just as good as gold. Quite terrible, isn't it? And all those poor freaks in sideshows, too—dwarfs and giants, you know—all pineal or pituitary, and they come right again. Though I daresay they make a great deal more money as they are, which throws such a distressing light on unemployment, does it not?"

Wimsey said that everything had the defects of its qualities.

"Yes, indeed," agreed Mrs. Rushworth. "But I think it is so infinitely more heartening to look at it from the opposite point of view. Everything has the qualities of its defects, too, has it not? It is so important to see these things in their true light. It will be such a joy for Naomi to be able to help dear Walter in this great work. I hope you will feel eager to subscribe to the establishment of the new Clinic."

Wimsey asked, what new Clinic.

"Oh! hasn't Marjorie told you about it? The new Clinic to make everybody good by glands. That is what dear Walter is going to speak about. He is so keen and so is Naomi. It was such a joy to me when Naomi told me that they were really engaged, you know. Not that her old mother hadn't suspected something, of course," added Mrs. Rushworth, archly. "But young people are so odd nowadays and keep their affairs so much to themselves."

Wimsey said that he thought both parties were heartily to be congratulated. And indeed, from what he had seen of Naomi Rushworth, he felt that she at least deserved congratulation, for she was a singularly plain girl, with a face like a weasel.

"You will excuse me if I run off and speak to some of these other people, won't you?" went on Mrs. Rushworth. "I'm sure you will be able to amuse yourself. No doubt you have many friends in my little gathering."

Wimsey glanced round and was about to felicitate himself on knowing nobody, when a familiar face caught his eye.

"Why," said he, "there is Dr. Penberthy."

"Dear Walter!" cried Mrs. Rushworth, turning hurriedly in the direction indicated. "I declare, so he is. Ah, well—now we shall be able to begin. He should have been here before, but a doctor's time is never his own."

"Penberthy?" said Wimsey, half aloud, "good lord!"

"Very sound man," said a voice beside him. "Don't think the worse of his work from seeing him in this crowd. Beggars in a good cause can't be choosers, as we parsons know too well."

Wimsey turned to face a tall, lean man, with a handsome, humourous face, whom he recognized as a well-known slum padre.

"Father Whittington, isn't it?"

"The same. You're Lord Peter Wimsey, I know. We've got an interest in crime in common, haven't we? I'm interested in this glandular theory. It may throw a great light on some of our heartbreaking problems."

"Glad to see there's no antagonism between religion and science," said Wimsey.

"Of course not. Why should there be? We are all searching for Truth."

"And all these?" asked Wimsey, indicating the curious crowd with a wave of the hand.

"In their way. They mean well. They do what they can, like the woman in the Gospels, and they are surprisingly generous. Here's Penberthy, looking for you, I fancy. Well, Dr. Penberthy, I've come, you see, to hear you make mincemeat of original sin."

"That's very open-minded of you," said Penberthy, with a rather strained smile. "I hope you are not hostile. We've no quarrel with the Church, you know, if she'll stick to her business and leave us to ours."

"My dear man, if you can cure sin with an injection, I shall be only too pleased. Only be sure you don't pump in something worse in the process. You know the parable of the swept and garnished house."

"I'll be as careful as I can," said Penberthy. "Excuse me one moment. I say, Wimsey, you've heard all about Lubbock's analysis, I suppose."

"Yes. Bit of a startler, isn't it?"

"It's going to make things damnably awkward for me, Wimsey. I wish to God you'd given me a hint at the time. Such a thing never once occurred to me."

"Why should it? You were expecting the old boy to pop off from heart, and he did pop off from heart. Nobody could possibly blame you."

"Couldn't they? That's all you know about juries. I wouldn't have had this happen, just at this moment, for a fortune. It couldn't have chosen a more unfortunate time."

"It'll blow over, Penberthy. That sort of mistake happens a hundred times a week. By the way, I gather I'm to congratulate you. When did this get settled? You've been very quiet about it."

"I was starting to tell you up at that infernal exhumation business, only somebody barged in. Yes. Thanks very much. We fixed it up—oh! about a fortnight or three weeks ago. You have met Naomi?"

"Only for a moment this evening. My friend Miss Phelps carried her off to hear all about you."

"Oh, yes. Well, you must come along and talk to her. She's a sweet girl, and very intelligent. The old lady's a bit of a trial, I don't mind saying, but her heart's in the right place. And there's no doubt she gets hold of people whom it's very useful to meet."

"I didn't know you were such an authority on glands."

"I only wish I could afford to be. I've done a certain amount of experimental work under Professor Sligo. It's the Science of the Future, as they say in the press. There really isn't any doubt about

338

that. It puts biology in quite a new light. We're on the verge of some really interesting discoveries, no doubt about it. Only what with the anti-vivisectors and the parsons and the other old women, one doesn't make the progress one ought. Oh, lord—they're waiting for me to begin. See you later."

"Half a jiff. I really came here—no, dash it, that's rude! But I'd no idea you were the lecturer till I spotted you. I originally came here (that sounds better) to get a look at Miss Dorland of Fentiman fame. But my trusty guide has abandoned me. Do you know Miss Dorland? Can you tell me which she is?"

"I know her to speak to. I haven't seen her this evening. She may not turn up, you know."

"I thought she was very keen on—on glands and things."

"I believe she is—or thinks she is. Anything does for these women, as long as it's new—especially if it's sexual. By the way, I don't intend to be sexual."

"Bless you for that. Well, possibly Miss Dorland will show up later."

"Perhaps. But—I say, Wimsey. She's in rather a queer position, isn't she? She may not feel inclined to face it. It's all in the papers, you know."

"Dash it, don't I know it? That inspired tippler, Salcombe Hardy, got hold of it somehow. I think he bribes the cemetery officials to give him advance news of exhumations. He's worth his weight in pound notes to the *Yell*. Cheerio! Speak your bit nicely. You don't mind if I'm not in the front row, do you? I always take up a strategic position near the door that leads to the grub."

. . . . .

Penberthy's paper struck Wimsey as being original and well-delivered. The subject was not altogether unfamiliar to him, for Wimsey had a number of distinguished scientific friends who found him a good listener, but some of the experiments mentioned were new and the conclusions suggestive. True to his principles, Wimsey made a bolt for the supper-room, while polite hands were still applauding. He was not the first, however. A large figure in a hard-worked looking dress-suit was already engaged with a pile of savoury sandwiches and a whisky-and-soda. It turned at his approach and beamed at him from its liquid and innocent blue eyes. Sally Hardy—never quite drunk and never quite sober—was on the job, as usual. He held out the sandwich-plate invitingly.

"Damn good, these are," he said. "What are you doing here?"

"What are you, if it comes to that?" asked Wimsey.

Hardy laid a fat hand on his sleeve.

"Two birds with one stone," he said, impressively. "Smart fellow, that Penberthy. Glands are news, you know. He knows it. He'll be one of these fashionable practitioners"—Sally repeated this phrase once or twice, as it seemed to have got mixed up with the soda—"before long. Doing us poor bloody journalists out of a job like . . . and . . ." (He mentioned two gentlemen whose signed contributions to popular dailies were a continual source of annoyance to the G.M.C.)

"Provided he doesn't damage his reputation over this Fentiman affair," rejoined Wimsey, in a refined shriek which did duty for a whisper amid the noisy stampede which had followed them up to the refreshment-table.

"Ah! there you are," said Hardy. "Penberthy's news in himself. He's a story, don't you see. We'll have to sit on the fence a bit, of course, till we see which way the cat jumps. I'll have a par. about it at the end, mentioning that he attended old Fentiman. Presently we'll be able to work up a little thing on the magazine page about the advisability of a p.m. in all cases of sudden death. You know—even experienced doctors may be deceived. If he comes off very badly in cross-examination, there can be something about specialists not always being trustworthy—a kind word for the poor downtrodden G.P. and all that. Anyhow, he's worth a story. It doesn't matter what you say about him, provided you say something. You couldn't do us a little thing—about eight hundred words, could you—about rigor mortis or something? Only make it snappy."

"I could not," said Wimsey. "I haven't time and I don't want the money. Why should I? I'm not a dean or an actress."

"No, but you're news. You can give me the money, if you're so beastly flush. Look here, have you got a line on this case at all? That police friend of yours won't give anything away. I want to get something in before there's an arrest, because after that it's contempt. I suppose it's the girl you're after, isn't it? Can you tell me anything about her?"

"No—I came here to-night to get a look at her, but she hasn't turned up. I wish you could dig up her hideous past for me. The Rushworths must know something about her, I should think. She used to paint or something. Can't you get on to that?"

Hardy's face lighted up.

"Waffles Newton will probably know something," he said. "I'll see what I can dig out. Thanks very much, old man. That's given me an idea. We might get one of her pictures on the back pages. The old lady seems to have been a queer old soul. Odd will, wasn't it?"

"Oh, I can tell you all about that," said Wimsey. "I thought you probably knew."

He gave Hardy the history of Lady Dormer as he had heard it from Mr. Murbles. The journalist was enthralled.

"Great stuff!" he said. "That'll get 'em. Romance there! This'll be a scoop for the *Yell*. Excuse me. I want to 'phone it through to 'em before somebody else gets it. Don't hand it out to any of the other fellows."

"They can get it from Robert or George Fentiman," warned Wimsey.

"Not much, they won't," said Salcombe Hardy, feelingly. "Robert Fentiman gave old Barton of the *Banner* such a clip under the ear this morning that he had to go and see a dentist. And George has gone down to the Bellona, and they won't let anybody in. I'm all right on this. If there's anything I can do for you, I will, you bet. So long."

He faded away. A hand was laid on Peter's arm.

"You're neglecting me shockingly," said Marjorie Phelps. "And I'm frightfully hungry. I've been doing my best to find things out for you."

"That's top-hole of you. Look here. Come and sit out in the hall; it's quieter. I'll scrounge some grub and bring it along."

He secured a quantity of curious little stuffed buns, four *petitsfours,* some dubious claret-cup and some coffee and brought them with him on a tray, snatched while the waitress's back was turned.

"Thanks," said Marjorie, "I deserve all I can get for having talked to Naomi Rushworth. I cannot like that girl. She hints things."

"What, particularly?"

"Well, I started to ask about Ann Dorland. So she said she wasn't coming. So I said, 'Oh, why?' and she said, 'She *said* she wasn't well.'"

"Who said?"

"Naomi Rushworth said Ann Dorland said she couldn't come because she wasn't well. But she said that was only an excuse, of course."

341

"Who said?"

"Naomi said. So I said, was it? And she said yes, she didn't suppose she felt like facing people very much. So I said, 'I thought you were such friends.' So she said, 'Well, we are, but of course Ann always was a little abnormal, you see.' So I said that was the first I had heard of it. And she gave me one of her catty looks and said, 'Well, there was Ambrose Ledbury, wasn't there? But of course you had other things to think of then, hadn't you?' The little beast. She meant Komski. And after all, everybody knows how obvious she's made herself over this man Penberthy."

"I'm sorry, I've got mixed."

"Well, I was rather fond of Komski. And I did almost promise to live with him, till I found that his last three women had all got fed up with him and left him, and I felt there must be something wrong with a man who continually got left, and I've discovered since that he was a dreadful bully when he dropped that touching lost-dog manner of his. So I was well out of it. Still, seeing that Naomi had been going about for the last year nearly, looking at Dr. Penberthy like a female spaniel that thinks it's going to be whipped, I can't see why she need throw Komski in my face. And as for Ambrose Ledbury, anybody might have been mistaken in him."

"Who was Ambrose Ledbury?"

"Oh, he was the man who had that studio over Boulter's Mews. Powerfulness was his strong suit, and being above worldly considerations. He was rugged and wore homespun and painted craggy people in bedrooms, but his colour was amazing. He really could paint and so we could excuse a lot, but he was a professional heart-breaker. He used to gather people up hungrily in his great arms, you know—that's always rather irresistible. But he had no discrimination. It was just a habit, and his affairs never lasted long. But Ann Dorland was really rather overcome, you know. She tried the craggy style herself, but it wasn't at all her line—she hasn't any colour-sense, so there was nothing to make up for the bad drawing."

"I thought you said she didn't have any affairs."

"It wasn't an affair. I expect Ledbury gathered her up at some time or other when there wasn't anybody else handy, but he did demand good looks for anything serious. He went off to Poland a year ago with a woman called Natasha somebody. After that, Ann Dorland began to chuck painting. The trouble was, she took things seriously. A few little passions would have put her right, but she isn't the sort of person a man can enjoy flirting with. Heavy-handed. I don't think she would have gone on worrying about Ledbury if he hadn't happened to be the one and only episode. Because, as I say, she did make a few efforts, but she couldn't bring 'em off."

"I see."

"But that's no reason why Naomi should turn round like that. The fact is, the little brute's so proud of having landed a man—*and* an engagement ring—for herself, that she's out to patronize everybody else."

"Oh?"

"Yes; besides, everything is looked at from dear Walter's point of view now, and naturally Walter isn't feeling very loving towards Ann Dorland."

"Why not?"

"My dear man, you're being very discreet, aren't you? Naturally, everybody's saying that she did it."

"Are they?"

"Who else could they think did it?"

Wimsey realized, indeed, that everybody must be thinking it. He was exceedingly inclined to think it himself.

"Probably that's why she didn't turn up."

"Of course it is. She's not a fool. She must know."

"That's true. Look here, will you do something for me? Something more, I mean?"

"What?"

"From what you say, it looks as though Miss Dorland might find herself rather short of friends in the near future. If she comes to you . . ."

"I'm not going to spy on her. Not if she had poisoned fifty old generals."

"I don't want you to. But I want you to keep an open mind, and tell me what you think. Because I don't want to make a mistake over this. And I'm prejudiced. I want Miss Dorland to be guilty. So I'm very likely to persuade myself she is when she isn't. See?"

"Why do you want her to be guilty?"

"I oughtn't to have mentioned that. Of course, I don't want her found guilty if she isn't really."

"All right. I won't ask questions. And I'll try and see Ann. But I won't try to worm anything out of her. That's definite. I'm standing by Ann."

"My dear girl," said Wimsey, "you're not keeping an open mind. You think she did it."

Marjorie Phelps flushed.

"I don't. Why do you think that?"

"Because you're so anxious not to worm anything out of her. Worming couldn't hurt an innocent person."

"Peter Wimsey! You sit there, looking a perfectly well-bred imbecile, and then in the most underhand way you twist people into doing things they ought to blush for. No wonder you detect things. I will *not* do your worming for you!"

"Well, if you don't, I shall know your opinion, shan't I?"

The girl was silent for a moment. Then she said:

"It's all so beastly."

"Poisoning is a beastly crime, don't you think?" said Wimsey.

He got up quickly. Father Whittington was approaching, with Penberthy.

"Well," said Lord Peter, "have the altars reeled?"

"Dr. Penberthy has just informed me that they haven't a leg to stand on," replied the priest, smiling. "We have been spending a pleasant quarter of an hour abolishing good and evil. Unhappily, I understand his dogma as little as he understands mine. But I exercised myself in Christian humility. I said I was willing to learn."

Penberthy laughed.

"You don't object, then, to my casting out devils with a syringe," he said, "when they have proved obdurate to prayer and fasting?"

"Not at all. Why should I? So long as they *are* cast out. And provided you are certain of your diagnosis."

Penberthy crimsoned and turned away sharply.

"Oh, lord!" said Wimsey. "That was a nasty one. From a Christian priest, too!"

"What have I said?" cried Father Whittington, much disconcerted.

"You have reminded Science," said Wimsey, "that only the Pope is infallible."

CHAPTER XVII

PARKER PLAYS A HAND

"NOW, MRS. MITCHAM," said Inspector Parker, affably. He was always saying "Now, Mrs. Somebody," and he always remembered to say it affably. It was part of the routine.

The late Lady Dormer's housekeeper bowed frigidly, to indicate that she would submit to questioning.

"We want just to get the exact details of every little thing that happened to General Fentiman the day before he was found dead. I am sure you will help us. Do you recollect exactly what time he got here?"

"It would be round about a quarter to four—not later; I am sure I could not say exactly to the minute."

"Who let him in?"

"The footman."

"Did you see him then?"

"Yes; he was shown into the drawing-room, and I came down to him and brought him upstairs to her ladyship's bedroom."

"Miss Dorland did not see him then?"

"No; she was sitting with her ladyship. She sent her excuses by me, and begged General Fentiman to come up."

"Did the General seem quite well when you saw him?"

"So far as I could say he seemed well—always bearing in mind that he was a very old gentleman and had heard bad news."

"He was not bluish about the lips, or breathing very heavily, or anything of that kind?"

"Well, going up the stairs tried him rather."

"Yes, of course it would."

"He stood still on the landing for a few minutes to get his breath. I asked him whether he would like to take something, but he said no, he was all right."

"Ah! I daresay it would have been a good thing if he had accepted your very wise suggestion, Mrs. Mitcham."

"No doubt he knew best," replied the housekeeper, primly. She considered that in making observations the policeman was stepping out of his sphere.

"And then you showed him in. Did you witness the meeting between himself and Lady Dormer?"

"I did not" (emphatically). "Miss Dorland got up and said 'How do you do, General Fentiman?' and shook hands with him, and then I left the room, as it was my place to do."

"Just so. Was Miss Dorland alone with Lady Dormer when General Fentiman was announced?"

"Oh, no—the nurse was there."

"The nurse—yes, of course. Did Miss Dorland and the nurse stay in the room all the time that the General was there?"

"No. Miss Dorland came out again in about five minutes and came downstairs. She came to me in the housekeeper's room, and she looked rather sad. She said, 'Poor old dears,'—just like that."

"Did she say any more?"

"She said: 'They quarrelled, Mrs. Mitcham, ages and ages ago, when they were quite young, and they've never seen each other since.' Of course, I was aware of that, having been with her ladyship all these years, and so was Miss Dorland."

"I expect it would seem very pitiful to a young lady like Miss Dorland?"

"No doubt; she is a young lady with feelings; not like some of those you see nowadays."

Parker wagged his head sympathetically.

"And then?"

"Then Miss Dorland went away again, after a little talk with me, and presently Nellie came in—that's the housemaid."

"How long after was that?"

"Oh, some time. I had just finished my cup of tea which I have at four o'clock. It would be about half past. She came to ask for some brandy for the General, as he was feeling badly. The spirits are kept in my room, you see, and I have the key."

Parker showed nothing of his special interest in this piece of news.

"Did you see the General when you took the brandy?"

"I did not take it." Mrs. Mitcham's tone implied that fetching and carrying was not part of her duty. "I sent it by Nellie."

"I see. So you did not see the General again before he left?"

"No. Miss Dorland informed me later that he had had a heart attack."

"I am very much obliged to you, Mrs. Mitcham. Now I should like just to ask Nellie a few questions."

Mrs. Mitcham touched a bell. A fresh-faced pleasant-looking girl appeared in answer.

"Nellie, this police-officer wants you to give him some information about that time General Fentiman came here. You must tell him what he wants to know, but remember he is busy and don't start your chattering. You can speak to Nellie here, officer."

And she sailed out.

"A bit stiff, isn't she?" murmured Parker, in an awestruck whisper.

"She's one of the old-fashioned sort, I don't mind saying," agreed Nellie with a laugh.

"She put the wind up me. Now, Nellie—" he took up the old formula, "I hear you were sent to get some brandy for the old gentleman. Who told you about it?"

"Why, it was like this. After the General had been with Lady Dormer getting on for an hour, the bell rang in her ladyship's room. It was my business to answer that, so I went up, and Nurse Armstrong put her head out and said, 'Get me a drop of brandy, Nellie, quick, and ask Miss Dorland to come here. General Fentiman's rather unwell.' So I went for the brandy to Mrs. Mitcham, and on the way up with it, I knocked at the studio door where Miss Dorland was."

"Where's that, Nellie?"

"It's a big room on the first floor—built over the kitchen. It used to be a billiard-room in the old days, with a glass roof. That's where Miss Dorland does her painting and messing about with bottles and things, and she uses it as a sitting-room, too."

"Messing about with bottles?"

"Well, chemists' stuff and things. Ladies have to have their hobbies, you know, not having any work to do. It makes a lot to clear up."

"I'm sure it does. Well, go on, Nellie—I didn't mean to interrupt."

"Well, I gave Nurse Armstrong's message, and Miss Dorland said, 'Oh, dear, Nellie,' she said, 'poor old gentleman. It's been too much for him. Give me the brandy, I'll take it along. And run along and get Dr. Penberthy on the telephone.' So I gave her the brandy and she took it upstairs."

"Half a moment. Did you see her take it upstairs?"

"Well, no, I don't think I actually saw her go up—but I thought she did. But I was going down to the telephone, so I didn't exactly notice."

"No—why should you?"

"I had to look Dr. Penberthy's number up in the book, of course.

347

There was two numbers, and when I got his private house, they told me he was in Harley Street. While I was trying to get the second number Miss Dorland called over the stairs to me. She said 'Have you got the doctor, Nellie?' And I said, 'No, miss, not yet. The doctor's round in Harley Street.' And she said, 'Oh! well, when you get him, say General Fentiman's had a bad turn and he's coming round to see him at once.' So I said, 'Isn't the doctor to come here, miss?' And she said, 'No; the General's better now and he says he would rather go round there. Tell William to get a taxi.' So she went back, and just then I got through to the surgery and said to Dr. Penberthy's man to expect General Fentiman at once. And then he came downstairs with Miss Dorland and Nurse Armstrong holding on to him, and he looked mortal bad, poor old gentleman. William—the footman, you know, came in then and said he'd got the taxi, and he put General Fentiman into it, and then Miss Dorland and Nurse went upstairs again, and that was the end of it."

"I see. How long have you been here, Nellie?"

"Three years—sir." The "sir" was a concession to Parker's nice manners and educated way of speech. "Quite the gentleman," as Nellie remarked afterwards to Mrs. Mitcham, who replied, "No, Nellie—gentlemanlike I will not deny, but a policeman is a person, and I will trouble you to remember it."

"Three years? That's a long time as things go nowadays. Is it a comfortable place?"

"Not bad. There's Mrs. Mitcham, of course, but I know how to keep the right side of her. And the old lady—well, she was a real lady in every way."

"And Miss Dorland?"

"Oh, she gives no trouble, except clearing up after her. But she always speaks nicely and says please and thank you. I haven't any complaints."

"Modified rapture," thought Parker. Apparently Ann Dorland had not the knack of inspiring passionate devotion. "Not a very lively house, is it, for a young girl like yourself?"

"Dull as ditchwater," agreed Nellie, frankly. "Miss Dorland would have what they called studio parties sometimes, but not at all smart and nearly all young ladies—artists and such-like."

"And naturally it's been quieter still since Lady Dormer died. Was Miss Dorland very much distressed at her death?"

Nellie hesitated.

"She was very sorry, of course; her ladyship was the only one she had in the world. And then she was worried with all this lawyer's business—something about the will, I expect you know, sir?"

"Yes, I know about that. Worried, was she?"

"Yes, and that angry—you wouldn't believe. There was one day Mr. Pritchard came, I remember particular, because I happened to be dusting the hall at the time, you see, and she was speaking that quick and loud I couldn't help hearing. 'I'll fight it for all I'm worth,' that was what she said and 'a . . . something—to defraud'—what would that be, now?"

"Plot?" suggested Parker.

"No—a—a conspiracy, that's it. A conspiracy to defraud. And then I didn't hear any more till Mr. Pritchard came out, and he said to her, 'Very well, Miss Dorland, we will make an independent inquiry.' And Miss Dorland looked so eager and angry, I was surprised. But it all seemed to wear off, like. She hasn't been the same person the last week or so."

"How do you mean?"

"Well, don't you notice it yourself, sir? She seems so quiet and almost frightened-like. As if she'd had a shock. And she cries a dreadful lot. She didn't do that at first."

"How long has she been so upset?"

"Well, I think it was when all this dreadful business came out about the poor old gentleman being murdered. It is awful, sir, isn't it? Do you think you'll catch the one as did it?"

"Oh, I expect so," said Parker, cheerfully. "That came as a shock to Miss Dorland, did it?"

"Well, I should say so. There was a little bit in the paper, you know, sir, about Sir James Lubbock having found out about the poisoning, and when I called Miss Dorland in the morning I took leave to point it out. I said, 'That's a funny thing, miss, isn't it, about General Fentiman being poisoned,' just like that, I said. And she said, 'Poisoned, Nellie? you must be mistaken'. So I showed her the bit in the paper and she looked just dreadful."

"Well, well," said Parker, "it's a very horrid thing to hear about a person one knows. Anybody would be upset."

"Yes, sir; me and Mrs. Mitcham was quite overcome. 'Poor old gentleman,' I said, 'whatever should anybody want to do him in for? He must have gone off his head and made away with himself,' I said. Do you think that was it, sir?"

349

"It's quite possible, of course," said Parker, genially.

"Cut up about his sister dying like that, don't you think? That's what I said to Mrs. Mitcham. But she said a gentleman like General Fentiman wouldn't make away with himself and leave his affairs in confusion like he did. So I said, 'Was his affairs in confusion then?' and she said, 'They're not your affairs, Nellie, so you needn't be discussing them.' What do you think yourself, sir?"

"I don't think anything yet," said Parker, "but you have been very helpful. Now, would you kindly run and ask Miss Dorland if she could spare me a few minutes?"

Ann Dorland received him in the back drawing-room. He thought what an unattractive girl she was, with her sullen manner and gracelessness of form and movement. She sat huddled on one end of the sofa, in a black dress which made the worst of her sallow, blotched complexion. She had certainly been crying Parker thought, and when she spoke to him, it was curtly, in a voice roughened and hoarse and curiously lifeless.

"I am sorry to trouble you again," said Parker, politely.

"You can't help yourself, I suppose." She avoided his eye, and lit a fresh cigarette from the stump of the last.

"I just want to have any details you can give me about General Fentiman's visit to his sister. Mrs. Mitcham brought him up to her bedroom, I understand."

She gave a sulky nod.

"You were there?"

She made no answer.

"Were you with Lady Dormer?" he insisted, rather more sharply. "Yes."

"And the nurse was there too?"

"Yes."

She would not help him at all.

"What happened?"

"Nothing happened. I took him up to the bed and said, 'Auntie, here's General Fentiman.'"

"Lady Dormer was conscious, then?"

"Yes."

"Very weak, of course?"

"Yes."

"Did she say anything?"

"She said 'Arthur!' that's all. And he said, 'Felicity!' And I said, 'You'd like to be alone,' and went out."

"Leaving the nurse there?"

"I couldn't dictate to the nurse. She had to look after her patient."

"Quite so. Did she stay there throughout the interview?"

"I haven't the least idea."

"Well," said Parker, patiently, "you can tell me this. When you went in with the brandy, the nurse was in the bedroom then?"

"Yes, she was."

"Now, about the brandy. Nellie brought that up to you in the studio, she tells me."

"Yes."

"Did she come into the studio?"

"I don't understand."

"Did she come right into the room, or did she knock at the door and did you come out to her on the landing?"

This roused the girl a little. "Decent servants don't knock at doors," she said, with a contemptuous rudeness; "she came in, of course."

"I beg your pardon," retorted Parker, stung. "I thought she might have knocked at the door of your private room."

"No."

"What did she say to you?"

"Can't you ask *her* all these questions?"

"I have done so. But servants are not always accurate; I should like your corroboration." Parker had himself in hand again now, and spoke pleasantly.

"She said that Nurse Armstrong had sent her for some brandy, because General Fentiman was feeling faint, and told her to call me. So I said she had better go and telephone Dr. Penberthy while I took the brandy."

All this was muttered hurriedly, and in such a low tone that the detective could hardly catch the words.

"And then did you take the brandy straight upstairs?"

"Yes, of course."

"Taking it straight out of Nellie's hands? Or did she put it down on the table or anywhere?"

"How the hell should I remember?"

Parker disliked a swearing woman, but he tried hard not to let this prejudice him.

"You can't remember—at any rate, you know you went straight on up with it? You didn't wait to do anything else?"

She seemed to pull herself together and make an effort to remember.

"If it's so important as that, I think I stopped to turn down something that was boiling."

"Boiling? On the fire?"

"On the gas-ring," she said, impatiently.

"What sort of thing?"

"Oh, nothing—some stuff."

"Tea or cocoa, or something like that, do you mean?"

"No—some chemical things," she said, letting the words go reluctantly.

"Were you making chemical experiments?"

"Yes—I did a bit—just for fun—a hobby, you know—I don't do anything at it now. I took up the brandy——"

Her anxiety to shelve the subject of chemistry seemed to be conquering her reluctance to get on with the story.

"You were making chemical experiments—although Lady Dormer was so ill?" said Parker, severely.

"It was just to occupy my mind," she muttered.

"What was the experiment?"

"I don't remember."

"You can't remember at all?"

"NO!" she almost shouted at him.

"Never mind. You took the brandy upstairs?"

"Yes—at least, it isn't really upstairs. It's all on the same landing, only there are six steps up to Auntie's room. Nurse Armstrong met me at the door, and said 'He's better now,' and I went in and saw General Fentiman sitting in a chair, looking very queer and gray. He was behind a screen where Auntie couldn't see him, or it would have been a great shock to her. Nurse said, 'I've given him his drops and I think a little brandy will put him right again.' So we gave him the brandy—only a small dose, and after a bit, he got less deathly-looking and seemed to be breathing better. I told him we were sending for the doctor, and he said he'd rather go round to Harley Street. I thought it was rash, but Nurse Armstrong said he seemed really better, and it would be a mistake to worry him into doing what he didn't want. So I told Nellie to warn the doctor and send William for a taxi.

General Fentiman seemed stronger then, so we helped him downstairs and he went off in the taxi."

Out of this spate of words, Parker fixed on the one thing he had not heard before.

"What drops were those the Nurse gave him?"

"His own. He had them in his pocket."

"Do you think she could possibly have given him too much? Was the quantity marked on the bottle?"

"I haven't the remotest idea. You'd better ask her."

"Yes, I shall want to see her, if you will kindly tell me where to find her."

"I've got the address upstairs. Is that all you want?"

"I should just like, if I may, to see Lady Dormer's room and the studio."

"What for?"

"It's just a matter of routine. We are under orders to see everything there is to see," replied Parker, reassuringly.

They went upstairs. A door on the first-floor landing immediately opposite the head of the staircase led into a pleasant, lofty room, with old-fashioned bedroom furniture in it.

"This is my aunt's room. She wasn't really my aunt, of course, but I called her so."

"Quite. Where does that second door lead to?"

"That's the dressing-room. Nurse Armstrong slept there while Auntie was ill."

Parker glanced in to the dressing-room, took in the arrangement of the bedroom and expressed himself satisfied.

She walked past him without acknowledgment while he held the door open. She was a sturdily-built girl, but moved with a languor distressing to watch—slouching, almost aggressively unalluring.

"You want to see the studio?"

"Please."

She led the way down the six steps and along a short passage to the room which, as Parker already knew, was built out at the back over the kitchen premises. He mentally calculated the distance as he went.

The studio was large and well-lit by its glass roof. One end was furnished like a sitting-room; the other was left bare, and devoted to what Nellie called "mess." A very ugly picture (in Parker's opinion) stood on an easel. Other canvases were stacked round the walls. In one corner was a table covered with American cloth, on which stood a gas-ring, protected by a tin plate, and a Bunsen burner.

"I'll look up that address," said Miss Dorland, indifferently, "I've got it here somewhere."

She began to rummage in an untidy desk. Parker strolled up to the business end of the room, and explored it with eyes, nose and fingers.

The ugly picture on the easel was newly-painted; the smell told him that, and the dabs of paint on the palette were still soft and sticky. Work had been done there within the last two days, he was sure. The brushes had been stuck at random into a small pot of turpentine. He lifted them out; they were still clogged with paint. The picture itself was a landscape, he thought, roughly drawn and hot and restless in colour. Parker was no judge of art; he would have liked to get Wimsey's opinion. He explored further. The table with the Bunsen burner was bare, but in a cupboard close by he discovered a quantity of chemical apparatus of the kind he remembered using at school. Everything had been tidily washed and stacked away. Nellie's job, he imagined. There were a number of simple and familiar chemical substances in jars and packages, occupying a couple of shelves. They would probably have to be analyzed, he thought, to see if they were all they seemed. And what useless nonsense it all was, he thought to himself; anything suspicious would obviously have been destroyed weeks before. Still, there it was. A book in several volumes on the top shelf caught his attention: it was Quain's Dictionary of Medicine. He took down a volume in which he noticed a paper mark. Opening it at the marked place, his eye fell upon the words: "Rigor mortis," and, a little later on—"action of certain poisons." He was about to read more, when he heard Miss Dorland's voice just behind him.

"That's all nothing," she said, "I don't do any of that muck now. It was just a passing craze. I paint, really. What do you think of this?" She indicated the unpleasant landscape.

Parker said it was very good.

"Are these your work, too?" he asked, indicating the other canvases.

"Yes," she said.

He turned a few of them to the light, noticing at the same time how dusty they were. Nellie had scamped this bit of the work—or perhaps had been told not to touch. Miss Dorland showed a trifle more animation than she had done hitherto, while displaying her works. Landscape seemed to be rather a new departure; most of the canvases were figure-studies. Mr. Parker thought that, on the whole, the artist had done wisely to turn to landscape. He was not well acquainted with the modern school of thought in painting, and had difficulty in expressing his opinion of these curious figures, with their faces like eggs and their limbs like rubber.

"That is the Judgment of Paris," said Miss Dorland.

"Oh, yes," said Parker. "And this?"

"Oh, just a study of a woman dressing. It's not very good. I think this portrait of Mrs. Mitcham is rather decent, though."

Parker stared aghast; it might possibly be a symbolic representation of Mrs. Mitcham's character, for it was very hard and spiky; but it looked more like a Dutch doll, with its triangular nose, like a sharp-edged block of wood, and its eyes mere dots in an expanse of liver-coloured cheek.

"It's not very like her," he said, doubtfully.

"It's not meant to be."

"This seems better—I mean, I like this better," said Parker, turning the next picture up hurriedly.

"Oh, that's nothing—just a fancy head."

Evidently this picture—the head of a rather cadaverous man, with a sinister smile and a slight cast in the eye—was despised—a Philistine backsliding, almost like a human being. It was put away, and Parker tried to concentrate his attention on a "Madonna and Child" which, to Parker's simple evangelical mind, seemed an abominable blasphemy.

Happily, Miss Dorland soon wearied, even of her paintings, and flung them all back into the corner.

"D'you want anything else?" she demanded abruptly. "Here's that address."

Parker took it.

"Just one more question," he said, looking her hard in the eyes. "Before Lady Dormer died—before General Fentiman came to see her—did you know what provision she had made for you and for him in her will?"

The girl stared back at him, and he saw panic come into her eyes. It seemed to flow all over her like a wave. She clenched her hands at her sides, and her miserable eyes dropped beneath his gaze, shifting as though looking for a way out.

"Well?" said Parker.

"No!" she said. "No! of course not. Why should I?" Then, surprisingly, a dull crimson flush flooded her sallow cheeks and ebbed away, leaving her looking like death.

"Go away," she said, furiously, "you make me sick."

CHAPTER XVIII

PICTURE-CARDS

"SO I'VE PUT a man in and had all the things in that cupboard taken away for examination," said Parker.

Lord Peter shook his head.

"I wish I had been there," he said, "I should have liked to see those paintings. However——"

"They might have conveyed something to you," said Parker, "you're artistic. You can come along and look at them any time, of course. But it's the time factor that's worrying me, you know. Supposing she gave the old boy digitalin in his B and S, why should it wait all that time before working? According to the books, it ought to have popped him off in about an hour's time. It was a biggish dose, according to Lubbock."

"I know. I think you're up against a snag there. That's why I should have liked to see the pictures."

Parker considered this apparent *non sequitur* for a few moments and gave it up.

"George Fentiman—" he began.

"Yes," said Wimsey, "George Fentiman. I must be getting emotional in my old age, Charles, for I have an unconquerable dislike to examining the question of George Fentiman's opportunities."

"Bar Robert," pursued Parker, ruthlessly, "he was the last interested person to see General Fentiman."

"Yes—by the way, we have only Robert's unsupported word for what happened in that last interview between him and the old man."

"Come, Wimsey—you're not going to pretend that Robert had any interest in his grandfather's dying before Lady Dormer. On the contrary."

"No—but he might have had some interest in his dying before he

356

made a will. Those notes on that bit of paper. The larger share was to go to George. That doesn't entirely agree with what Robert said. And if there was no will, Robert stood to get everything."

"So he did. But by killing the General then, he made sure of getting nothing at all."

"That's the awkwardness. Unless he thought Lady Dormer was already dead. But I don't see how he could have thought that. Or unless——"

"Well?"

"Unless he gave his grandfather a pill or something to be taken at some future time, and the old boy took it too soon by mistake."

"That idea of a delayed-action pill is the most tiresome thing about this case. It makes almost anything possible."

"Including, of course, the theory of its being given to him by Miss Dorland."

"That's what I'm going to interview the nurse about, the minute I can get hold of her. But we've got away from George."

"You're right. Let's face George. I don't want to, though. Like the lady in Maeterlinck who's running round the table while her husband tries to polish her off with a hatchet, I am not gay. George is the nearest in point of time. In fact he fits very well in point of time. He parted from General Fentiman at about half-past six, and Robert found Fentiman dead at about eight o'clock. So allowing that the stuff was given in a pill——"

"Which it would have to be, in a taxi," interjected Parker.

"As you say—in a pill, which would take a bit longer to get working than the same stuff taken in solution—why then the General might quite well have been able to get to the Bellona and see Robert before collapsing."

"Very nice. But how did George get the drug?"

"I know, that's the first difficulty."

"And how did he happen to have it on him just at that time? He couldn't possibly have known that General Fentiman would run across him just at that moment. Even if he'd known of his being at Lady Dormer's, he couldn't be expecting him to go from there to Harley Street."

"He might have been carrying the stuff about with him, waiting for a good opportunity to use it. And when the old man called him up and started jawing him about his conduct and all that, he thought he'd better do the job quick, before he was cut out of the will."

"Um!—but why should George be such a fool, then, as to admit he'd never heard about Lady Dormer's will? If he had heard of it, we couldn't possibly suspect him. He'd only to say the General told him about it in the taxi."

"I suppose it hadn't struck him in that light."

"Then George is a bigger ass than I took him for."

"Possibly he is," said Parker, dryly. "At any rate, I have put a man on to make inquiries at his home."

"Oh! have you? I say, do you know, I wish I'd left this case alone. What the deuce did it matter if old Fentiman was pushed painlessly off a bit before his time? He was simply indecently ancient."

"We'll see if you say that in sixty years' time," said Parker.

"By that time we shall, I hope, be moving in different circles. I shall be in the one devoted to murderers and you in the much lower and hotter one devoted for those who tempt others to murder them. I wash my hands of this case, Charles. There's nothing for me to do now you have come into it. It bores and annoys me. Let's talk about something else."

Wimsey might wash his hands, but, like Pontius Pilate, he found society irrationally determined to connect him with an irritating and unsatisfactory case.

At midnight, the telephone bell rang.

He had just gone to bed, and cursed it.

"Tell them I'm out," he shouted to Bunter, and cursed again on hearing the man assure the unknown caller that he would see whether his lordship had returned. Disobedience in Bunter spelt urgent necessity.

"Well?"

"It is Mrs. George Fentiman, my lord; she appears to be in great distress. If your lordship wasn't in I was to beg you to communicate with her as soon as you arrived."

"Punk! they're not on the 'phone."

"No, my lord."

"Did she say what the matter was?"

"She began by asking if Mr. George Fentiman was here, my lord."

"Oh, hades!"

Bunter advanced gently with his master's dressing-gown and slippers. Wimsey thrust himself into them savagely and padded away to the telephone.

"Hullo!"

"Is that Lord Peter?—Oh, *good!*" The line sighed with relief—a harsh sound, like a death-rattle. "Do you know where George is?"

"No idea. Hasn't he come home?"

"No—and I'm frightened. Some people were here this morning . . ."

"The police."

"Yes . . . George . . . they found something . . . I can't say it all over the 'phone . . . but George went off to Walmisley-Hubbard's with the car . . . and they say he never came back there . . . and . . . you remember that time he was so funny before . . . and got lost . . ."

"Your six minutes are up," boomed the voice of the Exchange, "will you have another call?"

"Yes, please . . . oh, don't cut us off . . . wait . . . oh! I haven't any more pennies . . . Lord Peter . . ."

"I'll come round at once," said Wimsey, with a groan.

"Oh, thank you—thank you so much!"

"I say—where's Robert?"

"Your six minutes are up," said the voice, finally, and the line went dead with a metallic crash.

"Get me my clothes," said Wimsey, bitterly—"give me those loathsome and despicable rags which I hoped to have put off forever. Get me a taxi. Get me a drink. Macbeth has murdered sleep. Oh! and get me Robert Fentiman, first."

Major Fentiman was not in town, said Woodward. He had gone back to Richmond again. Wimsey tried to get through to Richmond. After a long time, a female voice, choked with sleep and fury, replied. Major Fentiman had not come home. Major Fentiman kept very late hours. Would she give Major Fentiman a message when he did come in? Indeed she would not. She had other things to do than to stay up all night answering telephone calls and giving messages to Major Fentiman. This was the second time that night, and she had told the other party that she could not be responsible for telling Major Fentiman this, that and the other. Would she leave a note for Major Fentiman, asking him to go round to his brother's house at once? Well now, was it reasonable to expect her to sit up on a bitter cold night writing letters? Of course not, but this was a case of urgent illness. It would be a very great kindness. Just that—to go round to his brother's house and say the call came from Lord Peter Wimsey.

"Who?"

"Lord Peter Wimsey."

"Very well, sir. I beg your pardon if I was a bit short, but really——"

"You weren't, you snobby old cat, you were infernally long," breathed his lordship inaudibly. He thanked her, and rang off.

Sheila Fentiman was anxiously waiting for him on the doorstep, so that he was saved the embarrassment of trying to remember which was the right number of rings to give. She clasped his hand eagerly as she drew him in.

"Oh! it is good of you. I'm so worried. I say, don't make a noise, will you? They complain, you know." She spoke in a harassed whisper.

"Blast them, let them complain," said Wimsey, cheerfully. "Why shouldn't you make a row when George is upset? Besides, if we whisper, they'll think we're no better than we ought to be. Now, my child, what's all this? You're as cold as a *pêche Melba*. That won't do. Fire half out—where's the whisky?"

"Hush! I'm all right, really. George——"

"You're not all right. Nor am I. As George Robey says, this getting up from my warm bed and going into the cold night air doesn't suit me." He flung a generous shovelful of coals on the fire and thrust the poker between the bars. "And you've had no grub. No wonder you're feeling awful."

Two places were set at the table—untouched—waiting for George. Wimsey plunged into the kitchen premises, followed by Sheila uttering agitated remonstrances. He found some disagreeable remnants— a watery stew, cold and sodden; a basin half-full of some kind of tinned soup; a chill suet pudding put away on a shelf.

"Does your woman cook for you? I suppose she does, as you're both out all day. Well, she can't cook, my child. No matter, here's some Bovril—she can't have hurt that. You go and sit down and I'll make you some."

"Mrs. Munns——"

"Blow Mrs. Munns!"

"But I must tell you about George."

He looked at her, and decided that she really must tell him about George.

"I'm sorry. I didn't mean to bully. One has an ancestral idea that women must be treated like imbeciles in a crisis. Centuries of the 'women-and-children-first' idea, I suppose. Poor devils!"

"Who, the women?"

"Yes. No wonder they sometimes lose their heads. Pushed into corners, told nothing of what's happening and made to sit quiet and do nothing. Strong men would go dotty in the circs. I suppose that's why we've always grabbed the privilege of rushing about and doing the heroic bits."

"That's quite true. Give me the kettle."

"No, no, I'll do that. You sit down and—I mean, sorry, *take* the kettle. Fill it, light the gas, put it on. And tell me about George."

The trouble, it seemed, had begun at breakfast. Ever since the story of the murder had come out, George had been very nervy and jumpy, and, to Sheila's horror, had "started muttering again." "Muttering," Wimsey remembered, had formerly been the prelude to one of George's "queer fits." These had been a form of shell-shock, and they had generally ended in his going off and wandering about in a distraught manner for several days, sometimes with partial and occasionally with complete temporary loss of memory. There was the time when he had been found dancing naked in a field among a flock of sheep, and singing to them. It had been the more ludicrously painful in that George was altogether tone-deaf, so that his singing, though loud, was like a hoarse and rumbling wind in the chimney. Then there was a dreadful time when George had deliberately walked into a bonfire. That was when they had been staying down in the country. George had been badly burnt, and the shock of the pain had brought him round. He never remembered afterwards why he had tried to do these things, and had only the faintest recollection of having done them at all. The next vagary might be even more disconcerting.

At any rate, George had been "muttering."

They were at breakfast that morning, when they saw two men coming up the path. Sheila, who sat opposite the window, saw them first, and said carelessly: "Hullo! who are these? They look like plain-clothes policemen." George took one look, jumped up and rushed out of the room. She called to him to know what was the matter, but he did not answer, and she heard him "rummaging" in the back room, which was the bedroom. She was going to him, when she heard Mr. Munns open the door to the policemen and then heard them inquiring for George. Mr. Munns ushered them into the front room with a grim face on which "police" seemed written in capital letters. George——

At this point the kettle boiled. Sheila was taking it off the stove to make the Bovril, when Wimsey became aware of a hand on his coat-collar. He looked round into the face of a gentleman who appeared not to have shaved for several days.

"Now then," said this apparition, "what's the meaning of this?"

"Which," added an indignant voice from the door, "I thought as there was something behind all this talk of the Captain being missing. You didn't expect him to be missing, I suppose, ma'am. Oh, dear no! Nor your gentleman friend, neither, sneaking up in a taxi and you waiting at the door so's Munns and me shouldn't hear. But I'd have you know this is a respectable house, Lord Knows Who or whatever you call yourself—more likely one of these low-down confidence fellers, I expect, if the truth was known. With a monocle too, like that man we was reading about in the News of the World. And in my kitchen too, and drinking my Bovril in the middle of the night, the impudence! Not to speak of the goings-in-and-out all day, banging the front door, and that was the police come here this morning, you think I didn't know? Up to something, that's what they've been, the pair of them, and the Captain as he says he is but that's as may be, I daresay he had his reasons for clearing off, and the sooner you goes after him my fine madam, the better I'll be pleased, I can tell you."

"That's right," said Mr. Munns—"ow!"

Lord Peter had removed the intrusive hand from his collar with a sharp jerk which appeared to cause anguish out of all proportion to the force used.

"I'm glad you've come along," he said. "In fact, I was just going to give you a call. Have you anything to drink in the house, by the way?"

"Drink?" cried Mrs. Munns on a high note, "the impudence! And if I see you, Joe, giving drinks to thieves and worse in the middle of the night in my kitchen, you'll get a piece of my mind. Coming in here as bold as brass, and the Captain run away, and asking for a drink——"

"Because," said Wimsey, fingering his note-case, "the public houses in this law-abiding neighbourhood are of course closed. Otherwise a bottle of Scotch——"

Mr. Munns appeared to hesitate.

"Call yourself a man!" said Mrs. Munns.

"Of course," said Mr. Munns, "if I was to go in a friendly manner to Jimmy Rowe at the Dragon, and ask him to give me a bottle of Johnny Walker as a friend to a friend, and provided no money was to pass between him and me, that is——"

"A good idea," said Wimsey, cordially.

Mrs. Munns gave a loud shriek.

"The ladies," said Mr. Munns, "gets nervous at times." He shrugged his shoulders.

"I daresay a drop of Scotch wouldn't do Mrs. Munns's nerves any harm," said Wimsey.

"If you dare, Joe Munns," said the landlady, "if you dare to go out at this time of night, hobnobbing with Jimmy Rowe and making a fool of yourself with burglars and such——"

Mr. Munns executed a sudden volte-face.

"You shut up!" he shouted. "Always sticking your face in where you aren't wanted."

"Are you speaking to me?"

"Yes. Shut up!"

Mrs. Munns sat down suddenly on a kitchen chair and began to sniff.

"I'll just hop round to the Dragon now, sir," said Mr. Munns, "before old Jimmy goes to bed. And then we'll go into this here."

He departed. Possibly he forgot what he had said about no money passing, for he certainly took the note which Wimsey absent-mindedly held out to him.

"Your drink's getting cold," said Wimsey to Sheila.

She came across to him.

"Can't we get rid of these people?"

"In half a jiff. It's no good having a row with them. I'd do it like a shot, only, you see, you've got to stay on here for a bit, in case George comes back."

"Of course. I'm sorry for all this upset, Mrs. Munns," she added, a little stiffly, "but I'm so worried about my husband."

"Husband?" snorted Mrs. Munns. "A lot husbands are to worry about. Look at that Joe. Off he goes to the Dragon, never mind what I say to him. They're dirt, that's what husbands are, the whole pack of them. And I don't care what anybody says."

"Are they?" said Wimsey. "Well, I'm not one—yet—so you needn't mind what you say to me."

"It's the same thing," said the lady, viciously, "husbands and parricides, there's not a half-penny to choose between them. Only parricides aren't respectable—but then, they're easier got rid of."

"Oh!" replied Wimsey, "but I'm not a parricide either—not Mrs. Fentiman's parricide at any rate, I assure you. Hullo! here's Joe. Did

363

you get the doings, old man? You did? Good work. Now, Mrs. Munns, have just a spot with us. You'll feel all the better for it. And why shouldn't we go into the sitting-room where it's warmer?"

Mrs. Munns complied. "Oh, well," she said, "here's friends all round. But you'll allow it all looked a bit queer, now, didn't it? And the police this morning, asking all those questions, and emptying the dust-bin all over the backyard."

"Whatever did they want with the dust-bin?"

"Lord knows; and that Cummins woman looking on all the time over the wall. I can tell you, I was vexed. 'Why, Mrs. Munns,' she said, 'have you been poisoning people?' she said. 'I always told you,' she said, 'your cooking 'ud do for somebody one of these days.' The nasty cat."

"What a rotten thing to say," said Wimsey, sympathetically. "Just jealousy, I expect. But what did the police find in the dust-bin?"

"Find? Them find anything? I should like to see them finding things in my dust-bin. The less I see of their interfering ways the better I'm pleased. I told them so. I said, 'If you want to come upsetting my dust-bin,' I said, 'you'll have to come with a search-warrant,' I said. That's the law and they couldn't deny it. They said Mrs. Fentiman had given them leave to look, so I told them Mrs. Fentiman had no leave to give them. It was my dust-bin, I told them, not hers. So they went off with a flea in their ear."

"That's the stuff to give 'em, Mrs. Munns."

"Not but what I'm respectable. If the police come to me in a right and lawful manner, I'll gladly give them any help they want. I don't want to get into trouble, not for any number of captains. But interference with a free-born woman and no search-warrant I will *not* stand. And they can either come to me in a fitting way or they can go and whistle for their bottle."

"What bottle?" asked Wimsey, quickly.

"The bottle they were looking for in my dust-bin, what the Captain put there after breakfast."

Sheila gave a faint cry.

"What bottle was that, Mrs. Munns?"

"One of them little tablet bottles," said Mrs. Munns, "same as you have standing on the wash-hand stand, Mrs. Fentiman. When I saw the Captain smashing it up in the yard with a poker——"

"There now, Primrose," said Mr. Munns, "can't you see as Mrs. Fentiman ain't well?"

"I'm quite all right," said Sheila, hastily, pushing away the hair which clung damply to her forehead. "What was my husband doing?"

"I saw him," said Mrs. Munns, "run out into the back yard—just after your breakfast it was, because I recollect Munns was letting the officers into the house at the time. Not that I knew then who it was, for, if you will excuse me mentioning of it, I was in the outside lavatory, and that was how I come to see the Captain. Which ordinarily, you can't see the dust-bin from the house, my lord I should say, I suppose, if you really are one, but you meet so many bad characters nowadays that one can't be too careful—on account of the lavatory standing out as you may say and hiding it."

"Just so," said Wimsey.

"So when I saw the Captain breaking the bottle as I said, and throwing the bits into the dust-bin, 'Hullo!' I said, 'that's funny,' and I went to see what it was and I put it in an envelope, thinking, you see, as it might be something poisonous, and the cat such a dreadful thief as he is, I never can keep him out of that dust-bin. And when I came in, I found the police here. So after a bit, I found them poking about in the yard and I asked them what they were doing there. Such a mess as they'd made, you never would believe. So they showed me a little cap they'd found, same as it might be off that tablet bottle. 'Did I know where the rest of it was?' they said. And I said, what business had they got with the dust-bin at all. So they said——"

"Yes, I know," said Wimsey. "I think you acted very sensibly, Mrs. Munns. And what did you do with the envelope and things?"

"I kept it," replied Mrs. Munns, nodding her head, "I kept it. Because, you see, if they *did* return *with* a warrant and I'd destroyed that bottle, where should *I* be?"

"Quite right," said Wimsey, with his eye on Sheila.

"Always keep on the right side of the law," agreed Mr. Munns, "and nobody can't interfere with you. That's what I say. I'm a Conservative, I am. I don't hold with these Socialist games. Have another."

"Not just now," said Wimsey. "And we really must not keep you and Mrs. Munns up any longer. But, look here! You see, Captain Fentiman had shell-shock after the War, and he is liable to do these little odd things at times—break things up, I mean, and lose his memory and go wandering about. So Mrs. Fentiman is naturally anxious about his not having turned up this evening."

"Ay," said Mr. Munns, with relish, "I knew a fellow like that. Went clean off his rocker he did one night. Smashed up his family with a beetle—a paviour he was by profession, and that's how he came to have a beetle in the house—pounded 'em to a jelly, he did, his wife and five little children, and went off and drownded himself in the Regent's Canal. And, what's more, when they got him out, he didn't remember a word about it, not one word. So they sent him to—what's that place? Dartmoor? no, Broadmoor, that's it, where Ronnie True went to with his little toys and all."

"Shut up, you fool," said Wimsey, savagely.

"Haven't you got feelings?" demanded his wife.

Sheila got up, and made a blind effort in the direction of the door.

"Come and lie down," said Wimsey, "you're worn out. Hullo! there's Robert, I expect. I left a message for him to come round as soon as he got home."

Mr. Munns went to answer the bell.

"We'd better get her to bed as quick as possible," said Wimsey to the landlady. "Have you got such a thing as a hot-water bottle?"

Mrs. Munns departed to fetch one, and Sheila caught Wimsey's hand.

"Can't you get hold of that bottle? Make her give it you. You can. You can do anything. Make her."

"Better not," said Wimsey. "Look suspicious. Look here, Sheila, what *is* the bottle?"

"My heart medicine. I missed it. It's something to do with digitalin."

"Oh, lord," said Wimsey, as Robert came in.

. . . . . .

"It's all pretty damnable," said Robert.

He thumped the fire gloomily; it was burning badly, the lower bars were choked with the ashes of a day and night.

"I've been having a talk with Frobisher," he added. "All this talk in the Club—and the papers—naturally he couldn't overlook it."

"Was he decent?"

"Very decent. But of course I couldn't explain the thing. I'm sending in my papers."

Wimsey nodded. Colonel Frobisher could scarcely overlook an attempted fraud—not after things had been said in the papers.

"If I'd only let the old man alone. Too late now. He'd have been buried. Nobody would have asked questions."

"I didn't *want* to interfere," said Wimsey, defending himself against the unspoken reproach.

"Oh, I know. I'm not blaming you. People . . . money oughtn't to depend on people's deaths . . . old people, with no use for their lives . . . it's a devil of a temptation. Look here, Wimsey, what are we to do about this woman?"

"The Munns female?"

"Yes. It's the devil and all she should have got hold of the stuff. If they find out what it's supposed to be, we shall be blackmailed for the rest of our lives."

"No," said Wimsey, "I'm sorry, old man, but the police have got to know about it."

Robert sprang to his feet.

"My God!—you wouldn't——"

"Sit down, Fentiman. Yes, I must. Don't you see I must? We can't suppress things. It always means trouble. It's not even as though they hadn't got their eye on us already. They're suspicious——"

"Yes, and why?" burst out Robert, violently. "Who put it into their heads? . . . For God's sake don't start talking about law and justice! Law and justice! You'd sell your best friend for the sake of making a sensational appearance in the witness-box, you infernal little police spy!"

"Chuck that, Fentiman!"

"I'll not chuck it! You'd go and give away a man to the police—when you know perfectly well he isn't responsible—just because you can't afford to be mixed up in anything unpleasant. I know you. Nothing's too dirty for you to meddle in, provided you can pose as the pious little friend of justice. You make me sick!"

"I tried to keep out of this——"

"You tried!—don't be a blasted hypocrite! You get out of it now, and stay out—do you hear?"

"Yes, but listen a moment——"

"Get out!" said Robert.

Wimsey stood up.

"I know how you feel, Fentiman——"

"Don't stand there being righteous and forebearing, you sickening prig. For the last time—are you going to shut up, or are you going to

367

trot round to your policeman friend and earn the thanks of a grateful country for splitting on George? Get on! Which is it to be?"

"You won't do George any good——"

"Never mind that. Are you going to hold your tongue?"

"Be reasonable, Fentiman."

"Reasonable be damned. Are you going to the police? No shuffling. Yes or no?"

"Yes."

"You dirty little squirt," said Robert, striking out passionately. Wimsey's return blow caught him neatly on the chin and landed him in the waste-paper basket.

"And now, look here," said Wimsey, standing over him, hat and stick in hand. "It's no odds to me what you do or say. You think your brother murdered your grandfather. I don't know whether he did or not. But the worst thing you can do for him is to try and destroy evidence. And the worst thing you can possibly do for his wife is to make her a party to anything of the sort. And next time you try to smash anybody's face in, remember to cover up your chin. That's all. I can let myself out. Good-bye."

.   .   .   .   .

He went round to 12 Great Ormond Street and routed Parker out of bed.

Parker listened thoughtfully to what he had to say.

"I wish we'd stopped Fentiman before he bolted," he said.

"Yes; why didn't you?"

"Well, Dykes seems to have muffed it rather. I wasn't there myself. But everything seemed all right. Fentiman looked a bit nervy, but many people do when they're interviewed by the police—think of their hideous pasts, I suppose, and wonder what's coming next. Or else it's just stage-fright. He stuck to the same tale he told you—said he was quite sure the old General hadn't taken any pills or anything in the taxi—didn't attempt to pretend he knew anything about Lady Dormer's will. There was nothing to detain him for. He said he had to get to his job in Great Portland Street. So they let him go. Dykes sent a man to follow him up, and he went along to Walmisley-Hubbard's all right. Dykes said, might he just have a look round the place before he went, and Mrs. Fentiman said certainly. He didn't expect to find anything, really. Just happened to step into the back-yard, and saw a bit of broken glass. He then had a look round, and there was the cap of the tablet-bottle in the dust-bin. Well, then, of course, he started to get interested, and was just having a hunt through for the rest of it, when old mother Munns appeared and said the dust-bin was her property. So they had to clear out. But Dykes oughtn't to have let Fentiman go till they'd finished going over the place. He 'phoned through to Walmisley-Hubbard's at once, and heard that Fentiman had arrived and immediately gone out with the car, to visit a prospective customer in Herts. The fellow who was supposed to be trailing Fentiman got carburetor trouble just beyond St. Albans, and by the time he was fixed, he'd lost Fentiman."

"Did Fentiman go to the customer's house?"

"Not he. Disappeared completely. We shall find the car, of course —it's only a matter of time."

"Yes," said Wimsey. His voice sounded tired and constrained.

"This alters the look of things a bit," said Parker, "doesn't it?"

"Yes."

"What have you done to your face, old man?"

Wimsey glanced at the looking-glass, and saw that an angry red flush had come up on the cheekbone.

"Had a bit of a dust-up with Robert," he said.

"Oh!"

Parker was aware of a thin veil of hostility, drawn between himself and the friend he valued. He knew that for the first time, Wimsey was seeing him as the police. Wimsey was ashamed and his shame made Parker ashamed too.

"You'd better have some breakfast," said Parker. His voice sounded awkward to himself.

"No—no thanks, old man. I'll go home and get a bath and shave."

"Oh, right-oh!"

There was a pause.

"Well, I'd better be going," said Wimsey.

"Oh, yes," said Parker again. "Right-oh!"

"Er—cheerio!" said Wimsey at the door.

"Cheerio!" said Parker.

The bedroom door shut. The flat-door shut. The front-door shut.

Parker pulled the telephone towards him and called up Scotland Yard.

.   .   .   .   .

The atmosphere of his own office was bracing to Parker when he got down there. For one thing, he was taken aside by a friend and congratulated in conspiratorial whispers.

"Your promotion's gone through," said the friend. "Dead certainty. The Chief's no end pleased. Between you and me, of course. But you've got your Chief-Inspectorship all right. Damn good."

Then, at ten o'clock, the news came through that the missing Walmisley-Hubbard had turned up. It had been abandoned in a remote Hertfordshire lane. It was in perfectly good order, the gear-lever in neutral and the tank full of petrol. Evidently, Fentiman had left it and wandered away somewhere, but he could not be far off. Parker made the necessary arrangements for combing out the neighbourhood. The bustle and occupation soothed his mind. Guilty or insane or both, George Fentiman had to be found; it was just a job to be done.

The man who had been sent to interview Mrs. Munns (armed this time with a warrant) returned with the fragments of the bottle and tablets. Parker duly passed these along to the police analyst. One of the detectives who was shadowing Miss Dorland rang up to announce that a young woman had come to see her, and that the two had then come out carrying a suit-case and driven away in a taxi. Maddison, the other detective, was following them. Parker said, "All right; stay where you are for the present," and considered this new development. The telephone rang again. He thought it would be Maddison, but it was Wimsey—a determinedly brisk and cheerful Wimsey this time.

"I say, Charles. I want something."

"What?"

"I want to go and see Miss Dorland."

"You can't. She's gone off somewhere. My man hasn't reported yet."

"Oh! Well, never mind her. What I really want to see is her studio."

"Yes? Well, there's no reason why you shouldn't."

"Will they let me in?"

"Probably not. I'll meet you there and take you in with me. I was going out any way. I've got to interview the nurse. We've just got hold of her."

"Thanks awfully. Sure you can spare the time?"

"Yes. I'd like your opinion."

"I'm glad somebody wants it. I'm beginning to feel like a pelican in the wilderness."

"Rot! I'll be round in ten minutes."

"Of course," explained Parker, as he ushered Wimsey into the studio, "we've taken away all the chemicals and things. There's not much to look at, really."

"Well, you can deal best with all that. It's the books and paintings I want to look at. H'm! Books, you know, Charles, are like lobster-shells. We surround ourselves with 'em, and then we grow out of 'em and leave 'em behind, as evidences of our earlier stages of development."

"That's a fact," said Parker. "I've got rows of school-boy stuff at home—never touch it now, of course. And W. J. Locke—read everything he wrote once upon a time. And Le Queux, and Conan Doyle, and all that stuff."

"And now you read theology. And what else?"

"Well, I read Hardy a good bit. And when I'm not too tired, I have a go at Henry James."

"The refined self-examinations of the infinitely-sophisticated. 'M-m. Well now. Let's start with the shelves by the fireplace. Dorothy Richardson—Virginia Woolf—E. B. C. Jones—May Sinclair—Katherine Mansfield—the modern female writers are well represented, aren't they? Galsworthy. Yes. No J. D. Beresford—no Wells—no Bennett. Dear me, quite a row of D. H. Lawrence. I wonder if she reads him very often."

He pulled down "Women in Love" at random, and slapped the pages open and shut.

"Not kept very well dusted, are they? But they have been read. Compton Mackenzie—Storm Jameson—yes—I see."

"The medical stuff is over here."

"Oh!—a few text-books—first steps in chemistry. What's that tumbled down at the back of the book-case? Louis Berman, eh? *The Personal Equation*. And here's *Why We Behave Like Human Beings*. And Julian Huxley's essays. A determined effort at self-education here, what?"

"Girls seem to go in for that sort of thing nowadays."

"Yes—hardly nice, is it? Hullo!"

"What?"

"Over here by the couch. This represents the latest of our lobster-shells, I fancy. Austin Freeman, Austin Freeman, Austin Freeman—

371

bless me! she must have ordered him in wholesale. *Through the Wall*
—that's a good 'tec story, Charles—all about the third degree—Isabel
Ostrander—three Edgar Wallaces—the girl's been indulging in an orgy
of crime!"

"I shouldn't wonder," said Parker, with emphasis. "That fellow
Freeman is full of plots about poisonings and wills and survivorship,
isn't he?"

"Yes"—Wimsey balanced *A Silent Witness* gently in his hand, and
laid it down again. "This one, for instance, is all about a bloke who
murdered somebody and kept him in cold storage till he was ready
to dispose of him. It would suit Robert Fentiman."

Parker grinned.

"A bit elaborate for the ordinary criminal. But I daresay people
do get ideas out of these books. Like to look at the pictures? They're
pretty awful."

"Don't try to break it gently. Show us the worst at once. . . . Oh,
lord!"

"Well, it gives *me* a pain," said Parker. "But I thought perhaps
that was my lack of artistic education."

"It was your natural good taste. What vile colour, and viler
drawing."

"But nobody cares about drawing nowadays, do they?"

"Ah! but there's a difference between the man who can draw and
won't draw, and the man who can't draw at all. Go on. Let's see the
rest."

Parker produced them, one after the other. Wimsey glanced quickly
at each. He had picked up the brush and palette and was fingering
them as he talked.

"These," he said, "are the paintings of a completely untalented
person, who is, moreover, trying to copy the mannerisms of a very
advanced school. By the way, you have noticed, of course, that she
has been painting within the last few days, but chucked it in sudden
disgust. She has left the paints on the palette, and the brushes are still
stuck in the turps, turning their ends up and generally ruining themselves. Suggestive, I fancy. The—stop a minute! Let's look at that
again."

Parker had brought forward the head of the sallow, squinting man
which he had mentioned to Wimsey before.

"Put that up on the easel. That's very interesting. The others, you
see, are all an effort to imitate other people's art, but this—this is an

effort to imitate nature. Why?—it's very bad, but it's meant for some-body. And it's been worked on a lot. Now what was it made her do that?"

"Well, it wasn't for *his* beauty, I should think."

"No?—but there must have been a reason. Dante, you may remember, once painted an angel. Do you know the limerick about the old man of Khartoum?"

"What did he do?"

"He kept two black sheep in his room. They remind me (he said) Of two friends who are dead, But I cannot remember of whom."

"If that reminds you of anybody you know, I don't care much for your friends. I never saw an uglier mug."

"He's not beautiful. But I think the sinister squint is chiefly due to bad drawing. It's very difficult to get eyes looking the same way, when you can't draw. Cover up one eye, Charles—not yours, the portrait's."

Parker did so.

Wimsey looked again, and shook his head.

"It escapes me for the moment," he said. "Probably it's nobody I know after all. But, whoever it is, surely this room tells you something."

"It suggests to me," said Parker, "that the girl's been taking more interest in crimes and chemistry stuff than is altogether healthy in the circumstances."

Wimsey looked at him for a moment.

"I wish I could think as you do."

"What *do* you think?" demanded Parker, impatiently.

"No," said Wimsey. "I told you about that George business this morning, because glass bottles are facts, and one mustn't conceal facts. But I'm not obliged to tell you what I think."

"You don't think, then, that Ann Dorland did the murder?"

"I don't know about that, Charles. I came here hoping that this room would tell me the same thing that it told you. But it hasn't. It's told me different. It's told me what I thought all along."

"A penny for your thoughts, then," said Parker, trying desperately to keep the conversation on a jocular footing.

"Not even thirty pieces of silver," replied Wimsey, mournfully.

Parker stacked the canvases away without another word.

CHAPTER XIX

LORD PETER PLAYS DUMMY

"DO YOU WANT to come with me to the Armstrong woman?"

"May as well," said Wimsey, "you never know."

Nurse Armstrong belonged to an expensive nursing home in Great Wimpole Street. She had not been interviewed before, having only returned the previous evening from escorting an invalid lady to Italy. She was a large, good-looking, imperturbable woman, rather like the Venus of Milo, and she answered Parker's questions in a cheerful, matter-of-fact tone, as though they had been about bandages or temperatures.

"Oh, yes, constable; I remember the poor old gentleman being brought in, perfectly."

Parker had a natural dislike to being called constable. However, a detective must not let little things like that irritate him.

"Was Miss Dorland present at the interview between your patient and her brother?"

"Only for a few moments. She said good afternoon to the old gentleman and led him up to the bed, and then, when she saw them comfortable together, she went out."

"How do you mean, comfortable together?"

"Well, the patient called the old gentleman by his name, and he answered, and then he took her hand and said, 'I'm sorry, Felicity; forgive me,' or something of that sort, and she said, 'There's nothing to forgive; don't distress yourself, Arthur,'—crying, he was, the poor old man. So he sat down on the chair by the bed, and Miss Dorland went out."

"Nothing was said about the will?"

"Not while Miss Dorland was in the room, if that's what you mean."

"Suppose anybody had listened at the door afterwards—could they have heard what was said?"

"Oh, no! The patient was very weak and spoke very low. I couldn't hear myself half she said."

"Where were you?"

"Well, I went away, because I thought they'd like to be alone. But I was in my own room with the door open between, and I was looking in most of the time. She was so ill, you see, and the old gentleman looked so frail, I didn't like to go out of earshot. In our work, you see, we often have to see and hear a lot that we don't say anything about."

"Of course, Nurse—I am sure you did quite right. Now when Miss Dorland brought the brandy up—the General was feeling very ill?"

"Yes—he had a nasty turn. I put him in the big chair and bent him over till the spasm went off. He asked for his own medicine, and I gave it to him—no, it wasn't drops—it was amyl nitrate; you inhale it. Then I rang the bell and sent the girl for the brandy."

"Amyl nitrate—you're sure that's all he had?"

"Positive; there wasn't anything else. Lady Dormer had been having strychnine injections to keep her heart going, of course, and we'd tried oxygen; but we shouldn't give him those, you know."

She smiled, competently, condescendingly.

"Now, you say Lady Dormer had been having this, that and the other. Were there any medicines lying about that General Fentiman might have accidentally taken up and swallowed?"

"Oh, dear no."

"No drops or tabloids or anything of that kind?"

"Certainly not; the medicines were kept in my room."

"Nothing on the bedside table or the mantelpiece?"

"There was a cup of diluted Listerine by the bed, for washing out the patient's mouth from time to time, that was all."

"And there's no digitalin in Listerine—no, of course not. Well now, who brought up the brandy-and-water?"

"The housemaid went to Mrs. Mitcham for it. I should have had some upstairs, as a matter of fact, but the patient couldn't keep it down. Some of them can't, you know."

"Did the girl bring it straight up to you?"

"No—she stopped to call Miss Dorland on the way. Of course, she ought to have brought the brandy at once and gone to Miss Dorland afterwards—but it's anything to save trouble with these girls, as I daresay you know."

"Did Miss Dorland bring it straight up—?" began Parker. Nurse Armstrong broke in upon him.

"If you're thinking, did she put the digitalin into the brandy, you can dismiss that from your mind, constable. If he'd had as big a dose

375

as that in solution at half past four, he'd have been taken ill ever so much earlier than he was."

"You seem to be well up in the case, Nurse."

"Oh, I am. Naturally I was interested, Lady Dormer being my patient and all."

"Of course. But all the same, *did* Miss Dorland bring the brandy straight along to you?"

"I think so. I heard Nellie go along the passage on the half landing, and looked out to call to her, but by the time I'd got the door open, I saw Miss Dorland coming out of the studio with the brandy in her hand."

"And where was Nellie then?"

"Just got back to the end of the passage and starting downstairs to the telephone."

"At that rate, Miss Dorland couldn't have been more than ten seconds alone with the brandy," said Peter, thoughtfully. "And who gave it to General Fentiman?"

"I did. I took it out of Miss Dorland's hand at the door and gave it to him at once. He seemed better then, and only took a little of it."

"Did you leave him again?"

"I did not. Miss Dorland went out on to the landing presently to see if the taxi was coming."

"She was never alone with him?"

"Not for a moment."

"Did you like Miss Dorland, Nurse? Is she a nice girl, I mean?" Wimsey had not spoken for so long that Parker quite started.

"She was always very pleasant to me," said Nurse Armstrong. "I shouldn't call her an attractive girl, not to my mind."

"Did she ever mention Lady Dormer's testamentary arrangements in your hearing?" asked Parker, picking up what he conceived to be Wimsey's train of thought.

"Well—not exactly. But I remember her once talking about her painting, and saying she did it for a hobby, as her aunt would see she always had enough to live on."

"That's true enough," said Parker. "At the worst, she would get fifteen thousand pounds, which carefully invested, might mean six or seven hundred a year. She didn't say she expected to be very rich?"

"No."

"Nor anything about the General?"

"Not a word."

"Was she happy?" asked Wimsey.

"She was upset, naturally, with her aunt being so ill."

"I don't mean that. You are the sort of person who observes a lot —nurses are awfully quick about that kind of thing, I've noticed. Did she strike you as a person who—who felt right with life, as you might say?"

"She was one of the quiet ones. But—yes—I should say she was satisfied with things all right."

"Did she sleep well?"

"Oh, she was a very sound sleeper. It was a job to wake her if anything was wanted in the night."

"Did she cry much?"

"She cried over the old lady's death; she had very nice feelings."

"Some natural tears she shed, and all that. She didn't lie about and have awful howling fits or anything like that?"

"Good gracious, no!"

"How did she walk?"

"Walk?"

"Yes, walk. Was she what you'd call droopy?"

"Oh, no—quick and brisk."

"What was her voice like?"

"Well, now, that was one of the nice things about her. Rather deep for a woman, but with what I might call a tune in it. Melodious," said Nurse Armstrong, with a faint giggle, "that's what they call it in novels."

Parker opened his mouth and shut it again.

"How long did you stay on at the house after Lady Dormer died?" pursued Wimsey.

"I waited on till after the funeral, just in case Miss Dorland should need anybody."

"Before you left, did you hear anything of this trouble about the lawyers and the wills?"

"They were talking about it downstairs. Miss Dorland said nothing to me herself."

"Did she seem worried?"

"Not to notice."

"Had she any friends with her at the time?"

"Not staying in the house. She went out to see some friends one evening, I think—the evening before I left. She didn't say who they were."

"I see. Thank you, Nurse."

Parker had no more questions to put, and they took their leave.

"Well," said Parker, "how anybody could admire that girl's voice——"

"You noticed that! My theory is coming out right, Charles. I wish it wasn't. I'd *rather* be wrong. I should like to have you look pitifully at me and say, 'I told you so.' I can't speak more strongly than that."

"Hang your theories!" said Parker. "It looks to me as if we shall have to wash out the idea that General Fentiman got his dose in Portman Square. By the way, didn't you say you'd met the Dorland girl at the Rushworths?"

"No. I said I went hoping to meet her, but she wasn't there."

"Oh, I see. Well, that'll do for the moment. How about a spot of lunch?"

At which point they turned the corner and ran slap into Salcombe Hardy, emerging from Harley Street. Wimsey clutched Parker's arm suddenly. "I've remembered," he said.

"What?"

"Who that portrait reminds me of. Tell you later."

Sally, it appeared, was also thinking of grub. He was, in fact, due to meet Waffles Newton at the Falstaff. It ended in their all going to the Falstaff.

"And how's it all going?" demanded Sally, ordering boiled beef and carrots.

He looked limpidly at Parker, who shook his head.

"Discreet man, your friend," said Sally to Peter. "I suppose the police are engaged in following up a clew—or have we reached the point when they are completely baffled? Or do we say that an arrest is imminent, eh?"

"Tell us your own version, Sally. Your opinion's as good as anybody's."

"Oh, mine!—Same as yours—same as everybody's. The girl was in league with the doctor, of course. Pretty obvious, isn't it?"

"Maybe," said Parker, cautiously. "But that's a hard thing to prove. We know, of course, that they both sometimes went to Mrs. Rushworth's house, but there's no evidence that they knew each other well."

"But, you ass, she—" Wimsey blurted out. He shut his mouth again with a snap. "No, I won't. Fish it out for yourselves."

Illumination was flooding in on him in great waves. Each point of light touched off a myriad others. Now a date was lit up, and now a sentence. The relief in his mind would have been overwhelming, had it not been for that nagging central uncertainty. It was the portrait that worried him most. Painted as a record, painted to recall beloved features—thrust face to the wall and covered with dust.

Sally and Parker were talking.

". . . moral certainty is not the same thing as proof."

"Unless we can show that she knew the terms of the will. . . ."

". . . why wait till the last minute? It could have been done safely any time. . . ."

"They probably thought it wasn't necessary. The old lady looked like seeing him into his grave easily. If it hadn't been for the pneumonia."

"Even so, they had five days."

"Yes—well, say she didn't know till the very day of Lady Dormer's death. . . ."

"She might have told her then. Explained . . . seeing the thing had become a probability. . . ."

"And the Dorland girl arranged for the visit to Harley Street. . . ."

". . . plain as the nose on your face."

Hardy chuckled.

"They must have got a thundering shock when the body turned up the next morning at the Bellona. I suppose you gave Penberthy a good grueling about that rigor."

"Pretty fair. He fell back on professional caution, naturally."

"It's coming to him in the witness-box. Does he admit knowing the girl?"

"He says he just knows her to speak to. But one's got to find somebody who has seen them together. You remember the Thompson case. It was the interview in the tea-shop that clinched it."

"What I want to know," said Wimsey, "is why——"

"Why what?"

"Why didn't they compromise?" It was not what he had been going to say, but he felt defeated, and those words would end the sentence as well as any others.

"What's that?" asked Hardy, quickly.

Peter explained.

"When the question of survivorship came up, the Fentimans were ready to compromise and split the money. Why didn't Miss Dorland agree? If your idea is the right one, it was much the safest way. But it was she who insisted on an inquiry."

"I didn't know that," said Hardy. He was annoyed. All kinds of "stories" were coming his way to-day, and to-morrow there would probably be an arrest, and he wouldn't be able to use them.

"They *did* agree to compromise in the end," said Parker. "When was that?"

"After I told Penberthy there was going to be an exhumation," said Wimsey, as though in spite of himself.

"There you are! They saw it was getting too dangerous."

"Do you remember how nervous Penberthy was at the exhumation?" said Parker. "That man—what's his name's—joke about Palmer, and knocking over the jar?"

"What was that?" demanded Hardy again. Parker told him, and he listened, grinding his teeth. Another good story gone west. But it would all come out at the trial, and would be worth a headline.

"Robert Fentiman ought to be given a medal," said Hardy. "If he hadn't gone butting in——"

"Robert Fentiman?" inquired Parker, distantly.

Hardy grinned.

"If he didn't fix up the old boy's body, who did? Give us credit for a little intelligence."

"One admits nothing," said Parker, "but——"

"But everybody says he did it. Leave it at that. Somebody did it. If Somebody hadn't butted in, it would have been jam for the Dorland."

"Well, yes. Old Fentiman would just have gone home and pegged out quietly—and Penberthy would have given the certificate."

"I'd like to know how many inconvenient people are polished off that way. Damn it—it's so easy."

"I wonder how Penberthy's share of the boodle was to be transferred to him."

"I don't," said Hardy. "Look here—here's this girl. Calls herself an artist. Paints bad pictures. Right. Then she meets this doctor fellow. He's mad on glands. Shrewd man—knows there's money in glands. *She* starts taking up glands. Why?"

"That was a year ago."

"Precisely. Penberthy isn't a rich man. Retired Army surgeon, with a brass plate and a consulting-room in Harley Street—shares the house with two other hard-up brass-platers. Lives on a few old dodderers down at the Bellona. Has an idea, if only he could start one of these clinics for rejuvenating people, he could be a millionaire. All these giddy old goats who want their gay time over again—why, they're a perfect fortune to the man with a bit of capital and a hell of a lot of cheek. Then this girl comes along—rich old woman's heiress—and he goes after her. It's all fixed up. He's to accommodate her by removing the obstacle to the fortune, and she obligingly responds by putting the money into his clinic. In order not to make it too obvious, she has to pretend to get a dickens of an interest in glands. So she drops painting and takes to medicine. What could be clearer?"

"But that means," put in Wimsey, "that she must have known all about the will at least a year ago."

"Why not?"

"Well that brings us back to the old question: Why the delay?"

"And it gives us the answer," said Parker. "They waited till the interest in the glands and things was so firmly established and recognized by everybody that nobody would connect it with the General's death."

"Of course," said Wimsey. He felt that matters were rushing past him at a bewildering rate. But George was safe, anyhow.

"How soon do you think you'll be able to take action?" asked Hardy. "I suppose you'll want a bit more solid proof before you actually arrest them."

"I'd have to be certain that they don't wriggle out of it," said Parker, slowly. "It's not enough to prove that they were acquainted. There may be letters, of course, when we go over the girl's things. Or Penberthy's—though he's hardly the man to leave compromising documents lying about."

"You haven't detained Miss Dorland?"

"No; we've let her loose—on a string. I don't mind telling you one thing. There's been no communication of any kind with Penberthy."

"Of course there hasn't," said Wimsey. "They've quarreled."

The others stared at him.

"How do you know that?" demanded Parker, annoyed.

"Oh, well—it doesn't matter—I *think* so, that's all. And any way, they would take jolly good care not to communicate, once the alarm was given."

"Hullo!" broke in Hardy, "here's Waffles. Late again. Waffles!— what *have* you been doing, old boy?"

"Interviewing the Rushworths," said Waffles, edging his way into a chair by Hardy. He was a thin, sandy person, with a tired manner. Hardy introduced him to Wimsey and Parker.

"Got your story in?"

"Oh, yes. Awful lot of cats these women are. Ma Rushworth—she's the sloppy sort of woman with her head in the clouds all the time, who never sees anything till it's stuck right under her nose—she pretends, of course, that she always thought Ann Dorland was an unwholesome kind of girl. I nearly asked why, in that case, she had her about the house; but I didn't. Anyway, Mrs. Rushworth said, they didn't know her very intimately. They wouldn't, of course. Wonderful how these soulful people sheer off at the least suggestion of unpleasantness."

"Did you get anything about Penberthy?"

"Oh, yes—I got something."

"Good?"

"Oh, yes."

Hardy, with Fleet Street's delicate reticence towards the man with an exclusive story, did not press the question. The talk turned back and went over the old ground. Waffles Newton agreed with Salcombe Hardy's theory.

"The Rushworths must surely know something. Not the mother, perhaps—but the girl. If she's engaged to Penberthy, she'll have noticed any other woman who seemed to have an understanding with him. Women see these things."

"You don't suppose that they're going to confess that dear Dr. Penberthy ever had an understanding with anybody but dear Naomi," retorted Newton. "Besides, they aren't such fools as not to know that Penberthy's connection with the Dorland girl must be smothered up at all costs. They know she did it, all right, but they aren't going to compromise him."

"Of course not," said Parker, rather shortly. "The mother probably knows nothing, anyway. It's a different matter if we get the girl in the witness-box——"

"You won't," said Waffles Newton. "At least, you'll have to be jolly quick."

"Why?"

Newton waved an apologetic hand.

"They're being married to-morrow," he said, "special license. I say, that's not to go further, Sally."

"That's all right, old man."

"Married?" said Parker. "Good lord! that forces our hand a bit. Perhaps I'd better pop off. So long—and thanks very much for the tip, old man."

Wimsey followed him into the street.

"We'll have to put the stopper on this marriage business, quick," said Parker, madly waving to a taxi, which swooped past and ignored him. "I didn't want to move just at present, because I wasn't ready, but it'll be the devil and all if the Rushworth girl gets hitched up to Penberthy and we can't take her evidence. Devil of it is, if she's determined to go on with it, we can't stop it without arresting Penberthy. Very dangerous, when there's no real proof. I think we'd better have him down to the Yard for interrogation and detain him."

"Yes," said Wimsey. "But—look here, Charles."

A taxi drew up.

"What?" said Parker, sharply, with his foot on the step. "I can't wait, old man. What is it?"

"I—look here, Charles—this is all wrong," pleaded Wimsey. "You may have got the right solution, but the working of the sum's all wrong. Same as mine used to be at school, when I'd looked up the answer in the crib and had to fudge in the middle part. I've been a fool. I ought to have known about Penberthy. But I don't believe this story about bribing and corrupting him, and getting him to do the murder. It doesn't fit."

"Doesn't fit what?"

"Doesn't fit the portrait. Or the books. Or the way Nurse Armstrong described Ann Dorland. Or your description of her. It's a mechanically perfect explanation, but I swear it's all wrong."

"If it's mechanically perfect," said Parker, "that's good enough. It's far more than most explanations are. You've got that portrait on the brain. It's because you're artistic, I suppose."

For some reason, the word "artistic" produces the most alarming reactions in people who know anything about art.

"Artistic be damned!" said Wimsey, spluttering with fury, "it's because I'm an ordinary person, and have met women, and talked to them like ordinary human beings——"

"You and your women," said Parker, rudely.

"Well—I and my women, what about it? One learns something. You're on the wrong tack about this girl."

"I've met her and you haven't," objected Parker. "Unless you're

383

suppressing something. You keep on hinting things. Anyhow, I've met the girl, and she impressed me as being guilty."

"And I haven't met her, and I'll swear she isn't guilty."

"You must know, of course."

"I do happen to know about this."

"I'm afraid your unsupported opinion will hardly be sufficient to refute the weight of evidence."

"You haven't any real evidence, if it comes to that. You don't know that they were ever alone together; you don't know that Ann Dorland knew about the will; you can't prove that Penberthy administered the poison——"

"I don't despair of getting all the evidence necessary," said Parker, coldly, "provided you don't keep me here *all* day." He slammed the taxi-door.

"What a beast of a case this is," thought Wimsey. "That makes two silly, sordid rows to-day. Well, what next?" He considered a moment.

"My spirit needs soothing," he decided. "Feminine society is indicated. Virtuous feminine society. No emotions. I'll go and have tea with Marjorie Phelps."

CHAPTER XX

ANN DORLAND GOES MISERE

THE STUDIO DOOR was opened by a girl he did not know. She was not tall, but compactly and generously built. He noticed the wide shoulders and the strong swing of the thighs before he had taken in her face. The uncurtained window behind her threw her features into shadow, he was only aware of thick black hair, cut in a square bob, with a bang across the forehead.

"Miss Phelps is out."

"Oh!—will she be long?"

"Don't know. She'll be in to supper."

"Do you think I might come in and wait?"

"I expect so, if you're a friend of hers."

The girl fell back from the doorway and let him pass. He laid his hat and stick on the table and turned to her. She took no notice of him, but walked over to the fireplace and stood with one hand on the mantelpiece. Unable to sit down, since she was still standing, Wimsey moved to the modeling-board, and raised the wet cloth that covered the little mound of clay.

He was gazing with an assumption of great interest at the half-modeled figure of an old flower-seller, when the girl said:

"I say!"

She had taken up Marjorie Phelps' figurine of himself, and was twisting it over in her fingers.

"Is this you?"

"Yes—rather good of me, don't you think?"

"What do you want?"

"Want?"

"You've come here to have a look at me, haven't you?"

"I came to see Miss Phelps."

"I suppose the policeman at the corner comes to see Miss Phelps too."

Wimsey glanced out of the window. There *was* a man at the corner —an elaborately indifferent lounger.

"I am sorry," said Wimsey, with sudden enlightenment. "I'm really awfully sorry to seem so stupid, and so intrusive. But honestly, I had no idea who you were till this moment."

"Hadn't you? Oh, well, it doesn't matter."

"Shall I go?"

"You can please yourself."

"If you really mean that, Miss Dorland, I should like to stay. I've been wanting to meet you, you know."

"That was nice of you," she mocked. "First you wanted to defraud me, and now you're trying to——"

"To what?"

She shrugged her wide shoulders.

"Yours is not a pleasant hobby, Lord Peter Wimsey."

"Will you believe me," said Wimsey, "when I assure you that I was never a party to the fraud. In fact, I showed it up. I did, really."

"Oh, well. It doesn't matter now."

"But do please believe that."

"Very well. If you say so, I must believe it."

She threw herself on the couch near the fire.

"That's better," said Wimsey. "Napoleon or somebody said that you could always turn a tragedy into a comedy, by sittin' down. Perfectly true, isn't it? Let's talk about something ordinary till Miss Phelps comes in. Shall we?"

"What do you want to talk about?"

"Oh, well—that's rather embarrassin'. Books." He waved a vague hand. "What have you been readin' lately?"

"Nothing much."

"Don't know what I should do without books. Fact, I always wonder what people did in the old days. Just think of it. All sorts of bothers goin' on—matrimonial rows and love-affairs—prodigal sons and servants and worries—and no books to turn to."

"People worked with their hands instead."

"Yes—that's frightfully jolly for the people who can do it. I envy them myself. You paint, don't you?"

"I try to."

"Portraits?"

"Oh, no—figure and landscape chiefly."

"Oh! . . . A friend of mine—well, it's no use disguising it—he's a detective—you've met him, I think . . ."

"That man? Oh, yes. Quite a polite sort of detective."

"He told me he'd seen some stuff of yours. It rather surprised him, I think. He's not exactly a modernist. He seemed to think your portraits were your best work."

"There weren't many portraits. A few figure-studies . . ."

"They worried him a bit." Wimsey laughed. "The only thing he understood, he said, was a man's head in oils. . . ."

"Oh, that!—just an experiment—a fancy thing. My best stuff is some sketches I did of the Wiltshire Downs a year or two ago. Direct painting, without any preliminary sketch."

She described a number of these works.

"They sound ever so jolly," said Wimsey. "Great stuff. I wish I could do something of that kind. As I say, I have to fall back on books for my escape. Reading *is* an escape to me. Is it to you?"

"How do you mean?"

"Well—it is to most people, I think. Servants and factory hands read about beautiful girls loved by dark, handsome men, all covered over with jewels and moving in scenes of gilded splendour. And passionate spinsters read Ethel M. Dell. And dull men in offices read detective stories. They wouldn't, if murder and police entered into their lives."

"I don't know," she said. "When Crippen and Le Neve were taken on the steamer, they were reading Edgar Wallace." Her voice was losing its dull harshness; she sounded almost interested.

"Le Neve was reading it," said Wimsey, "but I've never believed she knew about the murder. I think she was fighting desperately to know nothing about it—reading horrors, and persuading herself that nothing of that kind had happened, or could happen, to her. I think one might do that, don't you?"

"I don't know," said Ann Dorland. "Of course, a detective story keeps your brain occupied. Rather like chess. Do you play chess?"

"No good at it. I like it—but I keep on thinking about the history of the various pieces, and the picturesqueness of the moves. So I get beaten. I'm not a player."

"Nor am I. I wish I were."

"Yes—that would keep one's mind off things with a vengeance. Draughts or dominoes or patience would be even better. No connection with anything. I remember," added Wimsey, "one time when something perfectly grinding and hateful had happened to me. I played patience all day. I was in a nursing home—with shell-shock—and other things. I only played one game, the very simplest . . . the demon . . . a silly game with no ideas in it at all. I just went on laying it out and gathering it up . . . hundred times in an evening . . . so as to stop thinking."

"Then you too . . ."

Wimsey waited; but she did not finish the sentence.

"It's a kind of drug, of course. That's an awfully trite thing to say, but it's quite true."

"Yes, quite."

"I read detective stories too. They were about the only thing I could read. All the others had the war in them—or love . . . or some damn thing I didn't want to think about."

She moved restlessly.

"You've been through it, haven't you?" said Wimsey, gently.

"Me? . . . well . . . all this . . . it isn't pleasant, you know . . . the police . . . and . . . and everything."

"You're not really worried about the police, are you?"

She had cause to be, if she only knew it, but he buried this knowledge at the bottom of his mind, defying it to show itself.

"Everything's pretty hateful, isn't it?"

"Something's hurt you . . . all right . . . don't talk about it if you don't want to . . . a man?"

"It usually is a man, isn't it?"

Her eyes were turned away from him, and she answered with a kind of shamefaced defiance.

"Practically always," said Wimsey. "Fortunately, one gets over it."

"Depends what it is."

"One gets over everything," repeated Wimsey, firmly. "Particularly if one tells somebody about it."

"One can't always tell things."

"I can't imagine anything really untellable."

"Some things are so beastly."

"Oh, yes—quite a lot of things. Birth is beastly—and death—and digestion, if it comes to that. Sometimes when I think of what's happening inside me to a beautiful *suprème de sole,* with the caviare in boats, and the *croûtons* and the jolly little twists of potato and all the gadgets—I could cry. But there it is, don't you know."

Ann Dorland suddenly laughed.

"That's better," said Wimsey. "Look here, you've been brooding over this and you're seeing it all out of proportion. Let's be practical and frightfully ordinary. Is it a baby?"

"Oh, no!"

"Well—that's rather a good thing, because babies, though no doubt excellent in their way, take a long time and come expensive. Is it blackmail?"

"Good heavens, no!"

"Good. Because blackmail is even longer and more expensive than babies. Is it Freudian, or sadistic, or any of those popular modern amusements?"

"I don't believe you'd turn a hair if it was."

"Why should I?—I can't think of anything worse to suggest, except what Rose Macaulay refers to as 'nameless orgies.' Or diseases, of course. It's not leprosy or anything?"

"What a mind you've got," she said, beginning to laugh. "No, it isn't leprosy."

"Well, what *did* the blighter do?"

Ann Dorland smiled faintly: "It's nothing, really."

"If only Heaven prevents Marjorie Phelps from coming in," thought Wimsey, "I'm going to get it now . . . It must have been something, to upset you like this," he pursued aloud, "you're not the kind of woman to be upset about nothing."

"You don't think I am?" She got up and faced him squarely. "He said . . . he said . . . I imagined things . . . he said . . . he said I had a mania about sex. I suppose you would call it Freudian, really," she added hastily, flushing an ugly crimson.

"Is that all?" said Wimsey. "I know plenty of people who would take that as a compliment . . . But obviously you don't. What exact form of mania did he suggest . . . ?"

"Oh, the gibbering sort that hangs round church doors for curates," she broke out, fiercely. "It's a lie. He did—he *did*—pretend to—want me and all that. The beast! . . . I can't tell you the things he said . . . and I'd made such a fool of myself. . . ."

She was back on the couch, crying, with large, ugly, streaming tears, and snorting into the cushions. Wimsey sat down beside her.

"Poor kid," he said. This, then, was at the back of Marjorie's mysterious hints, and those scratch-cat sneers of Naomi Rushworth's. The girl had wanted love-affairs, that was certain; imagined them perhaps. There had been Ambrose Ledbury. Between the normal and the abnormal, the gulf is deep, but so narrow that misrepresentation is made easy.

"Look here." He put a comforting arm round Ann's heaving shoulders. "This fellow—was it Penberthy, by the way?"

"How did you know?"

"Oh!—the portrait, and lots of things. The things you liked once, and then wanted to hide away and forget. He's a rotter, anyway, for saying that kind of thing—even if it was true, which it isn't. You got to know him at the Rushworths', I take it—when?"

"Nearly two years ago."

"Were you keen on him then?"

"No. I—well, I was keen on somebody else. Only that was a mistake too. He—he was one of those people, you know."

"They can't help themselves," said Wimsey, soothingly. "When did the change-over happen?"

"The other man went away. And later on, Dr. Penberthy—oh! I don't know! He walked home with me once or twice, and then he asked me to dine with him—in Soho."

"Had you at that time told any one about this comic will of Lady Dormer's?"

"Of course not. How could I? I never knew anything about it till after she died."

Her surprise sounded genuine enough.

389

"What did you think? Did you think the money would come to you?"

"I knew that some of it would; Auntie told me she would see me provided for."

"There were the grandsons, of course."

"Yes; I thought she would leave most of it to them. It's a pity she didn't, poor dear. Then there wouldn't have been all this dreadful bother."

"People so often seem to lose their heads when they make wills. So you were a sort of dark horse at that time. H'm. Did this precious Penberthy ask you to marry him?"

"I thought he did. But he says he didn't. We talked about founding his clinic; I was to help him."

"And that was when you chucked painting for books about medicine and first-aid classes. Did your aunt know about the engagement?"

"He didn't want her told. It was to be our secret, till he got a better position. He was afraid she might think he was after the money."

"I daresay he was."

"He made out he was fond of me," she said, miserably.

"Of course, my dear child; your case is not unique. Didn't you tell any of your friends?"

"No." Wimsey reflected that the Ledbury episode had probably left a scar. Besides—did women tell things to other women? He had long doubted it.

"You were still engaged when Lady Dormer died, I take it?"

"As engaged as we ever were. Of course, he told me that there was something funny about the body. He said you and the Fentimans were trying to defraud me of the money. I shouldn't have minded for myself—it was more money than I should have known what to do with. But it would have meant the clinic, you see."

"Yes, you could start a pretty decent clinic with half a million. So that was why you shot me out of the house."

He grinned—and then reflected a few moments.

"Look here," he said, "I'm going to give you a bit of a shock, but it'll have to come sooner or later. Has it ever occurred to you that it was Penberthy who murdered General Fentiman?"

"I—wondered," she said, slowly. "I couldn't think—who else—But you know they suspect *me?*"

"Oh, well—*cui bono* and all that—they couldn't overlook you. They have to suspect every possible person, you know."

"I don't blame them at all. But I didn't, you know."

"Of course not. It was Penberthy. I look at it like this. Penberthy wanted money; he was sick of being poor, and he knew you would be certain to get *some* of Lady Dormer's money. He'd probably heard about the family quarrel with the General, and expected it would be the lot. So he started to make your acquaintance. But he was careful. He asked you to keep it quiet—just in case, you see. The money might be so tied up that you couldn't give it him, or you might lose it if you married, or it might only be quite a small annuity, in which case he'd want to look for somebody richer."

"We considered those points when we talked it over about the clinic."

"Yes. Well, then, Lady Dormer fell ill. The General went round and heard about the legacy that was coming to him. And then he toddled along to Penberthy, feeling very groggy, and promptly told him all about it. You can imagine him saying: 'You've got to patch me up long enough to get the money.' That must have been a nasty jar for Penberthy."

"It was. You see, he didn't even hear about my twelve thousand."

"Oh?"

"No. Apparently what the General said was, 'If only I last out poor Felicity, all the money comes to me. Otherwise it goes to the girl and my boys only get seven thousand apiece.' That was why——"

"Just a moment. When did Penberthy tell you about that?"

"Why, later—when he said I was to compromise with the Fentimans."

"That explains it. I wondered why you gave in so suddenly. I thought, then, that you—Well, anyhow, Penberthy hears this, and gets the brilliant idea of putting General Fentiman out of the way. So he gives him a slow-working kind of a pill——"

"Probably a powder in a very tough capsule that would take a long time to digest."

"Good idea. Yes, very likely. And then the General, instead of heading straight for home, as he expected, goes off to the Club and dies there. And then Robert——"

He explained in detail what Robert had done, and resumed.

"Well, now—Penberthy was in a bad fix. If he drew attention at the time to the peculiar appearance of the corpse, he couldn't reasonably give a certificate. In which case there would be a post-mortem and an analysis, and the digitalin would be found. If he kept quiet, the money might be lost and all his trouble would be wasted. Maddenin' for him, wasn't it? So he did what he could. He put the time of the death as early as he dared, and hoped for the best."

"He told me he thought there would be some attempt to make it seem later than it really was. I thought it was *you* who were trying to hush everything up. And I was so furious that of course I told Mr. Pritchard to have a proper inquiry made and on no account to compromise."

"Thank God you did," said Wimsey.

"Why?"

"I'll tell you presently. But Penberthy now—I can't think why *he* didn't persuade you to compromise. That would have made him absolutely safe."

"But he did! That's what started our first quarrel. As soon as he heard about it, he said I was a fool not to compromise. I couldn't understand his saying that, since he himself had said there was something wrong. We had a fearful row. That was the time I mentioned the twelve thousand that was coming to me anyway."

"What did he say?"

" 'I didn't know that.' Just like that. And then he apologized and said that the law was so uncertain, it would be best to agree to divide the money anyhow. So I rang up Mr. Pritchard and told him not to make any more fuss. And we were friends again."

"Was it the day after that, that Penberthy—er—said things to you?"

"Yes."

"Right. Then I can tell you one thing: he would never have been so brutal if he hadn't been in fear of his life. Do you know what had happened in between?"

She shook her head.

"I had been on the 'phone to him, and told him there was going to be an autopsy."

"Oh!"

"Yes—listen—you needn't worry any more about it. He knew that the poison would be discovered, and that if he was known to be engaged to you, he was absolutely bound to be suspected. So he hurried to cut the connection with you—purely in self-defense."

"But why do it in that brutal way?"

"Because, my dear, he knew that that particular accusation would be the very last thing a girl of your sort would tell people about. He made it absolutely impossible for you to claim him publicly. And he bolstered it up by engaging himself to the Rushworth female."

"He didn't care how *I* suffered."

"He was in a beast of a hole," said Wimsey, apologetically. "Mind you, it was a perfectly diabolical thing to do. I daresay he's feeling pretty rotten about it."

Ann Dorland clenched her hands.

"I've been so horribly ashamed——"

"Well, you aren't any more, are you?"

"No—but——" A thought seemed to strike her. "Lord Peter—I can't *prove* a word of this. Everybody will think I was in league with him. And they'll think that our quarrel and his getting engaged to Naomi was just a put-up job between us to get us both out of a difficulty."

"You've got brains," said Wimsey, admiringly. "*Now* you see why I thanked God you'd been so keen on an inquiry at first. Pritchard can make it pretty certain that you weren't an accessory before the fact, anyhow."

"Of course—so he can. Oh, I'm so glad! I *am* so glad." She burst into excited sobs and clutched Wimsey's hand. "I wrote him a letter —right at the beginning—saying I'd read about a case in which they'd proved the time of somebody's death by looking into his stomach, and asking if General Fentiman couldn't be dug up."

"Did you? Splendid girl! You *have* got a head on your shoulders! . . . No, I observe that it's on my shoulders. Go on. Have a real, good howl—I feel rather like howling myself. I've been quite worried about it all. But it's all right now, isn't it?"

"I am a fool . . . but I'm so thankful you came."

"So am I. Here, have a hanky. Poor old dear! . . . Hullo! there's Marjorie."

He released her and went out to meet Marjorie Phelps at the door.

"Lord Peter! Good lord!"

"Thank you, Marjorie," said Wimsey, gravely.

"No, but listen! Have you seen Ann?—I took her away. She's frightfully queer—and there's a policeman outside. But whatever she's done, I couldn't leave her alone in that awful house. You haven't come to—to——"

"Marjorie!" said Wimsey, "don't you ever talk to me again about feminine intuition. You've been thinking all this time that that girl

393

was suffering from guilty conscience. Well, she wasn't. It was a man, my child—a MAN!"

"How do you know?"

"My experienced eye told me as much at the first glance. It's all right now. Sorrow and sighing have fled away. I am going to take your young friend out to dinner."

"But why didn't she tell me what it was all about?"

"Because," said Wimsey, mincingly, "it wasn't the kind of thing one woman tells another."

CHAPTER XXI

LORD PETER CALLS A BLUFF

"IT IS NEW TO ME," said Lord Peter, glancing from the back window of the taxi at the other taxi which was following them, "to be shadowed by the police, but it amuses them and doesn't hurt us."

He was revolving ways and means of proof in his mind. Unhappily, all the evidence in favour of Ann Dorland was evidence against her as well—except, indeed, the letter to Pritchard. Damn Penberthy. The best that could be hoped for now was that the girl should escape from public inquiry with a verdict of 'Not proven.' Even if acquitted —even if never charged with the murder—she would always be suspect. The question was not one which could be conveniently settled by a brilliant flash of deductive logic, or the discovery of a blood-stained thumb-mark. It was a case for lawyers to argue—for a weighing of the emotional situation by twelve good and lawful persons. Presumably the association could be proved—the couple had met and dined together; probably the quarrel could be proved—but what next? Would a jury believe in the cause of the quarrel? Would they think it a pre-arranged blind, or perhaps—or mistake it for the falling-out of rogues among themselves? What would they think of this plain, sulky, inarticulate girl, who had never had any real friends, and whose clumsy and tentative graspings after passion had been so obscure, so disastrous?

Penberthy, too—but Penberthy was easier to understand. Penberthy, cynical and bored with poverty, found himself in contact

394

with this girl, who might be so well-off some day. And Penberthy, the physician, would not mistake the need for passion that made the girl such easy stuff to work on. So he carried on—bored with the girl, of course—keeping it all secret, till he saw which way the cat was going to jump. Then the old man—the truth about the will—the opportunity. And then, upsettingly, Robert . . . Would the jury see it like that?

Wimsey leaned out of the cab window and told the driver to go to the Savoy. When they arrived, he handed the girl over to the cloak-room attendant. "I am going up to change," he added, and turning, had the pleasure of seeing his sleuth arguing with the porter in the entrance-hall.

Bunter, previously summoned by telephone, was already in attendance with his master's dress clothes. Having changed, Wimsey passed through the hall again. The sleuth was there, quietly waiting. Wimsey grinned at him, and offered him a drink.

"I can't help it, my lord," said the detective.

"Of course not; you've sent for a bloke in a boiled shirt to take your place, I suppose?"

"Yes, my lord."

"More power to his elbow. So long."

He rejoined his charge and they went into the dining-room. Dressed in a green which did not suit her, she was undoubtedly plain. But she had character; he was not ashamed of her. He offered her the menu.

"What shall it be?" he asked. "Lobster and champagne?"

She laughed at him.

"Marjorie says you are an authority on food. I don't believe authorities on food ever take lobster and champagne. Anyway, I don't like lobster, much. Surely there's something they do best here, isn't there? Let's have that."

"You show the right spirit," said Wimsey. "I will compose a dinner for you."

He called the head waiter, and went into the question scientifically.

"*Huîtres Musgrave*—I am opposed on principle to the cooking of oysters—but it is a dish so excellent that one may depart from the rules in its favour. Fried in their shells, Miss Dorland, with little strips of bacon. Shall we try it?—The soup must be *Tortue Vraie,* of course. The fish—oh! just a *Filet de Sole,* the merest mouthful, a hyphen between the prologue and the main theme."

395

"That all sounds delightful. And what is the main theme to be?"

"I think a *Faisan Rôti* with *Pommes Byron*. And a salad to promote digestion. And, waiter—be sure the salad is dry and perfectly crisp. A *Soufflé Glace* to finish up with. And bring me the wine-list."

They talked. When she was not on the defensive, the girl was pleasant enough in manner; a trifle downright and aggressive, perhaps, in her opinions, but needing only mellowing.

"What do you think of the *Romanée Conti?*" he asked, suddenly.

"I don't know much about wine. It's good. Not sweet, like Sauterne. It's a little—well—harsh. But it's harsh without being thin—quite different from that horrid Chianti people always seem to drink at Chelsea parties."

"You're right; it's rather unfinished, but it has plenty of body—it'll be a grand wine in ten years' time. It's 1915. Now, you see. Waiter, take this away and bring me a bottle of the 1908."

He leaned towards his companion.

"Miss Dorland—may I be impertinent?"

"How? Why?"

"Not an artist, not a bohemian, and not a professional man;—a man of the world."

"What *do* you mean by those cryptic words?"

"For you. That is the kind of man who is going to like you very much. Look! that wine I've sent away—it's no good for champagne-and-lobster sort of person, nor for very young people—it's too big and rough. But it's got the essential guts. So have you. It takes a fairly experienced palate to appreciate it. But you and it will come into your own one day. Get me?"

"Do you think so?"

"Yes. But your man won't be at all the sort of person you're expecting. You have always thought of being dominated by somebody, haven't you?"

"Well——"

"But you'll find that yours will be the leading brain of the two. He will take great pride in the fact. And you will find the man reliable and kind, and it will turn out quite well."

"I didn't know you were a prophet."

"I am, though."

Wimsey took the bottle of 1908 from the waiter and glanced over the girl's head at the door. A man in a boiled shirt was making his way in, accompanied by the manager.

"I am a prophet," said Wimsey. "Listen. Something tiresome is going to happen—now, this minute. But don't worry. Drink your wine, and trust."

The manager had brought the man to their table. It was Parker.

"Ah!" said Wimsey, brightly. "You'll forgive our starting without you, old man. Sit down. I think you know Miss Dorland."

Parker bowed and sat down.

"Have you come to arrest me?" asked Ann.

"Just to ask you to come down to the Yard with me," said Parker, smiling pleasantly and unfolding his napkin.

Ann looked palely at Wimsey, and took a gulp of the wine.

"Right," said Wimsey. "Miss Dorland has quite a lot to tell you. After dinner will suit us charmingly. What will you have?"

Parker, who was not imaginative, demanded a grilled steak.

"Shall we find any other friends at the Yard?" pursued Wimsey.

"Possibly," said Parker.

"Well, cheer up! You put me off my food, looking so grim. Hullo! Yes, waiter, what is it?"

"Excuse me, my lord; is this gentleman Detective-Inspector Parker?"

"Yes, yes," said Parker, "what's the matter?"

"You're wanted on the 'phone, sir."

Parker departed.

"It's all right," said Wimsey to the girl. "I know you're straight, and I'll damn well see you through."

"What am I to do?"

"Tell the truth."

"It sounds so silly."

"They've heard lots of very much sillier stories than that."

"But—I don't want to—to be the one to——"

"You're still fond of him, then?"

"*No!*—but I'd rather it wasn't me."

"I'll be frank with you. I think it's going to be between you and him that suspicion will lie."

"In that case"—she set her teeth—"he can have what's coming to him."

"Thank the lord! I thought you were going to be noble and self-sacrificing and tiresome. You know. Like the people whose noble motives are misunderstood in chapter one and who get dozens of

397

people tangled up in their miserable affairs till the family lawyer solves everything on the last page but two."

Parker had come back from the telephone.

"Just a moment!" He spoke in Peter's ear.

"Hullo?"

"Look here; this is awkward. George Fentiman——"

"Yes?"

"He's been found in Clerkenwell."

"Clerkenwell?"

"Yes; must have wandered back by 'bus or something. He's at the police-station; in fact he's given himself up."

"Good lord!"

"For the murder of his grandfather."

"The devil he has!"

"It's a nuisance; of course it must be looked into. I think perhaps I'd better put off interrogating Dorland and Penberthy. What are you doing with the girl, by the way?"

"I'll explain later. Look here—I'll take Miss Dorland back to Marjorie Phelps' place, and then come along and join you. The girl won't run away; I know that. And anyhow, you've got a man looking after her."

"Yes, I rather wish you would come with me; Fentiman is pretty queer, by all accounts. We've sent for his wife."

"Right. You buzz off, and I'll join you in—say in three quarters of an hour. What address? Oh, yes, righty-ho! Sorry you're missing your dinner."

"It's all in the day's work," growled Parker, and took his leave.

.   .   .   .   .

George Fentiman greeted them with a tired white smile.

"Hush!" he said. "I've told them all about it. *He's* asleep; don't wake him."

"Who's asleep, dearest?" said Sheila.

"I mustn't say the name," said George, cunningly. "He'd hear it —even in his sleep—even if you whispered it. But he's tired, and he nodded off. So I ran in here and told them all about it while he snored."

The police superintendent tapped his forehead significantly behind Sheila's back.

"Has he made any statement?" asked Parker.

"Yes, he insisted on writing it himself. Here it is. Of course . . ." the Superintendent shrugged his shoulders.

"That's all right," said George. "I'm getting sleepy myself. I've been watching him for a day and a night, you know. I'm going to bed. Sheila—it's time to go to bed."

"Yes, dear."

"We'll have to keep him here to-night, I suppose," muttered Parker. "Has the doctor seen him?"

"We've sent for him, sir."

"Well, Mrs. Fentiman, I think if you'd take your husband into the room the officer will show you, that would be the best way. And we'll send the doctor in to you when he arrives. Perhaps it would be as well that he should see his own medical man too. Whom would you like us to send for?"

"Dr. Penberthy has vetted him from time to time, I think," put in Wimsey, suddenly. "Why not send for him?"

Parker gasped involuntarily.

"He might be able to throw some light on the symptoms," said Wimsey, in a rigid voice.

Parker nodded.

"A good idea," he agreed. He moved to the telephone. George smiled as his wife put her arm about his shoulder.

"Tired," he said, "very tired. Off to bed, old girl."

A police-constable opened the door to them, and they started through it together; George leaned heavily on Sheila; his feet dragged.

"Let's have a look at his statement," said Parker.

It was written in a staggering handwriting, much blotted and erased, with words left out and repeated here and there.

"I am making this statement quickly while he is asleep, because if I wait he may wake up and stop me. You will say I was moved and seduced by instigation of but what they will not understand is that he is me and I am him. I killed my grandfather by giving him digitalin. I did not remember it till I saw the name on the bottle, but they have been looking for me ever since, so I know that he must have done it. That is why they began following me about, but he is very clever and misleads them. When he is awake. We were dancing all last night and that is why he is tired. He told me to smash the bottle so that you shouldn't find out, but they know I was the last person to see him. He is very cunning, but if you creep

399

on him quickly now that he is asleep you will be able to bind him in chains and cast him into the pit and then I shall be able to sleep.

George Fentiman."

"Off his head, poor devil," said Parker. "We can't pay much attention to this. What did he say to you, superintendent?"

"He just came in, sir, and said 'I'm George Fentiman and I've come to tell you about how I killed my grandfather.' So I questioned him, and he rambled a good bit and then he asked for a pen and paper to make his statement. I thought he ought to be detained, and I rang up the Yard, sir."

"Quite right," said Parker.

The door opened and Sheila came out.

"He's fallen asleep," she said. "It's the old trouble come back again. He thinks he's the devil, you know. He's been like that twice before," she added, simply. "I'll go back to him till the doctors come."

The police-surgeon arrived first and went in; then, after a wait of a quarter of an hour, Penberthy came. He looked worried, and greeted Wimsey abruptly. Then he, too, went into the inner room. The others stood vaguely about, and were presently joined by Robert Fentiman, whom an urgent summons had traced to a friend's house.

Presently the two doctors came out again.

"Nervous shock with well-marked delusions," said the police-surgeon, briefly. "Probably be all right to-morrow. Sleeping it off now. Been this way before, I understand. Just so. A hundred years ago they'd have called it diabolic possession, but *we* know better."

"Yes," said Parker, "but do you think he is under a delusion in saying he murdered his grandfather? Or did he actually murder him under the influence of this diabolical delusion? That's the point."

"Can't say just at present. Might be the one—might be the other. Much better wait till the attack passes off. You'll be able to find out better then."

"You don't think he's permanently—insane, then?" demanded Robert, with brusque anxiety.

"No—I don't. I think it's what you'd call a nerve-storm. That is your opinion, too, I believe?" he added, turning to Penberthy.

"Yes; that is my opinion."

"And what do you think about this delusion, Dr. Penberthy?" went on Parker. "Did he do this insane act?"

"He certainly thinks he did it," said Penberthy; "I couldn't possibly say for certain whether he has any foundation for the belief. From time to time he undoubtedly gets these fits of thinking that the devil has taken hold of him, and of course it's hard to say what a man might or might not do under the influence of such a delusion."

He avoided Robert's distressed eyes, and addressed himself exclusively to Parker.

"It seems to me," said Wimsey, "if you'll excuse me pushin' my opinion forward and all that—it seems to me that's a question of fact that can be settled without reference to Fentiman and his delusions. There's only the one occasion on which the pill could have been administered—would it have produced the effect that was produced at that particular time, or wouldn't it? If it couldn't take effect at 8 o'clock, then it couldn't, and there's an end of it."

He kept his eyes fixed on Penberthy, and saw him pass his tongue over his dry lips before speaking.

"I can't answer that off-hand," he said.

"The pill might have been introduced into General Fentiman's stock of pills at some other time," suggested Parker.

"So it might," agreed Penberthy.

"Had it the same shape and appearance as his ordinary pills?" demanded Wimsey, again fixing his eyes on Penberthy.

"Not having seen the pill in question, I can't say," said the latter.

"In any case," said Wimsey, "the pill in question, which was one of Mrs. Fentiman's, I understand, had strychnine in it as well as digitalin. The analysis of the stomach would no doubt have revealed strychnine if present. That can be looked into."

"Of course," said the police-surgeon. "Well, gentlemen, I don't think we can do much more to-night. I have written out a prescription for the patient, with Dr. Penberthy's entire agreement"—he bowed; Penberthy bowed—"I will have it made up, and you will no doubt see that it is given to him. I shall be here in the morning."

He looked interrogatively at Parker, who nodded.

"Thank you, doctor; we will ask you for a further report to-morrow morning. You'll see that Mrs. Fentiman is properly looked after, Superintendent. If you wish to stay here and look after your brother and Mrs. Fentiman, Major, of course you may, and the Superintendent will make you as comfortable as he can."

Wimsey took Penberthy by the arm.

"Come round to the Club with me for a moment, Penberthy," he said. "I want to have a word with you."

CHAPTER XXII

THE CARDS ON THE TABLE

THERE WAS NOBODY in the library at the Bellona Club; there never is. Wimsey led Penberthy into the farthest bay and sent a waiter for two double whiskies.

"Here's luck!" he said.

"Good luck," replied Penberthy. "What is it?"

"Look here," said Wimsey. "You've been a soldier. I think you're a decent fellow. You've seen George Fentiman. It's a pity, isn't it?"

"What about it?"

"If George Fentiman hadn't turned up with that delusion of his," said Wimsey, "you would have been arrested for the murder this evening. Now the point is this. When you are arrested, nothing, as things are, can prevent Miss Dorland's being arrested on the same charge. She's quite a decent girl, and you haven't treated her any too well, have you? Don't you think you might make things right for her by telling the truth straight away?"

Penberthy sat with a white face and said nothing.

"You see," went on Wimsey, "if once they get her into the dock, she'll always be a suspected person. Even if the jury believe her story —and they may not, because juries are often rather stupid—people will always think there was 'something in it.' They'll say she was a very lucky woman to get off. That's damning for a girl, isn't it? They might even bring her in guilty. You and I know she isn't—but—you don't want the girl hanged, Penberthy, do you?"

Penberthy drummed on the table.

"What do you want me to do?" he said at last.

"Write a clear account of what actually happened," said Wimsey. "Make a clean job of it for these other people. Make it clear that Miss Dorland had nothing to do with it."

"And then?"

"Then do as you like. In your place I know what I should do."

Penberthy propped his chin on his hands and sat for some minutes staring at the works of Dickens in the leather-and-gold binding.

"Very well," he said at last. "You're quite right. I ought to have done it before. But—damn it!—if ever a man had rotten luck . . .

"If only Robert Fentiman hadn't been a rogue. It's funny, isn't it? That's your wonderful poetic justice, isn't it? If Robert Fentiman had been an honest man, I should have got my half-million, and Ann Dorland would have got a perfectly good husband, and the world would have gained a fine clinic, incidentally. But as Robert was a rogue—here we are . . .

"I didn't intend to be such a sweep to the Dorland girl. I'd have been decent to her if I'd married her. Mind you, she did sicken me a bit. Always wanting to be sentimental. It's true, what I said—she's a bit cracked about sex. Lots of 'em are. Naomi Rushworth, for instance. That's why I asked her to marry me. I had to be engaged to somebody, and I knew she'd take any one who asked her . . .

"It was so hideously easy, you see . . . that was the devil of it. The old man came along and put himself into my hands. Told me with one breath that I hadn't a dog's chance of the money, and in the next, asked me for a dose. I just had to put the stuff into a couple of capsules and tell him to take them at 7 o'clock. He put them in his spectacle-case, to make sure he wouldn't forget them. Not even a bit of paper to give me away. And the next day I'd only to get a fresh supply of the stuff and fill up the bottle. I'll give you the address of the chemist who sold it. Easy?—it was laughable . . . people put such power in our hands. . . .

"I never meant to get led into all this rotten way of doing things—it was just self-defense. I still don't care a damn about having killed the old man. I could have made better use of the money than Robert Fentiman. He hasn't got two ideas in his head, and he's perfectly happy where he is. Though I suppose he'll be leaving the Army now . . . As for Ann, she ought to be grateful to me in a way. I've secured her the money, anyhow."

"Not unless you make it clear that she had no part in the crime," Wimsey reminded him.

"That's true. All right. I'll put it all on paper for you. Give me half an hour, will you?"

"Right you are," said Wimsey.

He left the library and wandered into the smoking-room. Colonel Marchbanks was there, and greeted him with a friendly smile.

"Glad you're here, Colonel. Mind if I come and chat to you for a moment?"

"By all means, my dear boy. I'm in no hurry to get home. My wife's away. What can I do for you?"

Wimsey told him, in a lowered voice. The Colonel was distressed.

"Ah, well," he said, "you've done the best thing, to my mind. I look at these matters from a soldier's point of view, of course. Much better to make a clean job of it all. Dear, dear! Sometimes, Lord Peter, I think that the War has had a bad effect on some of our young men. But then, of course, all are not soldiers by training, and that makes a great difference. I certainly notice a less fine sense of honour in these days than we had when I was a boy. There were not so many excuses made then for people; there were things that were done and things that were not done. Nowadays men—and, I am sorry to say, women too—let themselves go in a way that is to me quite incomprehensible. I can understand a man's committing murder in hot blood —but poisoning—and then putting a good, ladylike girl into such an equivocal position—no! I fail to understand it. Still, as you say, the right course is being taken at last."

"Yes," said Wimsey.

"Excuse me for a moment," said the Colonel, and went out.

When he returned, he went with Wimsey into the library. Penberthy had finished writing and was reading his statement through.

"Will that do?" he asked.

Wimsey read it, Colonel Marchbanks looking over the pages with him.

"That is quite all right," he said. "Colonel Marchbanks will witness it with me."

This was done. Wimsey gathered the sheets together and put them in his breast-pocket. Then he turned silently to the Colonel, as though passing the word to him.

"Dr. Penberthy," said the old man, "now that that paper is in Lord Peter Wimsey's hands, you understand that he can only take the course of communicating with the police. But as that would cause a great deal of unpleasantness to yourself and to other people, you may wish to take another way out of the situation. As a doctor, you will perhaps prefer to make your own arrangements. If not——"

He drew out from his jacket-pocket the thing which he had fetched.

"If not, I happen to have brought this with me from my private locker. I am placing it here, in the table-drawer, preparatory to taking it down into the country to-morrow. It is loaded."

"Thank you," said Penberthy.

The Colonel closed the drawer slowly, stepped back a couple of paces and bowed gravely. Wimsey put his hand on Penberthy's shoulder for a moment, then took the Colonel's arm. Their shadows moved, lengthened, shortened, doubled and crossed as they passed the seven lights in the seven bays of the library. The door shut after them.

"How about a drink, Colonel?" said Wimsey.

They went into the bar, which was just preparing to close for the night. Several other men were there, talking over their plans for Christmas.

"I'm getting away south," said Tin-Tummy Challoner. "I'm fed up with this climate and this country."

"I wish you'd look us up, Wimsey," said another man. "We could give you some very decent shooting. We're having a sort of house-party; my wife, you know—must have all these young people round— awful crowd of women. But I'm getting one or two men who can play bridge and handle a gun, and it would be a positive charity to see me through. Deadly season, Christmas. Can't think why they invented it."

"It's all right if you've got kids," interrupted a large, red-faced man with a bald head. "The little beggars enjoy it. You ought to start a family, Anstruther."

"All very well," said Anstruther, "you're cut out by nature to dress up as Father Christmas. I tell you, what with one thing and another, entertaining and going about, and the servants we have to keep in a place like ours, it's a job to keep things going. If you know of a good thing, I wish you'd put me onto it. It's not as though——"

"Hullo!" said Challoner, "what was that?"

"Motor-bike, probably," said Anstruther. "As I was saying, it's not as though——"

"Something's happened," broke in the red-faced man, setting down his glass.

There were voices, and the running to and fro of feet. The door was flung open. Startled faces turned towards it. Wetheridge burst in, pale and angry.

"I say, you fellows," he cried, "here's another unpleasantness. Penberthy's shot himself in the library. People ought to have more consideration for the members. Where's Culyer?"

Wimsey pushed his way out into the entrance-hall. There, as he

405

had expected, he found the plain-clothes detective who had been told off to shadow Penberthy.

"Send for Inspector Parker," he said. "I have a paper to give him. Your job's over; it's the end of the case."

POST-MORTEM

"AND GEORGE IS ALL RIGHT again now?"

"Thank heaven, yes—getting on splendidly. The doctor says he worked himself into it, just out of worry lest he should be suspected. It never occurred to me—but then George is very quick at putting two and two together."

"Of course he knew he was one of the last people to see his grand-father."

"Yes, and seeing the name on the bottle—and the police com-ing——"

"That did it. And you're sure he's all right?"

"Oh, rather. The minute he knew that it was all cleared up, he seemed to come out from under a blanket. He sent you all sorts of messages, by the way."

"Well, as soon as he's fit you must come and dine with me . . ."

.   .   .   .   .

". . . A simple case, of course, as soon as you had disentangled the Robert part of it."

"A damned unsatisfactory case, Charles. Not the kind I like. No real proof."

"Nothing in it for us, of course. Just as well it never came to trial, though. With juries you never know."

"No; they might have let Penberthy off; or convicted them both."

"Exactly. If you ask me, I think Ann Dorland is a very lucky young woman."

"Oh, God!—you *would* say that . . ."

.   .   .   .   .

". . . Yes, of course, I'm sorry for Naomi Rushworth. But she needn't be so spiteful. She goes about hinting that of course dear Walter was got over by that Dorland girl and sacrificed himself to save her."

"Well, that's natural, I suppose. You thought Miss Dorland had done it yourself at one time, you know, Marjorie."

"I didn't know then about her being engaged to Penberthy. And I think he deserved all he got . . . Well, I know he's dead, but it was a rotten way to treat a girl, and Ann's far too good for that kind of thing. People have a perfect right to want love-affairs. You men always think . . ."

"Not me, Marjorie. I don't think."

"Oh, you! You're almost human. I'd almost take you on myself if you asked me. You don't feel inclined that way, I suppose?"

"My dear—if a great liking and friendship were enough, I would—like a shot. But that wouldn't satisfy you, would it?"

"It wouldn't satisfy *you*, Peter. I'm sorry. Forget it."

"I won't forget it. It's the biggest compliment I've ever had paid me. Great Scott! I only wish . . ."

"There! that's all right, you needn't make a speech. And you won't go away tactfully forever, will you?"

"Not if you don't want me to."

"And you won't be embarrassed?"

"No, I won't be embarrassed. Portrait of a young man poking the fire to bits to indicate complete freedom from embarrassment. Let's go and feed somewhere, shall we? . . ."

.   .   .   .   .   .

". . . Well, and how did you get on with the heiress and the lawyers and all that lot?"

"Oh! there was a long argument. Miss Dorland insisted on dividing the money, and I said no, I couldn't think of it. She said it was only hers as the result of a crime, and Pritchard and Murbles said she wasn't responsible for other people's crimes. And I said it would look like my profiting by my own attempt at fraud, and she said, not at all, and we went on and on, don't you know. That's a damned decent girl, Wimsey."

"Yes, I know. The moment I found she preferred burgundy to champagne I had the highest opinion of her."

407

"No, really—there's something very fine and straightforward about her."

"Oh, yes—not a bad girl at all; though I shouldn't have said she was quite your sort."

"Why not?"

"Well—arty and all that. And her looks aren't her strong point."

"You needn't be offensive, Wimsey. Surely I may be allowed to appreciate a woman of intelligence and character. I may not be high-brow, but I have *some* ideas beyond the front row of the chorus. And what that girl went through with that blighter Penberthy makes my blood boil."

"Oh, you've heard all about that?"

"I have. She told me, and I respected her for it. I thought it most courageous of her. It's about time somebody brought a little bright-ness into that poor girl's life. You don't realize how desperately lonely she has been. She had to take up that art business to give her an in-terest, poor child, but she's really cut out for an ordinary, sensible, feminine life. You may not understand that, with your ideas, but she has really a very sweet nature."

"Sorry, Fentiman."

"She made me ashamed, the way she took the whole thing. When I think of the trouble I got her into, owing to my damned dishonest tinkering about with—you know——"

"My dear man, you were perfectly providential. If you hadn't tinkered about, as you say, she'd be married to Penberthy by now."

"That's true—and that makes it so amazing of her to forgive me. She *loved* that blighter, Wimsey. You don't know. It's absolutely pa-thetic."

"Well, you'll have to do your best to make her forget it."

"I look on that as a duty, Wimsey."

"Just so. Doing anything to-night? Care to come and look at a show?"

"Sorry—I'm booked. Taking Miss Dorland to the new thing at the Palladium, in fact. Thought it'd do her good—buck her up and so on."

"Oh?—good work!—Here's luck to it . . ."

.   .   .   .   .

". . . and the cooking is getting perfectly disgraceful. I spoke to Culyer about it only yesterday. But he won't do anything. I don't know what's the good of the committee. This club isn't half what it used to be. In fact, Wimsey, I'm thinking of resigning."

"Oh, don't do that, Wetheridge. It wouldn't be the same place without you."

"Look at all the disturbance there has been lately. Police and reporters—and then Penberthy blowing his brains out in the library. And the coal's all slate. Only yesterday something exploded like a shell—I assure you, exactly like a shell—in the card-room; and as nearly as possible got me in the eye. I said to Culyer, 'This must *not* occur again.' You may laugh, but I knew a man who was blinded by a thing popping out suddenly like that. These things never happened before the War, and—great heavens! William! Look at this wine! Smell it! *Taste* it! Corked? Yes, I should think it *was* corked! My God! I don't know what's come to this Club."